SHARK TANK

SHARK TANK

A Novel

by

TOM O'NEILL

ibooks
new york

DISTRIBUTED BY PUBLISHERS GROUP WEST

A Publication of ibooks, inc.

Copyright © 2004 by Tom O'Neill

Distributed by Publisher's Group West
1700 First Street
Berkeley, CA 94710
www.pgw.com

ibooks, inc.
24 West 25th Street
New York, NY 10010

The ibooks World Wide Web Site Address is:
http://www.ibooks.net

ISBN: 1-59687-101-6
First ibooks, inc. printing September 2005
10 9 8 7 6 5 4 3 2 1

Cover design: M. Postawa

Printed in the U.S.A.

*This book exists because of
my great friend Hadley.*

*Anyone would do well
to have such a friend.*

SHARK TANK

Prologue

1995

Jimmy slipped on the wet sidewalk and tumbled. A couple ahead of him pressed closer to a building. The woman shrank behind her date. He rolled to his feet in a continuation of the fall and ran past them.

His shoes were slick.

"New half-soles and heels," his wife had said to him just the night before, looking after him as usual.

She's dead now. What are you gonna do about it?

It wasn't far, less than a block. It was getting late—the bums were pissing out in the open instead of in the alleys. He turned the last corner and could see the light spilling from the lobby. Another couple saw him and stopped short.

"What happened?" the man asked.

He kept going.

"Where were you?"

That's what she had asked.

"Where were you? Where have you been?"

Wasting all your time, all your life, on that asshole.

Good job.

That's what they can put on her headstone: "Good job, Jimmy."

He crashed into the lobby door. It was locked. He pounded for the guard inside and dropped his wallet looking for his pass. It was wet, covered with her blood. He swiped the pass and the door unlatched. The wide-eyed guard behind the desk reached for the telephone. Jimmy ran into the elevator.

The floors blinked by. He remembered the ambulance ride, the hospital, her only words.

"Where were you?"

Sorry, honey, I was at the office working on something I can't even remember.

What had it been?

Discovery?

Pre–trial motion?

General ranting?

It all ran together.

The doors slid open. He exploded through the gap.

Sorry I missed your homicide, honey. I know it must have been a big deal for you.

Someone was opening the door. He turned at the noise. It was Bard.

Bard's eyes grew wide. "Jimmy, I just heard."

It's her blood. You're covered in it.

Bard stood in the way of the door, arms reaching out to embrace him.

Nice tux. You hired me. Why couldn't I have worked for you instead?

He thrust his elbow up. Bard crumpled.

He walked down the corridor toward the corner office. The door was open. He could hear him. He could smell him.

Walter stood in the hall ahead of him. His face drained of color.

What is it with all these people? Haven't they ever seen blood before?

"Jimmy," Walter said. "My God."

Walter has a god.

That's good.

Good for him.

"Get out of the way, Walt."

The sound of his own voice stopped him more than Walter did. He hadn't said anything since the emergency room. He had told them to stop.

"Where were you?"

I was there for the part when they were playing pinochle in your chest, the part when they asked if it was okay to stop.

The voice came from the office. "Wally, who the fuck is out there with you?"

"We just heard," Walter said. "I was going to head for the hospital."

"If it's that cocksucker Bard, tell him we're through."

Walter turned to the corner office to say something, but Jimmy hit him first. Walter dropped like a stone.

"Sorry, Walter."

"Who the fuck is out there?"

He stepped into the light of the office. Dennis sat behind the desk, collar open, chopsticks poised over a paper carton. Their eyes met.

"Oh, fuck," Dennis said.

He dropped the carton and reached for his top drawer, but it was too late. Jimmy catapulted over the desk and hauled Dennis into a choke hold. He squeezed Dennis's neck. The stink of Dennis's cologne and Cubans was strong. Jimmy watched the manicured fingernails digging into his forearm, drawing blood. The clench was textbook. He just needed some rotation to snap the neck.

This is too quick.

You need to see his face.

He spun Dennis around.

Wake up, you son of a bitch.

Dennis's eyes fluttered and then opened wide when Jimmy applied his hands to the throat.

There. That's much better.

Dennis's face was red, almost purple. His eyes were huge. His fingernails dug in again, but Jimmy did not feel it. Someone kicked him in the back, but he didn't let go. There it was again, and again.

He couldn't stand up. Dennis was dragging him down.

Dennis dragging you down. How perfect is that? That was her expression. She loved to say that.

"How perfect is that?"

What was the other thing she said?

"Where were you?"

Part I

2000

Chapter 1

"Well, what the hell is that?" R. W. said.

"It's a synthetic, man, for partying." The driver of the Mercedes rocked his head as he spoke.

"I never heard of it." R. W. said, gritting his teeth. It was late. He was cold.

"It's awesome." He squirmed in his seat. "You should stock some."

"Yeah, well, I'll talk to my inventory manager." R. W. glanced down the street for the night's next customer, but hoped this was the last. Robert "R. W." Wilson did not want to be out on the street working retail. He wanted to be in the house counting the money, diluting the dope. He squatted next to the driver's window and peered across at the passenger.

"What about her?"

The Mercedes driver wobbled his head toward his unconscious passenger before returning to face R. W.

"What about her?" he asked.

"What does she need?"

The driver laughed. "Whatever I give her."

"Well, lookit, I don't want to be out here all motherfuckin' night. You want party synthetics, all I got left is some X."

"Man, that is so over."

1

"Look, I know. That's why I still got it. Can give it to you cheap, but as far as I concerned, it's just like ground-up aspirin, or some shit."

"You got that right."

"That's right, it's shit. Now you not at some motherfuckin' boutique. You at the drive-through in the middle the night. What I can do for you tonight, right now, is some serious shit." R. W. looked down the empty street yet again. "You want smack? Crack? Coke? Crank? What?"

R. W.'s phone chirped its alert tone even as he noticed the headlights at the end of the block.

The driver squinted against the oncoming lights. "How much is the heroin?"

"Get the fuck outta here," R. W. said as the driver shielded his eyes from the lights.

The driver grabbed at R. W.'s arm. "Isn't this a one-way street?"

"It's the cops, dumb shit." R. W. stood to his full height and hit the roof of the car with his hand. "Back the fuck outta here."

R. W. stepped toward the curb as the Mercedes lurched backward. It sideswiped two hulks before the end of the block. R. W. could see Von, one of his lookouts, ambling away down the street after sending the phone alert.

R. W. turned to his runners, Lonnie and Feebie. "Okay, niggers, empty your motherfuckin' pockets."

R. W. did not feel rushed to dump anything. The cash he carried was untraceable and the runners carried the drugs. R. W. had a 9mm Glock taped behind the wheel of a derelict Buick, but he could deny any knowledge of it in the unlikely event the police recovered it. Lonnie and Feebie were new. He wanted to make sure they did not have anything damning, but he was out of time. The police car stopped without tire noise. The speed and bulk of the sedan gave the maneuver enough authority that the three men all looked up in unison.

"Excuse me, sir, this is a one-way street." R. W. said, hoping to ease the tension emanating from Lonnie and Feebie. He did not want them to run and get him killed in the process.

A man in a suit stepped out of the Crown Victoria. He had a badge pinned to his coat and brandished a shotgun.

"Hey, no problem here, man." R. W. held his hands up at shoulder height and backed toward the front of house number 1623. Feebie and Lonnie gravitated to number 1627, but glanced toward R. W. R. W.

checked for his lookout. Von was long gone. White cops with big guns scared him even though he would never admit as much.

"Up against the wall, nigger."

R. W.'s eyes scanned the street. "Are you by yourself? 'Cause this is a really dangerous neighborhood."

"It's shake-down time." The cop came around the car with the shotgun leveled at R. W. "Where's the money?"

"Oh, man! Why didn't you say so, cous'? You scared the shit outta me!" R. W. invoked his best impression of a compliant black man. Or was he African-American at the moment? No matter. R. W. was a businessman at heart, regardless of his color, and this was another cop to be dealt with, though his methods were somewhat crude. He relaxed and started to let his hands down.

The cop shoved the muzzle of the shotgun into R. W.'s cheek and pushed him against the wall.

"I said: up against the wall. Get them, too, or I'll do all of you on the spot."

"Okay! Okay! Okay!" R. W. suppressed the quivering in his voice. "Feeb! Lonnie! It's cool! Do what he says."

"Relax, man. We can do business."

Lonnie and Feebie joined R. W. at the wall. At twenty-one, R. W. was older and more experienced than the others. He was the street group's leader and they were supposed to do what he said. All three men faced the front of 1623 and leaned against the wall in a familiar, if not comfortable, spread-eagle position.

The cop frisked all three and confiscated a large wad of cash from R. W.; three pagers; two wireless telephones; and a Glock semiautomatic pistol from Feebie. R. W. noted that the cop missed the dope that Lonnie had had in his pockets just a few minutes earlier. It was too bad Feebie wasn't smart enough to hide the Glock, but, then again, his lack of intelligence was what qualified him to carry it. The cop handcuffed them together in a string. R. W. noticed through the corner of his eye that the cop wore a nice watch, which he checked at least three times, even though the search only took a minute. He also put some type of shoulder bag on the ground next to his shotgun that leaned against the wall. He looked to be about forty, with glasses and a moustache. He wore a hat like Elliott Ness used to wear.

R. W. had never been robbed by a cop, but he thought a cop was not likely to kill a dealer he could come back to and rob again, perhaps on a more familiar basis without the need to be so forceful. Now that he thought about it, though, he could not recall ever speaking with anyone the police actually robbed. The cop hoisted the shotgun in his hands.

R. W. started to sweat and told himself to keep cool. Something was wrong. The gun was right—a big grayish, black thing that appeared to have some kind of tag on the trigger guard, probably from the property room. The raincoat was all right. But he certainly wasn't a narcotics cop. They were scraggly things who stood out through their efforts to fit in as some type of unkempt druggy. And this guy just wasn't pasty-faced and tired-looking enough to be a cop. He was square, strong, too healthy looking. R. W. felt his suspicion grow when he noticed the cop was wearing basketball shoes—black ones like the refs wear. He stole a look at the badge pinned to the cop's raincoat and turned back to the wall.

"Yo, nice shoes," R. W. said.

Get this over with.

He looked over his shoulder. "You work out? 'Cause, man you look tough and I like that hat! Is that one of them Indiana Jones deals? I been lookin' all around for—"

"Where's the money?" As he spoke, R. W. noticed the cop watched Feebie even though the question was directed to R. W.

"You got my money! There's at least fifteen K there. What do I look like—fuckin' Chase Manhattan Bank? Motherfuckin' cops operate under a—a—ah, a misperception that—"

The shotgun blast stopped R. W. in midsentence, or maybe he simply couldn't hear the rest of it as he pressed his face into the bricks and turned from the flash. He felt warm liquid all over his side as he was dragged to the sidewalk. The ringing in his ears was phenomenal.

Shit. I'm dead.

He opened his eyes and saw Lonnie crouched down in front of him. The length of the dark street was visible beyond him, a street that had never looked longer or clearer. R. W. got low and tried to run around Lonnie, but had not completed a single step when he felt the tug of the handcuff on his wrist and something pushing into the right side of his head. He stopped short. The pressure left the side of his head and R. W. turned in time to see the shotgun's stock swing into his face.

The blow knocked R. W. back onto the ground. He now sat with his free right hand in something both sharp and gelatinous. He looked down to see it stuck in a shattered mess of bone, hair, and blood where Feebie's head should have been.

R. W. screamed and choked on the teeth the cop had knocked out. He spat out a mouthful of blood and teeth and looked back toward his intended escape route to see the cop pointing the shotgun at Lonnie's head. The cop was talking, but R. W. couldn't hear him over the ringing in his ears. He saw that Lonnie said something.

The shotgun erupted and R. W. watched Lonnie's head explode across the front of number 1623.

The cop pumped the forearm of the shotgun to eject the spent shell and load a new one into the chamber as he faced R. W. He put the hot shotgun against R. W.'s forehead.

"Where's the money?"

With his ears still ringing, R. W. realized that this is what the cop must have said to Lonnie, just as he had asked him before he started killing everybody. Lonnie must not have told him. R. W. always knew that Lonnie was a stupid fuck.

"Sixteen-seventeen! Sixteen-seventeen! Sixteen-seventeen! Sixteen-seventeen! Sixteen-seventeen!"

"Very good. Where in sixteen-seventeen?"

"Upstairs in the back! Upstairs in the back! Upstairs in—"

"How many are there with it?"

"How... what... how... how many what?"

"How many brothers are in there with the money?"

"Two! Two!"

"Are the drugs there, too?"

"Yeah! I mean yes!"

"How many weapons?"

"What?"

"Guns. How many guns?"

"Uhmmm... a couple nines, and an AK!"

"Anything else?"

"No! Fuck! Please don't fuckin' shoot me, man! I got three babies!"

"Wait right here." The cop picked up his satchel and walked toward the door of number 1617. R. W. looked the length of the street. Most of the houses were ripe for demolition. The few residents left were hostile to his activities, so he did not expect any help. R. W. looked back toward 1617 in time to see the door explode.

R. W. could hear only a flat tone. He opened his eyes and looked over his shoulder again to see the cop jump through the hole where the door used to be. A streak of tracers from the Kalashnikov ripped through the doorway.

"You get him, Alf!" R. W. shouted the words, but he could barely hear them. He rolled over and tried to get up. The handcuff and a pain in his leg stopped him. He looked down to see a piece of the doorframe stuck in his calf. He tried his left arm against the weight of the two bodies.

"He all alone, Alf! Kill the motherfucker!"

R. W. did not like Alf, the senior man who functioned as his boss. He liked Bobby even less since he was the reason everyone called him R. W. instead of Robert. The men had more experience, but they were not as smart as he was. He was left to freeze his ass off working customers while they stayed inside blocking his upward mobility. He heard shooting inside.

"Get him, Bobby! He all alone!"

R. W. looked around. He was about thirty feet from the derelict Buick where his own Glock was stashed. His right hand was free. He crawled toward the car, dragging the bodies of his companions behind. A long stream of tracers flew from the doorway and ricocheted off the sidewalk. R. W. felt some of them thump into the bodies behind him.

"Motherfuckers are good for something at least," R. W. said. As he looked back to address the corpses, R. W. saw Bobby reach the doorway with the AK in hand. Even as he started to leap from the building, Bobby's face exploded. His body tumbled onto the sidewalk.

"Fuck." R. W. redoubled his effort to reach his gun. The bodies were heavy. His leg felt like it was filled with broken glass. He stopped to listen a couple times, but heard no more shooting.

"Motherfuckin' Alf better not have run out on me." R. W. strained against the load. He smelled smoke and saw fire licking at one of the upstairs windows inside 1617.

"Fuckin' Von, wait till I get his ass." He was almost to the Buick.

R. W. got to his knees and reached behind the Buick's wheel. His hand grasped the Glock.

"Whatcha got there?"

R. W. spun his head to see the cop. He had a pistol in one hand and a gym bag over his shoulder. R. W. knew what was in the bag: money—his money.

He could not have this sort of shit happening on his turf.

R. W. pulled out the Glock as fast as he could.

"Really bad idea," the cop said.

Chapter 2

Detective Sergeant Joseph Macuzak awoke with the second ring of the phone. He held the receiver in his hand by the fourth. A dispatcher from the radio room confirmed who he was and started to rattle a location and some generalities, which he scrawled across the pad he kept on the bed stand.

"Okay. Tell them I'll be there in twenty minutes."

He hung up the telephone and creaked out of bed. He felt every one of his fifty-five years, and reminisced about long-gone days when he wasn't important enough to get called out of bed. His wife, Liz, rolled over to face her husband.

"You've gotta go out? Of course you do. I just heard you tell them you'd be over. I thought you didn't have to go out on these right before you retire."

"It's not my case. Looks like a bad one, so they want my help."

"Why don't they call George?"

"He'll be in it tomorrow. Besides, it's my turn."

"I'll make coffee while you shower."

"No time for a shower. I gotta get moving."

"You know, I always thought that was a gimmick for TV with cops answering the phone in the middle of the night and saying, 'I'll be there in twenty minutes.' I always wondered how they got ready so quick."

"Now you know it's because we all have poor hygiene."

"Maybe that's why they call you pigs."

"Hey, no one under the age of fifty calls us that anymore."

"I'll make coffee. You go brush your teeth at least."

She rolled out of bed and headed for the kitchen. On her way out the bedroom door she oinked at him and ran from the playful hand he aimed at her behind.

Forty minutes later Macuzak pulled to the end of the 1600 block of some street whose name he did not recall. He couldn't read most of what he wrote when he got the telephone call, but remembered forming a picture of the neighborhood in his mind while on the phone. All the street signs at the corners were gone, so he still didn't know precisely where he was, but being a police officer in Camden, New Jersey, for twenty-four years and three hundred four days meant he knew where he was within fifty yards or so. He figured the flashing lights about halfway down the block marked his assignment.

The street was closed at the corner but he drove his unmarked Ford past the barricade moved for him by some uniformed cop. He parked in the middle of the street about thirty yards from number 1617, a figure he could read on his note. Fire apparatus and police cars clogged the street. Macuzak sat on the sill of his trunk and changed into high rubber boots. He retrieved a large flashlight from the trunk. The fire department illuminated the area in front of the house. As he walked toward the light, Macuzak looked at the row houses. Most were vacant, but a few people peered into the street from opened front doors.

"Hey, Joe," more than one of the uniforms said as he approached. The firemen were in the process of rolling hoses and gathering other equipment. The pavement was wet and slippery from their efforts, but it was just warm enough that ice had not formed. Nonetheless, the detective almost fell when he slipped on some of the water.

"Oh! My back!" Macuzak yelled as he twisted and slipped. "Get me a lawyer!"

"Funny. Very funny," Detective Mike McLaughlin said. His face contorted for just a second. "Actually, I might be able to help you there."

"Yeah, right. Show me a cop who doesn't already know too many lawyers! What have we got?"

"Let's start at the beginning." He read from his notes. "At two-oh-three A.M. there was an anonymous call on nine-one-one of shots fired at this location. Dispatch put the call on the air at two-oh-four. Unfortunately, the sector car, which would have been only a couple blocks away, was already on an assist-officer call fifteen blocks away."

"Was that founded?"

"No, and every operational car rolled on the call—"

"So, no one was anywhere near here." Macuzak knew that no call received a more robust response than a call to assist a fellow officer. Prowl cars hurtled across the city to get to such a call, creating gaps in patrol coverage.

"Okay, so what time did someone get here?" Macuzak took his own notes.

"No, wait. There's more. At two-twelve there was a call of fire made to dispatch from Alva Mables, who lives at sixteen-thirty-eight. She tells the operator that the police have already been here and left. So dispatch calls the fire department after checking and confirming that there was no response made to the scene. The first fire truck rolls at two-fifteen and got here at two-twenty-three."

"When did we get here?"

"Two-thirty-six A.M."

"I thought you said we were already here, according to Mabel what's-her-name."

"Well, yeah, she says we were, but there is no record of a unit being here. So the first city people at the scene are the fire department guys from what we can tell."

"The fire department beat us here? I hate when that happens!"

"So, when they get here, there's four bodies in the street and the upper floor of the house is fully evolved in flames."

"*In*volved in flames. It's *in*volved, not *e*volved."

McLaughlin stopped interpreting his notes and stared at Macuzak. "Whatever."

"Hey, look—I don't want you to look like a total asshole when you talk to Lois Lane and friends." Macuzak gestured down the block toward a television reporter from the New Jersey bureau of a Philadelphia station who was busy trying to comb the tangles from her hair before going on camera.

"That's all I'm about here. I'm not trying to bust 'em for ya. I retire in a few weeks. This is gonna be your case, not mine. They just called me out to back you up while I'm still around." Macuzak supposed his words were false even before he completed them. As the most experienced detectives on the force, he and his partner probably would catch this case despite their pending departures. Macuzak watched another television news van arrive. A uniformed officer stopped it from moving down the street, so its crew began offloading gear at the end of the block. The story of a multiple homicide and fire would be on the morning news broadcasts.

At least it's too late for the papers.

"Now what else you got?"

McLaughlin returned to his notes. "All right, the firemen get here and there's four stiffs in the street. There's one in the way, so they move him. The other three are over there, also in the way, but clearly part of a crime scene, so they tarped them in place."

"Moved one from where?"

"I don't know. I guess in front of the house."

"Did they run him in an ambulance?"

"Who?"

"The victim they moved. Did they pronounce him here, or what?"

"The fire captain says they were all dead. They had their heads blown off."

"Has the medical examiner already left?"

"I didn't see him," McLaughlin said.

"Where are the bodies?"

"The three are over here by the car. The one near the house is across the street under another tarp."

"So, as we stand here right now, the bodies are here, but you're not sure which ones are from where."

"Lookit. They moved the one near the house before I got here. He's across the street. The scene is spoiled anyway because of the fire. The three over here are still in place, but they got wet with the firefighting."

Macuzak looked around to avoid showing his disgust to McLaughlin. The fire touched at least three of the houses and others were soaked. There was not much light on the street apart from what the firemen had brought with them.

"Place is abandoned?" Macuzak walked toward the Buick with its bright blue tarp.

"Yeah."

"Why did they bother fighting it?"

"Thought maybe there were vagrants inside." McLaughlin pulled the tarp aside. Macuzak surveyed the scene.

"Looks like the guy with the Glock dragged the other two over here. See the streaks?"

"Yeah. They got wet, but they're still visible. This is brain tissue here." McLaughlin pointed to the sidewalk.

"The Glock is probably a stash piece. See the tape? Probably under the car or in the wheel well. This guy got capped here. See the spray pattern?" Macuzak put his light and nose close to the Buick's fender.

"High caliber?" McLaughlin turned away and wrote notes.

"Did the job, whatever it was."

Macuzak turned back toward the houses. "Do we know who lived here?"

"No one. I mean they're crack houses. All hooked together inside— see the steel doors that are all the same? Most of the action was in number sixteen-seventeen. It looks like they blew the door in."

"I assume we have no witnesses—and we have four stiffs. Any—"

"Five."

"What?"

"Five stiffs. One was in the house. And you're right. No witnesses, but some uniform heard the name 'Vaughn' from the bystanders a couple times. We also have some spent shotgun shells, which are right here." McLaughlin held up a Ziploc bag with two shells in it.

"Where were they found?"

"Floating around somewhere. We also think we have what's left of the shotgun."

"Any ID on the bodies?"

"Not yet."

"What about what's-her-name—Mabel—?"

"Alva Mables."

"Yeah, right. Did we talk to her?"

"Briefly. She went to the hospital with chest pains. She insists there was a police car here, an unmarked police car. She even gave me a partial tag number."

"Did you run that?"

"It's only a partial and she don't know what kind of car it was. I figured we'd do it first thing."

"Do it now against the municipal index. Any town that gets close to a hit you call and see if they know where their car is."

"Right."

"Do that right away."

"I said I would."

"Okay. Is the guy still inside?"

"Yeah. He's up in the back. Crime lab is on the way."

"This is gonna shake out to be some kind of gang bullshit. Maybe locals or some guys from Philly or New York, but let's go take a look."

As the detectives walked up the steps from the sidewalk to where the front door had stood, McLaughlin stopped Macuzak and said, "Oh, yeah! Look at this."

"What?"

"Over here."

Macuzak looked at part of what he guessed was the doorframe. He put on his reading glasses and squinted at the water-logged business card tacked to the wood.

Macuzak turned to McLaughlin. "What is this—a joke?"

Macuzak shone his light on the card and read aloud. "James Sullivan, Attorney at Law."

Chapter 3

"Yeah. Okay. Hey, thanks a lot. Bye-bye," Macuzak said into the telephone. "We got a match on the prints."

It was 8:50 A.M. He sat at his desk in his rumpled overcoat and rubbed his eyes. His partner, George Whitcomb, sat at the next desk, impeccably groomed as always, even after those nights when he was called to a murder scene instead of Macuzak. Macuzak stifled a yawn. "Gettin' too old for this shit."

Whitcomb studied his partner until Macuzak turned to meet his stare.

"What? What did I do, Georgie?"

"I thought we talked about the 'bye-bye' thing before."

"Oh, jeez, here we go. Look, I've been up all night on this. Cut me the smallest of breaks on my diction this morning. Besides, I haven't told you about my trip."

"It is unprofessional for detectives to speak over the telephone as though their intellectual development halted at the preschool level. If you are serious about our mutual retirement plans of operating a private investigative and consulting firm then we must curb some of these tendencies. Further, did I or did I not ask you to stop calling me 'Georgie' in the context of the workplace?"

Macuzak said a semi–silent thank-you to the ceiling when the telephone rang on Whitcomb's desk. Whitcomb answered it, but scowled his disapproval at Macuzak. After a few minutes of writing notes, he said, "Very well, and I thank you."

"Well, what have you got?" Macuzak asked as Whitcomb set down the telephone.

"Did you notice my telephone manner? You should try to emulate it."

"Between you and my wife, I don't know how it is I survived all these years."

"How is Elizabeth? Well, I hope. Please give her my regards. But enough small talk, would you not like to hear what I learned?"

"Do tell."

"The decedents are identified as—have you a pencil?"

"Yes. Shoot. No pun intended."

"Robert Johnson, L. Andrew Johnson, Robert Wilson, Frederick Douglass Jefferson, and Alvin Whittaker. He is the one who burned. So his identification is somewhat more tentative than the others."

"Alf Whittaker? I know Alf. He went to Rahway about five years back for a murder during a robbery. I guess he got out."

"Indeed. I will check the criminal histories on these names."

"I'll do it. Alf was tied up in the gangs as far as I know. Wanta hear about my trip?"

"Do tell."

Macuzak grinned.

"I'm at the scene and I get a call at five-thirty from dispatch telling me that Newark PD has my car at their airport up there. So, I figure my trail's hot and I bolt."

"This was the unit stolen from the New Brunswick PD."

"Right. Guess how long it took me to get there?"

"New Brunswick or Newark?"

"Newark Airport."

Whitcomb straightened papers on his desk. "One hour."

Macuzak doffed his coat. "Thirty-six minutes."

Whitcomb arched his eyebrows. "Lights and siren?"

"All the way up the turnpike."

"Only way to fly."

"So, I get there and the bomb squad is just finishing up."

"Why were they there?"

"There was a friggin' bomb in the car. Guy left it idling in a tow zone. They shut down the whole terminal."

"Yes, but how did they know there was a bomb?"

Macuzak rummaged through his briefcase. "That's the best part. The second best part. Where the hell is it? Here it is."

Whitcomb read the photocopy Macuzak twirled toward him:

> HELLO.
>
> PLEASE READ AND UNDERSTAND THIS MESSAGE IN ITS ENTIRETY BEFORE TAKING FURTHER ACTION.
>
> THIS IS A STOLEN VEHICLE PRESENTLY EQUIPPED WITH EXPLOSIVES.
>
> DO NOT PANIC.
>
> SINCE THE VEHICLE IS NOW ABANDONED, THE DETONATING DEVICE IS DISABLED, BUT PLEASE DO NOT ATTEMPT TO REMOVE THE DEVICE IN THIS VEHICLE WITHOUT PROPER TRAINING.
>
> TIME IS NOT OF THE ESSENCE.
>
> CONTACT THE BOMB DISPOSAL UNIT AND FURNISH THEM WITH THIS CARD. THE INFORMATION AND DIAGRAM ON THE BACK WILL FACILITATE SAFE REMOVAL OF EXPLOSIVES FROM THE TRUNK AND/OR ENGINE COMPARTMENT. THIS VEHICLE MAY BE DRIVEN OR TOWED FROM THE AREA PRIOR TO REMOVING ANY EXPLOSIVES TO MINIMIZE INCONVENIENCE.
>
> SORRY FOR ANY DISRUPTION.
>
> HAVE A NICE DAY.

Whitcomb turned over the copy. "What was this? An index card?"

"Right. On the back there was a wiring diagram and instructions on how to disarm the car bomb."

"Considerate. What's the best part?"

Macuzak squinted. "What?"

"You said the note was the second best part. That implies that there is another best part or, if you will, a better than best part."

"Right," Macuzak said, leaning back in his chair. "The note was pinned to the dashboard by a cheap brass badge that says 'Sheriff Jimmy' right across the front."

"A novelty item, I presume."

"Looked like it. Newark still has it, but right on the back is a visible print. It's like the guy rolled his thumb across it on purpose. They shot a copy of the lift down to our guys who already matched it to a latent from one of the cuffs left at our scene."

"McLaughlin said he found some lawyer's card at the scene."

"McLaughlin would be lucky to find his ass with both hands. This case is perfect for him. It's practically solving itself. Friggin' card was pinned to the doorway. It lists some lawyer named Sullivan. Probably represents whoever did the shooting."

"It would seem the case has enough gravity that they re-assigned it to us." Whitcomb held aloft the clear evidence bag containing the business card.

"Shit."

"What's the matter?" Whitcomb asked. "You just said the case was practically solving itself."

"Now that it's ours it'll go through the friggin' looking glass one way or another."

Whitcomb donned his overcoat. "Don't be so pessimistic. Crime scene called to advise that the tag attached to the shotgun bears the name and address of a Leroy Buckwell."

"That's exactly the kind of thing I mean. Normal killers don't drop names at the scene. These whackos left us little notes for Christ's sake."

"You may be correct," Whitcomb said, wrapping his scarf. "Mr. Buckwell was killed in Louisiana last year."

"Par for the course. Taking yourself out to the scene?" Macuzak looked at the business card.

"Unless you are willing to bear the burden of all testimony at trial."

"Have fun. Maybe there will be some youngsters upon whom you can exert a positive influence."

"I thought I might first visit Mrs. Mables at the hospital. Perhaps you should telephone Mr. Sullivan in the unlikely event he is our perpetrator."

"Wouldn't that be a kick in the ass? They print all the lawyers in Jersey, right?"

"Correct."

"Maybe I'll have them express the lifts against that database."

"I, for one, would be stunned if there was a match."

"Yeah, that would be too easy, wouldn't it? It'll probably match the dead guy. What's his name? Buckwheat?"

"Buckwell. Leroy Buckwell."

"I wrote it down. You won't have to tell me again."

"Fabulous. Very well then, I will take my leave. We should confer this afternoon."

After Whitcomb left, Macuzak studied the business card inside the evidence envelope. The card was attributed to a lawyer named James Sullivan in Philadelphia who also had an office in New Jersey. He should have waited for the lab to check the scene prints against the lawyer noted on the card, but he doubted they would match. Macuzak picked up his phone and dialed the card's Philadelphia number.

"Hello?" asked a female voice at the other end of the line.

Macuzak hunted for a pencil. He had expected a recital of the firm's name rather than a simple "Hello."

"James Sullivan please."

"May I ask who is calling?"

"Joseph Macuzak."

"Will he know what your call concerns?"

Macuzak felt like he was fencing with Whitcomb. "It is confidential. Please put him on the line if he is available."

"One moment please."

Macuzak heard a number of clicks and hums through the line. He thought he was about to hear a recording to the effect that his call had not gone through when the line came alive at the other end.

"Hello?" It was a male voice.

"James Sullivan?"

"No. Mr. Sullivan is indisposed. May I help you, Mr. Menksak?"

"Macuzak. No. I think I will have to speak with Mr. Sullivan directly. I'll try again later. By the way, with whom am I speaking?"

"Roger Sorenson."

"And is this the law firm of O'Brien, Bard, Camby, and Scott?"

"It's not called that anymore. Bard is gone."

"Oh, okay. Well, thank you, Mr. Sorenson." Macuzak started to close the contact. He was already thinking of detectives he knew in the Philadelphia Police Department to call concerning Sullivan and his law firm. Macuzak reached for his Rolodex.

"Mr. Macsak?"

"Macuzak."

"Sorry. This call would not by chance concern a police matter, would it?"

Macuzak stopped his journey through his contact cards. "Mr. Sorenson, why would you ask that?"

"Just a guess. You're calling from the Camden police and I assume you are the detective who caught the case."

"I never said I was from Camden, or the police." Macuzak knew that the caller identification feature was blocked on his line as well as most others within the police department.

"Let's see here... five people dead. Our friend Mr. Sullivan has been busy. How did you get this number—from his card?"

"Who is this?"

"Roger Sorenson, special agent with the FBI. I'm looking at a wire service report of the shooting. Relax—I'll be up this afternoon and we'll talk. Where is your office so that we can meet?"

"At headquarters. You might have mentioned the FBI part a little sooner instead of making me into some kind of a grade-A asshole. Do you always leave your phone number at multiple homicides?"

"No. Sullivan did that. He just doesn't have the number anymore. I'll explain it this afternoon."

"Your info is that this guy is my shooter?"

"Yes. Case practically solved itself didn't it?"

"Way too easy. My guess is I won't find him sitting in his office."

"Hardly."

"Does that mean 'no' in fedspeak?"

"Correct. I'll see you this afternoon and lay it out for you."

"So, you'll find me?"

"Yes. Someone from the Philadelphia Field Office will get me there. I've got to run for a meeting soon. I'll see you later."

"Before you get off, have you got a photo you can fax me or a physical description so we can look for this guy?"

"Caucasian; thirty-three, he'll be thirty-four on Christmas Day; six feet tall; athletic build; brown hair. No photo. Don't worry about it—he's long gone."

Macuzak scribbled.

"Detective?"

"Yeah?"

"Try not to talk to any more reporters, okay?"

"Hey, I didn't talk to any." Macuzak stopped writing and focused on a point in space somewhere beyond his desk. "Look, we all know that

Camden is a first-class shit hole, but do you think it's a big secret here that five people got whacked and a city block burned down?"

"No. I guess it wouldn't be. My apologies."

"I got better things to do than talk to some reporter."

"I would hope so."

"Yeah, whatever."

"Listen, I'll see you later."

"Okay, sure."

"Thanks for calling now, you hear."

"Bye-bye," Macuzak spoke into the dead line.

Chapter 4

S orenson wore an expensive suit and highly polished shoes. Macuzak thought he looked like a fraternity brother on a job interview. Sorenson demanded that a telephone be placed in the interrogation room. He made a series of calls on it while Macuzak and Whitcomb gathered their files and some refreshments. A computer sprouted from Sorenson's briefcase to occupy part of the tabletop.

Whitcomb repeated a chronology similar to, but more refined than, McLaughlin's earlier that morning. Macuzak noticed that Sorenson seemed to be looking through Whitcomb rather than at him, and though his fingers furiously stroked computer keys, his eyes never scanned the machine's display. Macuzak started to discuss the victims of the shootings, but Sorenson's expression remained fixed on Whitcomb.

"The decedents are Robert Johnson, L. Andrew 'Lonnie' Johnson, Robert Wilson, Frederick Douglass 'Feebie' Jefferson, and Alvin 'Alf' Whittaker. We presume that the man in charge among them was Alf Whittaker, who has an extensive criminal history for drug offenses and some heavier stuff, including homicide."

"Let me just interject, if I may, Detective. You're going to tell me that all these victims have criminal records for drug and probably gang violence, right?"

Macuzak perused the record sheets. "Yeah, basically."

"They were operating a notorious drug distributorship at least at the retail, if not wholesale, level, right?"

"Yep. Both in this instance. Mostly heroin and crack plus some synthetics."

"Their operation was fixed at some location in a bad part of town and, as I think Detective Whitcomb said, the police were diverted from their normal patrol through the area by some type of unfounded call."

"Sounds like you've seen this pattern before."

"Among others. And our Mr. Sullivan left his card at the scene, right?"

"Correct."

"And you say the police car was rigged with explosives."

"Right again. You'll be moving on to our bonus round," Whitcomb said.

"That's totally new. No one was hurt by those?" Sorenson continued to type.

"No. In fact, he left a card stuck to the dashboard that gave instructions on how to defuse the bomb." Macuzak produced another photocopy.

"Well, now. That is more in character."

"They also found a handgun in the trunk."

"Nine-millimeter Beretta?"

"Correct."

"Well, he can't very well walk onto a plane with that."

"So, you believe he caught a flight."

"That's been his pattern. Either he catches a plane, or train, or simply disappears."

"What can you tell us about Mr. Sullivan?" Whitcomb asked.

"I can tell you that he is the subject of an FBI task force, which I head, and he has perpetrated this same type of crime many times throughout the country over the last three years. We've been chasing him and will take over this case for you so you can clear it off your books. If you like, you can just give me your original file or I can get it copied. What time is it?"

"It's a couple minutes past three," Macuzak said. "What do you mean you'll take it over from us? We don't just give over multiple homicides because someone says so."

"What's your jurisdiction?" Whitcomb asked.

"Well, it's really kind of simple. The shooter in your homicides is James Sullivan. There's really no dispute about it. He's wanted for a number of crimes in which he has done essentially the same thing, and we're running him to ground. The victims are generally minority members—if nothing else, we can describe this as a series of hate crimes. He moves around a lot and I will bet you that he is not anywhere near here at the moment and that he won't come back now that he has hit. In fact, we hope to get a position on him in a little while when he calls."

"Excuse me," Whitcomb said. "Apart from what sounds like a tenuous jurisdictional tie, I must have misunderstood what you said. I thought you just said that he was going to call."

"I did. He often telephones between twelve and fifteen hours after the crime. I came this close," Sorenson held up his index finger and thumb to indicate a minuscule gap, "to talking him into surrendering."

"You expect him to telephone you?"

"Yes. That's why the phone is here. If we can run the trace fast enough, we can close on him."

"What else can you tell us about him?"

"There's not too much to tell. He's a psychopath who kills drug dealers and takes their money when he gets the chance."

Whitcomb peered over his cheaters. "Have you any information on Leroy Buckwell?"

"Dead. Illegal arms dealer down south. Sullivan killed him after taking a load of weapons off him. Did us a favor on that one. Tagged one of his guns, did he?"

"Correct."

"How come we never heard anything about this?" Macuzak asked.

"It's all hush-hush so that we can close in. That's why I didn't want you to talk to any reporters. We don—"

The telephone rang. After three rings during which he drew deep breaths, Sorenson picked up the handset and punched the speaker button.

"Hello, Roger. It's Jim."

"Jim? Jim? Ohhh! Sheriff Jimmy?" Sorenson said.

"You liked that, huh?"

"Oh, yeah. I have to say that you are the most interesting serial murderer I deal with. Your sense of humor can be absolutely wry. By the way, where are you?"

"You know I won't answer that and you know I won't stay on the phone long enough for you to get a trace so stop wasting my time. I called to confirm Camden and claim the car at Newark, which I presume you know about since you know about the badge. Any problem with the Semtex? It's getting kind of old."

"I'll have to check on that."

Laughter barked from the speaker.

"You know that we'll catch you sooner or later, Jim. By the way, what's with impersonating a cop? The vagrant gig seemed to be working so well. Then again, you must be running low on ideas." Sorenson spoke without giving the caller a chance to answer. "Why don't you just hang it up and come on in?"

The line stayed quiet for a moment.

"Roger, you're full of shit. You know it and so do I. Have a nice day."

"Don't you want to hear about your latest victims?" Sorenson asked the now-dead line. A series of clicks were audible, and the caller was gone.

"Did you get him?" Sorenson said into the telephone. He massaged his head.

"No," a female voice said.

"Why the hell not?"

"He wasn't on long enough for a full contemporaneous trace. We'll have to reconstruct it, but I'll tell you we're going to find out he's coming off a satellite. If you would just call the right folks at NSA we'll be able to pin him."

"Did you get a town or at least a region?"

"Not really. I know he is west of the Mississippi River, probably in the Pacific Northwest, but he was off too quickly. From the background noise I would guess he was outside somewhere this time, maybe a wireless, maybe a satellite."

"Doc, are you there?" Sorenson asked.

"He wasn't on the line."

"Why not?"

"He was tied up, I guess."

"Get him. Play the tape for him and have him call me."

"Roger that."

Sorenson hung up the telephone and pounded the laptop. "Morons."

He turned to Macuzak and Whitcomb. "I'll need to know the terminal where the car was found so that I can check the flights. Do you folks have that?"

"Sure." Whitcomb said. "Of course, he may have used another terminal, or gone someplace else altogether. It was very early, even for the airlines."

"Who is this 'Doc'?" Macuzak held his pen poised.

"He's a psychiatrist working up a profile for us."

Whitcomb winked at Macuzak. "Why would the FBI want a psychological profile of you?"

"It's not for me. It's for Sullivan."

Macuzak and Whitcomb exchanged a glance.

"He doesn't sound too interested in the project," Macuzak said.

"He should be interested. He's been on this for months. Thinks he might get a book out of it."

The telephone rang and Sorenson punched the speaker button.

"Yes."

"Yes, this is Dr. Funtz. I am calling for Mr. Sorenson. Is he available?"

Sorenson sat up straighter. "Yes, Dr. Funtz, this is Roger Sorenson. I'm here with a couple of detectives who are working on the latest episode with our Mr. Sullivan. Have you had a chance to listen to his latest communication?"

"What? I can hardly hear you. Are you calling me on a speakerphone? You sound like you are at the bottom of a well."

Sorenson picked up the handset. "Is that better, Doctor?"

"Yes. Much better."

"Have you listened to the tape?"

"No. Not yet. I don't know that it makes much difference though. Oh, wait. My secretary tells me the man with the tape is on the other line. I will listen to it and call you back, or you can hold."

"I'll hold."

As Sorenson mouthed to the detectives that he was on hold, an instrumental version of "Raindrops Keep Falling on My Head" blared through the handset. Macuzak held up his empty coffee cup. Sorenson nodded his head and mouthed, "Thank you." Macuzak brushed Whitcomb's arm. He followed Macuzak down the hall to the coffee machine.

"Let me just interject, if I may, Detective Wilcox," Macuzak said, "or is it Watson? No matter. This guy's an asshole."

Whitcomb shook his head. "Am I missing something here, or has the Federal Bureau of Investigation lowered its standards? Don't they have in place some personality or at least an intelligence test?"

Macuzak poured coffee for Sorenson and himself. "I'm not sure if he's stupid, or just a prick. Maybe he's a token. They were hiring too many qualified blacks and women so they went out looking for dumb Nordic guys who look like male models to balance it out."

Whitcomb brewed his decaffeinated herbal tea. "I try to inject a small amount of levity into a serious matter—I mean we are still dealing with a multiple homicide believed to have been perpetrated by at least a constructive serial or spree killer. How old do you suppose he is?"

"Thirty, maybe."

"It's so hard to tell with you white people. You really all do look alike, you know."

They returned to find Sorenson leaning back in the chair with his feet on the desk. The phone was still propped on his shoulder. He was half-humming and half-singing "New York, New York" as his fingers danced across the laptop. Sorenson suddenly put his feet on the floor and replaced the computer on the table.

"Yes, Doctor. I'm still here. Wait while I put you back on speaker." Sorenson cradled the handset as he hit the speaker button.

"What do you want to know?" Funtz roared through the speaker.

"Well… what are your initial impressions from the call?"

"It wasn't very long was it?"

"What is the significance of that?"

"I guess he was in a hurry. He no doubt knew you were trying to trace his call."

"Doctor, you're not telling me anything I don't know. Is there anything additional?"

"He appears to be tired and annoyed, but my assumption is that he's still acting out this pathologic grief triggered by his wife's demise. However, it may be that his initial motivation is petering out. His psychosis may be decompensating, er, ah, may be becoming more unstable. He might be just as likely to kill somebody over a parking space, or subway seat as anything else. I'm speculating to a degree, but this pattern shouldn't be surprising. He may be reaching some resolution, or, more logically, realizing that there is no satisfactory resolution. He can pile up the bodies like cord wood and has nothing to show for it. He's killed what—sixty or eighty people over the last few years?"

Upon hearing the figures, Macuzak coughed so that his coffee rose into his sinuses. Whitcomb shook his head and sipped his tea.

"Anything else, Doctor?"

"No. Do you think there should be something else?"

"This call isn't about what I think, Doctor."

"So I gathered. I'll send you a report for your file."

"Excuse me, Doctor?" Whitcomb said.

"What? Yes? Who's this?"

"George Whitcomb. Doctor, what is the diagnosis that applies to Mr. Sullivan?"

"What is this, Roger? A press conference finally?"

"No, Doctor. Detective Whitcomb and his partner are working on the most recent homicides." Sorenson hesitated. "You can talk to them."

"Okay. My diagnosis? He's nuts! How's that for a succinct diagnosis?"

"I guess I was after something a bit more scientific."

A sigh came through the telephone.

"My apologies, Detective—?"

"Whitcomb."

"Whitcomb. My apologies, Detective Whitcomb. "Can I fit a specific diagnosis to Mr. Sullivan? The short answer is no, I can't. However, that's not an unusual circumstance in the field of psychiatry. In many ways it's an imprecise science.

"What do we know? We have someone who has killed a lot of people.

"Do I think that is aberrational behavior? Yes, I do.

"Do I think it is a manifestation of some psychosis? Yes, I do.

"Am I right? I don't know the answer to that yet because I have not had the opportunity to analyze the subject apart from tapes of these extraordinarily brief telephone conversations and his background as the All-American boy. By the way, Roger, you have to do something about keeping him on the telephone longer."

"I've tried. If I stall him, he simply hangs up."

"Well, whatever. Listen, I've got to run. Give my best to your father."

The line went dead before either detective could pose another question.

Chapter 5

John Gavigan passed two joggers and a woman walking her little dog. He guessed they lived nearby, but he didn't know anyone on the block except the homosexuals who lived upstairs on the third floor. He didn't even know the girl who rented the second-floor back apartment and dripped water on the hood of his Volvo when she watered the plants on her deck. He turned north to reach Market Street where a corridor of skyscrapers held most of the larger law firms in town. The morning was beautiful and cloudless. It would have been one of Philadelphia's two or three perfect days each fall, except the wind was not quite strong enough to dissipate the stench of urine wafting from the alleys.

Gavigan stopped at the vendor's cart across the street from his office. He paid the vendor for the steaming coffee inside his blue and yellow Parthenon cup and walked to his building's doors, where on Saturdays and other odd hours he had to sweep a card through a reader to get the door open. He managed this task despite the coffee, briefcase, and two newspapers he juggled.

"You know, you could take a Saturday off every once in a while," the security guard said, his eyes never leaving his sports page.

"Gotta get ready for trial." Gavigan swept his card through another reader on the massive reception desk.

"No rest for the weary, baby."

"Got that right." Gavigan said as the elevator doors shut.

He emerged onto the floor occupied by O'Brien, Camby & Scott where he punched a code into the keypad next to the doors. A green light flashed red as Gavigan heard the lock release. Once inside, he flicked on the lights, although he suspected he could find his office with his eyes shut. As he neared the corner suite of Dennis O'Brien, his heart raced. The lights were out, but the door to his boss's office stood open like the maw of some beast. A grandfather's clock inside chimed seven as Gavigan ducked past the open door into his adjacent office. He deposited his burdens among the piles of documents, which he deceived himself into believing had some order. Confident that Dennis O'Brien was not around, Gavigan sipped some coffee and strolled to the tiny room that housed the word processing center for the firm. There he found a secretary transcribing one of his tapes amid snaps of gum and blaring dance music. She was new and worked with one of the attorneys in another group, but she worked a lot after hours. His guess was that she would stay with the firm for a while and then leave when she found out that it inadequately rewarded overtime. In the meantime, she was chipper and efficient.

"Hi. I have your tape," she said. Everyone in the firm knew Gavigan, the big ex-linebacker who had to work with O'Brien and Cole.

"Great. Thanks. I'm John Gavigan. I'm sorry, but I don't know your name."

"Carmen."

"Okay, Carmen, let me know when you have something for me to review. My extension is two-five-seven. Do you want some coffee or something?"

"No. I'm good, thanks." She gestured at the Pepsi and hoagie on the workstation.

"All right, then." As he headed toward his office, a telephone rang. He ran down the hall and grabbed the phone at his secretary's station.

"Good morning, O'Brien, Camby, and Scott."

"Who's this?"

"Gavigan." He recognized Dennis O'Brien's voice and fear gripped his stomach. "What can I do for you, Dennis?"

"Who's there besides you?" Static crackled through O'Brien's mobile.

"I don't really know, I just got here myself. Are you looking for someone in particular?"

"Is Wally there?"

Gavigan looked across the hall toward Walter Cole's door.

"I don't know. His door is shut."

"Go see if he's there. I'll hold on."

Gavigan looked at the phone's blinking lights, sweating. It had three times the buttons his did.

What was he supposed to push to leave someone on hold? Where's a secretary when you need one?

He held his breath and punched a worn red button. All the phone's lights went out.

"Shit."

He jogged around the secretarial counter to Cole's door, opening and knocking at the same time. Cole slumped behind his desk, drumming his fingers on the temples of his balding head. He looked at Gavigan with an air of resignation, as though he expected the interruption.

"Sorry, I didn't think you were here or I'd have knocked for real. Denny is, or was, on the phone and wanted me to see if you were here for his call. Are you here?" Gavigan tumbled the words out as he noticed that one of the chairs opposite Cole's desk was occupied by Melinda Swayze, a young associate. The secretary's phone rang again.

"That's all right. I'll take it." Cole heaved himself toward his telephone.

"What's your extension? I'll try to transfer it."

"I think I can get it from here. Thanks."

"Okay."

Gavigan left them in the darkened office. He shook off the rumors of an affair between Cole and Swayze. It was more likely that she was helping Cole keep up with some project within O'Brien's compartmentalized practice, although that prospect provided little solace. Gavigan held a low opinion of Swayze's work and preferred that she stay as far away from his litigation group as possible.

Gavigan returned to his desk and reviewed a pile of outgoing correspondence. He extracted a pad imprinted with the format for recording his time and proceeded to jot client and matter numbers in the appropriate blocks as he read the letters. Recording time was mandatory and withholding time sheets resulted in financial penalties. Actually reading the letters was discouraged, for it consumed time that could be spent on more substantive tasks. Composing original correspondence was also discouraged in many cases, since the firm's word-processing system held a form letter for almost every occasion and their use was encouraged whenever possible.

Through his office doorway, Gavigan noticed a large pile of outgoing correspondence on the desk outside O'Brien's office. The secretary sent it out by rote and signed it with a signature stamp, but clients would be billed as though O'Brien had toiled over the letters. His secretary went so far as to complete his time sheets for him, so that he was spared the tedium of the task. Gavigan knew of at least one day on which O'Brien's time sheets credited him with over thirteen hours of work when he did not even appear in the office.

Beyond the piles of correspondence, Gavigan watched Swayze swinging her hips as she left Cole's office. Gavigan pondered the wisdom of wearing three-inch high heels with blue jeans, but supposed that the choice had not been made for practical locomotion. Cole put his head through the doorway to Gavigan's office. He looked down at a notepad.

"You would have been wise to let the phone ring," Cole said.

"Sorry, I thought it might be for me." Gavigan knew the call carried bad news as soon as he heard O'Brien ask for Cole. O'Brien had the habit of allowing his emotions to express themselves in the way he referred to people. For example, when he was irritated he would exchange the standard reference to Cole of "Walter" or "Cole" for "Wally," a name Cole hated. If he was pleased about something, he would use the familiar "Walt." If O'Brien was exuberant or excited, he would forget everyone's name.

"No problem, but now it knows you're here," Cole said.

"What does he want?"

"A meeting with everyone here in the fiefdom. Melinda kept her mouth shut, so it doesn't know she's here and she's gonna take off. Any problem with that?"

"No. I never saw her. You might want to warn anyone else who's here. Where is he anyway?"

"In the car, about ten minutes away. Of course, that means he's really about a half-hour away. You didn't hope to get any work done did you?"

"Well, I'm trying to catch up so that I can take some time at Thanksgiving and Christmas."

"Too bad. He knows you're here and specifically asked me to line you up for whatever it is he wants to discuss. So, you're stuck for the meeting, just like me. With any luck, I'll still get to pick up my kid on time."

"Probably more aquarium bullshit." Gavigan referred to O'Brien's interest in an aquatic attraction in town, shorthand for any topic other than the actual practice of law including O'Brien's multifarious schemes for accumulating wealth.

"I'm going to see who I can scare away before he gets here," Cole said.

"I'll be here."

Gavigan signed his letters and scanned his newspapers in the wake of his shattered concentration. Forty minutes later, he returned to Cole's office to ask about O'Brien's arrival, taking a paper with him as an icebreaker. A lurid article about shark attacks off Australia quoted a marine biologist they once used as an expert witness in an aquarium case.

During the brief trip across the hall, O'Brien swept into the office. "My office. Now."

Cole and Gavigan followed him. He flopped into the chair behind his desk.

"Anyone else around?" O'Brien said.

Gavigan and Cole exchanged glances. "No."

O'Brien leapt from his chair to stalk around the floor, dragging back a new associate named Audrey. Gavigan glanced at Cole and understood that he had found Audrey earlier. It was her bad luck she'd failed to clear out before O'Brien's arrival. Gavigan returned a sympathetic look.

The meeting commenced with the usual pointed questions about whether anyone had any ideas about how to make money. Gavigan remained silent, calculating whose turn it was to trigger O'Brien's wrath. Audrey said something to the effect that perhaps an educational seminar would be a good way to introduce the firm to new clients while reinforcing its position with established ones—not all that bad a suggestion for someone without a great deal of experience. However, the veneer containing O'Brien's personality disorder was thin today. He dismissed the suggestion, questioning how Audrey had managed to secure a position in the firm.

"Wally, aren't you on the fucking hiring committee?"

"Yes," Cole said. Gavigan watched his face and head turn red. *This could take awhile.*

"Did I or did I not tell you fuck knuckles to get me some people with brains in here?"

"We hire the best people we can get. Audrey is more than—"

"Bullshit the best people! You keep hiring a bunch of fucking drones! Good for nothing but practicing law! Technically competent, but with no ideas of their own! I'm fucking responsible for making payroll here for a bunch of fucking parasites! You're supposed to be supporting me, not the other way around!"

"We're fine. They're aren't any major financial issues at—"

"What do you fucking know about it? They're my clients. Mine! And the fucking clients! They're a bigger bunch of fucking assholes than *you*. I've gotta kiss their fat asses and then the fuckers write their own discounts. I should start writing discounts on you cocksuckers. Look, I don't want to fucking be here anymore. I shouldn't have to work this hard. I want you to work for me. I want to be a client, not serve them. You fuckers are killing me here!"

Gavigan stared at the building across the street, pondering whether O'Brien forgot to take his lithium or had broken through the prescribed level yet again. His stomach growled. Cole's son might like a Happy Meal for lunch. Gavigan would ask once this conference terminated. It bothered Gavigan that, like Cole, he was almost accustomed to the rage. Spittle gathered at the edge of O'Brien's mouth.

"What are you fucking doing sitting there?"

"Listening," Gavigan said.

Here we go.

"Listening. The great fucking wise man. You're not worth the sweat off my fucking balls."

Gavigan pushed his anger down. He stole a glance at Audrey, who he guessed was creating a list of firms to which she could send her résumé.

"Nothing to say?" O'Brien said.

No one answered. The meeting ended with the inevitable physical manifestation of Dennis O'Brien's loss of control. On this occasion, he threw a lamp against the wall and ordered everyone out. In closing, they learned they could all go to hell. Audrey ran from the room, but contained her tears until halfway down the hall.

"Lunch?" Gavigan whispered to Cole in the hall.

"Naw. Got plans," Cole answered. "Have a good weekend if I don't see you."

O'Brien's door slammed behind them.

Gavigan gathered his things with tension quivering in his chest. He realized that he had left part of his newspaper in O'Brien's office, but elected to forget it rather than attempt its retrieval. He stopped by Audrey's office on his way out, but she was gone. He wanted to reassure her that she was not at fault for what happened. O'Brien might even apologize before the weekend was over. If he had thought to look, he would have found her curled up in a stall in the ladies' room, where she sobbed for the next forty minutes.

O'Brien sat in his office and read Gavigan's newspaper, the storm over as quickly as it began. An article about shark attacks fascinated him so much that he read it three times.

Chapter 6

Ramirez had another headache. He did not know whether this was new or simply a continuation of the one that had dogged him for the last few weeks. He lit another Camel and blew the smoke toward the man on the telephone. For a moment he could not recall why he was annoyed or even who the other man was, but when it came flooding back, his annoyance advanced to anger.

"Why is the dog barking?" Stephens said into the telephone.

"What is it?" Ramirez asked. Although the caller was unintelligible, his excited tone carried into the room.

"Not a problem." Stephens held up a finger and turned his attention back to the call. "I know he a homeless bitch, but ask the motherfucker if he's the police."

"Police?" Ramirez felt the hairs on his neck rise. Stephens shook his head over the barking noise coming through his wireless.

"Then put the dog on him!"

"I'm gone." Ramirez stood.

"Look, just take care of it, motherfucker. Do him if you have to. Just keep it quiet."

Stephens blocked the door and held up a hand to stop Ramirez. The three bodyguards with Ramirez all had their hands under their jackets. Stephens shut the phone and smiled. Ramirez stared at the hand blocking his exit.

"Just a small question of a bum roaming around out back."

"A bum."

"Probaly just looking for a place to sleep." Stephens flashed a gold tooth.

"In the alley."

"Right. No cause for alarm." Stephens gestured for Ramirez to return to his seat.

After the slightest hesitation, Ramirez went back to the table and flipped open his briefcase. Stephens took the seat opposite him.

"This is the proposal." Ramirez spun the case with its packets of cash.

"Seed money. You use it to finance your first purchase from us. Rate is twenty-five percent. Keep your projected sales volume up and you'll have it paid off within six weeks. After that your cut will be ten percent of everything you can move with zero percent financing up to one million in gross sales biweekly. You move more than that and your cut climbs at the rate of two and a half percent for every hundred thousand in sales."

"How much is here?" Stephens peered into the case.

"One million clean cash." Ramirez sounded bored. He was.

He wondered why it was that he had to make pitches to these retail dealers when he had partners who were just as able except for the fact that they were all in Mexico.

"Have I got to use all of it to finance the buy?"

"No, you can have up to five hundred thousand up front for your own purposes. However," Ramirez waved a practiced finger, "you still have to pay it off on schedule. The interest rate doubles for every week a part of the principal is still outstanding."

"Well, I would have to make some capital expenditures." Stephens's arms swept the room of the dilapidated safe house. He had a sixth-grade education, but knew all about illicit finance.

"It's your choice, but some of my associates can be unforgiving." Ramirez was practiced at delivering such threats. This deal would close. His mind wandered to his daughter waiting in the car, to the private jet that would fly him back to California as soon as he was finished here. Why couldn't he remember his daughter's name?

"Why are you coming to me with this?"

"Our former distributors in this area ran into some difficulties with law enforcement. This creates an opportunity for you, but if you are not interested I have other appointments to keep." Ramirez did not bother to reach for the bag.

"I think we can do business, but I need a larger percentage."

"How much larger?" Ramirez remembered that he had an MBA, the reason why his partners sent him to do this sort of thing. Of late, recollections like this came upon him like a flash as though he forgot the most basic facts about himself. Too much stress, he told himself.

"Thirty."

"Impossible." Ramirez stood up and reached for the bag, the expected step in the choreography.

Ramirez felt the first few cracks before he heard them. It was when the staccato started that he recognized the gunfire for what it was. It was outside, but not far. Ramirez's bodyguards had their weapons drawn without firing, not recognizing any target. Ramirez grabbed his bag. He did not want to be here, but could not recall why. His head was splitting. His people swarmed around him.

Stephens was on his phone. "What the fuck is—"

When Stephens's people charged through the door, the shooting inside the room began.

Ramirez had no weapon. He had people who did his shooting for him. He tried to squeeze himself behind the briefcase and make for the door, but he tripped over a writhing body. He felt the house shudder and sat up, dizzy from the fall. It was quiet. His eyes stung. He fluttered them and saw blood and bodies. Stephens slumped against the opposite wall with blood pumping from his chest. Something ran into Ramirez's eyes. He wiped them with his hand. It came away covered with blood. He tried to stand, but his legs would not move. He felt dizzy and shut his eyes against the blood.

When he opened them again, the vagrant was looking in the briefcase.

"My daughter? Is she all right?" Ramirez tried to ask in English, but Spanish came out.

The bum leveled a rifle at Ramirez.

"Your daughter?" Ramirez heard Spanish.

"She's in the Mercedes outside. Is she all right?"

"I'll check. Where are the keys?"

"There's a set in the bag."

Ramirez watched the vagrant hoist his briefcase. Before he blacked out, he wondered if it was such a good idea to have this man check on his daughter.

———— •◆•◂ ————

Artetia Roosevelt, R.N., looked up from the triage area to see a homeless man charging through the door of her emergency room and concluded that she needed security.

A guard assigned to the emergency department was an absolute must, she'd told the meeting of the managing committee on personnel resources earlier that day. There had always been a guard, but budget cutbacks meant fewer of them, and now they had to roam the area rather than sit right by the door. The committee told her the recommendation would be taken "under advisement," but she knew that absent a crisis nothing further would happen on her request. So she had wasted her own personal time to talk to the committee just to have this animal come into her emergency room on her very next shift. This filthy looking man with the piercing eyes might present the opportunity to prove her right, but there was no point in taking chances. She pushed the panic button under the countertop of the nursing station.

"I need help. This child's been shot."

Only with his statement did Artetia notice the bundle in the vagrant's arm. She snapped on latex gloves and peeled back the cover with the expectation that a rabid ferret would assault her. Instead she saw a little Hispanic girl who looked to be sleeping.

"Where?" Artetia asked.

"Thigh. Possibly lodged in the hip. Probably nine millimeter." He pulled back the blanket to reveal a dressing with blood seeping through it. "She was crying in the car, but stopped a minute ago."

Artetia looked back at the man. She wondered what kind of a bum drives a car.

"Johnny! We got a live one here. Call Dr. Pierce." She did not have to say "stat" or "hurry" or express urgency in any other medical manner. If she asked for a doctor, Johnny knew it was important. He came from a room behind the nurses' counter sporting gloves and protective eyewear. The homeless man handed the child to Johnny who disappeared with her into the back.

"When did this happen?" Artetia shed her gloves and turned to a form on a metal clipboard.

"Perhaps eight minutes ago, but maybe as much as twelve."

"What's the child's name?" She had a lot of information to get. Artetia noticed the man's watch and wondered if it was real.

"I have no idea."

"She's not yours then?"

"No. She's not mine. I have to be going now." The vagrant turned to leave.

Artetia smiled at Boris when he entered the emergency room from outside just as the vagrant had a moment earlier. She liked Boris. He came from Romania or Russia or someplace like that where he worked as a miner. He seemed grateful to have the thankless job of security guard at a hospital in the capital of the United States of America. Artetia waved her fingers one at a time and pointed at the bum. Boris, at six feet, two inches tall and two hundred thirty-seven pounds, blocked the entire exit. The bum walked right for him and Artetia looked down at her form to ascertain which of the blocks were really important since the man would not know everything.

Artetia looked up only after she heard the snapping noise and Boris's scream. She saw Boris suspended in the air. Except for his contorted face, he looked perfectly relaxed although he was parallel to the ground at shoulder level with the bum, who seemed to have hold of Boris's arm. Artetia momentarily doubted that Boris could be in such a position as his hand appeared to be on backward. He hung there for a moment like he was lying in a hammock waiting for someone to bring him one of those German beers he liked so much. Then he just dropped like a stone and hit the floor so hard that Artetia thought the impact boosted her off the floor a few inches. Boris yelped, but only for an instant as the air rushed from his lungs.

The vagrant bent down and took Boris's pistol. He looked back at Artetia, smiled, waved his fingers as she had, and left.

Chapter 7

Macuzak and Whitcomb heard about the gang assault in Washington before they left New Jersey. Unlike most police cars, the one they requisitioned for the drive to Washington featured an AM/FM stereo. Whitcomb tuned it to National Public Radio after enduring Macuzak's oldies station until the reception faded. On the Delaware Memorial Bridge, they caught parts of a Baltimore station, which related that someone had fired a rocket into a Washington crack house at almost the same time as the shooting.

"Jesus Christ. These guys are shooting rockets at each other now," Macuzak said.

"You'd think that would make the national news."

"I guess they're just interested in the body count."

"The subtle nuance of heavy weapons escapes them."

"You think this is our guy?"

"We'll soon find out."

It had taken time to schedule the meeting with Roger Sorenson. He had come through Camden and disappeared in less than twenty-four hours. Whitcomb and Macuzak felt the FBI had more pertinent information than what little Sorenson furnished. After avoiding their telephone calls for several days, the FBI special agent agreed to a meeting in Washington only after the detectives mentioned to Sorenson's voice mail that the Camden chief of police planned to call the FBI director.

On their way to FBI headquarters this morning, they detoured to the scene of the previous evening's assault. To their surprise, their New Jersey badges got them past the yellow barrier tape without a second look. They spotted Sorenson among the multitude of people sporting FBI windbreakers. Sorenson saw them, but did not look happy. They closed the gap to the door where Sorenson stood.

"Good morning, gentlemen," Sorenson said. "As you can see, I'm a little busy at the moment. Why don't we reschedule our meeting for a different day?"

"Hello, Roger. We were in the neighborhood and thought we might stop by to compare notes, since we came all this way," Whitcomb said.

Sorenson's face hardened. "I'm up to my ass in alligators here. I don't have time to deal with you now."

Macuzak ignored Sorenson and walked into the house. "How many dead?"

An agent taking pictures answered. "Ten or twelve. One left the house alive and one from the roof across the street was still in surgery last I heard. Some of the bodies are diplomatic."

"Excuse me," Sorenson said. "Please don't divulge information. I'm in charge here."

The man shrugged at Macuzak and turned back to his photography. Macuzak came back to the front door and lit a cigarette. The smoke puffed out as he spoke to Sorenson.

"Did he call yet?"

"Seriously, let's do this some other time." Sorenson turned away.

"Asshole."

Sorenson spun to face Macuzak. "What did you say?"

"He asked if Sullivan called yet," Whitcomb said.

Sorenson's eyes shifted from one detective to the other before answering. "No. I expect he will after lunch, if it's him. He left no card that we can find. This also looks way too untidy for Sullivan."

"We can talk about our case some other time, but we might as well observe what's going on with this one since we're here," Whitcomb said. "Don't you agree, Joseph?"

"Absolutely. Maybe we can pick up a few pointers."

"Well, I don't," Sorenson said.

"Very well," Whitcomb said, turning to Macuzak. "Do you think we can find that news van? You recall the one with the attractive African-American reporter. It was around the corner, was it not?"

"We can probably just hit the siren and she'll find us."

"I visualize a multipart, award-winning story featuring that young lady. I'd wager she will secure an anchor position with the network before we're through."

"Roger here can be in it," Macuzak said. "He'll be walking through a parking lot saying: 'No Comment,' while he blocks the camera with his laptop."

"Fine," Sorenson said. "Look around all you want, but don't touch anything."

"Great." Macuzak glanced around. "Who's catering this gig?"

Sorenson turned his back on them and made a call on his wireless. Macuzak and Whitcomb separated themselves from Sorenson and sauntered through the scene. They asked around for another hour before following Sorenson back to his office, where they sat and ate sandwiches while watching the telephone. Sorenson confirmed that some of the dead at the house held diplomatic credentials from Latin America but refused to divulge more. A Mercedes-Benz found at the scene belonged to an embassy pool. He related the tale of the child in the hospital, complained about the quality of the hospital's surveillance tape and fielded six telephone calls within forty-five minutes while tapping away at his laptop between bites. Just as he hung up from the last of the six calls, the telephone rang again.

"Hi, Roger. I claim Washington. Two locations."

"Jimbo! Shooting little girls now?" Sorenson snapped his fingers at the New Jersey detectives.

"Ballistics will match it to someone in the street. First location was just an old RPG with no injuries. At the second, I shot two pieces of muscle out front, one out back and maybe one on the roof across the street. I got anyone who made it into the alley with a Claymore mine. They all shot one another inside. Got all that?"

"You bet."

"I'm taking time off. You should do the same."

"Well, you won't deny you beat up the hospital guard?"

"No. You might want to put on a seminar for the guards there teaching them that they don't have the right to lay their hands on someone just because of their appearance. There was one Hispanic guy alive when I left the house; the little girl is his in case you didn't make the linkage. Did he survive?"

"Where was he in the house? We pulled a couple out alive."

"Bullshit. He was alive and maybe the guy on the roof across the street."

"Let's see, hmmm, I think I have the report here somewhere." Sorenson ruffled papers on the desk and smiled at the two detectives.

"Three seconds, Roger. Don't waste time. I don't care that much."

"He must be the guy with the brain tumor."

"Say again."

"A brain tumor. Shot in the head. They scanned him to find the bullet and there it was next to a tumor. Doc says—"

The click of the line stopped Sorenson. He stayed on the line and listened to the snaps and pops of technical wizardry.

"Did you get him?" Sorenson asked.

"Not exactly." Macuzak recognized the woman's voice from the call in New Jersey.

"What the fuck does that mean?"

"He's close, but he's cellular... Hold on... hold on... Georgetown? Georgetown. He's in Georgetown somewhere. Do you hear me? He's in George—"

Sorenson hung up and called a dispatcher. Sorenson ended the call and ran into the hall after pushing through Macuzak and Whitcomb.

"Sullivan didn't run too far, did he?" Macuzak said.

"No. We better keep up with our illustrious host."

"I was waiting for him to snap his fingers at me again."

The detectives rode in the back of Sorenson's vehicle. Another special agent to whom they were never introduced drove while Sorenson worked the radio and his telephone. He broadcast a physical description that fit every fourth man on the street. They heard it carry over the radio as it did in other police and FBI cars weaving through the colonial town. Macuzak had never been to Georgetown and was hopeful of catching Sullivan on a picturesque side street, but when he saw the Key Bridge over the Potomac River he elbowed Whitcomb.

"Egress out the wazoo." Macuzak waved toward the traffic flowing over the bridge.

"I see it," Whitcomb said. "At least it's a nice day for a ride."

"He's not fucking here." Sorenson said over and over.

———◼▸◆◂◼———

That evening, at Whitcomb's insistence, Macuzak ate dinner with his hands in an Ethiopian restaurant in Georgetown. Afterward, Macuzak claimed continued hunger and licked an ice cream cone as they walked through the darkened side streets. Whitcomb puffed his pipe.

"What are the similar crime numbers we've come up with again?" Whitcomb asked.

"About two dozen other assaults like these last two that we've been able to shake out," Macuzak said. "Of course, we could be a lot more certain if Sorenson would just share his files."

"Probably locked inside his computer." Whitcomb fiddled with his pipe. "Are they all the same?"

"Pretty close. All the victims are scum. Looks like this kid last night was the first mushroom."

"They're not all black, you know. There were at least two hits on white meth labs." Whitcomb puffed.

"Yeah, well, we can't let the brothers have all the fun."

"All in illicit drug sales or production."

"Kinda makes you wonder why he hasn't been caught yet, what with the war on drugs and all."

"Or whether he should be caught."

"What do you think Funtz had to say?" Macuzak asked, finishing his ice cream and moving on to the cone.

"I think he told Sorenson what he thinks and then Sorenson ignored him. What do you think?"

"I think you're right, but what I mean to ask is do you think this guy's crazy?"

"No." Whitcomb exhaled the word with the pipe smoke. "I don't think he's insane, whatever that means from a legal standpoint. What is your impression?"

"I think you're right. You should write it down that I agreed with you twice in a row. He's too much on top of this to be delusional. What's his motive?"

"Anger. He's angry. Really, really angry. If he were crazy, he could not turn it off and on like he does. He has too much control to be insane. Presumably, we will extract more data from Mr. Sorenson and gain greater insight into what we are confronting. From what I gather, Mr. Sullivan paces himself and plans thoroughly. And twice is not a row. It's a pair."

"Agreed." Macuzak crunched through the last of his cone.   "He's crazy like a fox. Example: He could have offed that guard at the hospital, but he didn't. That's three times I agreed with you. That's enough for a row."

"That whole scenario with the child in the hospital indicates lucidity to me if not some residue of a conscience. It may have upset him, and that is why he's calling a truce. That seems to be a comparatively rational course of action to me."

"I don't know. He seems to move where and when he wants. Friggin' iceman is what he is. He might need a break for some other reason." Macuzak said.   "Maybe he doesn't think he can jerk Roger around anymore."

"Perhaps. Or maybe he's finished."

"Or maybe he's out of rockets."

They walked toward the shore of the Potomac River and down some steps to a segment of an old canal with a recreation path along it. They commandeered a bench and watched the slow waters of the canal.

"How many more days before we're off the job?" Whitcomb banged his pipe in his palm.

"Twenty-eight, if you deduct the accumulated vacation and sick time. You might be a little different, but we'll be off by Christmas."

"Four weeks. That is not enough time for this one."

"There isn't enough time in the world for this one, Georgie. The guy's a loner. We have no conspirators, so no leaks. He's proven he can move right under our noses. No one can catch this guy if he continues to operate this way. Now, he's fallen off the scope for God knows how long. Maybe forever."

Macuzak shifted in his coat. "Someone else is gonna have to clean up this mess. I suspect a whole boatload of people are gonna be needed to clean this up."

Whitcomb used a pipe cleaner and hunted through his pockets for his tobacco pouch.

"Do you ever actually smoke that thing?"

"As little as possible," Whitcomb said.

"You should go back to the Luckies."

"You should quit altogether."

Macuzak lit his last Marlboro for the day.

"Do you think Roger knows any of this?" Whitcomb said.

"I think Sorenson's enough of a prick that it doesn't matter what he knows."

"It's all about him?"

"Bingo."

Chapter 8

The sun was long down as Sullivan drove through the mountains. A diffuse light reflected against the low clouds to announce his destination. The casino slid into view as he followed a bend in the highway between two lesser peaks, but it disappeared as the road continued its search for the path of least resistance. After another curve, the road straightened so that he could see the complex two miles ahead to the right of the highway as it dropped from the mountain pass. It took another ten minutes to actually enter the parking lot of the casino and find a spot for the Chevy Suburban.

Sullivan rubbed his eyes and ran his hands over his face. He opened Ramirez's laptop and the Post-it notes spilled onto the floor. He gathered and flipped through them for the fortieth time since his last conversation with Sorenson. He was not reading them since their neat instructions, account numbers, and passwords had long since been committed to memory.

"A brain tumor," Sullivan said.

Guy must've had a hard time remembering what his name was.

In his odyssey with the computer, Sullivan had employed the information on the five large Post-it notes to embezzle just over forty-two million dollars. Paul Stewart, one of his alternate Canadian identities, became an even wealthier man as he liquidated Ramirez's assets and bounced funds from New York to Panama to Toronto to London to

Bermuda to Grand Cayman. Sullivan was careful not to completely drain any of the accounts or portfolios. He had some experience laundering funds, but never had dealt with such substantial sums. He assumed some oversight body somewhere would detect the massive liquidations and transfers, but Stewart was already gone. To the dismay of a very nice bank president, Stewart closed his accounts where he dumped this fortune and physically moved among a dozen other banks and brokerage houses first with bearer's instruments and ultimately with valises of cash. Sullivan spread the wealth among several identities at the risk of losing vast amounts to a mugger, customs inspector, or express company.

Easy come, easy go.

He reached into the backseat and swapped the computer for a large Resistol hat. He already sported a pair of well-worn boots peeking from the cuffs of his jeans. He pulled a sheepskin coat over his stylized western blazer. The snow had yet to come to the valley floor, but the night air stung to the point that he would be cold by the time he reached the door. He locked the Suburban and studied his reflection in the glass of the driver's door to make sure the hat was reasonably straight. The scraggly moustache and beard were genuine. Gradient tinted glasses completed the ensemble. He thought he looked the part of a westerner, or at least a Texan in the event anyone noticed the license on the Suburban.

Let's see how this gig works.

Although he was not anywhere near the state and had never used this particular disguise, Sullivan sometimes found it convenient to pretend he hailed from Texas. It was a large state with lots of occupants from numerous places no one had ever heard of or visited and, therefore, whose names would not be recalled through the course of casual conversation. If necessary, he could be loud and gregarious to satisfy the expectations of many non-Texans. While the listeners' attentions focused on endorsing their stereotypes they would pay less attention to him and disregard his actual features.

Friday night on the reservation. Yee-haw.

Sullivan crossed the parking lot crowded with dozens of tractor trailers. He noticed a few men and women here and there among the rumbling rigs, the only universal feature they shared were the glowing tips of their cigarettes. He assumed that most of the females were prostitutes meeting the demands of the truckers. A woman stepped out from behind a Kenworth not fifteen feet ahead of him.

Like many men, Sullivan had the habit of appraising women before focusing on their faces. She wore a short jacket fashioned from some hapless animal's hide, which was open to expose a low-cut lace top over a short, tight black skirt. Her hosiery was dark against her legs and descended into a pair of stylized cowboy boots, the only sign of local color that distinguished her from an urban prostitute. Her hair was long and of a brown-blond variety.

Look at her face, idiot.

When he looked at her face he concluded that the woman was probably far more attractive in the absence of the overdone makeup. The cold flushed her cheeks and reddened her nose. Sullivan guessed she was about twenty or so, but long ago he had learned that he was terrible at guessing the ages of women between the ages of sixteen and forty-five.

Cute. Very cute.

"Well, howdy partner," she greeted him breathlessly with a wriggle of her shoulders and tossing of her long hair.

That was a little overdone.

"Hi." Sullivan knew with the utterance that he didn't sound like he was from anywhere west of New Jersey.

Should've taken the time to work on the accent.

"Got a light?" She eased a cigarette between her lips.

"Don't smoke," Sullivan answered.

He kept walking.

"How about a date?"

She stood in his path, forcing him to a stop. She grabbed his hat and put it on her head at an angle.

"Not tonight, missy. I got to get inside and lose some money," Sullivan said with some hint of an accent.

*Missy? Who in the hell uses the word "missy" when speaking to a woman? Take it easy. This isn't an episode of **Gunsmoke** and you aren't playing Festus here.*

He stepped around her to the left and reached for his hat, but as he did she wrapped herself around his right arm and began walking with him. She must have brushed the Beretta on his hip since he felt the holster move. He caught a flash of concentration on her face as she matched his stride.

"Well, then, how about some plain old company? My name's Rose, like the Yellow Rose of Texas? What's yours?"

Sandalwood.

God, she smells good.

Sullivan stopped and disentangled himself to hold the woman at arm's length.

"Look, here. I'm not interested. You're just wastin' your..." Sullivan stopped talking as he looked into the woman's eyes.

Oh, Christ. Don't start crying on me.

"How old are you anyway?"

"Twenty-six," she said.

"Bullshit."

Sullivan looked around among the tractor trailers. He guessed she was seventeen under all the makeup.

"Look, have you got a vehicle or transport?"

"Well sure, honey. It's right over here," she said. "Come on over with me and we'll have us a party."

"No. We won't."

Sullivan reached into the pocket of his jeans and peeled bills from his roll.

What a freakin' fiasco. I can't even get in the door.

"Here's five hundred dollars..."

"Well, for that we can have a party right here."

"It's gas money. Get in your car and go home, wherever that is. Visit your momma for Christmas."

Sullivan pressed the money into her hand. He turned away and continued his walk to the casino. He did not look back for fear he would see the young woman approaching another man.

A garish sign six stories above the main entrance explained that the casino operator and owner was the local Indian nation, a point made on billboards that closed ranks to every thousand yards or so for the last five miles of the highway. Under the marquee, a man who did not appear to have any Native American blood opened the door for him. The doorman wore a buckskin suit fringed with glitter and sequined feathers.

"How," he said as he opened the door.

Sullivan shook his head and stepped inside. He checked his coat with a woman whose heavy makeup mimicked some type of stylized figurehead on a totem pole. Sullivan kept his hat on his head as that seemed acceptable behavior as far as cowboy hats were concerned. It also obscured the views of the security cameras sprinkled throughout the casino's ceiling. He left the coat check and chose one of the two escalators to the floor below the lobby level.

He descended into a dark room the size of a football field. Some light shone from the slot machines arranged in neat rows, but the only significant illumination came from the lights situated directly over the gaming tables which, like the machines, were too numerous to count. He strolled through the blackjack parlors and scanned the area. His quarry liked to play baccarat, rather than something as pedestrian as blackjack, roulette, or craps. Sullivan walked toward the rear of the casino where four baccarat tables sat on a dais separated from the main floor by a glass enclosure. He glanced back at the escalators so he could keep his bearings. Like all casinos, this one enveloped its patrons to make it difficult to leave without encountering a score of temptations contrived to separate the last dollar from any departing patron. The Indian theme had dwindled to a hint of native dress on the cocktail waitresses. The dealers sported costumes reminiscent of white settlers of the nineteenth century.

Better to lose your money to the white man than to the savages, but the squaws are good enough to fetch your liquor.

Clever people, the Indians, once they got the hang of all this bullshit.

Good for them.

At the baccarat enclosure, Sullivan could not see the players through the glass because there were spectators lined up to look inside. He found a gap where he could peer over the shoulders of two women. Inside he saw four players: two Asians, a Native American, and a bald Caucasian man with a red bandana tied on his head.

Bingo.

The bald man was Larry Withers.

You are one ugly bastard, Larry.

The cute girl from the parking lot pushed into Sullivan's thoughts.

Yeah, yeah. Compare and contrast. Get your head in the game.

Withers was close to sixty years old, but it was hard to tell. He looked fit and muscular in his leather jacket and turtleneck. Sullivan figured the physique was more than a remnant of the days when Withers was a Green Beret in the jungles of Laos, later a case study within the army's elite forces of a soldier gone bad. Many of the stories associated with him were complete fabrications, but there were some facts and rumors on which Sullivan made the decision to approach Withers.

Larry Withers, also known as Larry Watson; Larry Wilson; Claymore Withers; Claymore Watson; Claymore Wilson; Alfred Lutz; Garcia Watson; Mr. Clean; Lightning; and, to his closer acquaintances, Bolt.

1970: Medically discharged for a psychiatric problem first detected as a consequence of still-classified events in Laos.

1970: Narcotics charges. California. Dropped.

1971: Armed robbery; assault with a deadly weapon.   Kansas. Convicted.

1978: Narcotics charges. Oregon. Acquitted.

1978: Armed robbery. Utah. Convicted.

1970-1987: Followed Grateful Dead when not in prison.   Acquired lightning-bolt tattoo extending completely over his scalp.

1985: Charged with armed robbery and homicide, three counts. California. Acquitted after lone eyewitness disappeared.

1988-2000: Whereabouts unknown. Believed to associate with militia elements in northwest and Rocky Mountain states. Suspected of procuring and vending Class 2 firearms and explosives.

Beyond this information, Sullivan sought out a notorious retired soldier from Fort Benning who was believed to be in contact with Withers. The former soldier, a bigot from Alabama, was drunk when Sullivan approached him. He divulged that Withers was a source for illegal weaponry not just for the militias, but for anyone with the available currency. The old soldier had no contact information, but intimated that Withers played baccarat every Friday in this casino.

Sullivan found no outstanding arrest warrants for Withers but did pick up the aliases. He did not think Withers would be under surveillance and hoped that he might restock his depleted arsenal. Sullivan tried a similar purchase from a man in Louisiana named Leroy Buckwell who boasted he was a member of the Ku Klux Klan. Sullivan secured the weapons, including those he used in Camden and Washington, but only after Buckwell tried to rob him.

Another fiasco.

I ought to just walk on this and go for the hijacking in a couple weeks. Probably not gonna use the guns anyway.

All the players had cocktails in front of them and Sullivan guessed they were not their first drinks of the evening. The Asians were together. Withers and the Indian seemed to know each other as well. Sullivan did not understand baccarat, nor did he care to learn, but from what he saw, the Asians had the advantage over Withers and the Indian. The game closed with one of the Asians beaming over the presentation of a large pile of chips. He won big enough to warrant an escort to the cashier. The two Asians stood to leave. They bowed at Withers's scowl.

Well, I came all this way.

Sullivan had no set script in mind. Getting weapons was the weakest part of his enterprise. He elbowed through the dissipating observers into the enclosed area, where he pushed a hundred-dollar bill into the hand of the casino worker keeping out the lower orders of gamblers. Once inside he dropped his glasses on the table and flopped into the seat next to Withers.

"Howdy, Larry."

Withers paused for a moment, his whiskey glass at his lip. He sipped and returned the drink to the table.

"Are you talking to me?"

"Why, yes. You're Larry Withers and I am talking to you."

"I think you're mistaken," Withers met Sullivan's gaze.

"I don't think so. You look like a bald psychopath and I'll bet that when I take that bandana off your head and shove it up your ass I'll find a lightning bolt on top of your skull which, incidentally, is the brightest thing that ever traversed your thick head. So, why don't we cut the bullshit and do some business which you will find both interesting and lucrative."

Withers stared at Sullivan. The dealer and his pit boss shifted on their feet.

"Bolt, let's get outta here," the Indian said.

"Shut up, Tonto. I'm not talking to you and neither is the Dead Head here.

"What's the matter, Larry? Cat got your tongue or are you thinkin' about killing those two gooks who just took your money? Maybe you're havin' a flashback about bein' back in the jungle killin' women and kids."

"I never killed any women and kids." The answer came without hesitation.

"Really? That's not what I heard back when I wore a green beanie." His had been maroon, but Sullivan had enough common experience that he could fake it.

"What the fuck do you know about it? You weren't there."

"Right, Larry, I wasn't there. So? You wanna spend all night traveling down memory lane or do you want to know what motivates a crazy bastard like me to insult you like this?"

Why do I bother with this shit?

Withers smiled and gestured at the table. "Do you play?"

"What do I look like? James Bond? No. I don't play and from what I've seen neither do you. Besides, we need to take a walk. I've got Dick Clark sitting in my van with a giant check. So, what do you say? Walk with me, talk with me, or whatever the line is for the day."

Withers stared at Sullivan while the casino workers held their breath. The Indian shifted his eyes between Sullivan and Withers, who continued to stare at one another.

Perhaps the direct approach wasn't the best idea.

"Sure. Why not." Withers pushed back from the table.

"Wait a minute, Bolt. This stinks. You don't know this asshole. He might be a cop."

The Indian might make a meaningful contribution yet.

"He ain't a cop. Cops don't have the cojones to talk like that. Besides, you know all the cops around here and you haven't said shit. Do you recognize him?"

"No. He might be federal."

Withers smiled. "Well, for his sake, I hope he's got some good backup. Let's go."

They left the enclosure and walked toward the escalator, Sullivan and Withers next to one another with the Indian trailing. They did not talk much but did establish that they would ride together in Withers's vehicle to an undisclosed location. The Indian, Redfeather, had already had too much to drink that evening and Withers was not far behind him. Sullivan had no intention of encountering the police because he rode with a drunken driver. He guessed they were armed, but so was he. If necessary, Sullivan would kill Redfeather to convince Withers to cooperate. If Withers refused, he would die and it would be a small loss to the world.

Another cluster fuck brewing. I should just walk.

"I've got to get my coat," Sullivan told them as they reached the top of the escalator.

"Fuck your coat," Redfeather said. Since boarding the escalator, he mentioned three times that he thought Sullivan was a cop and this was some type of ambush. Withers just smiled and let him talk.

"Have you got a stub?" Sullivan asked Withers, ignoring Redfeather.

"No. I'm ready for action." Withers evidently also felt it appropriate to ignore Redfeather. "Hurry up. I'm gonna take a piss on the way out."

Sullivan peeled off to the left toward the coat-check window.

Grab the coat and keep moving. Leave the girl a nice tip.

When he was about thirty feet from Withers and Redfeather he heard someone scream, "Cops!"

Sullivan turned toward the sound in time to see Redfeather training a nickel-plated Colt Python with a four-inch barrel at him.

Big revolver. Expensive.

He reached for the Beretta on his hip.

Why do I bother appraising the weapon he's got? You'd think I was shopping for apples.

He slipped into a crouch as the Beretta cleared the holster.

There were Braeburns, Granny Smiths, Romes, but they were, after all, just apples.

He rotated the safety catch as he raised the handgun to firing position, when a flash and deafening report confirmed that Redfeather had fired just as Sullivan felt something slam into his chest. He fell backward and could not catch his breath.

I love Cortlands. Sullivan thought even as he gasped for air.

Chapter 9

Sergeant Stacey Smith heard shots when she was near the bottom of the ascending escalator. There were people above her on the moving stairway who were trying to come down against the machine's flow. She hopped over the rail onto the parallel staircase and drew her SIG. She ran up the steps and crouched as she got near the top.

She peered over some of the people huddled on the top steps to see the Indian aiming toward the door. He shot at Williams, one of her two backup officers. Williams was kneeling on the floor training and firing his weapon as the Indian did the same. Jenks, her regular partner, and the Texan were down. The biker was crawling for cover behind some kind of booth off to the right. People were screaming, but the gunfire muted their cries.

Sergeant Smith then did something that violated all the rules of training, experience, and common sense she possessed. She abandoned her cover, stood erect, and leapt up the last few steps with her weapon trained on the Indian. She screamed something about being a police officer and to drop the gun.

"I'm out!" Williams yelled.

Smith fired at the Indian. The Indian kept firing at Williams. Williams fell backward as the Indian wilted into a heap. Smith expended all her ammunition during her advance toward the Indian.

She did not have a spare magazine. She closed the gap with the Indian and took the weapon from his hand. He was still moving. She looked to her right, but the biker was nowhere in sight. There were people on the floor all around, but it looked as though many of them had simply dropped and were now scrambling for cover. She started toward Williams but stopped ten feet from him. Williams lay on his back with his right leg behind him in an impossible position. His face and most of his head were gone. She turned toward Jenks, but caught sight of the biker in her peripheral vision. He hobbled for an emergency exit at the far end of the lobby. She sprinted after him to close the distance and dropped onto her right knee. Smith extended her newfound weapon in a firm two-handed grip.

"Freeze!"

The biker turned as Smith leveled the sights on the Indian's Python. He raised a large pistol in his left hand, but Smith held the sights of the Python centered on his chest some fifteen yards away. She squeezed the trigger and the hammer fell without results. She squeezed the trigger twice more, the cylinder rotated, the hammer snapped.

"Shit!"

Smith dove left in search of shelter, but found herself sprawled on the floor looking back toward the front door where Williams lay. A deep burn rose from her right thigh, and her leg wouldn't respond; she struggled for cover, the burning intensifying to a sharp pain. When she looked over her shoulder, the biker was close by, pointing his weapon at her, smirking. He started to say something, but his head exploded.

———■◆■———

"Nice shot." Sullivan exhaled as he let his head and the Beretta drop back to the floor.

He sucked in two more breaths and sat up with a groan. His bullet-resistant vest had saved his life, but he guessed he had several broken ribs. Redfeather was either not as drunk as he had thought or a good shot despite it. His single shot hit the chest plate insert of the vest and would have been fatal in its absence.

Sullivan struggled to his feet and replaced his cowboy hat. He checked the two men near the door. One had been hit in the head. The other had been hit in the chest two or three times. The wounds bubbled some air but his stare was long fixed on the ceiling. Sullivan walked to where Redfeather lay on his back. He had several wounds in his abdomen and one of his legs. Sullivan guessed they were from the empty SIG on the carpet nearby. Redfeather was still breathing but seemed to be unconscious. Sullivan kicked him hard, but he did not stir. He felt around Redfeather to confirm he had no functional weapons and moved to the woman. She was conscious but bleeding from her right leg. Sullivan guessed her femoral artery was compromised by Withers's .45 automatic. Sullivan knelt down next to the woman as he activated the safety on his Beretta and holstered it.

"Hey, how ya' doin'?" He used his Swiss Army knife to cut away the tattered fabric over her right thigh. In his rush, he had given up on the accent.

"I'm fine. Check on my partners."

"Someone's got them already. Looks like you're stuck with me. What's your name?"

"Smith. Stacey—Sergeant Stacey Smith. Highway Patrol."

Sullivan looked to his left for some help. There were people milling around. He saw a man who looked like a Native American. He wore a blazer with some type of patch and had a radio held up to his face. Sullivan made eye contact and yelled for an ambulance. The man nodded his understanding and continued speaking into his radio.

Good job, James. Getting more innocent people shot.

He turned his attention back to the cop. "Well, Sergeant Stacey Smith, tell me where it hurts besides your leg."

"Nowhere. Just my leg." She tried to sit up, but fell back down.

"Whoah! Stay down." Sullivan pulled a combat dressing from his jacket, opened the packet, and pressed it on the wound with his left hand.

"Does that hurt?" He was surprised she had not screamed. The bandage was already saturated.

"What?"

"My pressing. Can you feel me pressing?"

"I guess. Something I feel. It feels far away."

Sullivan felt around with his right hand, but could not find an exit wound.

"Havin' a good time there?"

"Can you feel your foot?"

"Yeah. I'm cold."

"Can you wiggle your toes?"

"What?" Her head lolled around.

He knelt in a pool of her blood. The pressure seemed to slow the bleeding, but he wasn't sure if that was an effect from his effort or the fact that she had already lost so much blood that she was not losing it as fast. Sullivan was afraid she would go into shock.

"I'm gonna lift your legs."

Smith screamed and passed out as Sullivan shoved his leg under her buttocks and hung her calves over a shoulder. Sullivan plugged his little finger into the entry wound. His fingertip found the pulsing flow and obstructed it. He saw two emergency medical technicians come in the front door carrying bags of gear.

"Sergeant! You with me? Wake up!"

"What?"

"Wiggle your toes!"

She complied and seemed to focus. "Jesus, that hurts."

"Sergeant Smith, I need you to hold on 'cause the cavalry's almost here."

"Don't give me that accent shit! You ain't from Texas anymore than I am."

Sullivan studied her face.

"Hey, you're the hooker from the parking lot. You should've used the gas money."

"Yeah? And I'll tell you something else. You're under arrest."

"No kiddin'?"

"What are ya doin' with those guys?"

Keep her talking.

"What guys?"

"What guys! How 'bout the guy who shot me, for Christ's sake!"

"Ohhh, those guys?"

"Yeah, those guys. I saw you in the casino with them."

"Sergeant, did you follow me inside? Were you really trying to pick me up?"

No answer. Stay alive. Keep focused.

"So. Sergeant, how long have you been a cop?"

"What?"

"A cop. How long have you been a cop?"

"I don't know, uhhmm, six, no, seven years."

"You don't look old enough to be on that long."

"Yeah, right. You're full of shit. What's goin' on with Jenks?"

"Is Jenks your partner?"

"Yeah. I saw Williams. He's dead isn't he?"

"Yeah. I'm afraid so."

Let her think about that for a minute.

"Look. Go check on Jenks. He's got a wife and two boys."

"Jenks is taken care of."

"He's got a family."

"How old are his boys?"

"I'm not sure. Five and three, I think."

"That's good. They're funny when they're that small. Like little people with little personalities."

"I was over at their house not too long ago," She laughed and seemed to have forgotten that she was bleeding to death on the tasteless, drink-stained carpet of a casino. "And Kyle, he's the little one—"

"How do you spell that?"

"Kyle?"

"Yeah."

"K-I-L-E, I think."

"Are you sure? I thought that was spelled K-Y-L-E."

Thrash a little.

"No. They spell it with an 'i.'"

"Really? That's unusual. What's the other one's name?"

"Lucas." Her answer came slowly.

Don't slip away here.

"So what did Kile do?"

"What's that?" She actually smiled.

So much blood. Does she have any left?

"You were over Jenks's house and Kile did something."

"Oh, yeah. I was over there and Kile—they live way out in the country and there's lots of mud—so, the boys are always runnin' around with these big rubber boots on. So, I'm there and it's time to go, but it rained, so there's these big puddles out there and Kile's there rockin' back and forth and I turn to wave and he just plops right over into the mud." She started to laugh.

Where are those guys?

"He fell over on his face?" Sullivan thought the laughter was good.

She laughed and tried to cover her mouth to suppress it. Tears rose in her eyes. Sullivan laughed along with her. He looked behind him and saw the EMTs attending to Redfeather.

"Forget him! Over here! Now!" Sullivan shouted. One got up with a bag and came his way.

"Are you married, Sergeant? Is there someone you want me to call so they can meet you at the hospital?"

"That's not really any of your business, is it? Besides, I'm not gonna make it anyway."

Better pissed off than unconscious.

"Now, there you go. That is a perfect argument why women make lousy cops."

"What?" She assumed full command of her senses.

Ahhhh, found some second wind.

"Well, you're shooting your mouth off about things you don't know anything about. You just lay there and whine about not making it home alive and that's just pure unadulterated bullshit. Plus, you have these mood swings. One minute you're laughing and the next you're all bent out of shape."

"I'm bleeding out. Have you got a cigarette?"

"No you're not. I've been hit worse than this and here I am wasting my time trying to help you out and all you want to do is bitch like you're some kind of tragic hero. We should have some kind of background music for the bullshit you're slinging out there. And you ask me for a cigarette? Don't you know those are bad for you?"

"You know what? You are under arrest."

"Yeah, right. If you're real sweet, wear a short skirt, and make good coffee, maybe, just maybe, they'll let you type up the reports on this back at headquarters."

"You're such an asshole you must be a fed."

"Now with that attitude, I can see why you're not married."

"Fuck you."

"Never even engaged?"

"Fuck you."

"You'd probably get more dates if you stopped smoking and cursing."

The EMT knelt beside Sullivan. He was a Native American maybe thirty years of age. "What have we got?"

"This is the lovely Sergeant Rose—that was your first name right, dear?"

"Stacey, asshole."

"Sergeant Stacey 'Asshole' Smith who has been shot once in the right thigh with a forty-five automatic. She is cold but has feeling in her lower leg. I couldn't find any exit wound. My guess is that she needs lots and lots of expanders, an air cast or tourniquet, and a helicopter. I suggest that you get your partner over here to help you. You have a hemostat, or a clamp, or something?"

"Chopper's already been called. He's got the other one."

"The other one isn't going to make it. Call him over," Sullivan read the EMT's name tag, "Mr. Halfmoon."

Halfmoon looked into Sullivan's eyes as he repeated the command. "Call him over."

Halfmoon called to his partner, "Kermit, get over here!"

"Kermit? Like the frog? Wild." Smith's head rolled from side to side on the carpet.

Kermit came over and squatted on the other side of Sullivan with more gear. He, too, was a Native American, in his late twenties or early thirties, with huge hands that seemed to grow as he changed his rubber gloves. "What have you got?"

"We got a bleeder we need to clamp," Halfmoon said.

"Vitals?"

"Yeah. See if she's still good for morphine." Halfmoon had the clamp in his hand. He looked at the pool of blood.

Smith lost consciousness.

"Clamp her now," Sullivan said.

"Yeah, she's out."

Halfmoon slid the clamp along Sullivan's finger and pinched the vessel.

"Take my place, Kermit." Sullivan stood up with a grimace.

Halfmoon saw the hole in his shirt for the first time: "Are you okay, man?"

"I'm fine. Hey darlin', I'm takin' you dancin' in a few weeks. Okay?"

Smith did not answer. Sullivan turned toward the front door. He picked up speed as he walked. Without breaking stride Sullivan drew his Beretta and shot Redfeather twice in the head. The revolving door muffled the renewed screams as he stepped into the cool night with his sidearm already back in its holster.

Chapter 10

Neither man knew Commissioner Flynn although MacDonough had met him once. The commissioner was new to the job and had been hired from outside the ranks of the Highway Patrol. The secretary's telephone buzzed. She told the two men they could enter. MacDonough and Christenson found Commissioner Flynn seated behind his expansive old desk surrounded by still-packed boxes. He greeted them with handshakes and motioned them to a sofa while he took a seat away from his desk.

The commissioner spoke first. "Well, I'd love to sit here and tell you about the football games I watched yesterday, but I didn't see any because of this casino thing. I went to see Sergeant Smith again and the governor wanted to shoot the breeze on the phone and some chief what's-his-name from the Indian nation got my home number, too. So, I didn't do too much but try to keep people off your backs and let you do your jobs. How'd you make out?"

Captain MacDonough spoke. "Well, we got pretty far and we ran into some problems, but we have plenty of leads to allow us to inform you of what we think happened."

"Have we got enough to talk to these press people?"

"I think so, but there are some questions we don't know the answers to yet."

"Cover what you have and we'll address the other parts at the end. I think I know what's going on, but I don't want to say anything that'll cross us up. At the same time, I want to make sure that everything has been coming up the chain. And, so you know, the governor scheduled this damn press conference and I can't do anything about postponing it. So, let's get moving."

"Okay. During the late evening of this Friday past and early morning of Saturday we had in place at the casino an anti-vice operation with Sergeant Smith posing as a prostitute in the parking lot."

"What about that? Is that our jurisdiction?" The commissioner scrawled notes.

"We have jurisdiction in part of the parking lot because it's part of the highway right-of-way," said Lieutenant Christenson. "The parking lot occupies an area where equipment and materials were staged in the valley while the road was put through the mountains."

"Fine. Continue."

"Patrolmen Williams and Jenks were Smith's backup and surveillance team. They were set up in a motor home in the lot. At some point late Friday night, possibly early Saturday, Smith encountered a suspect who carried a concealed weapon. She believed he behaved suspiciously, so she elected to follow him into the casino for the purpose of observing his movements and possible arrest."

"Well, now wait a minute. She told me about this guy. She said he ignored her dangle and then she tried harder by grabbing his arm or something and she felt a weapon—which turned out to be true from what I gather—and the guy then threw money at her."

"Right. So she decided to follow him inside."

"Well, now that's a problem. What she actually did was follow him inside with the intent of making a stop of him when he came back out. You see she doesn't just want people carrying concealed weapons around and endangering citizens."

"Sir," Christenson said, "probably half the people in this state, the men at least, carry firearms at one time or another."

"Lieutenant Christenson, I have personally reviewed this matter with the only surviving officer from the incident and it is clear in our minds that she was going to stop this suspect outside. That's what happened. Do you understand?"

MacDonough flipped through his notes. "The suspect's vehicle was registered in Texas."

"Well, there you go, Lieutenant," the commissioner said. "We can't have a bunch of Texans with handguns running around our state. What's next?"

MacDonough continued. "All right, she changes out of her hooker rig and followed him in while she had Williams and Jenks check on the Texan's truck, a Suburban, which was stolen and has been found."

"It's been located? I didn't hear that. Where was it?"

"It never left the lot; we impounded it Saturday morning and have processed it already. We found another vehicle we think the Texan used to escape."

"I'm sorry. Am I screwing you up with these questions? Why don't you give me the whole thing and I'll ask questions at the end. We were at the part where Williams and Jenks checked on the truck and learned it was stolen. They decided they should do their duty and back up the officer who was merely conducting surveillance of a legitimate suspect to be arrested on exit from the casino. Clearly, they went in due to the exigency of the circumstances of a fellow officer being in peril. Continue, Captain."

"Okay. Smith went inside and saw the Texan in the baccarat room on the lower floor of the casino. He met with two men positively identified as Lawrence Withers and Claude Frontenac. Both men have sheets and aliases. Withers is—was white and Frontenac a Native American from New York."

"Did we ID the Texan?"

"Yes and no. He's—"

"I'm interrupting again. I'll stop, but you'll get to that part right?"

"Yes, sir."

"Incidentally—funny story—did you ever hear those guys on the radio Click and Clack or Tip and Tack or whatever the hell their names are?"

"*Car Talk,*" Christenson said.

"Right. Right. *Car Talk.* Have you ever heard that show, Phil?"

"No, sir."

"Anyway. These guys, who are absolutely nuts, state that the official car of Texas is the Suburban, which is what we have here."

"Yes, sir."

"Well, I guess you have to hear it. It's a lot funnier when they do it."

"Tell him about the Donna Theory," Christenson said.

"Oh yeah, yeah, yeah," Flynn said. "They have this other, eh, hypothesis that whenever you see a woman—"

"A young woman," Christenson said.

"Yeah, yeah. A *young* woman with big hair speeding down the highway in a Camaro or Firebird doin' her makeup in the mirror that her name is Donna."

"Hand to God," Christenson said, "Shortly after I heard that I pulled over a woman under those identical circumstances and she was snappin' the gum and the whole deal and her name was Donna. I near about busted a gut tryin' to keep from laughin' when I looked at her license."

"Did you give her a ticket?"

"Hell, no."

"They're there in my hometown there in Cambridge."

"Do you know them, sir?"

"Well, Massachusetts is small, but it's not that small. Okay. I'm sorry, I interrupted again. We've got to do some more business."

MacDonough picked up the briefing. "Smith observed the Texan, Withers, and Frontenac at the table for about two minutes and had been in the casino for a total of less than fifteen minutes when they got up to leave. In the meantime, Williams and Jenks determined that the Suburban was stolen. They apparently decided that they should go tell Smith or offer her assistance. We'll never know for sure."

"I think we can safely assume they performed in accord with the high standards of our force as I've already outlined. Continue."

"The Texan, Withers, and Frontenac started to leave the casino and that's when the shooting started. We have video on that if you want to see it; I gather there is a video setup available here somewhere."

"Yes. They have something set up down in the training office. It's some type of big reel, right? One of you spoke to the technical fellow downstairs?"

"Yes, sir. I did," Christenson said. He extracted a large reel of tape from his briefcase.

"Well, let's go see it and you can talk over it."

Christenson and MacDonough went ahead while the commissioner dealt with some fresh telephone messages. In the training room, they met a video technician who threaded the tape onto a massive machine. Also in the room was Malcolm Welch, the chief of the crime lab. He had two large evidence bags with him.

"Hey, buddy, how you doin'?" Christenson said. "Good weekend?"

"The best. No sleep and now it's hurry up and wait. Old Ira and I have been waiting to start this briefing for twenty minutes."

"Hey, man, we already started. Where you been, boy?"

"Right here, where they told me to go."

"We started upstairs in the chief's office, but we're comin' down here now."

"Shoot. They told me to show up here. Did I miss anything?"

"I don't think so. I think the boss is goin' to handle everything with the press and we follow what he tells us and we'll be okay. It all boils down to there being one shooter unaccounted for and we just run him down."

"How is the boss?" Welch asked. "Is he okay?"

"Okay," both detectives said.

"Hey, have you ever heard of some radio program called *Car Talk*?" MacDonough asked Welch.

"Funny show. I listen to it every week."

"I never heard of it."

"You better move out of that cave. They're on public radio."

"The ones always beggin' for money?"

"That's why you never heard the show," Christenson said. "As soon as they ask for money you turn them off."

"I wouldn't if they didn't ask so much."

Commissioner Flynn strode in with his notepad and shirtsleeves rolled up. "Okay. We're gonna watch some films. Who's this?"

"Malcolm Welch, Commissioner. I'm head of the crime lab."

"Oh, excellent! Of course we've met a couple times. I didn't recognize you. You need some sleep I gather. Sit down and we can watch this and see what you have. Then you can rack out and get some rest. Ira, let's go."

A massive television in the corner jumped from solid gray to black-and-white interior views of the casino as seen from ceiling-mounted cameras. The screen showed twenty-five parts of the casino simultaneously in five rows of five images. Ira turned out the lights.

"What am I watching?"

"This is the surveillance tape from the casino," Christenson said. "As you can see, it picks up feeds from twenty-five camera locations inside the casino. There is another tape we have that takes into account the five cameras outside and another twenty cameras inside, plus others with all the table cameras, but this tape is the one that covers most of the pertinent area. There are other tapes, but this shows us what happened. We had to raise hell to get them from the Indians."

"Ira, can we zoom in on the parts we want if we have to?"

"Sure."

"Excellent. Let's get to the pertinent parts."

"Okay," Christenson said. "We have a few views of the Texan, but they are useless for identification because he wears a hat all through them. We have some shots of him coming in and checking a coat. Eight minutes later he's in the baccarat area sitting down with Withers and Frontenac, but still no good picture of his face."

"Did we talk to the dealer?"

"Yes, sir," MacDonough said. "He said the Texan came on really strong. The dealer knew Withers 'cause he was a regular. Thinks he saw Frontenac around once, maybe twice, but he never saw this guy before. The dealer said the guy wasn't from Texas. He guessed he was from back east and puttin' on some type of accent. The dealer is from New Jersey and worked in Atlantic City. We have him, the pit boss, the coat-check girl, and two cocktail waitresses going through mug books looking for the guy. We put together a composite, but it looks like every other guy on the street."

"Talk to Sergeant Smith and the two EMTs and see what you can do."

"Sergeant Smith was still sort of out of it each time we went to see her and the EMTs are scheduled to come back this afternoon."

"Okay. Stay on it. What else is on the tape?"

"We have them leaving the gambling area and then footage from upstairs where the shooting was," Christenson said.

"Let's see that," Flynn said.

"Watch the Texan walk away from the other two halfway down on the left side of the screen and the next thing you know he turns and Frontenac shoots him."

They watched the display as the events transpired as promised.

"Ouch. That hurt." Flynn said. "What did he use? Is that a magnum?"

"Colt Python, three-fifty-seven magnum."

"This is the one who was drunk?"

"Yes, sir. Mr. Frontenac. Point two one."

"Do we have sound?"

"No, sir, but we know from interviews that Frontenac yelled 'cops' before he started shooting. Ira, freeze it there. If you look on the next row higher on the right side of the screen you can see Williams and Jenks have just come in the door and you can still see Frontenac and Withers over here. It seems that Frontenac or Withers must have recognized Williams, or Jenks, or both. We're guessing they thought the Texan was setting them up so Frontenac shot him first. Okay, Ira."

They watched the gunfight play out. Withers gunned down Jenks while he took a round fired from one or both officers. Withers crawled. Frontenac seemed to jerk around, and with the disintegration of Williams's head the commissioner whispered, "Jesus."

Ira stopped the tape after Frontenac fell.

"Okay," Flynn said after a pause, "Let's see it again."

Ira replayed the tape six more times. The action consumed only twelve seconds in real time, but was slowed for clarity and expanded.

"Tell me this is the only tape," Flynn said. "I don't want to see this on the news. My cops getting killed by a goddamned cliché."

"Yes, sir. This is the original tape."

"That doesn't matter," Ira said.

"What?"

"I said that doesn't matter," Ira said it louder, "sir."

"Why not?" Christenson asked.

"Because these tapes are probably copied from a hard drive, which can reproduce the images. You don't need the tapes to make the pictures because the computer can do it. The images are digital. The tapes are only copies."

"Do you know if the Indians have that system?" Flynn's eyes bored into Ira.

"No. My guess would be they do since they spent the money on so many cameras and the images are kind of jumpy."

"Okay," Flynn said. "You fellows see to it that we get any computer imagery, if they have it. If they give you a hard time, call me. I don't want Mrs. Williams to have to watch her husband's head explode a million friggin' times while some anchorman tells us how terrible it is."

"They tried to chase us off the scene while we were processing," Christenson said. "We might have a hard time going back."

"Yeah, I know, but I'm not having any of this jurisdictional bullshit. They want to get territorial and I'll blockade their goddamned driveway."

"Yes, sir."

"I'll call the AG just to be safe, but they should be cooperative."

"Right."

Flynn waved at the screen. "Where's Sergeant Smith when all this is happening?"

"She's not in these frames, but if you look up here in the right corner you can see her come out of the stairway. You can also see the Texan on his back and Withers taking cover. It's a long view of the lobby from the far end opposite the entrance and lacks definition, but we can see things better when we make it full screen."

Ira made the image full screen and played the tape. It portrayed Smith emerging and gunning down Frontenac. She retrieved his weapon and looked for Withers who was closer to the foreground of the image taking cover. Smith checked Williams and then pursued the fleeing Withers.

"Jesus, balls of brass," Flynn said.

Smith fell from a shot fired by Withers who stood and walked toward her as she crawled for cover. As he stopped over her and took aim, his head blew apart and he dropped in place.

"What happened? Who shot him?"

Ira stopped the tape and rewound it.

"Watch the shape of the Texan in the frame." Christenson said. "And this, incidentally, is the only picture where he isn't wearing that damn hat."

The tape replayed and the Texan raised his arm along with his head. There was a flash near his hand at the same time Withers was hit.

"Jesus. How far is that shot?" Flynn was scribbling.

"One hundred and twenty-three feet. He hit him almost right between the eyes." MacDonough said.

The tape continued playing.

"Now watch what happens," Christenson said.

The Texan got up and ministered to Smith for several minutes. The EMTs came over and the Texan headed for the door.

"Ira, switch back to Frontenac," Christenson said.

The image showed the Texan stride past and execute Frontenac so quickly that it was almost missed. Ira replayed it slowly to show that the Texan shot the prone man in the head without even looking at him.

"He's pretty friggin' casual about that," Flynn said. "Got to be a pro."

"Especially when you consider he got shot in the chest and must have been hurting pretty good," MacDonald said. "Malcolm, do you have the vest?"

"Yeah," Welch said.

He pulled from one of his bags a piece of body armor.

"Where did you get that?" Flynn asked.

"It was recovered from a Porsche nine-twenty-eight at the Spokane airport along with this." Welch held up a 9mm Beretta. "We also have the cowboy hat, the shirt with the hole in it, and some really bloody clothes and boots."

"The Porsche was stolen from the casino," Christenson said, "but not reported for almost two hours because the owner didn't want to leave and miss any of the excitement. The valets had taken cover and didn't see who stole it. The pistol matches on the ballistics."

"Well, it's a seventy percent match at the moment," Welch said. "We have to run a couple more tests. He fired three rounds of Glaser Safety Slugs that basically disintegrate on impact. Frontenac's shot ran square into the ceramic insert in the vest and stopped there, but the shock probably broke some of his ribs. The blood on the clothes all belongs to Sergeant Smith."

"I guess so," MacDonough said. "They told me she got—what? Twelve or thirteen units of blood?"

"I heard fifteen through the surgery," Christenson said. "The EMT said she would've bled out except for this guy."

"Okay," the commissioner said. "This boils down to who in the hell is this guy with the cowboy hat and Beretta and where is he. The EMTs and Smith can ID him and help the sketch artist."

"I don't know about the EMTs," said Christenson. "One only saw him for an instant and he spooked the other one."

"What do you mean?"

"He told this EMT Halfmoon that the other EMT should help with Smith because Frontenac wasn't gonna make it, as in he was gonna do him on the spot. Now, this guy Halfmoon is no lightweight. He was one of those pararescue commandos back in the service who go and pick up injured pilots behind enemy lines. It sounded to me like this guy scared the shit out of him. I asked if he could identify him and he said he wasn't sure, but the guy had cold eyes even through his sunglasses."

"Did we get any prints?"

"Yes and no," Welch said. "We got a million lifts from the vehicles and casino, but a lot of them match nothing on file. We got a bunch of hairs from the hat, clothes, and cars, but they'll take a while to process."

"We got a hit with the FBI on a pattern crime database using the head shot, the Beretta, and the Glaser Slugs," MacDonough said. "The name furnished is James Sullivan. Then we ran the name James Sullivan and got a hit with the New Jersey Bar Association and the United States Army. The New Jersey lawyer is noted as inactive and the army guy is a captain listed as discharged on a medical. Malcolm's people lifted his partials from the Porsche and baccarat table. We're pretty sure he's our guy."

"Not enough points to testify to, but if you can grab him for some DNA, we'll get him with a hair," Welch said.

"What about the FBI file?" Flynn asked.

"Well, now, there's the rub," MacDonough said. "The file is coded inaccessible and we can't get it. Additionally, no one over there will tell us why we can't get it."

"Bullshit!" Flynn exploded from his chair. "Where's the phone?"

"There." Ira pointed.

Flynn dialed, covered the mouthpiece, and asked, "What's my secretary's name?"

"Lois," Ira said.

"Lois, can you do me a favor, dear?" Flynn spoke into the line. "Go to my Rolodex and get the number for Matty Feldman in Washington. I'll hold."

Flynn waited. "Okay, dial that office number and conference me in down here, and when you get off the line can you have sent down some more coffee and some doughnuts or danish? Just get what you think is good. Yeah, I'll hold on. How do I put this on speaker without hanging up?"

"Just hit the green button," Ira said.

Flynn hit the button and ringing filled the room.

"Matthew Feldman."

"Holy Christmas, is that you in the flesh? I expected voice mail or some comely wench answering your phone."

"Who is this?"

"Joe Flynn, Matty, how the hell are you?"

"Joe Flyyyynnnnnnnn. I should've known because of your reference to an obscure holiday in that pagan religion you follow. Don't you owe me money?"

"Blood from a stone if I do."

"I hear ya. How are things in Beantown?"

"Forget Beantown. I'm way out west where men are men and sheep are nervous."

"You sound funny and I don't mean the joke. Are you on a speaker?"

"Yeah. I have some investigators in the room with me and that's why the jokes aren't very good this morning. Hey, I thought you were a big deal down there. How come you answered your own phone?"

"Hey, listen. I'm lucky if they don't throw my sorry ass out of this corner office and put me in a cubicle with no windows so I can't look at the girls anymore."

"It's called re-engineering."

"I hear ya. Well, what's up? I presume you're up to your neck in our bullshit for no apparent reason."

"Matty, I got two dead cops, one wounded, and two dead suspects in a shoot-out. There's a suspect who escaped and we're havin' a hard time getting an ID on him in part because the Bureau has labeled his file 'inaccessible.' So we have a match based on the pattern of the shooting, but your computer won't tell us who he is. At the same time, we're getting a match on some lawyer from New Jersey named—" Flynn looked at the detectives.

"James Sullivan," MacDonough said.

"James Sullivan," Flynn said.

"James Sullivan. James Sullivan. James Sullivan. Another worthless Irishman. Hold on while I punch that in. I can't do anything on actually freeing the file without checking with someone. Here we go. Oooohhhhhh. This guy. I heard about this guy. We have a task force on this guy. What did he do? Kill some cops in a drug deal?"

"No. Our guys were in a casino and they were actually killed by two other suspects, both of whom were in turn shot by this Sullivan."

"Who did he shoot?"

"Sullivan killed the two guys who shot my cops."

"Oh, well. Can't bitch too much about that. Listen, I'll give you the contact on the task force and he can fill you in. Basically, from what I know, this guy is some half-baked vigilante who we're trying to run to ground. The guy you want to talk to is named Roger Sorenson. I'll transfer you, but here's his direct dial in case I lose you."

There was silence on the phone for a moment.

"Take me off the box will you, Joe?" Feldman said.

Flynn snatched the receiver. "How's that?"

The room's occupants could hear only Flynn's half of the discussion spaced over a few minutes.

"Oh yeah?" the commissioner said.

"Uh-huh."

"The old man, or the son?"

"Uh-huh."

"How much drag?"

"Right."

"Well, I've run into that kind of shit before, but the bottom line is I have two dead cops. End of story."

"Okay."

"I will."

"Okay, Matty, thanks an awful lot and give my best to Lorraine."

"Awwww, Matty, I'm sorry to hear that."

"I'll call you later this week."

"Bye, Matty."

The commissioner reached Sorenson's voice mail. Flynn left his name and number and selected options to indicate that the message was urgent. The FBI's telephone system disconnected him after the call.

"Okay. So our Texan is a lawyer and former soldier from New Jersey named Sullivan who kills drug dealers and the FBI hasn't been able to find him for at least a year. Have you guys heard about any of this before?"

"No, sir," MacDonough said, "and I'm the department liaison on nationwide manhunts. This is weird enough that I would've remembered it if it came across my desk. Although I don't know that I'd have looked too hard for him based on what I know so far."

"What about the two he shot?"

"Withers has—had—a number of aliases and old charges including assault, aggravated assault, robbery, kidnapping, and bank robbery. He was paroled out of both Utah and Kansas penitentiaries. He was rumored among some of the casino people to have ties to one or more of the militia groups. Our people who track what's left of the militias confirm that information and add that Withers was a weapons supplier. We checked his listed residence on one of the aliases and found an empty slot in a trailer park. The manager there said he was a gun dealer who paid his rent and moved on to God knows where."

MacDonough flipped a page. "Frontenac also had aliases and charges including aggravated assault, assault on a police officer, aggravated sexual assault, burglary, armed robbery, rape, and a bunch of drug stuff. He was paroled out of California and there are outstanding warrants for him in Oregon. He had woman trouble over there with someone named Larissa Frontenac—I guess that's his wife—who has a protection from abuse order that he is—was—alleged to have violated. In fact, it seems he beat her up right before his untimely demise."

"Sound like a couple of real winners," Flynn said. "Well, our trail is still hot so let's see if we can do what the FBI can't. If this guy flew out of Spokane on Saturday, he could be in Bangkok by now. See if the airport people have any surveillance footage that might show him and make sure you get that computer stuff from the casino. In fact, take Ira with you to make sure you have the right thing. When you go to Spokane, check the area hotels because the car at the airport might be a red herring. Also check the hospitals for anyone who might have come in over the weekend with a chest injury like this one from the vest. He might have tried to pass it off as motor vehicle related. Work with Smith and the EMTs to get a better composite together and have Sorenson send a photo over the fax machine. We'll use whichever one is better. Take the picture with you to Spokane. Have you done some of this stuff already?"

"Most of it," MacDonough said.

"Excellent. Run with it and keep me posted. Anything else?"

Heads shook.

"Let's try Sorenson again," Flynn said. "I'd like to talk to him before I feed the vultures. What time is it?"

"Nine-thirty," Christenson said.

"Shit. I really would like to know what the hell I'm talking about before I actually do it."

Flynn, MacDonough, and Christenson tried to reach Sorenson six times over the next thirty minutes. Flynn attempted to reschedule the press conference, but the governor wanted to be present for it and a postponement conflicted with his scheduled flight to Portugal for a trade conference addressing cutting-edge developments in the porcelain industry.

Chapter 11

Sullivan finished his huge, late breakfast while reading the newspaper. The shoot-out at the casino made the Sunday and now the Monday papers, but no suspect was identified except a Caucasian male with a moustache and light beard, both of which were gone. Now he looked like a soldier on leave to visit the natural wonders surrounding Jackson, Wyoming. Today he planned to visit some famous center for wildlife art north of town, maybe see if the elk were on their way. He stood up without groaning against the pain in his ribs. He guessed several were broken, but knew that a hospital would do nothing to treat him other than confirm that he had broken some ribs.

Back in his room, he turned on the television before going into the bathroom. He reversed course when he realized there was a news conference about the casino shootings. The speaker was identified as Joseph Flin of the Highway Patrol. He had a heavy Boston accent.

At least he isn't trying to fake that Texas thing.

Flin. What the hell kind of name is that?

Most of the information was old news: the pretty cop had survived; one of the dead cops was married with two kids; Redfeather's real name was Claude Frontenac. As he recited their criminal histories, Flin left the impression that neither Frontenac nor Withers had been a loss to society. Redfeather was wanted even as he died because he had beaten

77

the hell out of his wife on Friday morning. The police sought a suspect for questioning who might be wounded. Sullivan was surprised to hear his name mentioned. At present they would not release a photo, but a composite would be forthcoming that afternoon. With the news conference over, Flin ignored the shouted questions of the reporters and walked out of the room.

Uh-oh. Looks like someone with more than half a brain is looking for me now. I knew I should have called that asshole Sorenson. They didn't say anything about the Porsche in Spokane and they think I'm wounded so they probably didn't find the car or the vest.

A handsome face filled the screen and repeated some of the things Flin had said while drawing incorrect inferences about others. The talking head switched to an attractive woman standing outside in the rain with a caption of Seattle, Washington, under her pointy chin. She related that her sources told her the police had recovered the vehicle used in the "desperado's" escape.

Desperado? They have no idea.

Seattle is not particularly close to Spokane, but it's close enough that some Seattle cop might know about finding the Porsche. The cops have the car. Flin is keeping his mouth shut because he thinks he has a shot at catching me or flushing me into an airport terminal. Thank God for cute reporters and stupid cops who open their mouths in an effort to impress them.

Sullivan started to pack. The Husky waited at the Jackson airport. He still had a lead on more weapons to chase down back east. He stopped for a minute and looked out the window at the mountains.

Well, I guess Sorenson is gonna catch hell.

It's about time.

◆

Larissa Frontenac made her television debut about twelve hours after Commissioner Flynn concluded his press conference. The reporter at the news desk was an attractive blonde. She had been recalled from a Caribbean vacation for the interview because she had presented a five-part story on spousal abuse earlier in the year. Through a leading dialogue, she outlined the Frontenacs' history. Parental warnings about the graphic nature of the story flashed across the screen. Larissa was interviewed live from a hospital bed in Portland, Oregon. She had two black eyes, facial lacerations, her upper front teeth were missing, and her right arm was in a cast.

Born and raised in Plattsburgh, New York, Larissa met Claude Frontenac at a bar in Montreal. He courted her. She sparked for him. Although she was not a Native American they married in a ceremony crafted at the site of the Battle of the Little Big Horn. Together, they drifted to northern California where her husband had "friends." She knew he had been in prison but believed his proclamations of being reformed.

Claude Frontenac, who liked to be called "Redfeather," was ten years older than she and old problems with alcohol abuse and the law reemerged. His pattern, when not committing crimes, was to become intoxicated and then abusive toward Larissa. She abandoned Frontenac in California for a fresh start. Redfeather, as she called him, found her in Oregon and threatened her. She secured a court order. He violated the order twice. Redfeather beat and raped her the second time. She filed charges, but the police could not find him. Larissa bought a gun from a coworker, a Colt revolver. She changed apartments.

Redfeather found her a third time the Thursday before, probably by following her home from her night shift as a waitress. He broke into her apartment when she was in the shower. She found him drunk and belligerent in her bed. He came after her as she tried to flee the room. She screamed and went for her gun in the nightstand. He took it from her and broke her arm. He shoved the gun in her mouth, breaking her teeth in the process, and told her he was going to kill her. Then he sodomized her with the gun at the back of her head. Redfeather left, but promised he would be back to kill her later.

After Larissa Frontenac outlined this story, the reporter posed more generalized questions about spousal abuse to a woman from a shelter who turned out to have been in the hospital room with Larissa. The woman stressed the related problems of alcohol and spousal abuse. With obvious emotion in her voice, the reporter returned to Larissa Frontenac to ask how she felt now that her husband was dead.

"Good. I wish I killed him myself. Maybe those cops would still be alive."

"Do you think that there could have been some further type of program or intervention by the courts or the government that could have protected you as well as other women?"

"No. I been to the courts and the cops. They didn't do shit. Redfeather was just a badass and deserved killin' and that's all there is to it."

"Do you feel any remorse or sadness at all over his loss?"

"I feel sorry for them poor people, them cops he killed in that casino. I'm sorry for their families for what Redfeather done and I know in my heart and soul that he'll burn in hell forever for what he done to them people and what he done to me. I'm layin' here with a broken arm, a broken face, and stitches —eight stitches in my asshole because of that son of a bitch. And, and, and, and, I'll tell you this too—that guy that they say killed him, he deserves a medal. If they want, I'll pin it on him myself. I'm only sorry I didn't shoot that bastard Redfeather myself."

"Do you have any advice to offer to other women who may be in an abusive relationship and how they might avoid the plight you suffered?" The reporter paced the question to give the camera a chance to zoom in on Mrs. Frontenac's face.

"Don't run. Don't scream. Just kill the bastard when the time comes."

"Thank you, Mrs. Redfeather, and good luck in your recovery." The reporter looked into the camera with moist eyes and said, "We'll be right back."

She won an Emmy that year for her reporting on spousal abuse.

Larissa Frontenac landed a contract for a talk show.

On Tuesday morning, the FBI released a brief written statement pertaining to James Sullivan buried among a host of other press releases on various subjects. It related that James Sullivan was wanted for questioning in connection with assaults on twenty-seven drug establishments characterized as "drug-counting houses," immediately deemed "crack houses" by the media. Sixty-one homicides were linked to these attacks. No figures on the amount of drugs or cash involved were available.

On Wednesday, the photos from inside the casino started to appear in the mass media.

Some months before the shoot-out, a gifted fifteen-year-old in Boise learned how to hack his way through the casino computer's defenses. He used this access to search for some advantage over the house on a future gambling foray once he was old enough to get by the doormen. With word of the casino shooting, he used his talents to gather imagery from the casino's security cameras. He purloined the gruesome scenes Flynn hoped would never come to light and posted them on the Internet under the moniker "Really cool snuff footage."

Professional media people did not hesitate to use the photographs. Chief Flynn was outraged, but could do nothing to stop the publication and republication of the imagery. The press was self-absorbed enough to consider the morality of showing such morbid photos, but this ended when a plane crash offered even more grisly sights.

On Thursday afternoon, two Wharton School seniors incorporated Captain Crack Attack, Inc. Their products were trading cards, comics, shirts, posters, and action figures associated with the exploits of James Sullivan. The fact that there were no recognizable photographs of Sullivan did little to hamper production. The casino imagery provided enough material for initial product lines. In two months, gross sales exceeded six million dollars.

Not long after the casino shoot-out, a railroad policeman in Baltimore walked a draft of six rail cars contracted to the Department of Defense that required seal checks immediately after their arrival from Pennsylvania. He easily located the cars on the assigned track, since the containers to be checked sat atop rail chassis coupled to adjacent flatcars holding no fewer than six Abrams main battle tanks thinly disguised by olive drab tarps. He trudged through three inches of fresh snow while he reviewed his manifest with his flashlight. The listing showed there were eleven intermodal containers spread over the three rail cars. Two cars had full loads of four and one carried three. He walked by the cars with their stacked containers and passed his light across them.

He tilted his head down into the wind and scurried for the flatcars supporting the tanks. Although he had never been in the military, he was obsessed with its equipment and owned a collection of videotapes portraying military equipment in action. One of his favorite tapes showed Abrams tanks maneuvering through the deserts of Kuwait and Iraq during Operation Desert Storm. He liked to sit in his recliner after work and watch the videotapes while drinking Budweiser. Before she left him, his wife said that he loved his tapes more than he loved her.

He spent almost twenty minutes poking around the tanks before the subfreezing weather commanded that he return to his vehicle. He dismounted the flatcar and started to trot back past the containers. As he did so he looked up again. Two cars held three containers while one carried four. He checked his documents and flashed the light across the numbers on the railcars and containers.

The policeman stepped back and whistled. He extracted his radio from the case on his belt to double-check the information on his listing. After ten minutes, he heard confirming information to the effect that there were eleven containers shipped. He replied that there had been a theft. He walked back to his vehicle to wait for the inevitable supervisor. He knew that someone was going to catch hell for this. That was okay by him; he was in the clear since no one could have taken the shipment that quickly in this yard. Besides, there were no tracks in the snow. They must have been taken somewhere upstream. He would come out of this thing okay, but someone was in trouble for losing one whole hell of a lot of weapons.

Chapter 12

Stacey Smith awoke late on December 24, almost noon. As the cobwebs cleared, guilt over the deaths of Williams and Jenks settled in worse than usual. Henry Williams's widow, Amanda, had visited the previous afternoon. It turned out that the Williamses had succeeded in conceiving their first child just days before Henry's death. Smith was not certain whether this turn of events worsened Amanda's position, although, she had presented the news in an effort to brighten Stacey's disposition. Stacey acted happy, but both women wound up crying before Amanda ended the visit with some semblance of composure.

She rolled out of bed and stretched for the cane leaning at the far side of the bed stand. After visiting the bathroom, she limped to the kitchen, thankful that she lived in a single-story house. She was glad to be home, a thought that helped her make the leap to being glad that she was still alive. She even had two legs and had been assured that the injured one would recover a full level of function. Chief Flynn promised her that she had a job waiting. As for the rest of her, the psychologist told her she needed time.

Smith had visited Jenks's house the last two Christmases. That would not be the case this year since his widow and boys were at her sister's place some three hundred miles away. Stacey attended the funeral in a wheelchair and wondered if it was the last time she would see the remnants of the Jenks family. For now, she sat alone in her little house far from her neighbors and rode her emotions. She obsessed about following Sullivan into the casino, about letting Jenks and Williams get killed, about her poor marksmanship, about surviving, and about her less-than-comprehensive description of the suspect. She remembered her morphine-influenced description being comprised of three words: "He smelled good."

"Very professional, Stacey." She groaned into her coffee loudly enough that she did not hear the doorbell on the first ring. The second ring got her attention and she maneuvered her way to the door. It took her long enough that a third ring sounded before she was even close. She checked the security of her robe and opened the door to spy a man turning away. She recognized him as one of the doctors from the hospital. He had something to do with reconstructive surgery and had come with some others to look at her leg. He wore surgical scrubs under his jacket, which was accessorized with a Christmas tree slung over his shoulder.

"Hi, I'm not sure you remember me."

"Sure," Stacey said. "You're doctor—"

"Stone. Jeff Stone. I'm the plastics fellow."

"Right, right."

"I just got off call and thought that maybe you might not have had a chance to get set with a tree." He rolled his eyes toward the burden.

"Some guys from work set one up for me, but I appreciate the thought. Why don't you come in for some coffee?"

"I'd like that if it's not too much trouble. I've been up for the last thirty-six hours."

"No trouble. I just made a pot. Why don't you set the tree down next to the door? Listen, I should pay you for that."

"No that's stupid. Besides, I got it free. They just give them away this late in the game."

Stacey remembered that Jeff Stone was single. The younger nurses were all hot on his trail. She felt ashamed to be measuring this man for his relationship potential when she had planned to wallow in depression for the bulk of the day. He made himself so comfortable on the sofa that he was sound asleep by the time she got back with his coffee. Smith felt glad for the distraction of having a strange man sitting sound asleep on her sofa on Christmas Eve.

She had plenty of time for guilt later.

Roger Sorenson told his mother he was between relationships. In a way it was true. He was not committed to any one woman, but never had been. No woman he met seemed to appreciate him. He tossed down the rest of the Glenfiddich and stared into the fire. His father returned to the living room with fresh drinks.

In his father, Roger saw himself in thirty years. They both worked for the Federal Bureau of Investigation. They even shared the same name, the suffix Junior dropped from view in law school. The only woman in the nuclear family, universally known as Mrs. Sorenson, referred to them as "Roger the Father" and "Roger the Younger." A corollary professional distinction could have been "Roger the assistant director," and "Roger the special agent."

"Sit." Roger the father settled into a leather chair, his chair, near the fireplace.

They sat and studied the fire. Mrs. Sorenson was in the kitchen preparing their Christmas Eve feast. Scout, the ancient Irish Setter, curled at Roger the Father's feet. Special Agent Sorenson waited what he thought was enough time.

Roger the Father leaned close. "Make sure you compliment your mother's cooking. She doesn't do it that much."

"Of course. Dad, about the investigation—"

The older man set himself back in the chair. "Roger, it's out of your hands, now. That son of a bitch Flynn has seen to that."

"Do you have a read on what will happen? They pulled my files, my computer."

"Matty Feldman is doing something with it. Heathen is probably going over it right now. My guess is he'll give the case to one of his up-and-coming tribesmen, just like I kicked it to you."

"No one gave it to me. Sullivan called me. Remember?"

"Sullivan played you like a fish. He played me, too. Hell, if you hadn't gone to law school together, he'd have never known who I was, or that I had enough drag to put you in charge of catching him."

"And I will catch him."

"Don't be a dumbass!" Roger the Father looked toward the kitchen and lowered his voice.

"How many times have I told you? It's never a question of catching someone. It's a matter of being around when they fuck up."

"And he will."

"You don't know that. He hasn't so far and sometimes they never do. There's no trap he's vulnerable to. Everything he cares about is gone. You need to worry about your position. That's something you can control."

Roger the Younger felt exposed. He was not used to being with someone who knew his ambitions, shared them. Roger the Father broke his musings.

"Look, I'll do what I can to keep you on this if that's what you really want, but you want to distance yourself."

"Why?"

"Sullivan's the invisible man. Now that things are public, that's going to be more obvious. Your career will be tied to success or failure of the hunt. It probably already is. Frankly, I wouldn't want to be Feldman right now. He's got his work cut out for him."

"I'm the only one who can catch him."

Roger the Father popped from his chair. "Bullshit."

Scout lifted his head from the rug to sniff the drama.

"I know him better than anyone. They need me for this. I at least should be there for the takedown."

"Takedown? You've been watching too much television."

Roger the Father walked to the window so that he could peer at the other suburban Virginia homes. Roger the Younger had a better sense of theater than most. He rose and touched his father's arm.

"You're screwing this up, son. You're trying to hit a home run when you need to be whacking singles. That's how you get by, build up chits, move up the ladder."

"I want this, Dad. I really do." Special Agent Sorenson applied the piercing look he used to some effect in interviews and the seduction of women.

"You want what's not good for you."

"I want to hit that home run."

"I'm retiring, Roger."

"What?" Roger the Younger feigned surprise. He spied on his father just as he did his other colleagues.

"It's past time for me to go. I've already lined up a consulting position.

"Don't worry. Before I go, I'll see if I can put you into Matty's plans." With these words Roger the Father pushed the Special Agent from the nest in the hope that he had learned to fly. Scout barked to signal Mrs. Sorenson's approach. She beamed through the doorway.

"Hey, you two, ready for dinner?" Her unearthly smile and exuberance belied the hefty regime of antidepressants that had sustained her through the last decade.

"Mrs. Sorenson, I'm famished!" Roger the Father closed the discussion with his only son.

———•◆•———

Dennis O'Brien snorted another line from the desktop and tilted his head back. His eyes fluttered and he caught a trickle of blood from his nostril. After a few minutes, he was ready to resume his meeting.

"Sure you don't want any?"

"Shit'll kill you, man," Reggie Washington said.

"Hasn't yet."

"Give it time."

"You reformed types are the worst."

"Do what you want. Just don't ask me to come along."

"You're no fun since you found Jesus."

"Allah."

Dennis poured himself a drink. "Whatever."

"You should stay away from that shit. It's just a commodity, the profit engine."

Dennis sipped and smiled. "Listen to little Reggie, a fucking MBA all of a sudden."

Reggie leaned back into the sofa. His eyes wandered across the photos of fish he had seen a thousand times before. He hunched forward and waited for Dennis to focus.

"So, Denny, why am I here?"

"Because I fucking told you to be here."

Reggie flopped back on the sofa. "Listen, man, I got shit to do. It's like Christmas and I got shit to do for my family, my kids."

Dennis was out of his chair looking for more scotch. "I didn't think Muslims celebrated Christmas."

"Well, it's for my kids. Their mothers are into that church shit, at least one is. The other kid is with her grandma. Anyway, I got places to be. Ain't you?"

Dennis knocked back most of his fresh drink. "What I fucking need is to know how to solve this fucking hemorrhage of money I have happening. The cause of which, I hasten to add, is in your fucking department. So, in short, we're here because you're not doing your fucking job."

Reggie spread his arms. "What do you want from me, man? The spics have always had other connections for product and now they got a new setup for washing the money. It's competition. American way."

"Wrong." Dennis leaned across the desk. "This shit's not legal and, therefore, that American way bullshit is out the window. We need to resort to other means."

Reggie guessed where this was headed. "So, what do you want to do? You gotta sweeten the pie if you want 'em back."

Dennis rocked back in his chair and lit a cigar. "I don't gotta do shit. They're gonna meet my terms."

"What do you think? You gonna go to war with 'em? We don't have the muscle for that shit."

"I've gotta win-win worked out for us provided you know where the root of the problem is."

Reggie was losing patience. "Whatcha talkin' about?"

Dennis poured himself another scotch. "Can you finger the individuals who have bypassed us?"

"Yeah. I know who they are."

"How many?"

"Like two."

"Just two really, or more than two?"

"Two. The others will fall in line."

"Excellent. Can you detain these two?"

"Detain? You mean snatch 'em up? Are you fuckin' nuts?"

"You've done this kind of thing before. Don't pussy out on me now."

"I don't do that gang-banging shit anymore. I'm too old for that."

Dennis stared at Reggie through his cloud of smoke. "Bullshit. You're a murdering motherfucker now as much as ever."

Reggie squirmed a little in his seat. Dennis knew him too well.

"Besides," Dennis rolled his cigar, "you haven't heard my plan."

"Let's have it." Reggie knew he would hear it no matter what he said.

Dennis outlined the plan. Reggie paced and looked out a window over the big fish tank. When he was done, Dennis shoved his cigar back into the corner of his mouth. "Whatdya think?"

Reggie turned from the window and looked back at Dennis O'Brien. "Man, you are fucked up."

"Yeah, but will it work?"

Reggie turned back to the window. He had sworn off the dope, drink, and smokes that his partner wallowed in, but not the money. He never could give up the money. After a while he answered.

"I'll have to hire some help."

Late on Christmas afternoon, Joseph Murphy looked into the mirror. He straightened the burgundy tie and approved of the gray suit.

"All dressed up for your birthday," he said to his reflection.

A cat he did not recognize wrapped itself around his calves. It was a Maine coon with dense dark fur and a youthful air. It wore a collar with tags that confirmed it belonged in his house. He deduced that his neighbors Mona or Wanda had rescued it from somewhere and decided it should live on the farm.

He looked at the tag and read the cat's name: "Isildur."

Mona tended to name animals after obscure authors of English literature from the nineteenth century or peripheral characters from novels of similar vintage. This name was too weird for Wanda, Mona's mother. She would have named the cat "Bear" or "Coon" or some other monosyllable that would have been more than adequate. Murphy thought Isildur had something to do with *Beowulf* or some equally removed work. He liked Wanda a lot more than her daughter or son-in-law. Mona was a flake and her husband, Arthur, smoked too much dope.

"Well, it's the wrong century, but I guess Mona stuck me with you." He scratched the animal. "I'll call you Bob."

Murphy pulled a walnut case from a bottom desk drawer. It held a large revolver, an old Smith & Wesson Model 27. He wiped its mirror finish with a silicone-impregnated cloth and walked out onto the deck with the pistol in his hand.

Murphy stood on the deck and surveyed the hillside's mix of forest and field. Solid clouds hung at about two thousand feet so that they consumed the top halves of the looming mountains. The compact disc player blared, but he still heard the occasional whine of tires on the road down near the river, some three-quarters of a mile distant. Bob the cat leapt onto the rail of the deck and commenced a vigorous cleaning.

"Beautiful, eh, Bob?"

Jenks and Williams won't get to see anything like this ever again. Too bad, really.

A snow squall marched eastward from the direction of Lake Champlain. He could see sunlight beyond it. A sheet of ice floated on the surface of the pond just down the hill from where he stood. The coming snowfall pleased him. The Vermont winter was brutal enough that its victims should get a white Christmas as partial compensation.

Without further delay, Murphy placed the muzzle of the handgun against his right temple and squeezed the trigger. He never heard the hammer fall, but felt the transfer of mechanical force from it travel through the weapon to the bones of his skull and into his jaw.

———➤◆◆———

They play Lou Reed in hell. How appropriate.

Sullivan brought the weapon away from his head. He did not open the action.

"Happy birthday, James." Sullivan said.

He stood in the falling snow. This was the first time in the four years he had performed this ritual that he was glad the gun had not discharged. The second Christmas he did it, he pulled the trigger twice before stopping. His odds this Christmas were one in two that the gun would fire. Next year, he was guaranteed results.

Guns don't kill people. Statistics do.

"I'll tell you, Bob, the taxpayers in this country can't catch a break."

Bob punctuated Sullivan's musings by leaping from the rail and rubbing against his calf. Sullivan bent down to scratch the belly of the outstretched animal and sharpened the pain in his back. He had been busy: flying and driving too many miles, setting up anonymous trusts for the Jenks boys, stealing weapons from the rail yard. He hoped they would not be too hard on the clerk he bribed for information on the shipment.

His name was Peter Sizlewicz. Sullivan had found Sizlewicz by looking at the automobiles in the parking lot of the huge Department of Defense warehouse and transshipment facility not far from Harrisburg.

Sizlewicz drove a rusty Volkswagen Campmobile sporting Grateful Dead decals next to bumper stickers about the Air Force having to hold bake sales for bombers. Sullivan scouted the man over the previous five months and learned that Sizlewicz was a charismatic Christian who went to Mass every morning at six A.M. and picketed abortion clinics when he wasn't earning his GS-7 wages. He approached Sizlewicz in the guise of a defrocked priest turned activist and convinced the clerk to furnish information about a shipment of weapons so that a protest for peace could occur with the blocking of a train. Sizlewicz had agreed more easily than Sullivan had hoped and fostered a suspicion that the police would be waiting for him, but the clerk seemed to pray with even greater joy once armed with this mission. Nevertheless, Sullivan had been apprehensive enough about Sizlewicz's potential for double dealing that he had pursued Larry Withers.

Big mistake, James.

It didn't have to happen.

Should've left Withers alone.

At least I took care of Jenks's two sons.

A container with the last of the weapons from the railroad rested adjacent to his barn. He needed to hide its contents as he had hid the bulk of the shipment snatched from a switching yard along the Susquehanna. His back would have to hold up a bit longer.

That's the next step. Hide the rest of the guns. Slip over the border to Montreal and become someone else for a while. Spend the rest of the winter rehabbing on a Cuban beach.

For present purposes, Joseph Murphy was due at Wanda's for Christmas dinner. He had gifts packed in the car. Sullivan recovered a pager from the office where it sat in a charger for Joseph Murphy, the volunteer firefighter with enough social conscience that he had been approached to run for selectman. He pulled the suicide note from his suit jacket and shredded it like so many of the other papers associated with a man maintaining six distinct identities. The letter was rather articulate in its description of overwhelming depression and had been heartfelt when he drafted it years ago.

Maybe I'm dead already.

For right now, he would put the revolver away.

He would put all the guns away.

Part II

2001

Chapter 13

Gavigan knocked the telephone from the night stand. His hand fumbled along the floor as he leaned out of the bed until he grasped the dislodged handset and hauled it to his head.

"Hello?"

"John?"

Gavigan's eyes fluttered. This was not a misdialed call for Tamika or Shaquilla or some other imaginatively named person entirely unknown to him. He knew this voice.

It was Brother Joseph from the Christian Brothers who was calling to say there had been a terrible mistake. John Gavigan had never really graduated from high school after all. The Brothers just realized this as a consequence of a routine review of their records between kegs of Schlitz. Time to get back to school. Better hurry up about it, too, before someone else discovers the error. He would have to repeat undergraduate and law schools, of course, but if he acted immediately he could still make it to the office before anyone noticed he was gone. Time to stop living the lie.

"Yes?"

"It's Walt. Are you awake?"

Gavigan heaved himself to an upright position and focused on the clock's green numerals, which read 2:23.

"I am now. What's up, Walt? Did Dennis finally kill someone?"

There was silence on the telephone.

"Walter, are you still there?"

"We have a problem. We need you at the aquarium."

"Okay. Right now?" This was not so bad. He'd rather go to the aquarium than high school.

"Yeah. Right away."

"What's the matter?" Maybe Brother Joseph would ambush him there.

"There's been an accident. Just get here right away."

"Where are you? Is there a door open?"

"I guess. I'll meet you at the service entrance just in case. Call me on my cell when you're close."

Gavigan hung up and found his car keys and clothes without waking his wife. With briefcase in hand, he shuffled out the back door toward the Volvo. It was January but must have been sixty degrees with a light breeze. The woman upstairs even had some flowers spilling off her deck. As he opened the rear door to put his bag in the back, he noticed the glass in the door had been broken for the eighth time.

"Shit!"

He ignored the damage for the moment and started the car. The streets were deserted at this hour, the trip quick, but Gavigan almost sideswiped a car that was exiting the aquarium's parking lot. He caught a glimpse of a passenger in a uniform shirt. Gavigan circled to the rear of the building and saw Cole on the loading dock. He parked next to Cole's battered Subaru and noted that O'Brien's Lexus stood beside it.

"What's up, Walter? Did a burglar slip and fall?"

There had been burglaries and vandalism at the aquarium in the past. One incident just the week before was attributed to some Hispanic gang members based on the graffiti deposited on the walls. Cole did not answer from his post next to the loading dock. Another car pulled in next to Gavigan. He recognized it as the ancient Chevrolet station wagon belonging to Darryl Carfagno, a photographer the firm used in many cases. He coughed a greeting through a cloud of cigarette smoke and burrowed into the rear of the wagon. Gavigan grabbed his bag and lent Carfagno a hand with a tripod.

Cole had disappeared somewhere within the building. They caught a glimpse of him in the interior's gloom and followed his reflection on the polished floor. They passed tanks imbedded within walls that displayed many small species of fish. Gavigan noticed the puddles of water here and there that had spawned a plethora of slip and fall claims.

They followed Cole at a distance toward the heart of the building where a massive horseshoe tank stood three stories tall. It held a number of fish species, including the aquarium's main attraction, the East Coast's largest captive school of tiger sharks. The sharks all had names and ranged in length from five to twelve feet. Despite their bulk and menacing appearances, the sharks were generally relaxed except at feeding time. In the center of the open horseshoe, a ramp ascended in switchback fashion to an elevated platform where the surface of the tank's water was visible.

By the time they reached the diorama of a polar bear attacking a seal that sat at the bottom of the ramp, they had lost sight of Cole around the first switchback but could hear him ascending the ramp. As they trudged up the ramp, Gavigan saw a number of fish in the shadowy water but did not detect the bulk of any of the sharks. Gavigan did not ask Carfagno why they were there; he wanted to conceal his own ignorance on the topic. Cole was out of earshot, but Gavigan presumed he must be waiting either at the top of the ramp or in the administrative offices accessible through a hallway near the top of the tank. Gavigan heard splashing and then the voice of Dennis O'Brien.

Gavigan raced to the conclusion that Walter had finally had it with Dennis. He was going to feed him to the sharks and had called him here to witness it. Gavigan wondered if Walter still carried a gun. He quickened his steps as they neared the top and strained to hear O'Brien's plea for mercy.

"Where the fuck are they, Wally? There isn't going to be anything left if they don't move their fucking asses!"

"They're coming." Cole said.

Gavigan and Carfagno reached the level platform. O'Brien was not in the water. He perched in the gloom on a metal scaffold extending over the water. It was designed to enhance the drama when attendants fed the fish. Something big moved in the water nearby.

"What's up?" Gavigan huffed.

"It's about fucking time." O'Brien backed off the platform to the far wall. "Is your camera ready?"

"I need a minute to set up." Carfagno said.

"Well, fucking set up. We haven't got much time."

"Is this the light we're shooting in?"

"No, idiot. I have the lights off so they're more relaxed. Tell me when you're ready and I'll hit the lights."

Carfagno thundered through some cases and clicked things together. Gavigan looked at Cole, who would not take his eyes from the water, and then at O'Brien, whose eyes seemed to carry their own light. Neither man said anything.

"Somebody want to tell me what's going on?" Gavigan said.

"There are two of them." Cole's voice was a whisper.

"Ready!" Carfagno shouted while still kneeling among his pile of bags.

The lights in the water blasted to life as O'Brien threw switches on his side of the tank. Gavigan shielded his eyes from the sudden brightness. Cole continued to stare at the water.

"Jesus Christ," Carfagno said.

"Here he comes! Here he comes!" O'Brien jumped up and down across the water.

A large shark's back broke through the surface of the water and rolled to one side as it bit one of the torsos. The fish thrashed and tore the flesh near a tattooed bicep. Blood oozed from the wound to join the oily brown slick near the remains. As the shark separated with its morsel, the remnant rolled to reveal a face, a young face with a hint of hair and acne.

"Holy shit," Gavigan managed.

O'Brien was back out on the catwalk. "Did you get that? Did you get that?"

Carfagno already had his lighter up to a cigarette. The flame trembled before he inhaled deeply.

"Are you out of your fucking mind? No. No. I didn't get it."

"I need pictures!" O'Brien spread his arms. "Lots of pictures before anything is disturbed."

"Jesus Christ, Dennis. Get the net and we'll fish him out." Gavigan looked to his right to see something bob in the water where another shark thrashed.

"No fucking way! Not until I preserve the scene. These motherfuckers shouldn't be in here. I don't want to destroy any evidence."

"Did you call the cops?" Gavigan asked Cole.

"No. Not yet." Cole lit his own cigarette.

"No fucking cops!" O'Brien waved his arms. "Not yet, anyway. That's all I need is a bunch of fucking morons who have to be told to swallow their own spit tramping through the place. You can bet those motherfuckers will take all kinds of pictures. I got two dead guys in my tank and I need to cover my ass.

"Look! He's getting ready to come again! Get ready!"

"You're outta your fuckin' mind." Carfagno packed his gear.

"Wait, wait, Darren, don't go. We need pictures in case there's a claim."

"Name's Darryl. Get someone else." The last camera case clicked shut.

"Hundred dollars a frame."

Darryl hesitated. He looked back at the water.

"A thousand." Darryl exhaled a blue cloud.

"Two fifty." Dennis said.

"Five and that's my lowest."

"Done."

"Color okay?"

"Yes. Yes. Color is perfect. Now, hurry up."

"I don't believe this." Gavigan pushed his hair straight back and looked away before another bite.

"Why don't you fucking relax?" O'Brien said. "You've seen worse than this."

O'Brien was correct. Gavigan had seen people battered to pieces in auto accidents and burned to death in fires. He had seen much worse, but those circumstances had not seemed quite so bizarre. The people, men or boys, in the tank already exhibited an inhuman quality due to the portions removed from them. They resembled the sides of beef sometimes thrown into the tank as a treat for both the sharks and the patrons.

Cole looked up. "They came in through a skylight."

Gavigan followed his gaze up to the ceiling where a panel of a large skylight was broken out.

"I didn't see any glass in the tank, but it's probably in the bottom. They must have fallen right in."

Gavigan surveyed the ceiling. The hole where the glass had been was large enough for two men to fall through. If they fell straight, they would have landed in the tank. The legal technician in Gavigan's brain took over: two burglars on the roof looking for access who found it. A summary judgment or defense verdict should follow any claim. The men looked young, possibly Hispanic. The plaintiffs would be their estates, probably opened by their mothers.

"I don't suppose we have any ID on them," Gavigan said.

He tried to ignore the splashing and the whirling motor drive on Carfagno's camera.

"ID? *You* fucking reach in and get it," O'Brien said.

"I didn't see any extra cars in the lot. They probably parked nearby."

O'Brien looked across the water. "No. I didn't notice a car. Did you see one, Walt?"

"No. I didn't see anything."

Cole was back to staring into the tank.

"How about the guard? Did he find them?" Gavigan said.

"No guard tonight. He didn't show," O'Brien said.

"That's funny. I thought I passed him on the way in."

O'Brien almost fell in the tank.

"Watch yourself, Dennis," Gavigan said.

O'Brien stood upright and held the rail.

"No. There was supposed to be a new guy, but he never showed."

"Well, I almost had an accident with someone in a car wearing what looked like the guard's uniform."

"He never showed."

"Okay. So, who found them?"

"I did. I stopped by to get some paperwork when I heard the splashing."

O'Brien's head swung back and forth with the fish.

"Isn't the skylight alarmed?"

O'Brien focused on Gavigan. "No. I never replaced the sensor when it broke last year."

"How long ago did you find them?"

"Less than an hour ago."

Gavigan looked at his watch. Cole had called him forty minutes earlier.

"Look, Dennis, we have to call the cops, or we're looking at possible obstruction of justice or some other criminal bullshit."

"Okay. We can find a hook and drag the fuckers out. The cops will do it when they get here, but they may decide to shoot the fish along the way."

Carfagno started his third roll of film. It corresponded with what seemed to be his tenth cigarette. Cole went to look for a gaff to drag out the corpses. Carfagno focused on the broken skylight and used his flash for the first time.

"What the fuck are you doing?" O'Brien screamed.

"Don't you want shots to show ingress?"

"Fuck ingress! Shoot the fish. Shoot the fish. Nothing's gonna come of this."

Gavigan shook his head and dialed the police using the speed dial on his cellular telephone. It rang seven times.

"Nine-one-one. Do you have a life-threatening emergency?"

"No. Not at this point."

"Please hold."

He held and watched the awkward exercise of Cole and O'Brien trying to gaff the torsos. Gavigan's mind worked calmly under the stress of the situation. He covered the mouthpiece and called over to the other attorneys.

"They look Hispanic. Maybe they're Puerto Ricans, but they might be illegals. Maybe there'll be no claim."

O'Brien slipped, but regained his balance. He looked at Cole, who refused to make eye contact, and then over at Gavigan.

"Did you hear that, Wally? John's brain is working overtime. Good idea, John."

Gavigan looked through the broken skylight at the two stars that managed to shine through the city's light pollution. No viable case would come from this mess. Two guys were dead, but that happens. If they hadn't been trying to break in from the roof, they wouldn't have gotten killed. He looked at his watch and calculated the billable hours for the night's work so far. He'd be up the rest of the night. Carfagno exposed the last of his film while Gavigan waited on hold. Part of John's mind wondered if he could report the broken glass in his car during this call while other parts screamed against the madness that surrounded him.

Chapter 14

Early in the New Year, Matty Feldman plowed through the briefing binder Roger Sorenson had prepared. The matter of reforming the Bureau's investigation into the drug dealer slayings fell to him. In the words of one of his seniors: "You touched it, so you have it." Fresh analysis from the Investigative Support Unit and Dr. Funtz concluded that Sullivan was on a mission instead of deriving any pleasure from his actions, an assassin instead of a serial or spree killer. At least two of the contributors to the analysis opined that Sullivan had passed beyond the burnout point and would not voluntarily reemerge.

Feldman had pushed Sorenson to summarize his investigation through the Christmas holidays. As he reviewed the summary, Feldman realized he would still need Sorenson if for no other reason than to help find things. All the information and impressions gathered in the investigation of James Sullivan had passed through Sorenson's notebook computer at one time or another. The physical evidence was stored in a secure facility in New York but was indexed in such an arcane fashion that no one other than Sorenson could access it with any speed or reliability. Further, Sorenson's father was an assistant director who pushed to keep his son on the investigation. Although Feldman did not care for the father any more than the son, there were superiors he could not ignore who urged him to "give the boy a chance."

"Jackass." Feldman shook his head as he made notes.

Sorenson had accomplished little to date apart from traveling from crime scene to crime scene in what appeared to be an orchestrated campaign to alienate local police officials. He had been tempted to call Sorenson in an effort to plumb the depths of his arrogance but recalled the man's audacity in taking vacation this week. Sorenson's departure was even more bizarre in that Sullivan historically telephoned during the first few weeks of the year to announce the resumption of his mission.

"Mission."

There was that word again. Feldman had it written and underlined on his pad. His intercom buzzed.

"Yes?"

"Detectives Marzak and Whitcomb are here. Shall I go down to get them?"

"No. I'll do it. Thanks."

Feldman worked his way through the building toward the visitors' reception desk where he could take charge of the two freshly retired detectives. Sorenson's report denigrated the men, but Feldman spoke with the special agent who had driven them through Washington with Sorenson after Sullivan's last telephone call. That agent described the detectives as "old war horses" who "didn't get hysterical like some people in the car." The detectives chatted about the restaurants they passed in Georgetown while remaining vigilant for Sullivan. One of them suggested that Sullivan was in Virginia or might be sitting in some restaurant window watching them drive around. Sorenson had screamed at them to be quiet.

Feldman surveyed the two detectives as he approached. One was black and distinguished, almost professorial. The other was a pasty and rumpled white man who could stand to lose thirty pounds. Feldman guessed they had ten years on him. They could pass for luggage salesmen arriving at some convention. The telephone at the reception desk started ringing as Feldman approached.

"Gentlemen?" Feldman was not sure why he made his greeting sound like a question. "I'm Matty Feldman—"

"Director," the desk officer interrupted Feldman. "Urgent call, sir."

"Who?"

"Mr. Sullivan, sir."

"Shit."

Feldman pointed at a small security office off the reception area and motioned for the detectives to follow. They crammed into the room and displaced its occupants even as the phone started to ring. Feldman found the speaker button.

"Matty Feldman."

"James Sullivan. Are you in charge now?"

"Apparently," Feldman said. He gestured to the detectives that he needed to stretch the conversation.

"Here's the deal. I'm finished. Save your resources. You won't find me."

"They won't let me do that. I've already gotten the budget to find you approved."

Sullivan laughed.

"Besides, I've got two contract employees just on board here with me now."

"Send them home."

"What's the matter, Sullivan," Whitcomb said, "tired of decimating the African-American youth of our nation?"

"That's not what this has been about."

"What has it been about?" Macuzak said.

"It's not important anymore."

"What the hell kind of answer is that?" Whitcomb sounded astonished although he did not look it.

"The point is it's done."

"You sound burned out," Feldman said.

"Yeah, well, I guess that's one of the causes of the game being over."

"Game?" Feldman assumed Whitcomb's tone of indignation. "There are a couple of dead cops from the casino who didn't know they were playing."

"That was a cluster fuck."

"I'm sure that'll be a comfort to their widows and orphans," Macuzak said.

"The two cops, the three cops, belong to Withers and Redfeather. If you feel the need, you can add those two scumbags to my account, not that anyone would care. I did what I could for the cops."

"You were just on a salvage operation at that point." Macuzak sounded relaxed.

"Exactly."

"Is that why you took care of the kids?" Feldman asked. "Because you felt no responsibility?"

"You don't want me to talk about that, Mr. Feldman. As an agent, you may, but as a man you don't."

Feldman had ready techniques to camouflage any information he might uncover concerning Sullivan's involvement in the trusts established after the casino shootings. The trusts were irrelevant to Sullivan's arrest and prosecution. Feldman just wanted an answer for himself.

"How's the other cop? Smith?" Macuzak posed the question to Feldman in such a way that Sullivan would have to hear it. Feldman's eyes went wide and he gestured to draw Macuzak's attention to the telephone. Whitcomb and Macuzak both shook their heads and waved for an answer.

"She's doing well," Feldman spoke as though the telephone were not there.

"That's good to hear," Sullivan said.

"She'll be coming after you, too."

"Maybe you can teach her to shoot first."

"You think that will be necessary?"

"No," Sullivan said. "You'll come after me with a tactical team, if you ever find me."

"You sound a little less sure of yourself," Whitcomb said.

A deep, vibrating tone made the speaker hiss and crackle. Macuzak and Whitcomb each looked at their watches and scribbled the time.

"I'm confident enough that I'll tell you that noise was the horn of a tug pushing a barge through New Orleans, or as they insist on calling it down here, Nawlins."

"What's the name of the boat?" Whitcomb fired the question.

"I'm not that confident. Besides, my eyes aren't that good."

"You're lying," Macuzak said.

"Gentlemen, it's been a pleasure. You won't hear from me again. Ever. Mr. Feldman, it sounds like you might have gotten your money's worth from these two. Unfortunately, you're too late."

"What happened to Roger?" Macuzak asked Feldman with an eye toward the telephone. Feldman missed the signal. After a slight pause, Sullivan laughed and the line went dead.

"Shit," Feldman said. "I'm sorry."

"Excellent hang time, gentlemen!" a feminine voice erupted from the speaker. "We're running the trace and have scrambled New Orleans PD and the field office. Please stand by."

Feldman looked at his watch and did some mental arithmetic. The call that just ended lasted seven times longer than any prior one Sullivan placed. A trace was assured. Feldman felt uneasy since he assumed Sullivan must know that as well.

"Sorry I didn't pick up on that last gag about Sorenson," Feldman told Macuzak.

"Seattle. He's in Seattle. Elliott Bay to be more specific. He's using a sat phone." The technician's voice was calm and certain. "He may be on a boat, maybe one of the ferries."

"Please advise field office to respond. Have Seattle PD notified. Get SAC Seattle on the line and send the call to my office. Thank you. Good work." Feldman switched off the speaker and turned to his guests. "Okay, let's get to work."

Chapter 15

Macuzak drove twice around the building before selecting a parking space abutting a loading dock. He and Whitcomb had difficulty locating the old mill building among the score of others in the area. Matty Feldman said it was an old woolen mill that they could not miss. After thirty-five minutes driving around and through Fall River, Massachusetts, Whitcomb and Macuzak agreed that old mill buildings looked largely the same to the uneducated eye, irrespective of their original purpose. The buildings, like this one, were fieldstone structures four or five stories tall, consuming most of a city block. The macadam surrounding the building was littered with shards of glass from the countless broken windows. A cold rain had been falling since they arrived in Providence. Macuzak's eye measured the distance to the closest entrance, a gray steel door featuring an intercom and camera.

"Sure this is the place?" Macuzak asked.

"No," Whitcomb said looking at the directions he had transcribed from a telephone conversation he'd had just fifteen minutes earlier.

"I can't believe he beat us with call forwarding."

"Believe it. They found his satellite phone on the ferryboat."

"Still, you'd think the NSA people would be able to blow through call forwarding. I mean what are we paying taxes for?"

"If it helps, Matty said they seemed embarrassed."

Macuzak shook his head. "He's done if he let us tag him like that."

"Feldman seems to think it was our skill in keeping him engaged that held him on the line."

"That's bullshit on a bagel."

"I thank you for that imagery, but I suspect you are correct."

Macuzak switched off the ignition. "Sure is raining."

"A cogent observation, Joseph, but not one that completes our task."

"Got an umbrella?"

"No. I discarded it at the airport after the wind inverted it."

"Guess we get wet." Macuzak opened his door and ran for the entrance with Whitcomb following.

Macuzak rang the intercom's bell. "Know who has a nice umbrella?"

Whitcomb turned the collar of his coat up against the wind. "No one nearby, I suppose."

"The pope. It's probably twice the size of a regular umbrella and has extra stiffeners in it."

"You don't say." Whitcomb looked at the intercom. "Are you sure you pressed the right button?"

"Yeah," Macuzak hit the button again. "Plus, he's got a bishop to carry it around for him. You can bet your ass that the pope's umbrella never blows inside out."

Whitcomb looked at the half-dozen automobiles parked near their Ford. They included a Corvette, Mercedes Benz, Infiniti, and Volvo station wagon.

"Interesting assortment of vehicles."

"I think Don King would make a good pope." Macuzak said in the moment before the door's lock buzzed.

The detectives found themselves in a hallway showing their credentials to a large man wearing a shoulder holster. He led them to a freight elevator, which carried the trio to the top floor. The space was open with exceptional illumination from a series of skylights augmented with bright set lighting. In three pools of bright light women writhed in various lesbian encounters before automated cameras positioned around them. A few robed women stood away from the cameras, smoking, using the telephone, adjusting makeup. Other people lurked in the darkness behind tables loaded with computer equipment and displays.

A bald man with a fringe of long red hair rolled toward them in a wheelchair. The tattoos covering his muscular arms made him look as though he wore long sleeves. His glasses magnified his eyes.

"Who's Feldman?" the man in the wheelchair asked.

"Feldman couldn't come. He sent us in his place," Whitcomb said. He surveyed his surroundings.

"Did you check their papers?" The wheelchair man directed the question to the large armed man.

"FBI. Like you said was coming," the large man answered then walked away.

"Fucking eunuch." The man in the wheelchair shook his head. "Did you know there are still eunuchs? That guy's one there. Found him in the classifieds of *Soldier of Fortune.* Keeps him off the help while giving me an extra hand. I'd be all over them myself except I forgot to look right in London a few years back and got whacked by a Jag."

The wheelchair man extended his hand to Macuzak. "I'm Lenny Jones; sorry for the precautions, but we can get some major nutcases showing up."

"Joe Macuzak. This is my partner, George Whitcomb."

Whitcomb had moved a few steps away to survey the room. He did not acknowledge Jones's extended hand, which dropped to move the wheelchair.

"Now, you understand that my operation here is completely legitimate. I'm cooperating voluntarily."

"Legal. Not legitimate," Whitcomb said.

"What, are we gonna get into the fucking inquisition here?"

"No," Macuzak said. "We're here to get some info on a bug that someone might have picked up from your site."

"And, like I said, I'm trying to cooperate. I'm squeaky clean, or you wouldn't be here. Just because I forgot how to cross the street once doesn't mean I'm an idiot."

"Great. We're all on the same page."

"Come on over. I'm shorthanded so I have to run one of the consoles for a couple minutes." Jones rolled toward one of the tables supporting banks of computers and monitors. Macuzak followed and gestured for Whitcomb to relax.

"Is there someplace else we can talk?" Whitcomb asked. He fussed with his fountain pen and notebook.

"Yeah, but I've got to run this set for the next few minutes. You can wait, or we can talk as I work."

Macuzak looked at his watch. "We'll talk."

"Feldman said you had a problem with a couple of girls popping up in some word processing software." Jones rolled into the area behind some computers and donned a headset while he stroked keys.

"Yeah," Macuzak said.

Whitcomb peered at a screen displaying columns of changing numbers. "It seems that someone parked a bug in the program. Someone from inside the government tracked it back here. They could not repeat the infection. It was some sort of a one-shot deal."

"I've run my checks and don't show any bugs. Who found this out?" Jones spun his chair to look at the screen with the numerals.

Whitcomb stepped out of the way. "Can't tell you."

"NSA," Jones said. "Had to have been NSA. My firewalls are too good for anyone else to come rummaging around in here without me knowing."

"Still can't tell you," Macuzak said.

"No matter," Jones answered. "Bottom line is some wanker came in and caught something. So, what's the deal? Are these two chicks popping up on copies of the budget? Excuse me."

Jones spoke into his headset. "Veronica, client numbers are flying. We need you to piss on Barbara's ass. I'll use camera three. Barbara, on your hands and knees please and spread 'em."

Whitcomb and Macuzak watched a striking black woman mount an equally beautiful white one in the illuminated area ahead of them. Both women were nude except for their pumps. On Jones's monitor, they could see a close-up view of the black woman relieving herself on the buttocks of the white woman. The white woman manipulated her labia with her fingers and added to the flow of urine by relieving herself as well. Both women simulated orgasms.

"Beautiful, ladies. Nice touch, Barb. Do the cuddle thing for a couple minutes and hit the showers, Maxine will pick you up over there."

Jones turned back to his guests.

"Sorry about that. We run a demand site. When the numbers get to a certain point, we have to respond or we start losing subscribers."

"Many people pay to watch this in the middle of the afternoon?" Macuzak watched the large armed man move to the fringe of the set with a bucket and mop.

Whitcomb nodded at the screen with the numerals. "Lots of people, judging by those figures."

"School just got out in the Midwest. This is small-fry, a fetish site. Just about all lesbian, but we do some solo lead-ups, of course. Evidently there are a lot of folks hung up on urine, or as they say in the business 'golden showers.' Personally, I think it's disgusting, but it pays the bills even after all the disinfectant we have to use."

Whitcomb rubbed his eyes. "Joseph, do you have those prints Mr. Feldman furnished?"

"Sure."

Macuzak pulled some photos from a portfolio tucked under his arm and presented them to Jones. Jones examined the photos and arched his eyebrows.

"Oh, shit." Jones ran a hand over his head.

Whitcomb sighed. "You recognize them?"

"I know this one here, but not these photos. As you can see, both women are Asians. We don't do live Asian stuff here. It's not cost-effective stateside and can get the INS on your ass. We just take downloads and plop them on our site when the girls need a break, or whatever. Plus, we don't do that much bondage—too equipment intensive.

"This woman here, the one with the dragon on her back, she was into that and wanted to buy in here as a partner, but I said no. She made a pretty strong pitch about her programming background and said she could cut costs some by working out front with some of her friends, but I didn't need any partners. Besides, her English was horrible and her ink was all tribal. Would have driven me nuts. See, it's all black and gray. I like bright colors."

Whitcomb took the prints from Jones. "So, these aren't your images?"

"Nope. Never seen 'em before, which means they probably aren't on the Web. I'd have remembered the tattoos. Those photos are private stock."

"You don't display tattooed Asian lesbians urinating on one another?"

Jones shrugged. "I would if I had artistic control. There's definitely a market niche for it. I mean, I'd love to get hit every time someone types on their browser 'tattooed Asian lesbians pissing.' To run Asians live, I'd have to get simultaneous translation, probably more than one language, and there's the time-zone issue. How far ahead of us is Japan? Lot of sick fucks in that country. It's already, like, tomorrow, right? I'd never get any sleep. Not worth the hassle. Plus, you need excellent lighting and stark focus for our market, not that fuzzy Asian stuff.

"Anyway, it's not really so much about the images as getting the models to do what you want. It's a power trip more than a sex thing for the clients. They're out to get command of some part of their lives by getting these women to perform as they see fit. That's why we do so much live action. It's where the money is. If I wanted to double my staff, maybe, but I've got a good enough thing going right now. Shit, I've grown more than I like already. Two years ago, it was just me and the models."

"But this isn't your stuff?" Macuzak said.

"No."

"You're sure?" Macuzak's eyes wandered to where the eunuch was mopping.

"I'm sure."

"Positive?"

"Positive. Unless someone slipped it in here when I wasn't paying attention. Is that your guy in the picture they have next to them?"

Macuzak looked at the portrait next to the writhing women in the photograph. "Can't tell you."

"Any bugs here now?" Whitcomb asked.

"No. I just ran a systems check yesterday."

"When was the last one before yesterday?"

"Don't know. I run them most days so that I don't pick up any shit from some Christian commando types."

"Is there a time when you don't run a systems check?" Macuzak said.

"We shut down for the holidays: Christmas, New Year's. Girls spend time with their families. I do hardware upgrades and go to Vegas."

"Does anyone have access to the facility when you're shut down?"

Jones's hands roved over his skull. "We had a break-in over the holidays maybe two years ago, but nothing was taken. Didn't even report it to avoid contact with the local cops."

"When did the Asian woman try to buy in?"

"Right around Christmas, now that I think of it. Two, three? Maybe three Christmases back? More like two, I think. Shit." Jones's eyes grew behind his glasses.

"So, this was a couple years ago. Was there anyone with her when you met?"

"No. We had a meeting at a diner and then came back here. She drove herself."

"What kind of car?"

"Don't remember."

"You have any footage of her?" Whitcomb asked. "Surveillance from the cameras at the entrance?"

"No. It's all long gone."

"Résumé?"

"No. I don't even remember her name."

"Have you checked your machinery as far back as then?" Macuzak scribbled in his pad.

Jones sighed and rubbed his skull some more. "My mainframe fried itself better than eighteen months ago. I replaced it. Anything before then that wasn't on my master backups is gone."

"So, someone might have slipped this through the cracks at Christmas time a few years ago and now it would leave no trace?" Whitcomb asked.

"Correct." Jones's head was red where he kept touching it.

"If you wanted to infect a specific person's computer, how would you do it?" Macuzak asked.

"A specific person? I know who it is?"

"Yeah."

"I'd run an e-mail out to him with it. If I needed him to come here to infect himself, then I'd do teasers to him to get him to come and infect himself here. I guess it would depend on the nature of what I want to do to him."

"So, there are a number of ways," Whitcomb said.

"Well, yeah, I mean, if I know the guy has a proclivity to come to a site like this, I'll bait him in and nail him here. Later on he realizes he has a bug and the guilt factor takes over to keep him quiet about where he may have gotten it, if he even knows where he got it."

Macuzak put away his notepad. "Are your client lists from a few Christmases back still around?"

"Yeah, but those are proprietary," Jones said. "However, Feldman asked me to check for one name for the last five years. Used an alias, but he had identifiers on him. I wrote it on here with the dates of his visits."

Whitcomb took the pages from Jones. He glanced at them to see the name, number of dates and times. There was nothing complex about the list.

"So, we're clear," Macuzak said. He peered at a smaller piece of notepaper through his reading glasses. "You don't have any viruses here in your machines?"

"They're clean."

"Specifically, no 'borers' or 'Trojan horses', I think I'm reading this right."

Jones shook his head. "You've got problems, friend, but I don't have them here. If your guy caught something at this site, it's long gone from here but is no doubt all through anything he touched if someone was pissed off enough to go after him like that. Especially since they targeted him as an individual."

The interview coasted to an end in another few minutes. Macuzak kept things soothing while Whitcomb ground his teeth and looked like he was counting raindrops running down the skylight glass. The eunuch took them down in the elevator with Barbara the blonde. She was freshly showered, and even in the dim light of the elevator shaft, her hair glowed against her white turtleneck and Laura Ashley jumper. Macuzak helped her into her Burberry raincoat. A wedding band and massive diamond ring sparkled on her finger as she slipped a beret onto her hair.

Outside, the rain had stopped. Barbara unlocked the Volvo station wagon. A Chrysler minivan driven by another well-dressed, good-looking woman pulled in next to her. They exchanged warm pleasantries. Barbara said something about picking up her son at daycare. Macuzak was already in the car tapping the horn.

Whitcomb eased into the Ford. "Do you have any idea what your wife is doing right now?"

"Liz?" Macuzak dialed his wireless. "She only pisses on transgendered amputee bikers."

"I realize we have freedom of expression in this country, but there have to be some limits."

"Different strokes, George. Nobody says you have to be exposed to this shit if you don't want to."

"You touched her coat. You might want to wash your hands."

"You might want to worry about getting TMJ if you keep clenching your jaw like that."

"Something is just not right about all this. This paradox between who we're after and who we're working with just doesn't sit well."

"I got the voice mail." Macuzak rolled his eyes above his reading glasses and tilted the scrambled phone toward Whitcomb so he could overhear Feldman's recorded voice.

"So, what do you think about Don King?" Macuzak asked as the recording played.

"What?"

"As the pope. Uh-oh, here we go. Matty, it's Joe. George and I have checked that location we discussed and it's possible our friend caught his bug here. We have a list of his visits. The owner says that any evidence of it would be long gone by now, especially if it was a targeted type of thing. Since he doesn't have the bug on his system, he doesn't know what it is or how to get rid of it. He doesn't know where the women in the pictures are or how to reach them. One of them actually has technical knowledge and may be the source for the problem. The infection could be as much as three years old. That jives with what the techies told you. Sounds like a hit-and-run scenario. We'll be flying back to Washington tonight. Give George or me a call. Good-bye."

Macuzak looked at Whitcomb with raised eyebrows.

"I liked how you said 'good-bye' instead of 'bye-bye.' That was good," Whitcomb said as he watched the woman from the minivan walk into the building.

"I knew you'd like that. What about the hit-and-run analogy?"

Whitcomb nodded. "Strong imagery. Did you get that from one of the technical people?"

"No, no, no. That's all mine."

Both men sat for a moment contemplating the enormity of the problem Roger Sorenson had created. His indices of evidence, as well as every document he initiated or reviewed concerning James Sullivan, had been corrupted with the virus from the building in front of them. Interspersed among everything Sorenson's computer accessed were images of the two Asian women. Although none of the actual physical evidence was affected, any competent defense attorney would embarrass Sorenson and the FBI for weeks in the event of a trial. Any lawyer who prosecuted James Sullivan would have an enormous evidentiary problem. Feldman had confided to the detectives that the most intriguing piece of the puzzle was that the photos appeared to have been taken in Sorenson's apartment.

Whitcomb shook his head. "I can't believe we have to work with him after this."

"So, we've set to sea on a raft of shit. Not the first time."

"I know what the law is, but this is all so sordid."

"Feds pay quick. First deposit is already in the account."

"But the whole investigation is compromised. Feldman has us slinking around on damage control."

"Ours is not to question why."

"How could he have been so careless?"

"Roger's off on his own planet," Macuzak said. "He didn't give any thought to what he was doing, or if he did, he didn't give a rat's ass."

"What would Don do with his hair?" Whitcomb asked after a few minutes.

"That's the whole shooting match," Macuzak said as he slipped the car into gear. "He could just shape it into a point like one of those big hats they wear."

Chapter 16

S tacey Smith was tired. She blamed it on the pills she was taking but suspected that the airless conference room was not without some fault. She stifled a yawn to look around and caught Sorenson staring at her breasts again. Feldman was on the phone at the end of the room. Macuzak and Whitcomb whispered at the side table. There were no other agents in today's meeting, although she knew there were scores at Feldman's disposal. There was some technical woman at the far end of the table, but Smith knew nothing about her beyond her credentials dangling from her jacket.

Some task force. A bureaucrat, two retirees, a pig, and me.

Smith wondered if she could call Chief Flynn and go home. It had been almost a month since she had come to Washington. Apart from meetings and reviews of documents from field agents, they seemed to have accomplished little. At least she had learned to leave her cane back in the room so she could carry her briefing binders. Maybe she was ready to be back on the street. Maybe she was ready to go home to see Jeff Stone.

She perused the pile of fresh material in front of her. It comprised a lot of contact reports, mostly crank calls. This week's Captain Crack Attack Card was out. It showed her being carried out of a helicopter on a stretcher.

"Christ."

Sorenson leaned close. "What's that?"

"Nothing." Smith looked up. Everyone was at the table. She wondered when the meeting had started.

"He's done," Macuzak said.

Whitcomb nodded his agreement.

"Basically, that's what the profilers think, too," Feldman said. "Sullivan's not going to come out and play anymore. He burned his cover, one of his covers anyway, by giving us the satellite phone that we linked to an address in Fall River, Massachusetts. That turned out to be an empty apartment in a tripledecker."

"What about the landlord?" Whitcomb said.

Smith guessed she had not missed too much.

"Rented it to two Asian women right after Christmas," Feldman said. "They spoke little English and paid him in cash for the first three, last, and two months' security."

"Don't suppose they're around to be interviewed," Macuzak said.

"No. They're gone like smoke. He never saw them after they got their keys. Their description is generic except for some tribal tattooing."

"What about the rental application?" Smith asked.

"The landlord didn't even look at it until after our agents showed up. It's a fiction." Feldman looked at Sorenson.

"It seems Mr. Sullivan rented this abode and leased the satellite telephone using my identity," Sorenson said. He leaned back from his laptop.

Smith smiled. Macuzak and Whitcomb did not.

"In any event, agents are watching the location, but we've told the landlord he'll probably never see any more rent," Feldman said. "Okay, in your briefing books or binders or whatever you prefer to call them, you'll see that we have updated outlines of the victims and the crime locations. If you have any questions as we proceed, please feel free to stop me."

"Well, then, if I may interrupt," Whitcomb said. "I must confess that I have a small linguistic problem with the term 'victim' as utilized in the binder. The individuals Mr. Sullivan has dispatched do not appear to me to be the victims of anything other than their own vices. Further, as the only African-American on the team, I feel uniquely qualified to refute any implication that his crimes are racially motivated, despite accounts that may have so implied. That is a red herring which may be intended to divert our efforts or cloud our judgment. When conditions were right, he seems to have disposed of predatory elements irrespective of race, creed, or color."

"We needed the race angle to characterize this as a string of hate crimes," Sorenson said. "It gives us a firmer jurisdictional footing. We discussed this last week."

The table was silent.

"Your point is well taken, George," Feldman said. "Perhaps we rushed to judgment with that particular term, but I think we needed a common language to define the targets of Mr. Sullivan's wrath."

"Rage," Stacey Smith whispered.

Feldman whirled to face her.

"I'm sorry. I didn't hear you, Stacey."

"Sure, sorry."

"No. What did you say?"

"I said 'rage.' That's the word in Dr. Funtz's reports on Sullivan."

Smith wondered if the pills were loosening her tongue.

"Precisely," Whitcomb said. "Sullivan is enraged, just as the community at large is. He is fed up, for understandable reasons according to the history, and has taken matters into his own hands. However, he is not and I think this is a crucial point—acting without foresight. He picks and chooses where he will strike and he does so for maximum effect. He doesn't kill like some madman who randomly shoots everything and everyone in sight. Frankly, I am amazed that he did not kill anyone who was not a known criminal actor, specifically a drug dealer."

Sorenson looked at Smith.

"Except at the casino," he said. "He killed two cops."

"Well, the casino appears to be an exception," Macuzak said. "The police officers were killed by two perps tied to the militia or some terrorist-type group. Sullivan actually popped the two shooters when he got the chance."

Smith thought about how Sullivan had saved her life at the casino. She thought about that a lot in the last few weeks.

"Joseph is correct," Whitcomb said to Sorenson. "Apart from the casino incident, which he did not precipitate, the scenarios echo that which we faced in Camden. We are deceiving ourselves if we think that Sullivan acts from blind rage or kills indiscriminately, and if we take such an approach the credibility of our efforts will be undermined. Do you know what I saw the other day, Mr. Sorenson?"

"I have no idea."

"I witnessed a boy, perhaps eight or nine years of age, walk away from a drug dealer with an admonition. This is a little boy who lives in a project, who has been surrounded by drug-dealing gang members his whole life and who probably used to think they were the ultimate. He couldn't wait to grow up and be like them one day. Do you know what he said to the pusher, who, incidentally, wasn't much older than the boy? Do you know what he said, Mr. Sorenson?"

"How could I know?"

"He said this to the drug-pushing gang member, 'Captain Crack Attack is gonna get you.' Not the police. Not God. Not Allah. Not some antidrug or antigang task force. 'Captain Crack Attack.' He's a hero to some of these people. That's who we're after and after reviewing the material accumulated to date, I have some misgivings about whether you comprehend that."

"Two points," Sorenson said. "First, studies show a repudiation of drug dealers in the type of scenario you're describing wholly apart from Mr. Sullivan's efforts. Drugs have fallen out of fashion in the hardest hit communities. Second, I know him better than you think."

"I think we're getting away from the matter at hand, which remains the capture of Sullivan," Feldman said. He looked hard at Whitcomb. "Further, we're not here to argue semantics."

Smith doodled.

Did I miss something?

"I think what George is getting at is that we had some confusion about how this investigation got started," Macuzak said. "We've been at this a while and the materials are a little murky on how Roger started to get calls from Sullivan, and I wonder if we could clear that up."

"He called me because we know each other," Sorenson said.

Smith leaned forward.

"I'm sorry," she said. "Could you repeat that?"

"We know each other from law school. We were tracked together through school because his name came next to mine in the alphabet so we got to know each other pretty well."

"Excuse me. Excuse me," Whitcomb said, blinking. "You mean Sullivan called you?"

"Yes."

"It was not a matter that you somehow learned he was the perpetrator and contacted him, rather he initiated the contact?"

"Exactly. He called to confess and arrange a surrender because he knew I was with the FBI and the situation somehow changed or he decided not to surrender."

Macuzak was shaking his head.

"That wasn't in the binder," Smith said as she flipped through the book. She had read everything four times and kept up with all the supplements. Whitcomb looked like he was appraising Sorenson while Macuzak manipulated a pencil among the fingers of his right hand.

Feldman cleared his throat.

"With that one point as an exception, I think that all the information we have on Mr. Sullivan is in the binder. As I am sure you know, he has made no secret of the fact that he has taken down a location because he literally leaves his calling card."

"He also calls to tell us he's taking time off so that we don't waste taxpayer money chasing ghosts," Sorenson said. He looked at Macuzak and Whitcomb. Smith caught a flash of disgust cross Whitcomb's face.

What is going on?

"That's expressly why he calls according to the transcripts of the calls," Macuzak said, addressing Feldman. "He says that's why he's calling. And George mentioned earlier that he and I keep wandering back to this guy's motive. George thinks he's in a rage, but I disagree. I bet he's past that and may be operating on a monetary gain type of motive at this point."

"In any event, it appears that we have this down time," Feldman said. "If Sullivan is truly finished, we'll have to devise some method to engage him. We have lots of field agents at our disposal. As far as actual investigative work here in this group, we'll continue to work in teams. George and Joe should stay together. Stacey, you'll continue to be paired with Roger. Once you're completely back on your feet, we'll increase your field load."

"I can work now. As long as we aren't kicking in any doors in the immediate future, I'll be up to speed."

"Unfortunately, we're not at the point where we know what door to kick in, and when we get to that point, we'll summon a tactical team to take Sullivan."

"He won't fight us," Macuzak said.

"What?" Sorenson said.

"He said that Sullivan won't fight us," Whitcomb said.

"Why do you say that, Joe?" Feldman asked.

"Think about it. He takes pains to make sure no cops are around when he caps the dealers. I'll bet that he's passed on some targets because there were cops around who either might get hit or try to stop him. The history says his dad was a cop. The one time there are cops around, he pops the guys who shot the cops. He didn't have to do that. He could've waited for this Withers guy to shoot Stacey here, no offense intended."

"None taken," Stacey said.

Yeah, sure.

"And, after he does it, he stays and performs first aid. He did that when he could've boogied after layin' there and waiting for the smoke to clear."

"Captain Crack Attack," Whitcomb said.

"Interesting insight, but we'll cross that bridge when we come to it," Feldman said. "For now, I want you to go back and look at everything we have and conjure up practical things we can do for the purpose of closing in on Sullivan. If there is an interview you think should be done, let me know what it is and why. We'll continue to utilize field agents to the extent we have to, but if it's really important, then we'll send you out for it. I've already decided there will be a couple of repeat interviews at Sullivan's old law firm in Philadelphia and we'll visit with Sullivan's old army unit in an effort to see if someone there can help us with whatever criteria he uses to locate targets. For present purposes, I want you to take a step back and figure out what else we can do to locate our man or flush him into the open."

Whitcomb leaned forward.

"We as law-enforcement professionals are setting aside our assessment of whether Sullivan should be caught," he said. "I know that statement is implicit in what we do with respect to every case, but this time I think it is something we should contemplate so the issue is resolved before we arrive at some critical juncture. This perpetrator has committed crimes, unspeakable crimes in some instances, yet I, for one, cannot help but conclude that society has benefited and hope at some level that we are unsuccessful in our mission."

"What are you trying to say, Whitcomb?" Sorenson asked.

Smith sighed. "He's saying that we should think about whether, deep down inside, we really want to catch this guy."

"Make no mistake about it," Feldman said. "We will get Sullivan and if any of you are not up to it, then you are free to bow out."

Feldman looked at Sorenson like he wanted to skin him.

What is that about?

"It doesn't look to me like we have a great deal to do with the meat of an investigation," Macuzak said. "Usually, we spend most of our time trying to figure out who did the crime. This time that problem is solved and we just have to find the guy, and in some ways that's the hardest part. This Sullivan seems to work alone so he's increased his odds enormously."

"Right," Smith said. "He doesn't seem to have any help and he's not in bars trying to impress people with his tales of derring-do."

"What did you say?" Feldman asked.

Smith wondered if the medicine made her say something she did not intend.

"I said he works alone and isn't bragging in bars."

"No. You said 'derring-do' and that brings to mind the story of Robin Hood, who also had the appeal George described."

"Well, he doesn't give to the poor," Sorenson said. "He just robs from the rich."

"Only some of the time. It doesn't appear from what I read that money is the objective of every hit. It just looks to me like it's become a greater factor than it was before," Macuzak said.

"Plunder," Whitcomb said. "He's a buccaneer, a pirate really."

"A pirate?" Smith wondered why that sounded exciting.

"Certainly. He's a modern predator. In olden days, he could have sailed the Seven Seas and taken prizes, or destroyed them in the attempt to do so. He would have operated at the fringe of the known world just as he does now. He hits and he runs."

"More like a cannibal," Sorenson said.

Whitcomb cast a look at Sorenson before continuing.

"He operates at the fringe of our society in harassing the drug community. He is at the end of the earth when he strikes some of these locations. Although they tend to be in the urban milieu right under our noses, they are as remote as the American west or the Caribbean used to be."

"So, what are you saying?" Sorenson said. "We should be looking for someone wearing a cowboy hat and a Jimmy Buffett shirt?"

Feldman peered over reading glasses. "Change your tone, Roger."

"I don't think we're going to be able to catch him," Macuzak said. "We have to be ahead of him and be waiting when he hits."

"We can't possibly be at every crack house or drug corner to wait for him to hit," Sorenson said.

"If you think about it, that's our job," Smith said. "We shouldn't be out there waiting for him to hit, but we should be out there anyway because the dopers should be arrested."

Sorenson rolled his eyes.

"So, all we have to do is solve the drug problem in America and we can stop Sullivan although we may not catch him in the process. Well, let me tell you something. Out on the prairie, or hills, or wherever it is you come from, the problems are different—"

"Roger!" Feldman's voice boomed.

"I'm just trying to say—"

"You've said enough."

Smith shrugged. "I guess my point is that his targets are the same as ours in many instances. Maybe if we did our job better, he wouldn't be doing this."

Prick.

Was that out loud?

"This hearkens back to the subject I broached earlier," Whitcomb said. "While Sullivan's methods are draconian, they are not without some benefit to us all. So, the question becomes, in my mind, and I believe Joseph's, one of whether it is a good thing to capture or, let's face the more likely potential, kill Mr. Sullivan. As professionals, I know that Joseph and I have resolved the issue and I just want us all to affirmatively reflect on the task at hand."

"As I hoped I made clear, our mission is to stop James Sullivan and I will do whatever I can within the law to realize that result," Feldman said. "If that statement presents a problem to anyone, then you should not be here."

"We've all been on missions, Matthew," Whitcomb said. He fixed his gaze on Sorenson. "There comes a time in every mission, whether it be in a dark hallway or a revelation in the shower, where it's just you and the quarry. The notion of mission or duty is irrelevant. At those moments, we pursue because we want to or need to, not because someone is checking to see if we perform our jobs. Usually, it's not a problem because we're chasing a speeder, or a rapist, or a bank robber, or a dealer, but not this time. We are after the pirate everyone is pulling for at some level. This is someone who functions as our ally whether he intends to or not. In a small way he does the job that society—and we as individuals—are afraid to do."

Whitcomb pulled off his reading glasses.

"I'm sure we've all been on raids at one time or another. This place in Camden would have justified a raid team the size of a platoon if the police hit it, but he did it alone. Couple that type of commitment, that type of resolve, with a superior intellect and you have a formidable opponent. I seriously question whether he can be caught by any specific effort we may make. It seems more likely he might be picked up on a traffic stop or some other offense."

"The guy has no record we can find," Macuzak said. "And on the traffic stop thing, there hasn't even been a chase from one of these places he hits. Even if he's getting stopped a dozen times a week when he's just out toolin' around, he's got to have fake ID and unless he does something horrendous like wipe out a school bus, he's not gonna get printed. Unless he blunders, no one is gonna recognize him."

"That's why I'm here, isn't it?" Smith asked.

"In part," Feldman said. He ran his finger down the agenda. "Listen, we have a slide show that Roger put together in anticipation of those army and law firm interviews I want done. I think everything is covered in the binders, but let's sit through show and tell for a while and maybe it will spark some more thoughts as well as summarize what's been covered to date. Roger, are you set?"

"Just a second."

Sorenson got up and flicked a switch that lowered a projection screen at the far end of the room. He dimmed the lights and manipulated his computer. An image of James Sullivan's ROTC portrait shot from a projector onto the screen. His jaw was set. The visor of his hat obscured the eyes.

"As you know, this is the best photo we have of the suspect. It was taken eighteen years ago. There exist some later photographs, but none of them are of better or even equal quality to this one. We do have one composite that's being publicized and several others that have been developed but not circulated. The last time anyone saw him was at the time of the casino shoot-out involving Stacey."

Sorenson flashed still frames from the casino videotape across the screen. Smith looked down at her notepad.

Oh shit.

"I think we've all seen this, Roger," Feldman said. "We're familiar with the visual identification problem. Move along."

"Okay," Sorenson flashed back to the original image. "James Sullivan is thirty-four years of age. His birthday is Christmas, but I don't know if that gives rise to delusions of being the anti-Christ. He was born and raised in Philadelphia. He attended Drexel University where he studied electrical engineering on an army ROTC scholarship. He went into the active army as a second lieutenant and applied successfully for the airborne forces. He trained as a paratrooper and went on to what is known as ranger training before he was actually assigned a platoon at Fort Bragg in North Carolina. They also made him a supply officer. His fitness reports are in the appendices and they all say 'outstanding,' but I'm advised that such ratings are commonplace. He was promoted to first lieutenant slightly ahead of schedule and became a captain well ahead of schedule as a consequence of an accident his predecessor suffered. I would emphasize that contrary to some reports, Sullivan was never a Green Beret."

Sorenson stopped when he heard a snort.

"I'm sorry, Mr. Whitcomb, is something funny?"

"Sorry, Roger, that was me," Macuzak said. "I don't think it makes a lot of difference whether the guy was a Green Beret or not. He was an airborne ranger for Christ's sake. There's not a whole hell of a lot of difference. The guy is still trained to blow up things and kill people."

"Well, I want to point out that we aren't dealing with Rambo here."

"Have you ever been in the service, Roger?" Whitcomb asked.

"No. Not other than the FBI."

"I think Joseph is just trying to point out that our Mr. Sullivan has more than an adequate amount of expertise, as he has demonstrated, for the task of wreaking havoc when and where he desires. The point of whether he was a Green Beret is of little significance at a practical level to someone with his training and determination. It would be an interesting distinction for someone writing an article or pandering to the public, but the reality of the matter is that he is using skills which infantrymen learn in the first few months of training."

"Fine," Sorenson said. Smith saw his jaw clench. "While in the army, he met and married Ginger Phillip, the daughter of one of the sergeants in his battalion."

Pictures of an exotic dark-skinned woman flashed across the screen. Smith rubbed her eyes. For a fleeting moment, she thought she had seen two nude women in an embrace.

I really need to adjust my meds.

She glanced around the table and caught Feldman watching her. The technical lady at the far end wrote a note.

"She's Amerasian, is she not?" Whitcomb asked.

"Not exactly," corrected Sorenson. "Her father, Sergeant Phillip, is from Trinidad and is a naturalized citizen. He met her mother in the Philippines when he was stationed there. Ginger was their only daughter. She worked as an accountant. She was killed in a gang shooting just over five years ago. Dr. Funtz believes that event triggered Sullivan's killing spree in conjunction with other events."

Sorenson flashed a timeline across his screen. Smith thought she saw two women kissing for just an instant. She looked at Sorenson, but he did not miss a beat.

"Specifically, you will note that Sullivan's army career ended as a consequence of a motor vehicle accident in which his truck was struck by a driver operating under the influence of PCP. He got a service-related medical retirement because he was riding what they call drag on a convoy at the time of the accident. Apparently, he was in the last Hummer in line when he was rear-ended by this doper. The wreck must have been pretty severe in as much as Sullivan's radioman was killed and Sullivan suffered two herniated discs in his lumbar spine. He was laid up for better than a year. After his discharge he went to law school. He clerked for the firm of O'Brien, Bard, Camby & Scott in Philadelphia and secured a permanent position there upon graduation. He passed the bar in Pennsylvania and New Jersey. He worked as an associate and was supposedly on a partnership track when his wife was killed and he went crazy."

"Well, it's not quite that simple, is it?" Macuzak said.

"I'm just trying to give you the thumbnail sketch."

"His boss had him shot, didn't he?" Smith asked.

"Not exactly."

Feldman picked up the narrative. "This is one of the things I want to clear up. As I understand it, Sullivan was supposed to meet his wife for dinner. She was left waiting at the restaurant not far from the office because this Mr. O'Brien had some sort of professional crisis that held Sullivan up at work. Sullivan finally broke away and got to the restaurant as they were working on Ginger, the wife. She had gotten tired of waiting and started walking out of the restaurant in time to be caught in a hail of bullets fired at some dope dealer who was eating in the same place that night. Sullivan was in the ambulance and ER where she died. She was one of four people killed, two of them bystanders. Sullivan ran back to the office where O'Brien was still doing whatever it was he was doing that had caused him to be late, freaked out, and started to strangle O'Brien, but O'Brien's right-hand man was still there and he shot Sullivan. What is that guy's name, Roger?"

"Walter Cole."

"Right. Walter Cole shoots Sullivan two or three times to get him off O'Brien. Sullivan loses a couple feet of intestine, but O'Brien was basically okay."

"That infantry training didn't serve Sullivan too well in that encounter," Sorenson said.

"Well, he was out of his mind," Feldman said. "His wife just got blown away and, oh yeah, she was five months pregnant with their first child at the time."

"He wasn't too out of his mind to sue them," Sorenson said. "He held up that firm for three quarters of a million dollars."

Smith flipped pages. "That was a settlement, wasn't it?"

"Yeah," Macuzak said. "O'Brien made out like he didn't want to put Sullivan through anything else, but I bet he didn't want to go through a trial. From what I hear, he's a first-class horse's—"

"I think we get your meaning, Joseph," Whitcomb said. "Roger, do we know what happened to Cole?"

"Actually, O'Brien made him a partner, at least in name. Cole had kind of a funny job as O'Brien's lackey, but O'Brien was grateful enough that he rewarded Cole with a position of greater permanence, even though he still serves in pretty much the same way."

"What do you mean?" Smith asked.

Feldman answered. "Cole was in a dead-end type of job where he did nothing but work for O'Brien, as opposed to starting to get his own cases and his own destiny. He was never going to stand on his own within the firm apart from O'Brien, so he would not have made partner and probably would have been let go eventually. Instead, O'Brien rewarded him with a partnership, which means more money and prestige, but he's still really controlled by O'Brien."

"This was a civil firm, right?" Macuzak asked.

"Correct," Sorenson said.

"Why did Cole have a gun?"

"Good question," Sorenson said. He lifted a tab on his binder to shift the bulk of its contents.

"It turns out that O'Brien actually designated Cole as his informal bodyguard for a couple reasons. One, they would sometimes go into bad neighborhoods to do their work and O'Brien didn't want to go alone so he had Cole get a gun permit to go along with him; and two, O'Brien was so obnoxious that people, including employees, had threatened him in the past. So, Cole had his father's old police revolver in his desk when Sullivan came back from his wife's shooting. You'll find all this in the Memoranda of Interviews, Appendix Four."

"Cole's dad was a cop, too?"

"Something he had in common with Sullivan."

"Seven hundred and fifty thousand dollars will buy a good number of weapons for a start," Whitcomb said. "Do we know how much he cleared from the drug operations he's robbed?"

"In truth, we have no idea. We assume he has to have taken enough that profit is no longer his motive. He also sued the restaurant where the shooting happened and that was good for another three hundred thousand in settlement."

"So he's got a million dollars in his pocket," Macuzak said. "That's why Dr. Funtz concludes he's just angry."

"I don't know that I agree with that," Sorenson said.

"I don't know that I do either, but Funtz may have a point. Drugs have broken his back, killed his wife and unborn child, and ended his career. That's a lot to lay on a single source."

"Burned down his house, too," Smith said.

"Well, that happened when he was in the hospital," Sorenson said. "It was never related to any drug transaction or suspect."

Whitcomb flipped pages. "But it was arson."

"Correct," Sorenson said.

"He worked as a lawyer after the shooting, didn't he?" Smith asked.

Sorenson brought the lights back up in the room. "Yes. He went to work for a firm in Denver, but quit after six months and disappeared."

"Were you able to trace the funds?" Whitcomb asked.

"No. He disappeared with what was left of his money, close to seven hundred thousand after his lawyer took a cut. James Sullivan ceased to exist over three years ago."

"When did he first call you?" Smith asked.

"He called about a crack house in Chicago that he burned to the ground shortly after he disappeared. He killed six people in that one and has been on a roll ever since."

"Does he call all the time?"

"No."

"He calls to jerk your chain," Macuzak said.

"That thought occurred to us," Feldman said. "It's one reason why we've assembled this team to augment what Roger has already accomplished. Thank you for that presentation, Roger. Let's take a break."

Sorenson ambushed Smith on her way out of the ladies' room.

"Maybe we can do that dinner we talked about," he said.

"I don't think that would be such a great idea," Smith said.

Sorenson stopped her with a grip on her arm. He let go before she could pull away.

"Look, it's not anyone's business what we do outside of work, if that's what you're worried about."

"I'm involved with someone."

"You never mentioned that," Sorenson said. "Is it serious?"

Smith took a step away.

"It's complicated, long distance," she said. "Plus, I have all this stuff going on with my leg, and department. Now is just not a good time."

Sorenson stepped toward the conference room. Smith walked beside him.

"No problem," he said. "I was just thinking you're new to town and I'm the closest thing to a local you'll find to show you around."

Smith broke away to get coffee.

"Things are just a mess right now, Roger."

"Sure," he said. "I understand."

In reality, Smith was not sure she was involved with anyone at the moment, but she had seen Jeff Stone a half-dozen times since Christmas. She rebuked herself for failing to tell Sorenson that it was unprofessional for colleagues to date. In all her years as a cop, no fellow officer had ever asked her out, so the situation was foreign to her. She spent the rest of the briefing playing over the things she should have said to Sorenson to put him in his place, rather than create a block in his path. Her preoccupation cost her nothing as Sorenson simply plowed through materials she had already studied.

The naked women flashed back a couple of times. No one else gave any sign of seeing them. When she got back to her hotel, she would call about her medication.

Chapter 17

tacey Smith still had in her sinuses the aroma of men's cologne. She lost count of the number of different fragrances she had sampled in an effort to match that of the Texan in the casino. The technicians seemed happy that she was not realizing any success in finding a match. They said it meant that the cologne was obscure and, therefore, of more evidentiary value once Sullivan was caught. For her part, she was not convinced that she could identify the fragrance without it being installed on Sullivan.

Sorenson arranged for Whitcomb, Macuzak, and Smith to fly to Fort Bragg aboard an army C-12. Sorenson avoided the trip claiming more pressing obligations. Upon arrival, they met Major Paul Tibbetts, who functioned as some type of staff officer. He escorted them to a white van complete with driver and advised that he had a full agenda of activities planned for them. Smith saw Whitcomb and Macuzak exchange glances. Although it was only midmorning, Smith felt the humidity of North Carolina wilt her. She had never been east of Denver before this assignment and marveled at how hot and wet the air became as the spring progressed. Nevertheless, she kept her jacket on to cover the .40-caliber Smith & Wesson semiautomatic presented to her by Chief Flynn when she was promoted to lieutenant. The intense air conditioning inside the van coaxed a sigh from her as she took a seat on the middle bench. The heat assailed her once again during the short walk from the van to a dark conference room.

What followed was an overview briefing of the base and its units using videotape, slides, and the ubiquitous PowerPoint followed by a heavy lunch with a number of officers. They all wore camouflage with tiny insignia of rank, so it was difficult to sort out who was who among the soldiers. Between bites, Smith learned that few people remaining at the base were contemporaries of James Sullivan, and those who were had already provided statements to Roger Sorenson months, if not years, earlier. The army furnished the investigators with binders that seemed to replicate what Sorenson had provided.

Macuzak asked which noncommissioned officers had worked with Sullivan, but none of the officers knew the answer with any certainty. Several seemed to think that Sergeant Carl Corliss may have been the last NCO to work with Sullivan. One of the older officers promised to furnish this information.

After lunch they loaded back into the van and speculated on Sorenson's whereabouts. He had said he had to go to New York for some reason and expressed his opinion that a trip to Fort Bragg was a waste of time, but Feldman insisted. After another half hour in the van, Smith suspected that Sorenson may have been right.

A monologue flowed from the officer escorting them, who turned out to be the public affairs officer for the division. He talked ceaselessly as they progressed. A pattern developed. The van would stop and they would walk a short distance to where soldiers shot, helicopters flew, parachutes dropped, and explosives detonated. Occasionally they would ask questions that were answered, but that did not lead to anything enlightening as far as their quarry. Macuzak asked more questions than the others and at one point Smith thought she heard Whitcomb snoring in the seat behind her.

Everywhere soldiers ran. They ran in large groups. They ran in pairs. They ran alone. They ran in battle dress. They ran in T-shirts and shorts. When they stopped running, they lifted weights and performed calisthenics. They were young and fit, but mostly they sweated. They sweated a lot. They looked so hot it seemed that their tattoos might melt. Smith could understand why as the day progressed. Each time she exited the van, the air seemed to be thicker and heavier. She watched the towering clouds and wished for rain to relieve the humidity.

Smith guessed the tour was the same one they presented to journalists or congressional delegations seeking background information on airborne operations. At one point, she noticed the driver in his maroon beret lip-syncing along with the officer. All the investigators took notes, but she caught a glimpse of Macuzak's and saw he had drawn an intricate sea serpent together with a smaller doodling. Her notes were voluminous, but in glancing back through them she could not imagine how they related to the problem of finding James Sullivan. By three o'clock, Smith concluded this trip was a waste of time.

The final stop on the tour, or as Macuzak called it "The Grand Finale," was in what looked to be an abandoned village. Once out of the van, they witnessed a squad of camouflage-painted soldiers storm a pair of houses defended by another squad. There was a lot of shooting, smoke, and some blasts from what the officer called "thunder/flash grenades." The attacking squad prevailed with four mock casualties. As helicopters spun away with the victors aboard, the rain started to fall in big drops. It reached a downpour before they returned to the van where the officer declared the assault a success. Whitcomb spoke for the first time in hours.

"How would they perform that same assault if they were alone?"

"Excuse me, sir?" the officer said.

"If one of the soldiers was alone and tasked with the assignment of assaulting one of those houses, how would he go about it?"

"We here at the airborne are concerned with the safety of all our members and the circumstances you describe would be highly unlikely. You see, we operate under a team concept and—"

"Yes. I know about the team concept. By my count, you have mentioned it now a total of," Whitcomb counted strokes on his notepad, "thirty-seven times. Assume, for purposes of my question, that all other members of the squad are dead, yet you still must take the objective. What would happen then?"

"Sir, I find such a scenario hard to fathom. Why would a single soldier need to take the objective? He couldn't hold the territory. If anything, he should fall back and call for reinforcements."

"Assume that the only radio is controlled by people in the building. He needs to get to it to call for help."

The officer looked out the window and opened his mouth in an effort to formulate a sentence, which would not emerge. The driver mumbled something.

"What did you say?" Macuzak said to the driver.

"Me, sir? I didn't say nothing."

"Yeah, you did," Smith said. "Out with it."

"No, ma'am, I didn't say a word."

"Stop calling me 'ma'am' and just answer the damn question."

"He said 'Smash and grab,' a term we employ for such a scenario," the officer said. "It comes from the street term for—"

"We know what the street term means," Whitcomb said. "Do you have training for that type of situation?"

"Not specifically. Everything sort of comes into play. We don't push it in training because it undermines the—"

"Team concept," Macuzak and Whitcomb said in unison. Smith said it, too, but just a bit later.

"Exactly. It's difficult enough to get everyone working together smoothly. It is counterproductive to then teach the exact opposite in the interest of preparing for what is essentially a desperate, last-ditch type of assault. It's the type of thing John Wayne used to do in the movies when the bullets weren't real. We deal with real threats and value our people. We do not teach them or encourage them to throw their lives away."

"Has it ever been taught?" Whitcomb said.

"Not really, but I hear they used to have an informal contest in olden days. It was nothing sanctioned, but something guys would do during their off time. Some upper-echelon types thought the participants were too exuberant about it, so they put an end to it."

"Do you know who was involved in that contest?"

"No. I'm talking about years and years ago. Well before my time. I don't think anyone on base would know about it at this point. If they did, I don't know that they'd admit to it, since it flies in the face of current doctrine. Look. This isn't rocket science here. I suppose what you would do is throw as many grenades as you could carry or launch. You'd bust a lot of caps, I mean you'd use a lot of ammunition, and you'd hope for the best."

"You'd want to get close, too," the driver said over the roar of the air conditioner. "And you'd want to keep movin' so you wouldn't get hit. It would be a lot better if they didn't know you were coming."

"Let's go," the officer said.

"And they don't formally teach this anywhere?" Smith said.

"No, ma'am," the officer said as the van started to roll. "Unless you want to count the movies."

The officer lapsed back into his presentation, which Smith thought was timed to coincide with the drive back to the administration building from which they started. They piled from the van and fell under the charge of another officer. The investigators thanked the officer and driver from the van. Smith noticed that Whitcomb lingered in the slackening rain to speak with the officer and they parted with laughter. The new officer directed them to a different conference room inside and presented them with a sheet of paper containing the names, addresses, and telephone numbers of the last noncommissioned officers who worked with Captain Sullivan. He fielded a few redundant questions and, after receiving assurances of his helpfulness, dismissed himself to allow the investigators privacy to gather their thoughts and use the telephone in the conference room.

Smith broke the silence. "Well, what do you think?"

"I fear that we have wasted the taxpayers' money to some extent," Whitcomb said. "At the same time, I felt compelled to cover some of the same ground that Roger did in light of the fact that I question some of his preconceptions with respect to Mr. Sullivan."

"I think we've been totally wasting our time and should beat it back to D.C.," Smith said.

Macuzak had the telephone handset shoved in the crook of his shoulder with the list of new contacts in front of him.

"I think we should run this stuff to ground while it's still fresh," he said. "Besides, it doesn't look like Roger checked with any of these guys, or it would have been in the binders."

"Is it in the new one we got today?" Smith said.

"No," Whitcomb said. "I read through it between naps in the van. The new binder is identical to the military service information Sorenson furnished. I assume he never asked about the noncoms as Joseph did. It appears he stopped at the paper-gathering phase."

Smith felt she had to defend her absent colleague.

"Well, he got all the fitness reports and talked to his old commanding officer, who's up at the Pentagon now from what I remember."

"Fitness reports all read the same way," Macuzak said. "The interview he did is of a general who wouldn't have had day-to-day contact with Sullivan. We should run down the sergeants. If you want to know the real scoop, that's who you talk to."

Macuzak became engrossed in conversation over the telephone, an occurrence that Whitcomb and Smith exploited for bathroom breaks. When they returned, Macuzak was just replacing the handset in its cradle.

"Okay. Here's the scoop. One guy is dead from lung cancer, according to his daughter. Another guy is actually Sullivan's father-in-law who now lives in his native land of Trinidad. From what the binder says, Sorenson's binder I'm talkin' about, he won't talk to anyone about Sullivan, although Roger takes a trip to the islands once in a while to try again."

"Presumably he schedules those for the winter months," Whitcomb said.

"Now, now, ladies," Smith said.

"The third fella lives in Virginia. He's that Carl Corliss guy they were talkin' up at lunch. He's retired after thirty years in the army, but has a job at some tire place. He's at work, according to his wife. She didn't want to give me the number because his boss is a real prick."

"Where in Virginia?" Whitcomb said.

"Williamsburg."

"We should get moving."

"Didn't Roger already set up our return trip?" Smith said.

"I feel like I'm Japanese with this touring crap. I vote we cut loose." Macuzak said.

"Agreed," Whitcomb said. "Stacey?"

"Sounds good. How you wanta go?"

Whitcomb withdrew a telephone from his pocket and hit a speed-dial number. "We should be able to get a government rate on a rental. If we leave now, we'll get to Williamsburg, or at least Norfolk, before it's too late."

Chapter 18

Macuzak felt the humidity smother him as he exited the motel room. Although it was only 7:30 in the morning, a palpable haze hung in the air. He knew the real heat would come later. He loaded the trunk and stuffed himself behind the wheel of the convertible. He started the engine and air conditioner. The exhaust rattle irritated him.

Macuzak did not like Chryslers. He had heard of a police officer rendered a quadriplegic due to some design feature of a Dodge Monaco dating from the early '70s. He preferred Chevrolets and argued against taking the rental car because it was a Chrysler. Whitcomb extracted from the rental clerk an assurance that he had no vintage Dodge Monaco available. In fact, he had nothing available except for convertibles. Macuzak was sure that Whitcomb insisted upon a purple one to spite him. During the trip, Smith allied with Whitcomb in illustrating the superior features of the car. She even stroked the fender of the car like a spokesmodel while Whitcomb lowered the roof for the first time.

He stopped near the motel office where Whitcomb and Smith were still checking out. Whitcomb held the door open for Smith, who emerged wearing the sundress she had bought the night before at the mall.

"Jesus," Macuzak said.

Smith was stunning. As she dropped the sunglasses from the top of her head to the bridge of her nose, Macuzak thought of some movie star whose name he could not recall. Whitcomb was beaming. He carried her bag for her.

"George, you horny old bastard," Macuzak whispered.

Macuzak lowered the window. Whitcomb strode for the car.

"Joseph, please open the trunk and lower the top. It is not yet hot enough for the air conditioning."

Macuzak released the trunk, but Smith and Whitcomb were left to unlatch the roof as Macuzak pled ignorance of its function. Macuzak squinted against the strengthening sun as the top lowered.

"We're all gonna get skin cancer with that roof down. Besides, Stacey's gonna get all blown apart."

Smith tied up her hair as she climbed in back. "I'm not Betty Bouffant. I'll survive. Don't you worry about me, Joey."

"Did you get all the bags?" Whitcomb said.

"Yeah, but I couldn't find your crate of Viagra. You must have taken it all."

Smith laughed. Whitcomb hid behind his Ray-Bans.

"Breakfast," Whitcomb said.

"Breakfast and then Sergeant Corliss," Smith said.

At the Corliss's residence after breakfast the trio learned that the sergeant was not home. His wife told them where he worked. The investigators located the tire store, which occupied a low-slung building set back from a highway extending north from Williamsburg. Since Macuzak knew more about the circumstances of Corliss's employment than the others, he would initiate contact.

All three entered the storefront, but Macuzak approached the counter alone. In the waiting area furnished with dilapidated chairs and a sofa, a coffee table at the heart of the seating arrangement supported countless hunting, fishing, and auto-racing magazines. Windows set in an interior wall allowed a view into the garage where cars rested on lifts as their tires and wheels were removed and replaced. A counter inhabited the same wall as the windows, and tires and their associated displays occupied most of the floor space in the showroom.

"Hi there. I'm looking for Carl Corliss," Macuzak said.

The man behind the counter was Caucasian, about forty. His dark receding hair stood up due to the application of some oily substance. He featured large muttonchop-style sideburns. The man glanced at Whitcomb and leered in the direction of Smith.

"Carl's in back. I'm the manager. Is there somethin' I kin hep you with?"

"I'm an old friend of Carl's and I thought I'd stop by."

The man moved his wad of tobacco from one cheek to the other and gestured at the empty showroom.

"Well, we're pretty busy," he said.

Smith wandered toward the stacks of tires.

Macuzak squinted at the name tag on the man's shirt. "Well, Vic, I could use some tires, but I sure would like to talk with my ol' buddy Carl about it."

Vic hesitated then said, "I'll git 'im. What'd you say your name was?"

"I didn't. I want it to be a surprise. In fact, where is he? I'll just sneak up on him."

"He's down on the ind there. Y'all togitha, right?"

Macuzak turned and raised an eyebrow at Smith.

"Well," Smith was breathy and country, "I don't know about these gennelmen, but I was interested in learnin' about somma those all-weatha ti-ahs. Like the ones with the cute little baby sittin in 'im."

Vic shot from behind the counter and headed for Smith. "Carl's right down thay-ah on the ind."

Macuzak saw Smith roll her eyes over Vic's shoulder. She tapped her shoulder and mouthed something he could not interpret. He and Whitcomb went into the service bays.

Carl Corliss was short and sturdy. He was bathed in sweat, an impression enhanced by the glistening black skin of his shaved head and bulging arms. He glanced at Macuzak and Whitcomb approaching but continued removing a wheel from the Toyota pickup truck on the hydraulic lift. There were six workstations in the garage, but only two lifts were occupied and only one other mechanic was visible.

"Carl Corliss?" Macuzak asked and exhibited his credentials at waist level so no one other than Corliss would see.

"You didn't show those to Vic did you?" Corliss said.

"No. He thinks we're old buddies. Shake my hand and smile so it looks that way."

"Don't worry about it. He's watching the babe in the showroom. Besides, if he's not smart enough to make you guys for cops, he's even dumber than I thought. What did you tell him to get back here?"

"Told him me and George here are gonna buy some tires from my old friend Carl."

"You're here about Captain Sullivan I guess."

"That's right," Whitcomb said. "How'd you know?"

Corliss resumed work on the truck. "My wife gave me a call. Figured it was just a matter of time before you got around to talking to me."

"We'd like to set up an interview when we can sit and talk."

"Do I have to do that?"

"No. But we would appreciate it."

"Look. I don't know anything. I am out of the army so you can't beat me with that stick. Why don't you just ask me right now and we'll get this over with because I don't know anything. I'll answer your questions, but I'll tell you right up front that I hope you never catch him. Anybody who kills drug-dealing scum is okay in my book."

"This could take a while," Macuzak said.

"No, it won't, because I don't know anything."

"Fine. Do you know where he is?"

"No. Next question."

"When was the last time you saw him?"

"At a funeral after the convoy accident. Next question."

"Have you had any type of contact with him whatsoever since then?" Whitcomb said.

"On the telephone once or twice."

"When was the last time?"

"I don't recall."

"Was it recently?" Macuzak said.

"Negative. Years ago. It was before all this Captain Crack Attack stuff. I think he was living in Denver at the time we last spoke. What kind of car do you drive?"

"Chevy Caprice," Macuzak said. "Why?"

"I need to sell you some tires, remember?"

"Yeah. Okay."

"Set of four, I think."

"Okay, but don't give me Michelins or Pirellis or any foreign tires."

"Good man. I think you need rims, too?"

"I don't need any wheels, but do you ship?"

"Where?"

"Jersey."

"Done. What else do you want to know?"

"You're working pretty hard for a guy who has his twenty in," Whitcomb said.

"Thirty," Corliss said. "This is one of my three jobs. I have a daughter in her last year at Duke and a son with a start-up in my garage. So, between tuition and venture capital I'm all tapped out. I start teaching high school in the fall."

Corliss arched an eyebrow at the detectives. "You interested in investing in my son's start-up? He's got a program turns your laptop into a defibrillator. Working with a battery engineer to give the hardware the extra juice. Builds a viable prototype and cashes out to one of the big companies. What do you think?"

Whitcomb fingered Macuzak's jacket. "Does this look like the attire of a venture capitalist?"

"Hey, man, I got a master's in history and I'm puttin' on tires in this sweatbox. You never know."

"I'm gonna stop with the tires," Macuzak said. "What kind of guy was Sullivan?"

"Good guy. Lousy officer. They kind of go hand in hand."

"Explain the 'lousy officer' part a little more," Whitcomb said.

"He was one of these lead-from-the-front type of guys. That's okay if you're talking about a lieutenant or even a captain since they're expendable, but once you get above that, you've got to convert into one of these rear-echelon types. He was never going to be able to do that."

Whitcomb wiped his brow. "So his men did or didn't think he was a lousy officer?"

"Oh! His men loved him. They'd follow him anywhere. It was the army that didn't like him and vice versa, I suspect, but he never said so."

"Can you elaborate?"

"He would have had some problems moving up to a higher rank. For an officer to get above that platoon and company level where he was, he has to change his mindset so that he becomes less involved with the soldier and more involved with units of men. He maybe cared too much about the individuals. That's a big problem for the army. That's why we think we can fight wars where none of our soldiers get killed. Let me tell you that ain't the case. That whole bomb-the-bad-guy routine was the worst thing that could've happened to the army as far as I'm concerned. Makes people think we can win a war by pushing buttons. That's just not so."

Corliss flashed an enormous smile.

"But, I digress," he said. "Where was I?"

"Lead from the front," Macuzak said. "So, he was what? John Wayne?"

"No. He wasn't that. He didn't want to get killed more than anyone else. He was good at the fundamental unit stuff. The tactical type of thing. He wasn't eager to do the more strategic type of stuff. Sort of like 'show me my objective and I'll take it, but don't ask me to figure out what my objective is.' How was that? Pretty good?"

"Ever hear anything about soldiers running drills where they would take buildings alone?"

"Yeah, we used to do that. We even had contests once in a while, before they put a stop to it. Brass said it undermined the 'team approach' and I guess they were right about that."

"Did Sullivan ever participate in that contest?" Whitcomb asked.

"Oh, yeah. He won twice. Most of the other contestants were enlisted. That might be one reason why he had problems. He got in trouble for other training we did on the side. He used to set up these little optional training classes for us with some of the operators, the Special Ops people. They would teach us extra skills like how to steal a car, breaking and entering, tapping phones, false documentation, surveillance-stuff that we didn't normally learn but which might be handy behind enemy lines. Anyway, this is speculation on my part, you understand, because he never commanded above the company level. I don't think he would have been good at it. Plus he had some personal problems. All this didn't matter though, you see, because of the accident. You want whitewalls, right?"

Macuzak scribbled on a pad. "Yeah. That's fine."

"What kind of personal problems did Sullivan have? Was he a psycho or something?" Whitcomb asked.

Corliss laughed and then frowned. He hoisted a wheel back onto the Toyota.

"Captain Sullivan wasn't crazy. He just looked that way to some people who had higher rank than he did.

"Let's see, how would they put it? 'There existed some friction between Sullivan and command.' He was too much of a regular guy to be a senior officer. He didn't act like he was superior just because he was an officer. He didn't have a rod shoved up his ass like a lot of the other officers. His whole thing was that we were all in the same boat, so let's get the job done and not get killed in the process. And if the job didn't make any sense, he wouldn't take any risk to get it done. It was obvious that he was going to have to go because they weren't going to let him come up. I would guess that his wife wanted him to get out, too. The accident kind of sped up the process."

"Why was there 'friction'?"

"Couple of incidents."

Whitcomb had his pen poised. "What do you recall?"

"Well, one time, they call us out in the middle of the night. One of these full-blown deals where it's two in the morning and we don't know what's up. We're just out there putting on all our gear and scrambling for the apron where they load the planes. Now this happens, but when it does, you don't know if it's a drill or you're going to war, or what. They issue us live rounds and load up the C-141s and we go.

"Well, we were up in the air and when the sun comes up, we're out over an ocean and then the word comes that we're parachuting into Egypt, but we still don't know if it's real or just a drill. Some of the radio traffic starts to reach out of the drop zone and we find out the winds are blowing at thirty-five knots, with gusts to fifty. Sullivan hears this and gets on the radio for a definitive answer on whether this is real or a drill. He finds out it's a drill and decides we won't drop in those winds. You see if it was a real fight, we'd drop in anything. If it was a drill, it was too windy to jump safely."

"So? Did you jump?"

"Hell, no. Some of the other planes did and they had injuries. Serious injuries, like a couple broken backs. Even lost a guy in a sandstorm. We didn't jump. We rode to some airfield in the desert where Sullivan got his ass chewed by some colonel for not dumping the plane."

"Who was the colonel?" Macuzak asked.

"I don't know. He wasn't airborne. Nothing ever came of it though because Sullivan was right. If they charged him with something, then all he had to do was point at the injuries and he would have made all the other officers look like idiots."

"When did this happen?"

"Maybe three months before the accident. There was a whole other controversy came about from the accident."

"Tell us about that," Macuzak said.

"Let me run your credit card so I can set up delivery on your tires. I'll get you a discount."

Macuzak extracted a gold card from his wallet and gave it to Corliss along with the delivery address. They watched Corliss in the counter room where Smith and Vic still wandered among the stacks of tires. She was smiling a lot, tilting her head, and playing with her hair. Corliss walked back and returned the card.

"Anything else?"

"You were gonna tell us about the accident," Macuzak said.

"Oh, right. Well, one of the two guys who got killed, Torres his name was, wasn't supposed to be in the vehicle. I shouldn't say that. It was not normal for him to be in the Hummer. He usually rode in the back of a truck. Captain said he would ride with him and that's why he got killed."

"Where's the problem?"

"Torres, you see, went to see the captain along with his lieutenant to get a transfer. Rumor was that Torres was a fag. Someone saw him in a bar dancing with some guy, or some such shit. He denied it but wanted a transfer. That happened right before we did one of these deals where they roust us in the night and put us on a plane, only that time they sent us to California. Captain didn't have time to do the transfer before the trip. We drop in the desert and make camp. Next day, Torres is all beat up because someone kicked his ass. The captain keeps him close so no one will hurt Torres until we can get back and do the transfer. It didn't matter, though, because the accident happened like that second night or the next."

"What do you know about the accident?"

"Guy in a Corvette, no seat belt, driving over a hundred miles an hour. He's stoned or drunk or both. He's flyin' across the desert in the dark and rear ends the Hummer, which was at the back end of the convoy. It was desert camouflage but had a big orange triangle on the rear and a flashing yellow strobe, and this guy still hit it. He jammed his brakes and slowed down some, but he was still going pretty quick when impact happened. He goes flyin' into Torres who was in the back and then the two of them hit the Hummer driver. What the hell was his name?

"Anyway, the Corvette actually went all the way under the Hummer and slid into the tires of the last truck. We got back there double quick and thought everyone was dead, but the captain was just hurt."

"So the controversy was?" Whitcomb said.

"Oh, Torres wouldn't have gotten killed if he wasn't riding with the captain. Brass asked him later why he was in the vehicle and the captain just told them it was on his say-so. He didn't say anything about Torres getting beat up or being gay or any of that."

"Did Sullivan ever talk to you about the accident?" Macuzak said.

"No. Just about how he was doing with his injuries. He was hurt bad. They wanted to operate on his back, but he wouldn't let them. I heard he got better, then he got shot later on—you know that whole story."

"Parts of it."

"I didn't know anything about it. Sergeant Phillip told me about it later and I could hardly believe it. Guy got shot two or three times and now he's back kicking in doors. Always was a tough son of a bitch."

"Do you know of any places where Sullivan said he might want to move and settle down?" Whitcomb asked.

"No. We never talked about that kind of stuff. He wasn't one to hang out too much. When his day was over, he would hustle home to Ginger. She was a beautiful girl that one. Her daddy loved her for sure.

"Oh! That was another thing that caused some problems. The captain married the daughter of an enlisted man and a black one at that. Of course, he was a top sergeant, but you still got the feeling that some people in officer country didn't think that was kosher. Phillip didn't consider himself black either. He was darker than I am and he said he wasn't black. He used to say 'I'm Trinidadian, not black.' Ginger looked more like her mama. It was all just a damn shame the way it worked out."

"How about vacations? Where did Sullivan go?" Macuzak said.

"All over the place. He was a great one for hopping planes Space A. They would fly cargo planes all over the place: Japan, Germany, Hawaii, California, Philippines, Italy—they even went to Iceland once. They went all over the place. Captain used to talk it up with some of the troops. Tell them to spend their leave seeing the world instead of staying on base playing computer games and bowling. Look, are we about done?"

"Not really," Macuzak said.

"I don't know anything that can help you and I really don't want the guy to get caught. He's not hurting anybody but those who need it."

"We'd like to be able to call you if the need arises," Whitcomb said.

"Fine. Call me at home, but I go to bed at nine."

Macuzak wrote a Washington number on a slip of paper along with their names. "Here's where you can reach us. If we aren't there, just leave a message.

"Can you think of anyone we can talk to who might know more?" Whitcomb said.

"Ginger would know, but she's dead."

"Do you think Sergeant Phillip will talk to us?" Macuzak said.

"Not a chance. You should leave that man alone."

"Well, thanks for your help. Call us if anything comes to mind. We'll probably catch up with you later as the need arises."

They turned to leave, but Macuzak noticed an expression of revelation on Whitcomb. Whitcomb turned around.

"One more thing, Sergeant," Whitcomb said.

"Yes, sir?"

"Did Sullivan have any tattoos?"

Macuzak recalled that Sorenson's briefing binder detailed at least one that appeared in all the flyers seeking Sullivan's arrest. He remembered Smith tapping her shoulder.

"You heard about that, did you?" Corliss said.

"Tell us."

"Another point of friction. We had some go-getter captain—this was when Sullivan was still a lieutenant—wanted us all to get tattoos, even the officers. It was practically an order. He was even paying for them. He wanted us to get something on the shoulder appropriate for the airborne, like parachutes and skulls and knives and lightning bolts. So, these tattoos start popping up all over the place. Understand this is before college kids started doing this to themselves. There are tattoos all over the company and they've got sayings like 'Death from Above' and all this nonsense. Sullivan turns out to be the only guy in the company without a tattoo. So, the captain starts to lean on him and gives his platoon all the shitty assignments. Finally, Sullivan gives in and gets one."

"What did it show?"

"I'll show you. It said what being a soldier is all about, so I got one, too."

Corliss pulled up his left sleeve to reveal a massive deltoid muscle. There on his shoulder was a peace sign encircled with the words "Make Love, Not War."

Corliss grinned. "Pissed off the captain some good, but it didn't matter too much because he made major and was out of our hair. Of course, the real kicker was that it was fake."

"What was fake?" Macuzak said.

"Sullivan's tattoo. It was temporary."

"He didn't really have a tattoo?" Whitcomb said.

"No way. It washed off after a few weeks."

"Are you sure?" Macuzak said.

"Hey, I seen the man naked. No tattoo. It was a scam."

Macuzak pondered Sorenson's mistake, which now circulated on wanted posters together with the old ROTC photograph and composites. There was even a drawing on the poster identical to what Corliss sported on his shoulder. Tattoo artists were targeted with the flyers. Others had been consulted about how to modify or disguise what was presumed to be a key identifier.

Macuzak and Whitcomb left Corliss a few moments later with the understanding they could interview him at a later date if necessary. They found Smith walking north along the highway.

She said nothing for twenty minutes beyond her initial statement: "I'm driving."

Her raised hand silenced Macuzak and Whitcomb three times as they tried to recount the interview with Corliss. After a few miles, Smith pulled over, took off her sunglasses, and looked the two detectives in the eyes.

"He drooled down my dress," she said.

After a short silence, Whitcomb burst into laughter. Macuzak maintained his straight face and demanded to see the stain, thereby causing Whitcomb to laugh even harder.

"Was it drooling or did he spit?" Macuzak asked. "Because Vic had a pretty good chaw going when I saw him."

"It was drool; he tried to catch it with his hand, but some dripped off his chin."

"He was standing that close?"

"Yes. I can still feel it down there."

"Well, you probably get that a lot. Hell, I thought George was drooling on you this morning."

Whitcomb stopped laughing. Smith started.

"Pigs," she said. "You guys are as bad as Roger. Of course, he's much younger and a lot better looking and not married. It is a great dress though, isn't it?"

Smith pulled back onto the highway.

"Did you get my signal to ask about the tattoo?"

"There ain't no tattoo," Macuzak said. He and Whitcomb recounted the interview with Corliss. Smith asked some good questions. Macuzak decided that Smith was all right. He knew Whitcomb well enough that he could tell he had reached the same conclusion.

Stacey Smith drove through afternoon cloudbursts to the curb in front of the residential hotel where the investigators had booked their rooms. She volunteered to drop the rental car at the airport. The men protested at the inconvenience, but relented after she convinced them of her desire to use the car for a shopping stop on the way to the airport. They unloaded their bags and took them inside. Smith left the car running at the curbside while she ran in to check for messages at the desk.

<hr />

Angel leaned forward on the bench in the park across from the hotel. He adjusted his focus on the woman in the sundress and held the shutter button down. The motor drive affixed to his Nikon whirred. He cursed as the film magazine ran empty after a few frames. He had wasted too many shots on the old guys with the luggage but knew he had some excellent shots of the woman. She wore a fabulous dress and the sun backlit her figure. He leaned back on the park bench to reload, but looked up when he heard tires screech on the pavement. The convertible's tires cast off bluish smoke as the car's new operator tested its acceleration.

Angel spilled the camera bag and cursed some more as the trading cards fluttered onto the grass. The woman ran from inside the hotel. Angel grabbed another camera body and changed lenses. He fired the contents of that camera at the woman in the sundress. She fumed about the stolen car, and Angel smiled at the anger that animated her and gave him more poses. He shot another roll of film of the woman and the two men who joined her before some type of park policemen told him to move along. Angel was glad to leave. He knew he had plenty of excellent photographs of the woman and was eager to develop them.

As he gathered his things and the spilled cards Angel winced at the thought of his photographs appearing in the same format. He thought the cards crass and would take no credit for them, but the Philly boys would pay him good money for the pictures. He would get thousands of dollars for these shots as long as he got them to the boys at UPenn as fast as possible. He needed the money. He needed it for cigarettes. He needed it for more nose rings. He needed it to return his cobalt hair to the sulfurous yellow he preferred for the warmer months. Mostly, he needed the money for his art. Angel was not even halfway through his photographic study of public urinals in Major League Baseball stadiums.

Angel later regretted the deal he made for the photographs. Joel Karansky and Joshua Goldman paid him $2,750.00 for unlimited rights to them. Three of the candid photographs of Stacey Smith would prove to be among the most popular in the Captain Crack Attack series. Only the Larissa Frontenac lingerie and swimsuit cards, marketed with her consent for a percentage of gross sales, superseded the Stacey Smith series. However, Angel's remorse was short-lived. Someone strangled him with one of his camera straps in a men's room at Camden Yards less than two months later.

Chapter 19

Stacey Smith crossed her legs and looked at the office building across the street. The day was bright and some of the sunlight reflected from the windows across the way into the gritty office where she waited for Walter Cole. Her gaze wandered the room for the tenth time since she had sat down thirty minutes earlier.

Plants covered the windowsill. Some vines climbed the window frames while others spilled onto the floor. Piles of paper cluttered most flat surfaces. It appeared that the stacks had been straightened, perhaps in anticipation of her interview. Children's drawings filled a bulletin board screwed to one wall. The corners of the crayon-colored papers yellowed and curled from age. The wall near the chair behind the desk was littered with Post-it notes covered in indecipherable scrawl at all imaginable angles.

The side of a bookcase and the portion of the desk visible through the door featured signs pilfered, or purchased from unknown sources. Many of them were related to smoking. Prominent among them were those that read NO SMOKING; NOPE. NO SMOKING HERE; SMOKING? NO THAT'S NOT ALLOWED; SMOKING? NO. NOT ME; and, SMOKING? NOT IN HERE. WHY DO YOU ASK? There were also cartoons and some other signs that said WHIP ME! BEAT ME! TEACH ME LAW! And PLEASE USE TONGS. From the dropped ceiling hung dozens of automobile air fresheners that gave the room a smothering chemical atmosphere reminiscent of pine cleaner.

Cole walked in with a pile of paper under his arm. He was tall and thin. His shirtsleeves were rolled up crooked and mustard occupied a prominent location on his tie. His sharp features and intense black eyes drew attention away from his hairline, which seemed to retreat before Smith's gaze. Despite his lack of hair, he looked younger than his forty-three years. A short, young fellow wearing a suit jacket and carrying a briefcase followed him. Cole dropped the pile of papers next to another pile along the wall and extended his hand to Smith.

"Hi. Walt Cole. Sorry I'm late."

Cole's eyes widened as he struggled for the other man's name. "This is Larry—"

Smith detected the fatigue. It hung with Walter Cole like a separate entity.

The man extended his hand and took the chair next to Smith facing the desk.

"Larry Goldfein," he said.

Cole struggled to free his chair, the wheels of which seemed to be stuck on accumulated detritus, before bounding to close the door. Goldfein turned to face Smith. Some of the sunlight reflected off his glasses into Smith's eyes.

"Agent Smith, you know the rules of this interview?" Goldfein said.

"Yes."

Smith knew. She knew that she would be permitted to interview Cole for one hour or less. If the interview went longer than that, the firm would generate a bill for both Cole's and Goldfein's time to be sent to Matty Feldman with the full understanding that the bill would be satisfied within thirty days. Only one agent would question Cole. Goldfein would serve as Cole's attorney and advise his client during the interview. Feldman summarized the process as one agent/one hour. He said they had to live with the situation due to the extensive interviews Sorenson had conducted with these people before their involvement in the case. Additionally, debts were owed the firm for allowing the interception of Sullivan's calls.

In the next office, Feldman interviewed Dennis O'Brien who was represented by Sean O'Donnell, Esq., Goldfein's boss. O'Brien had engaged one of the city's most prominent criminal attorneys to represent him in his interview. Goldfein came along with the package. Smith had met O'Donnell earlier. He was about forty-five and polished. She had almost enjoyed the tour his eyes took. Goldfein was another matter, and Smith took an instant dislike to him.

Smith drew the interview with Cole to Sorenson's open disappointment. Smith guessed that Sorenson still thought he was in charge. She wondered if he, Macuzak, and Whitcomb were getting anything from the handful of paralegals and support staff who remembered Sullivan. None of those people had counsel. Goldfein talked while Cole pulled out and lit a cigarette.

"Just so you understand, the position we have taken with respect to these interviews is spawned by an atmosphere in which this firm's personnel have been interviewed repeatedly by Agent Sorenson. Not only has this been personally intrusive, but it has cost the firm monies due to the expenditure of time in conducting as well as preparing for the interviews themselves. You have extensive information in your files provided by Messrs. O'Brien, Cole, and other members of the firm— Walter, isn't this a no-smoking building?"

"What do you mean, Larry?" Cole extended his pack to Smith with hopeful eyes.

Smith had stopped smoking twelve hours earlier. She had quit smoking countless times in the last few months. She disliked anyone who used the words "monies" and "Messrs.," let alone in the same sentence. Goldfein was her adversary for at least the next hour. The smoke would annoy Goldfein.

Smith laid on the country-girl accent as she reached for the extended filter. "Why thank you, Walt."

Cole's hand trembled as the lighter came forward. He withdrew a massive ceramic ashtray from a drawer and floated it like a boat upon the sea of paper covering the desk. Goldfein moved his chair back a few inches, as if that would help him to escape the toxins spreading into the atmosphere. Cole laughed.

"That's not gonna save you, Larry."

Smith admired the ashtray.

"That's a nice heavy piece, Walt. Your kids make that?"

"Yeah. The older one did before I stopped smoking at home. The second one has asthma and the smoke is terrible for that."

"Have you got pictures?"

Cole flipped open his wallet with its compact portraits of his children wearing finery that Smith guessed fit for a few weeks before being passed to some cousin or acquaintance. Smith asked their ages and passed the photos to Goldfein. She noted the ages of the children and the driver's license number she had glimpsed in the wallet. Goldfein grunted at the photos.

"I'm sorry," he said. "Have we started here, or is this 'getting to know you' time?"

Cole accepted the wallet's return with a roll of his eyes.

"Relax, Larry," he said. "I'm not a suspect or anything. Right?"

"Right," Smith said.

"Walter, you know the program," Goldfein said. "They've wasted enough of our time."

"Time, time, time," Cole said. "They're gonna talk about time on my headstone. It's gonna say 'He billed a lot of hours.' But, you're right. Let's get down to it. I've got a brief due in Superior Court tomorrow. Besides, you folks know all about me by now."

Smith recalled the file Sorenson accumulated in his binders: height, weight, eye color, marital status, children, education, residences, bar admissions, and so forth. It must have taken hours to accumulate the data. She knew lots of facts about Walter Cole but knew nothing about him. She noticed yet another little sign affixed to his desk, which she recognized from her many recent flights, that said: YOUR SEAT CUSHION ALSO SERVES AS A FLOTATION DEVICE.

"Do the kids live with you now?" Smith said.

"Don't answer that," Goldfein said.

Cole shrugged and looked away. She had her answer.

"Why not, Walt?"

"Don't answer that," Goldfein said. "Agent, that's two strikes. One more and you're outta there."

Smith wondered how many times Goldfein practiced that line.

"Do you know where Sullivan went on vacation?"

Cole eyed Goldfein, but no instruction erupted. Goldfein wrote on his pad.

"Not specifically. He wasn't a Jersey shore kind of guy. Of course, we don't get much vacation."

"How about trips he took?"

"For pleasure?"

"Any trips at all."

"Christ. He was always getting on and off airplanes for one thing or another. He would have depositions all over the place and expert stuff. It was usually in some nondescript place. Nowhere sexy. Partners would do those themselves. They could suddenly become interested in the most mundane case if they had to meet a doctor in Florida or Arizona or California."

"You say 'they.' Aren't you a partner here?"

"Well, yeah. I am now, and that's why I can sit in here and not smoke, but I wasn't back when Jimmy was here. That all happened after."

"After you shot Sullivan?"

"Easy, Agent Smith," Goldfein said.

"I'm asking time frame and it's undisputed that he shot Sullivan."

"Just so the record is clear," Goldfein said. "You're not here investigating that shooting of James Sullivan."

"What record?"

Cole returned from the journey his gaze took across the walls.

"It's just lawyer bullshit. Lawyers always talk about 'the record,' like anyone gives a shit what they have to say about anything. To answer your question: Yes. I made partner here after I shot Jim Sullivan."

Goldfein started to stand. "Walter, let's talk outside."

"No. Sit down and represent me, but don't be such an asshole about it. Another smoke?"

"Sure," Smith said.

Cole's hands shook more than they had on the first pass with the lighter.

"The next question you want to ask is Did I make partner because I shot Jim Sullivan? The answer is I don't know."

"You put in enough time to become partner," Smith said.

"It's not that simple anymore. It used to be that you could work unreasonable hours and expect to be rewarded, but times have changed. Besides, I wasn't really on that partnership track."

"There's not really any need to get into this, Walter," Goldfein said.

"Well, I want to put this issue to rest to the extent that I can," Cole yammered around his cigarette. "When he was here, Jim Sullivan would probably have been the next associate to make partner absent them hiring someone laterally. He worked his ass off and was talented at what he did."

"What was his job?" Smith said.

"He was a trial lawyer. He had his own caseload assigned to him, but he also worked for Dennis. This meant that he worked with me because all of my work is with Dennis. I did, and still do, most of the paper work on Dennis's files, but Jim would go in and do the pretrial battles with the judges and opposing lawyers. It was a kind of symbiotic relationship. We would work on cases up to the time of trial and then Dennis would want to know what was happening on a particular file. Jim and I disposed of most cases by settling them well before Dennis ever became aware they existed. It was only the exceptional case that actually ever received his attention."

"So, you and Sullivan worked closely together?"

"Yes. Pretty closely."

"Were you friends?"

"That's hard to say. We worked together very well and shared a lot of the same miseries in this profession and in this firm. Most of our waking hours were spent together in one fashion or another, but we didn't see each other outside the office. For that matter, we didn't see anyone outside the office except our families. Most people don't believe it, but lawyers work pretty hard for their money. Plus, Dennis is not an easy man to work for."

"Why is that?"

"Don't answer that," Goldfein said. "Agent Smith, what does any of this have to do with Mr. Sullivan?"

"Let's put it this way," Cole said. "Since Jim left we've had six people try to fill his slot. Most of them were Prozac warriors or became them before they left."

"Walter, I've interposed an objection," Goldfein said.

"Prozac warriors?" Smith said.

"You know, Prozac stimulates production of serotonin to help them maintain some semblance of control despite the stresses they have in life. Like getting doped up before a fight except you do it all the time. A lot of people overcome their limitations that way. But, as far as I know, Sullivan was the genuine article. He naturally loved a good fight. Dennis is that way, too. Those guys don't need any chemicals to do their jobs. Real predators."

Goldfein was out of his seat saying something, but Cole motioned for him to sit.

"Relax, Larry," Cole said. "See. There's a perfect example. I take way too much of the stuff myself, but it allows me to tell abrasive bastards like Larry here to sit down and shut up. I never used to be able to do that. It was Jim's job and, of course, Dennis's joy in life."

"This is stopping now," Goldfein said.

"Who has Sullivan's job now?" Smith said.

"John Gavigan has parts of it, and so do I," Cole said.

"How's he holding up?"

"What am I?" Goldfein said. "Invisible?"

"John? He's hanging in there, but he doesn't like to lose. The reality is that defense lawyers like us usually lose and you have to be able to accept that to survive. Plus, Dennis will get to him eventually and he'll walk out, I suspect."

Goldfein rose from his chair, but Cole held up his hand.

"Dennis takes perverse pride in the fact that he's difficult to work for. He points it out to people who interview here, even if they aren't going to work with him."

"We've all worked with tough people, I'm sure," Smith said.

"Walter, please," Goldfein said.

"Not like Dennis," Cole said. "He's the consummate bastard. It's a badge of honor that Jim tried to strangle him. He introduces me sometimes as his bodyguard. Can you imagine? We are a law firm for Christ's sake. I only had the gun in my desk because he told me to get one after some witness threatened him."

"Are you his bodyguard?"

"God, no."

"Do you have a weapon?"

"Don't answer—" Goldfein said.

"I have my father's old Smith and Wesson locked in the desk, but haven't touched it since the police gave it back."

Smith stole a glance at Goldfein. He appeared to have given up and was scribbling notes.

"That's what you shot Sullivan with?" She said.

"Yes."

"Why did you do it?"

"That's it," Goldfein said.

Cole looked somewhere far beyond his lawyer and the walls. "I often ask myself the same question. I guess I felt I owed Den—"

Goldfein took to his feet. "Walter, shut up!"

He turned to Smith. "We're finished."

Smith blew smoke at him. "I don't think so."

Cole leaned back in his chair and smiled.

"Excuse me?" Goldfein said.

"I'm not done asking questions and you're wasting my time."

"I am counsel of record and we are through when I say we are."

"We covered this already. There isn't any record, and, let's face it, you're an errand boy. Now, go check with your boss if you've got a problem with me. Otherwise, sit down and be quiet."

Goldfein was apoplectic. The door seemed to explode as he opened it and stalked into the corridor. Smith knew that she had little time alone with Cole before Goldfein recovered or O'Donnell intervened. She turned to look at Cole who cleaned a shot glass with his tie.

He produced a half-empty bottle of Maker's Mark. "Drink?"

"Hell, why not?"

Cole poured her a shot to match the one he had already set out for himself. He held up his glass.

"To Jim Sullivan and his lovely bride," he said. "May God bless them both."

The whiskey went down in a single searing toss. Cole poured again.

"You're all right, Special Agent Smith."

"I'm not a special agent. I'm a contract employee for just this one case."

"Well, whatever. You want to know about Jimmy Sullivan? Come on, I'll show you something."

Cole rose to his feet as he tossed down his second shot. He reached into a file cabinet drawer and tugged loose a small leather suitcase. He turned for the door with the bag in hand. He made a show of stealth.

"Let's go," he said.

Smith followed Cole into the hall past the secretaries busy ignoring the tirade Goldfein spewed behind O'Brien's closed office door. Smith could hear lower tones that she assumed came from Feldman and the two older lawyers. Cole trotted down the hall toward the reception area. Smith caught him at the elevator. Cole made a show of allowing her to enter the car first. He followed and pressed the button for the highest numbered floor.

"Did you bring the bottle?" Cole said.

"Sorry, I forgot it."

Smith had also ignored the second shot of whiskey Cole set out for her. She watched the lights indicating the floors passed by the elevator.

"Jimmy really didn't drink much," Cole said. "Then, again, neither did I."

The elevator fell silent as Smith allowed Cole time to think. The doors opened on the top floor and Cole sprang into the hallway with a whispered admonition to follow and be quick about it. He turned a corner and went through a door into the fire tower. He ascended the steps two at a time. Smith kept up despite the burning in her leg and wondered whether she had pushed Cole just a bit too far. At the top of the steps Cole stopped short of an alarmed fire door. He turned with a look of supreme mischief focused upon a brass key.

"Jimmy gave me this. He was pretty resourceful about things like this."

The key slipped into the door to bypass the alarm. Cole and Smith stepped onto the rooftop as the wind caught the door and flung it wide open with a slam. Cole strode to the west edge of the roof. Smith wondered whether she would catch him before he walked off the edge. He stopped and pointed at something under a large air conditioning condenser.

"Grab that box if you would," he said.

Smith followed his finger toward a wooden box with rope handles. She slid it from its protected spot and hefted it. To her surprise, it was quite light. She carried it toward the spot where Cole squatted over the open suitcase. She heard the clicking as Cole assembled the forend and butt of an over-and-under shotgun. He slid a shell into each of the two chambers and closed the action before she could even think about dropping the box. Smith pondered what was about to happen.

Investigator Smith had little experience in sophisticated investigative technique in as much as she spent most of her career chasing speeders and entrapping sexually deprived truck drivers. She pushed an overly stressed witness who obviously had an alcohol and prescription drug problem. She smoked and drank with him while on duty in violation of God knows how many protocols. She spirited him away from his counsel. He blew her away on the roof before he shot himself.

Sorenson will get to write the reports.

They'll make a training film documenting everything I've done wrong.

Well, maybe not everything.

Cole opened the action.

Smith breathed.

"Are there any more shells in there?" he said.

She shrugged herself back to the rooftop and looked down at the top of the box. In faded letters were stenciled the words BLUE ROCK. Smith set the box down and opened it to reveal a few rows of clay pigeons and a hand launcher to set them in flight.

"No, sorry," she said.

"Damn. We only have two shots. Okay. We'll split 'em. I'll go first. Load up a bird and I'll let you know when to throw it. Make sure you throw it that way, toward the river."

Smith looked down at the box's contents and picked up the launcher and one of the yellow and black discs.

"You know, Walt, this probably isn't the greatest idea. The shot could hurt someone."

"Relax. Jimmy and I did this all the time. Two or three times anyway. Throw it that way and the shot will land in the Schuylkill. The pigeon fragments will land on the roof next door. He did all the math on it one day. It will be okay. I promise."

Smith walked toward the west edge of the roof. She could see the river in the distance. The wind blew straight into her face as she cocked her arm.

"Ready!" she yelled into the wind.

"Pull!" Cole screamed from her left rear.

Smith launched the pigeon and crouched. The howling of the wind muffled the shot. She saw the clay disc blow apart with a crack carried back on the wind. She could not track the shot past the target, but saw the remnants of the pigeon fall on the roof next door as Cole predicted.

Cole jumped up and down in delight. "Did you see that sucker blow apart?"

He struggled with the wind to light a smoke and offered one to Smith. Smith thought about telling Cole that it was time to stop playing, but he preempted her.

"This is where we talked. I mean seriously talked, Jimmy and me. This is where we decided to leave the firm."

That's not in the binders.

"How's that, Walt?"

"We were going to open our own shop. A couple institutional clients knew that Jimmy and I did all the work. They were going to leave Denny and follow us. Plus, Jimmy generated a lot of plaintiff cases. His dad was a cop here and it seemed he knew all the cops in town, and they steered cases to him."

Smith accepted the shotgun from Cole as he took the launcher. "You guys do defense work, don't you?"

"Yeah, but that sort of just pays the rent. The real money in any given year comes from a handful of high-value plaintiffs' cases that pan out. Jimmy was generating a lot of that work and Denny wasn't giving him his due. And, of course, there's the whole thing that Denny is just the biggest dick in the Western Hemisphere."

Cole looked off at the river.

"So what happened?" Smith asked.

"So, I shot him. Jimmy, I mean. That whole thing came a few days before we were going to tell Denny that we were history. But then there was this woman I was seeing, still am seeing. She's a lawyer here and wanted to go with us, but Jimmy sort of balked. I don't know if it would have worked out or not. When it came down to it, I sort of picked Denny by default when I shot Jimmy. Bunch of cannibals is what we are —lawyers that is."

"Say what?"

"Cannibals. Lawyers are cannibals. Just like the drug dealers. Except we pay taxes. Maybe that's what Jimmy is doing—taxing the drug dealers. Taxing the cannibals."

Smith made mental notes as she raised the shotgun to her shoulder. She did not want to push Cole. She asked Cole if he was ready, although she saw he still looked out at the river. After a moment, she heard his response.

"Ready!"

"Pull!"

Smith tracked the pigeon and aimed in advance of it. She squeezed the trigger and the shotgun recoiled lightly considering the fact that it was a 12-gauge. A chip from the edge of the clay pigeon separated, but its mass accelerated and continued its flight out and over the far edge of the lower roof next door.

"Winged it," Cole said. "I thought cops could shoot."

"I could make excuses about the breeze, or the length of the stock. Where do they land after they go over the edge of the building?"

"I don't know. The street, I guess. I never missed. Neither did Jimmy. You might want to keep that in mind if you run into him."

Smith extracted the two empty shells. Cole put the wooden box back in place and broke down the shotgun. They walked back down the steps and caught an elevator down.

"No one knows what I told you. Jimmy never said anything to anyone from what I can tell."

"I understand. O'Brien won't hear it from me."

"I don't care about that jackass."

Smith was about to ask why not when the doors opened and Cole handed her the suitcase.

"Here," he said. "This was Jimmy's. I've been holding it since he left. I haven't used it except for today. I don't know if it's considered evidence, or what, but I have no use for it anymore. Besides, it's probably one of his only remaining possessions."

Smith took the bag. "How's that?"

"Someone burned his house down while he was in the hospital after I shot him. He lost everything except his dog. Well, his wife's dog really. But you guys know all about that, right?"

"Yeah."

They entered the reception area to find a fuming Larry Goldfein. Sorenson, Macuzak and Whitcomb sat on couches and acted like they cared that Goldfein was upset.

Goldfein swung his arms while he spoke. "There you are. This meeting is over."

Cole shrugged his shoulders and shook Smith's hand before ambling back toward his office with Goldfein in tow. Smith flopped onto a sofa in the reception area.

"That was quick," Sorenson said.

Smith looked at her watch and realized she had used only thirty of her allotted sixty minutes.

"Looks like his lawyer threw me out."

"Why?"

"He didn't like my questions."

"That means you asked the right ones," Macuzak said without looking up from the sports section.

"Well, we know everything pertinent anyway," Sorenson said.

Guess again.

Smith disliked her partnership with Sorenson. She wished she worked with Macuzak or Whitcomb, but they seemed to function as a single unit.

"What's in the bag?" Sorenson asked.

"I'll tell you later. Did you guys find anything out?" Smith said in a voice she hoped the receptionist could not hear.

"Almost everyone who worked here when Sullivan did has since moved on to greener pastures," Whitcomb whispered.

"Sounds like a tough place to work."

"That's my impression, too."

The receptionist snorted. They stopped talking in the absence of more privacy and waited for Feldman to conclude his interview with O'Brien. He used his entire hour and then some before returning to the reception area with Dennis O'Brien patting him on the back. Sean O'Donnell followed a step or two behind with a grin on his face. Smiles and handshakes accompanied words of continued cooperation before the investigators found themselves in the elevator. Sorenson could not contain himself once the doors closed.

"Sir, how did it go?"

Feldman looked up and watched the numbers change as the car descended.

"Their story: One, O'Brien's admittedly difficult to work for, but that's only because he is a perfectionist; two, everyone who works for him owes him their lives; three, O'Brien is the greatest civil trial lawyer to stride the earth and, incidentally, O'Donnell is the world's greatest criminal defense attorney; four, Sullivan was an intellectual midget envious of O'Brien because of points one through three previously enumerated; and, finally, Sullivan snapped under the pressures of his own inadequacies as manifested in his failure to protect the life and safety of the thing he held most dear, his wife.

"O'Brien's handicap is five.

"O'Donnell's is three.

"They both prefer Cuban cigars and a massage therapist named Wendy. Isn't it funny that they've been friends for so long, but never seriously considered practicing together? They're going to discuss it further at dinner this week sometime."

Sorenson nodded. "Well, sir, that sounds like a very positive interview."

Feldman dropped his gaze to the opening doors and ever so subtly shook his head.

"I need a shower," he said.

Chapter 20

Joe Murphy's eyes flashed open. Sunlight struggled over the mountain. He looked at his watch to see that it was after seven A.M. Natalie Merchant sang "Carnival." The cats that kept him warm were gone to the barn where there would be food. When he swung into a seated position pain shot through his right buttock and part of the way down the back of his thigh.

"Shit."

He leaned back on the sofa and knew his pain would be worse when he tried to stand. Joe Murphy had a good orthopedic mattress for James Sullivan's bad back, but he had drifted off without climbing the stairs for the second time in as many nights. He groaned to his feet a few bars into Luciano Pavarotti's performance of *Nessun dorma* and shuffled to the kitchen where he started a pot of coffee big enough for six people.

Lydia brushed against his leg. She was a dark calico cat Murphy considered far more intelligent than most. She curled around his legs as Murphy sniffed the cream. It did not curdle in his coffee despite its age and the cat lapped it from a dish.

"Yeah, I know what you want," he said.

Joan Osborne's rasp returned for the umpteenth time since last night. Murphy activated the tuner to listen to Vermont Public Radio also known as VPR, or as his neighbor Wanda contemptuously referred to it "Viper." A strident homosexual lamented the fact that he had tested HIV-positive and belittled the sympathy tendered by those unaffected by the disease who could never understand what it was like to have it. He berated healthcare insurers and the government for delays and limits in paying for treatments and finding a cure. The speaker was so busy ranting about real or perceived injustice that his level of conviction sounded diminished. Sullivan looked down at the cat and scratched the animal under the chin.

"Boy, that was effective. He just doesn't know what he wants, not like you. You want cream? You come and hang around and act like you're my best pal and you eventually get cream, then you'll ignore me and sleep somewhere warm."

Listen to you. Criticizing the poor bastard.

At least he doesn't go around killing people.

Lydia hurled her shoulder against Murphy's calf. The sun broke from the clouds and shone through the large window to paint a patch of light on the floor. He looked down into his empty cup and pulled out more cream.

"You see, it's all about what you want. Since you can't handle the carton or take down a cow, you're left with manipulating me."

The cat lapped at the cream, but walked away leaving a fair amount in the saucer. Murphy watched the performance as the cat stopped a few feet away and reclined in the patch of sunlight to clean herself.

"Yep. It's all about knowing what you want and how to get it."

The telephone rang and Murphy studied it on the wall no more than an arm's length from him. It was not yet eight A.M. He picked up the handset on the fifth ring.

"Hello?"

"Are you decent?" It was Mona, Wanda's daughter.

"No."

He hung up, but continued to look at the telephone. The telephone rang again, which led him to conclude that Mona had programmed his number into some type of speed-dial apparatus, a major technical achievement for her. He sipped his coffee and took the handset from the cradle on the ninth ring.

"Hello?"

"Joe, don't hang up. There's a tractor trailer parked next to your barn."

"Yes. I put it there."

Sullivan was perturbed that his neighbor should be so observant of his activities. She could not see the barn from her house and must have come well up his driveway to see it. Her next question confirmed his suspicions.

"Can I stop by?"

"Mona, I have a lot to do and today is not a good day. How close are you?"

"I'm in the driveway outside."

"Come on in, but I warn you that I slept in my clothes."

Murphy extracted another mug from the cabinet and put on the tea kettle. As he rummaged in the pantry for a suitable herbal tea bag he heard the door open and looked back to see Lydia squint at the blast of air from the adjacent mudroom. He found an ancient decaffeinated herbal tea bag and exited the pantry to be confronted by Mona and another woman he did not recognize.

"Joe, this is my cousin, Carla. Carla, this is Joe."

He extended a hand.

"Pleased to meet you."

Carla was the notorious "Cousin Carla" to whom Mona had referred on countless occasions as the perfect match for the widower Joseph Murphy. She was petite, slim, and about his age. Sullivan knew she was two years older than he, but Joseph Murphy was almost her exact age. Carla's hair was dyed blond. She would be considered beautiful by many, and Murphy found himself agreeing with Mona's assertions that Carla was pretty.

Carla glared at Mona. "Sorry for barging in, but we were apparently in the neighborhood."

Mona tormented Lydia's peace by scratching her.

Murphy gritted his teeth a bit in his smile. "No problem. I'm used to Mona barging in. Please sit wherever you like. Can I get you some coffee?"

"Please. If it's no trouble."

"None, but Mona has to fend for herself."

Murphy poured Carla some coffee and they went to the living room with Mona in tow. Sullivan observed Carla's walk and compared it not to his wife's, but that of Stacey Smith in the parking lot of a casino. He apologized for the mess and folded the blanket under which he had slept. The television drew Carla's attention.

"Is that the television Wanda bought?"

"Yeah. Joe, you probably haven't even used it, have you?" Mona said. "He didn't even own a TV before this one."

"No. I'm not sure where the remote is. I don't think it works without one."

"Arthur borrowed it. We have the same set and he's too lazy to change the batteries. Didn't he give it back?"

"I haven't seen it, but I didn't really look for it yet."

"Let me call him and I'll check on it."

"That's okay. Ask him when you see him."

"No. I'll call him right now," Mona said. "He was supposed to drop it off weeks ago."

"That's okay. Don't bother now."

"I'll let you know later. If he didn't hide it here somewhere, I'll bring it over myself or Carla can do it. She knows where it is now."

"Mona, you haven't been showing people how you stalk me again have you?"

Carla laughed with an abrupt eruption, but Mona ignored the question and posed her own.

"What's with the semi at the barn?"

"I just had to move some stuff around and it got out of control. Is it spoiling your view or karma or something?"

"No. Just curious."

Sullivan spoke to Carla. "I keep some stuff for my business in the barn and Mona's always trying to steal it so I keep it locked up."

"Oh, is that the shop we passed down by the lake?" Carla said.

"Yeah. I think I pointed it out to you," Mona said.

Murphy knew this was nonsense. The shop occupied part of an old industrial building in Burlington's North End and one had to go to the end of a dead-end street to visit it. You did not pass by it on your way to anywhere other than the shop itself, which housed a small snowboard factory. He guessed that Mona had attempted to provide Carla with a gross, if not net, income figure from the business.

Mona no doubt had also emphasized the importance of Murphy's role as a business partner with Wanda in the snowboarding industry. That enterprise made rapid, substantial profits with very little effort. Two years earlier, Wanda had sought his advice and eventual equal contribution in backing a young man who turned out to be a prodigy in the snowboarding phenomenon. Sullivan thought there had been arithmetic mistakes on the balance sheet, but Wanda's smug smile confirmed that she could, as she proclaimed, "really pick 'em."

"What is it that you do?" Carla asked.

As Murphy considered the array of responses from "bush pilot" to "murderer," the telephone rang.

"Excuse me," he said.

Murphy walked to the kitchen and answered the telephone.

"Hello?"

"Is Mona there with that little bleached-blond murderess?" Wanda asked.

"Yes."

Wanda had warned him on more than one occasion that Carla cared only to marry a man who could provide an acceptable stream of income to replace that which she depleted from her first two husbands, both physicians who committed suicide within three years of their nuptials.

"Did you check out that little walk she has?"

"Yes. Yes, I did."

"She's fit that one. You could bounce a quarter off the cheeks of her ass."

"I can believe that."

"Forget the tits, though. Implants."

"Thanks for that information."

"I guess you're dead meat unless I save you."

"Looks like it."

"Shall I call off the witches?"

"That would be great."

"I'll call back in thirty seconds. You answer it and I'll talk to Mona to get you off the hook."

"Sounds great."

He replaced the telephone, which rang no sooner than ten minutes and another cup of coffee later.

"Hello?"

"Sweating yet? I bet you thought I forgot about you."

"You could say that."

"Okay. I'm ready. Put the Chief Shrew on."

Murphy called Mona to the telephone and rejoined Carla in the living room. She stood near the bookshelves. Bob, the Maine coon, perched atop a wing chair perhaps three feet from her and stared. It appeared that the cat was evaluating her potential as prey.

"Your house doesn't smell like cats. You know a lot of people with cats have apartments or houses that are virtually unbearable."

"Thank you. I try to avoid being unbearable when possible."

"What does Isildur mean?"

"It's old English for 'Bob.' Mona named him."

"Is this her cat? I thought she was allergic."

"Only when it's convenient."

Mona called out from the kitchen that they would have to depart. Murphy bade them farewell and went back to the kitchen, where he contemplated calling Wanda to thank her. Stacey Smith pushed her way into his thoughts. He thought about extracting the worn photo of his wife, but decided against it. He had not looked at it in months. The telephone rang. He assumed it was Wanda about to extract tribute.

"Hello?"

"Joe, it's Mona."

"Mona, you did much better with the telephone introduction that time. Did you forget something?"

"No. I just spoke with Arthur and he said he put the remote control between the storm door and the front door ages ago."

"Oh, okay. I never use that door since I have the mudroom. I'll go hunt for it. Thanks."

"Talk to you later."

"No doubt."

Murphy found the remote control and replaced the radio's distraction with that of the television. After switching through scores of channels he settled on an all-news channel. He studied the complex remote over his fourth cup of coffee before heading to the bathroom for a shower and shave, leaving the remote control on the kitchen counter. He stepped over Lydia, who had retreated to a sunny spot upstairs.

"Yeah. You know what you want. That's what it's all about isn't it?"

As he showered, he wondered what it was he wanted. The anger had dimmed. For a long time, he had wanted to wreak havoc and destroy someone, anyone he deemed valueless. His lack of focus cost some drug dealers their lives and money at great risk to himself, but he no longer felt the need to assault the class of people who had cost him his wife. There was no satisfaction in destroying small-time drug dealers, although it yielded the unintended benefit of profit. He thought back to the first men he killed. As far as he knew, they had nothing to do with drugs.

It was a Friday evening less than nine months after Ginger's death. He flew into Denver from three days of depositions in Tulsa. He wanted to retrieve his dog, Mimi, from the veterinarians' office where she boarded so that she would not be detained for the entire weekend. He got to the office after it closed, but one of the veterinarians was still there to release the dog to him.

The dog, a Pekingese, was the only remnant he possessed of Ginger. Mimi escaped the fire that consumed Sullivan's house while he was in the hospital recovering from the gunshot wounds Walter Cole had inflicted in defense of Dennis O'Brien. The dog predated Sullivan in Ginger's life. He never had cared for the animal while Ginger was alive, but the two shared some sort of bond after Ginger's death.

The dog was ecstatic over seeing Sullivan that Friday evening. She jumped around the front seat of his BMW, oblivious to the fact that her master was in the process of getting lost for the countless time in their new city. Sullivan found himself in a dark remote area with a dog that needed to relieve itself. He pulled off the road into a dirt area and let Mimi out on her leash. As he waited for the dog, Sullivan examined a map in his headlights. He did not notice the approaching pickup truck. The noise as the truck slid to a stop behind his car drew Sullivan's attention. Two men emerged from inside the cab, while two more jumped from the bed.

One of them spoke. "What we got here, man?"

They were all white, all young, all drunk by the smell of them.

"Looks like a faggot messin' up the scenree," another said.

They closed the distance to where Sullivan stood.

Sullivan turned his attention to collect the dog. "Fellas, I don't want any trouble. New in town. Lost. Just leaving."

They formed a semicircle around the front of the car. "Don't like faggots 'round here."

Mimi yapped and was tugging at the far end of her extended leash. "I'm sure you don't. So I just better be going."

One from the rear of the truck spoke for the first time and swayed from the effort. "Then you're a faggot?"

"No. Look guys, I was raised Catholic. I can barely accept the fact that I have a penis let alone thoughts about touching someone else's. I am just gonna get back in the car and—"

"Got any money?"

"Shut the fuck up, Curtis!"

Mimi growled.

"We're still tryin' to establish his fundamental faggotness."

Sullivan walked for the driver's door dragging Mimi at the end of her leash. "Again, fellas, no trouble here. I'm just leaving."

"Fag car. Fag suit. Fag dog. Fag glasses. Fag."

"Fag," two of the other three echoed.

Then Curtis shot Mimi. Sullivan jumped at the noise. He grabbed the dog, which had deflated into something resembling a wig splashed with blood. The others started to rebuke Curtis. Sullivan opened his door and put the dog inside. He reached under the front seat of his car and extracted the Colt .45 semiautomatic he kept there. Within five seconds he had slammed two rounds into the chest of each man. He then emptied Curtis's cheap little .380 into their heads and left. He buried Mimi in a park, took a shower, and slept well for the first time in months.

Sullivan read about the murders in the paper. Four men were dead; he could not have cared less. He resigned from the firm the following Monday, but stayed on for a month to clean up and transfer his caseload. The police never called. He sold his condominium, assumed two identities from deceased men, and disappeared. He had crossed some line because someone shot his dog.

Sullivan assaulted his first crack house fifty days after that night near Denver. He did not keep track of how much he took from the street dealers, but estimated that over the years he had extracted in excess of two million dollars apart from the massive profit from the Washington raid. Four or five houses had been particularly rich. They had looked like any other run-down house in a horrendous neighborhood, but were filled with cash, guns, and drugs.

He had regrets about the dead policemen in the casino. When kids and cops started to get shot, Sullivan crossed over another line. He was not sure where it put him, but decided he should now be defensive. No one would hear from James Sullivan unless they came looking and were able to invoke a miracle to find him. The next issue became what to do next.

He exited the shower to see a cat named Watson drinking from the toilet. "Yeah. I guess you know what you want, too. Everyone knows what they want around here except me."

As he lathered his face and started to shave he thought he heard voices downstairs. He stuck his head into the hall and realized he heard the television. He went back to shaving until he thought he recognized a voice. He listened and knew the voice.

Sullivan ran naked down the steps to the living room. The TV's large screen magnified the face of Dennis O'Brien. It spewed some nonsense Sullivan could not hear as anything other than a shrieking, nasal babble.

What are you doing here?

"Get out of my house!"

He searched the room for the remote control, but without success. Sullivan reached into the drawer of an old lowboy across the room from the television and extracted a revolver. He fired six shots into the place where Dennis O'Brien's face glimmered.

Long after his hair dried, Sullivan stood naked in his living room pointing the empty pistol at the destroyed television. After the smell from the gunfire dissipated, Lydia sniffed at the debris scattered on the floor. Sullivan looked at the cat.

"You just have to know what you want."

He lowered the revolver. Lydia rubbed against his calf. For the first time, he surveyed the remnants of the television.

"Boy, Wanda is gonna be pissed."

Chapter 21

S tacey Smith finished typing. They were still in Philadelphia and she had to hunt their temporary office for a copier. She would submit her report to Matty Feldman and have it circulated. He seemed pleased with her performance judging from his reaction to the oral summary she had given right after speaking with Walter Cole. As she watched the copier's light turn her eyelids red, Smith decided she would ask Feldman about a real job with the bureau.

She liked Feldman, but the FBI seemed encumbered with more administrative tasks than Smith preferred. Feldman justified the desk work as crucial to tracking its huge store of information. Sorenson took organization a few steps further and created a computerized flowchart with tiers to organize his thoughts. They had completed what Sorenson called all the tier one and two interviews. In his lexicon, this comprised those who had contact with James Sullivan, the criminal, and James Sullivan, the attorney. He spent weeks attempting to speak with Ramirez, the only known survivor of the Washington assault. Unfortunately, Ramirez had experienced some sort of religious conversion and refused to speak with anyone on advice of counsel until after his trial. His trial would start in about eight months, two months after his brain tumor was expected to kill him.

At the late-morning meeting, Macuzak and Whitcomb said they wanted to interview Dr. Julius Berman, who had served as an expert witness in many cases when Sullivan worked for the firm. Sorenson argued the interview was a waste of time, a tier five or lower. Whitcomb said that it was already scheduled for later in the afternoon. Feldman seemed happy and he praised the team's initiative over lunch at a place in South Philadelphia. Macuzak selected a sandwich shop renowned for cheese steaks. It was the greasiest thing Smith ever ate.

Feldman had no car and needed a ride to the airport after lunch. Sorenson volunteered to drive him. Smith went with Macuzak and Whitcomb rather than waste time at the airport. Feldman did not seem to have a problem with Sorenson wasting time. As Feldman recovered his luggage from the trunk of Whitcomb's vehicle, Smith had a sense of *déjà vu*. She realized that Feldman always rode with the two detectives from New Jersey.

Smith had indigestion from her cheese steak. Her skirt felt tight. She needed exercise that she was not getting on the road. There was a tiny gym at her hotel, but she had yet to find the time to use it. She remembered some reference to a health club in one of Sorenson's binders. She and Macuzak pored through the binders in the backseat while Whitcomb navigated Philadelphia traffic. Sorenson had put the data in a footnote.

"Tier fifteen, at least," Macuzak said.

They located the club on Broad Street tucked atop a parking garage.

Their credentials and Whitcomb's elegant demeanor afforded them access to the club's computerized membership file concerning James Sullivan. The membership associate who pulled it up said it was scant and old. She pointed out that many members provided more information than the club needed, as if they were trying to make the place into the friends they did not have in their everyday lives. A small black-and-white likeness appeared on a corner of her computer screen. Smith looked at the image, but the quality was poor. Perhaps some FBI technician could enhance it.

The investigators found Dr. Berman's massive brownstone a few blocks south of the O'Brien law firm on a side street named Delancey Place, about a mile from the health club. During that trip, Stacey Smith undermined her sense of accomplishment by counting no fewer than sixteen men who could have been identified as the man in the photograph.

After a futile search for a parking space, they left the car straddling the curb. Smith pointed out the brass plaque next to the entry that read JULIUS BERMAN, M.D., J.D.

"Overachiever," Macuzak said.

"Or glutton for punishment," Whitcomb said.

A small woman in her sixties let them inside. She exuded an air of sophistication with her expensive haircut and silk scarf. Smith decided she did not wear enough scarves. She was not sure she even owned any.

The woman offered her hand. "I'm Esther. You must be the people from the FBI."

Whitcomb made introductions. Esther took them to an office with a leather sofa and chairs far removed from an expansive desk piled high with books. Large medical texts occupied yards of shelving on all the walls. A skeleton holding a violin hung in the corner. Photographs arrayed here and there showed Esther posing with a man with white hair and a young woman with rich dark hair and glistening black eyes. In the photographs the young woman played the piano, went to the prom, graduated from school.

Suddenly, Smith wondered if she would be able to ask questions during the interview. Sorenson always established parameters for interviews and Smith realized she had not discussed this meeting in any depth with Macuzak or Whitcomb. Sorenson even went so far in one instance as to give Smith a reading assignment before an interview so that she would grasp what his technique would be during the discussion. Esther left them to fetch tea. Coffee was not offered.

"So, how you guys want to play this?" Smith said.

"What do you mean?" Macuzak said.

"The interview—what's the game plan?"

"Well, let's ask questions of the good doctor and see where it leads us," Whitcomb said. "Is that acceptable?"

"Sure. Do you mind if I ask any questions? I mean—I don't want to screw up any technique you have planned."

"How come we say that?" Macuzak said.

"What?" Whitcomb said.

"The 'good' doctor," Macuzak said. "I mean, how do we know if he's any good?"

Whitcomb turned to Smith. "Do you still presume that we'll be using any sophisticated interrogation techniques?"

"You know what was good?" Macuzak said. "Lunch was good."

"I think I'll try to keep up," Smith said.

"Let's just wing it," Macuzak said.

"We've realized some success with that approach," Whitcomb said.

The door opened and Esther returned. A man followed bearing a tea service. He set it upon the table in front of the sofa and introduced himself as Julius Berman. He stood just over six feet and looked quite fit in his golf shirt and pleated slacks. Smith guessed he was about fifty-five. He had glistening black eyes and a full head of white hair accentuated by a full but neat beard. This was the man from the photographs. He shared the eyes of the young woman in them. They fussed with tea and introductions.

Dr. Berman flopped onto his sofa. "So, what can I do for the FBI? By the way, Esther, did you check their credentials?"

Esther sat at the desk nursing her tea bag. "Jules, don't be rude."

"No problem," Macuzak said.

All three produced their identification which Berman examined.

"Esther, did you give them my CV?" he asked.

Esther was heading for the door. "No, dear. I'll fetch it."

Berman returned the credentials. "So, again, what can I do for you?"

"We're investigating James Sullivan and his potential involvement in a series of drug-related homicides. It's our understanding you and he were acquainted and we would like to interview you on that topic."

Smith thought these were the two most eloquent sentences she had ever heard Macuzak assemble.

"Should I have counsel for this interview? Silly question. Of course I should, but I am counsel so that's covered. Is this being recorded?"

"No."

"But we are taking notes," Whitcomb said.

"Very well. My cooperation will vary depending on the question."

Esther returned to distribute copies of Dr. Berman's lengthy *curriculum vitae*.

"First we should establish that you do know James Sullivan," Macuzak said.

Silence followed.

"Well?" Whitcomb said.

Berman leaned forward on the sofa. "Well what? Has a question been posed?"

Macuzak leaned back. "Look, doctor, we all know you're smart. We all know you're a professional witness. We all know that we're going to talk eventually. There's no margin in making this more difficult than it has to be."

"Mr. Macuzak," Berman said. "What you want to have is a conversation, rather than an interview. You need to be precise in your communication when dealing with someone like me. I will discuss Mr. Sullivan, but you should understand that I will not be responsible for any topics you may neglect in such a malleable mode of communication."

"Agreed," Macuzak said.

"Jules," Esther said from her perch on the end of the desk.

"Yes, dear?"

"Try not to be such an insufferable ass."

"Quite right," Berman said.

Esther's esteem soared in Smith's eyes.

"So, how'd you meet Sullivan?" Smith said.

"We met through the firm. I used to do rather a lot of work on their cases. Have you met Dennis?"

"Just in passing. Our boss interviewed him."

"Yes, of course your superior would have to interview him. I worked regularly with Dennis on the higher value cases. When James came on board I worked with him since he developed most of Dennis' cases. Later, I worked exclusively with James at the O'Brien firm. Of course, I work with other firms as well."

"Thank God," Esther said.

"Why do you say that?" Whitcomb asked.

Dr. Berman fielded the question. "I think Esther is referring to the fact that we no longer do any work for Dennis O'Brien's firm. We've been blacklisted, if you will."

"Why is that?"

"The stated reason is cost. I'm expensive."

"You get what you pay for," Macuzak said.

"Thank you. Money is how we keep score, don't you think? Fortunately, cost has not kept other firms from the door. At another level, Dennis felt that I became vulnerable on cross-examination because of my law degree. He thought jurors perceived me as too much of a mercenary. Additionally, I will not testify on videotape if at all possible, which was an asserted inconvenience despite the fact that I have never missed a trial call. As you probably know, most attorneys would kill to have their doctors testify live."

"I imagine it gives you a great deal of flexibility in your presentation," Whitcomb said.

"Of course. It is particularly valuable in the defense realm. Do you realize that it is common for some defense medical witnesses to be videotaped weeks before the plaintiff's treating physician?"

"No."

"It effectively gives away your entire medical defense before you even know what the evidence in chief is. It is tantamount to malpractice—legal malpractice."

"Do you just testify for defendants?"

Berman laughed. "God, no. I usually do plaintiff type analysis and testimony without actual treatment. That is what caused Dennis to use me in the first instance. I testified in a case against him in which the plaintiff recovered something in excess of four million dollars for a low-back disc herniation. He was impressed to the point that he called me in to do defense work."

"You must have a tight schedule with this legal work in addition to your orthopedic practice."

"Oh, I haven't performed surgery in twenty years."

Esther dropped from her perch to join Julius on the sofa. "Twenty-two."

"Why is that?" Smith asked.

She had a personal interest in this question in light of her snowballing relationship with Jeff Stone. She had spied him looking at her jewelry, trying to guess her ring size.

"Surgeons are like athletes," Berman said. "At least I think they are. You have a certain number of years when you are in your prime. After that, you are not doing the best in your craft and your patients can suffer. I believe I am almost alone in acting upon that assessment. There are surgeons who taught me that still operate. Again, malpractice. Institutional malpractice—this time medical."

"When did you get your law degree?"

"It is on the CV; ten years ago now I suppose."

"Thirteen," Esther said.

She stretched on the sofa and put her feet in the doctor's lap. He started to knead the soles.

"In any event, I have never practiced. I started to teach and testify extensively after retiring from the OR. I attended Temple Law School at night and had my degree in four years. You will note that this happened quite a while ago. It was never a problem with Dennis until much later."

"So you believe that was just an excuse he used to cut back on your work," Macuzak said.

"Of course. It was a pretext."

"What was the real reason you were cut out?"

"Our relationship—that between Dennis and me—evolved over time. Initially, it was all business. Then there was an ideal mixture of business and pleasure. Eventually, that was supplanted by one of almost purely social interaction with the excuse provided by the work. Dennis's ego and various other neuroses are high-maintenance commodities, which I think may explain why he is such an excellent trial attorney. However, it could and did interfere with our working relationship.

"For example, and he did this more than a few times, he would come into this office on the eve of trial on a case which I had attempted to bring to his attention for months. At that point it was really fish or cut bait on the case, but he would still avoid the issue. He would recline on this very davenport and talk about how awful his life was, rather than focus on the case."

"I suppose his work suffered," Whitcomb said.

"No, no, no. That was the true irony of things. It never really became apparent to anyone that he was in this state. He would be saved by either James, or Walter, who had prepared the matter in advance to give to him in abbreviated or bullet format. Alternatively, Dennis would manipulate the client into settling the case without ever letting on the real reason he did not want to try it. He was, and is, a master at manipulation of insurance companies."

"So, if this was working, what happened?" Smith said.

"Dennis had a lot of baggage, emotional and psychological. He was simply too burdensome and at a weak point, when I was exhausted, I suggested that he may want to seek some counseling to resolve some of the things that were bothering him."

"Like what?"

"Here's an area which I won't discuss because in some ways it violates the quasi-doctor-patient relationship we shared, although I am not a psychiatrist."

"And God knows he never paid for the hours he spent on your couch," Esther said.

Smith wondered what grade the doctor scored in law school concerning client confidentiality. He loved to talk and no doubt shared everything with Esther. Smith considered her a possible avenue to the information the doctor withheld.

"How about the other lawyers at the firm you worked with? Sullivan and Cole," Smith said.

"What about them?"

"You mentioned they would do a lot of Mr. O'Brien's work for him. That was really their job wasn't it?"

"I suppose, but I guess the point is that they were all very different people."

Berman the hopeless gossip returns.

"I'll say," Esther said.

"How's that?"

"Let me use a story to explain the three of them and in so describing them, I am not saying that this actually occurred."

Berman sipped his tea before beginning.

"Suppose that you have these three people, lawyers, who find themselves in an identical situation. Each one has gone off to the abyss of northern New Jersey to attend the videotaped deposition of Doctor Lyingwhore, the plaintiff's treating physician. After that event they are returning to Philadelphia but are caught in horrendous traffic on the New Jersey Turnpike. So, you have these three lawyers all in separate cars who are wondering how to make use of their time.

"Lawyer 'A,' let's call him... Winfield."

"For God's sake, Jules, just call him Walter or Cole," Esther said.

"Fine, I'll call them by name, but that's not to say this ever happened."

"Understood," Whitcomb said.

"Okay, Cole is in his car drumming his fingers on the wheel and running his fingers through where his hair used to be thinking that he cannot possibly bill the client for the time he spends sitting there in traffic. In fact he should not even bill the client for the time he's spent all day because he did such a terrible job cross-examining the plaintiff's doctor. The traffic report blaring from his radio is aggravating his ulcer.

"Lawyer B—"

Esther interrupted. "You forgot that Lawyer A is worried about getting back to his piece on the side before his wife calls and accidentally speaks with her since she's got her tight little behind in his office waiting for him."

"Walter Cole was having an affair?" Smith said.

"That's not really germane to what we're discussing," Berman said.

"Oh, please," Esther said. "Everyone knew about it except his wife. It's a disgrace. She's this little Twinkie not even half his age."

"She is more than half his age," Berman said. "It is not for us to judge what attracts people to one another."

"You know," Esther said. "Now that I think of it, isn't James the one who started to call her the Twinkie?"

"Krimpet," Berman said.

Macuzak laughed.

"I don't get it," Smith said.

"A Krimpet is like the local version of a Twinkie," Macuzak said.

"They're made by Tastykake, a local institution," Whitcomb said. "You're referring to Melinda Swayze?"

Esther's eyes opened. "Has he got another one?"

"That was the name we heard in some conversation at the firm."

"This is not really on point," Berman said.

"Tell us more about Sullivan sitting in traffic," Smith said.

"Anyway, James sits there in his car and, having planned ahead, he dictates reports interspersed with telephone calls. He resolves to make sure that the client pays for his time because it is not his fault he is stuck in traffic under those circumstances where the plaintiff selected a physician who has an office in New Jersey. He is also confident that he did a fine job in the deposition because he is a good lawyer. There is Vivaldi playing on his stereo.

"Lawyer C—"

"Dennis," Esther hissed.

Berman continued. "Dennis gets upset that he is sitting in traffic and telephones Esther to tell her that I did an inadequate job preparing him for the deposition, but that he was able to salvage the situation through his own brilliance—no thanks to me. He hangs up on her even as she utters an appropriate Yiddish epithet and calls Sullivan to scream at him about being stuck in traffic. James is smart enough to know who is calling and ignores the frantically ringing phone. In mounting frustration Dennis calls Walter and in a fury orders him to charter a helicopter to retrieve Dennis from traffic in the next five minutes. Dennis then hangs up on Walter who tumbles from his stopped car to vomit blood on the highway. O'Brien decides that his client will pay triple time for his added aggravation. The trial of the case is delayed two weeks because he takes to his sickbed, an event for which his client will also pay.

"Am I painting an understandable image for you about their personalities?"

"Sounds like a difficult dynamic to handle," Whitcomb said.

"No wonder you didn't mind losing the business," Macuzak said.

"I didn't lose James. I never lost him even when he went to Denver. He sent me a few cases to review and connected me to a couple of Colorado lawyers for whom I still do a bit of work now and then."

"Did you know anything about him leaving the firm?" Smith said.

"Well, of course, he left after Ginger died," Esther said.

"No. I mean before that. Did you ever hear anything about him leaving before his wife died?"

"I think we're back in that area where we cannot discuss this without possibly violating some privilege either real or perceived," Berman said.

Smith wrote a note that Dennis O'Brien knew of Sullivan's plans to leave.

Berman's eyes danced. "Let me add this. In the place that is Dennis O'Brien's world, things are about what he is owed. The economy owes him more than he can spend. His people owe him their allegiance. Society must pay him homage. It doesn't matter that he has enough. All that matters is that he collects in one fashion or another apart from whether he needs whatever the payment might be. My friend Mr. Sullivan will also collect if he feels he is owed. But he differs from Dennis in that he'll take it only to the point that he needs or expects payment."

"But you stayed in touch with Sullivan after he moved away?" Macuzak said.

"Yes. We were concerned with the grief he was suffering. In retrospect we were justified in thinking he might be explosive."

"We've had some experience with grief," Esther said.

She rolled to a sitting position next to the doctor and glanced at one of the photographs of the young woman who shared Dr. Berman's eyes.

"Pretty picture," Smith said.

"Our daughter."

"What happened to her?" Whitcomb said.

"She lived with a closet addict," Berman said. "Some of his dealer friends thought it would be a good idea to rape and kill her after she refused to give them money they were owed for drugs. It has taken us almost ten years to get to the point where we can articulate that sentence without completely breaking down, so we would like to close that subject."

"We're sorry for your loss," Macuzak said.

Smith hated that sentence, which all police officers use at some point in their careers, an aphorism appropriate for far too many occasions.

"Yes," Esther said. "We know."

"Did they catch them?" Smith said.

Dr. Berman answered with his voice starting to break. "No. No, they did not. Her paramour died of an overdose. God can work in mysterious ways sometimes."

"Why don't we take a break to compare notes? That way we can minimize any further intrusion," Whitcomb said.

Berman stood. "Excellent idea. If you need a rest room, there is one halfway down the hallway."

The doctor led the detectives toward the doorway. Smith sat still in her chair to scribble some more notes. She stopped to reach into her purse to provide Esther a tissue.

Esther wiped her eyes. "Maybe Jimmy killed them by now."

"Hope so," Smith said.

Shit. Was that out loud?

Esther smiled. "More tea, dear?"

Chapter 22

The Metroliner traveled through New Jersey with no stops save for Newark and Trenton. Sullivan knew he should be far from here, snug in the anonymity of one or more of his identities. Instead, he was slipping across New Jersey in all its rainy grayness on his way to Philadelphia, a loathsome city he, avoided for the last few years.

Driven by television, of all things.

After he shot his television, he checked into a motel to watch the broadcast that had triggered his fury. The story was about some men eaten alive by O'Brien's sharks. Someone filed claims and Dennis served as his own defense counsel and publicist. The cases settled; come see the man-eaters.

So, the cases settled. So, what?

Stay on the train to D.C. and catch a flight back north.

"Yeah, sure," he said.

An hour later, Sullivan stole a Porsche 911 from one of the garages on the Penn campus. He drove to the Four Seasons Hotel in the slackening drizzle and checked in under a false name. He looked up the old firm in the telephone directory and noted that the name had changed with the deletion of Bard's name. The firm he worked for had been called O'Brien, Bard, Camby & Scott, P.C. It was now O'Brien, Camby & Scott, P.C. Bard had hired Sullivan.

Bard got out. Good for him.

He imagined that one day the firm would be called O'Brien & Scott, P.C., and then O'Brien and Associates, P.C., and finally O'Brien and All the Rest of You Can Go to Hell, P.C.

The office building stood as he remembered, but appeared to have benefited from some renovations. He strode without hesitation to the elevators and pushed the buttons for the firm's floor as well as those above and below it. The doors shut and he was alone except for the camera in the corner of the ceiling. His fake beard, wig, and glasses disguised him to the point that he did not think he would be recognized even if he ran into someone he knew.

Sullivan could feel blood pulsing through his earlobes. He felt himself getting flushed and perspiring. The doors opened on the floor below the firm's. They were almost shut when he fired out his hand to knock them open. He lurched out and around the corner into a common hallway where he leaned against the wall.

Okay.

Relax.

This is no big deal.

You're just gonna take a peek.

You kill people. Remember? This is just a law firm. It isn't kryptonite and, by the way, you aren't Superman.

He looked back around the corner to the empty elevator lobby.

"Okay. Let's do it."

Sullivan hit the button to call an ascending elevator. A bell rang and doors opened. He walked into the elevator to find O'Brien yelling at the big bag man he had seen lurking in the background on television. The two of them occupied the elevator with a new trial bag and an old battered one. Sullivan's heart took off again, but he did not stutter in his steps. O'Brien stopped talking almost as soon as he entered, but stood red-faced not eight inches from his bag man. Sullivan turned his back to O'Brien and hit the button for the floor two stories up. Sullivan slouched in the front of the car with his face no more than six inches from the now-closed doors. He waited for O'Brien to recognize him.

The jig will be up then. He's gonna spot you in three seconds. You're gonna turn and kill him right in front of a camera and a witness, who may be big enough to break you in half. You've got no escape plan. You won't get three blocks before Philadelphia's finest gun you down.

"It's just a travesty," O'Brien said. "I shouldn't have to put up with this kind of shi—nonsense. It will not happen again. Do you understand?"

What was the bag man's name?

Gavigan? John or Jack? See. You're not prepared the way you should be.

O'Brien was in a rage, his dominant state. Sullivan was familiar with the condition. He had suffered from O'Brien's fits often enough that he had learned to accept them as normal back when he worked for him.

He's so pissed-off he doesn't see me.

Not that it really matters at this point.

Oh, well. You've gotta go sometime.

The bag man made noises like he was going to explain something, but O'Brien cut him off.

"You know, I just don't want to hear it; I just want you to assure me this will never happen again."

Kill him. Just do it now and get it over with. Gavigan will probably thank you.

Sullivan's right hand moved toward the Beretta under his left arm.

No. Wait for them to get off and pop him right before the doors shut.

His hand closed on the Beretta's grip.

"I mean it, John. I want to hear you say it will never happen again."

John! I knew it was something like that.

O'Brien's gonna erupt. Perfect. Just don't hit the bag man.

"It will never happen again," the bag man said.

Wow! This guy is as beaten down as Walter.

I wonder how Walter is.

The doors opened and Sullivan exploited the noise to unsnap the holster's thumb strap. O'Brien stalked off the car after Sullivan made way. Gavigan followed with a trial bag in each hand. He was big and took up most of the open doorway. The Beretta cleared the holster and Sullivan's thumb disengaged the safety.

He heard O'Brien retreating down the hall to the firm's entrance. O'Brien started to yell now that he was not constrained by the stranger on the elevator.

"This is just total fucking bullshit that I should not even have to worry about, but I have to, don't I? And do you know why? Because I'm the only one here with two fucking brain cells that fucking communicate with one another."

Three… two…

The battered trial bag in Gavigan's left hand ripped apart and spilled its contents all over the floor. The doors started to shut and the bag man bent to gather the spilled papers.

Sullivan would get a clean shot. He would use his left hand to block open the elevator doors. He noticed among the papers on the floor many photographs, big photographs, photographs of sharks. Gavigan was down out of the way.

Absolutely perfect.

"Why are you still carrying that fucking shit around?"

Sullivan heard the alarm in O'Brien's voice.

Dennis sounds like a little girl when he's scared.

He had never heard fear in that voice. Fear was not an emotion O'Brien allowed.

Not even when you're strangling him.

Sullivan stuffed the Beretta back into the shoulder holster and let the doors shut.

After what seemed like an hour, the doors opened one floor above the firm. Sullivan pressed the button for the lobby where he walked out of the building into what had become an afternoon thunderstorm. He walked north through the downpour to the Benjamin Franklin Parkway where he turned left, passed his hotel and headed toward the Philadelphia Museum of Art. He dumped his disguise in a trash can. Sullivan wandered through the museum for a few hours and pondered.

The shark photographs were foremost in his thoughts. He knew they related to the aquarium, or as it was referred to in his days with the firm, the fish store, or on days when it consumed extra time and effort, the shark tank. Dennis O'Brien became the principal shareholder in the aquarium about seven years ago. His career as an aquarium operator succeeded his brief career as a restaurateur.

Of immediate interest to Sullivan was the fact that O'Brien had reacted with such alarm to the fact that Gavigan had the pictures. In his day, Sullivan often carried material relating to the aquarium among his papers if for no other reason than he had failed to remove the items from his bag, or he had needed them for some reason. The aquarium always generated one legal problem or another at any given time. It would be standard procedure to have photos of the sharks in light of the claims he had learned of from the television. O'Brien had been afraid when he saw the pictures. The fear had been palpable, strong enough that Sullivan had passed on his chance to kill him.

Well, there's always tomorrow.

O'Brien had been obsessed with averting claims but was never able to do so. Patrons, children in particular, always seemed to find innovative ways to injure themselves. O'Brien even convinced the insurance carrier to allow the firm to serve as the exclusive designated defense counsel for the facility because of the prompt attention claims would receive. This time the event was publicized. He even called a news conference.

What the hell was that about?

Selling tickets.

Sullivan strolled into a long gallery and noticed a brilliant painting on the far wall. He was not yet close enough to see the detail, but was drawn to it even as he focused on more subtle works. He shortchanged the other paintings to reach the cacophony of color on the far wall.

As he drew closer, he saw it portrayed a circus scene in a large tent, an image dating to the late nineteenth or early twentieth century, judging by the clothing of the countless figures under the big top. It was a three-ring circus. In the left ring, clowns engaged in some type of antics. Over the right ring, there stood a trapeze with male artists sporting massive moustaches flying through space. In the third ring, the center ring, a suited man held his head within the jaws of a lion while others roared and pawed from their perches. Sullivan looked at the crowd and noticed that most of the opened mouth faces were young and watched the center ring regardless of where under the tent they sat.

Sullivan did not like the circus, never had. He turned his attention to the next painting, but found the circus painting commanded his attention like a car wreck, lurid and at some level compelling. He looked at the crowd and the lion. He thought about the aquarium and its sharks.

Oh, Denny, what have you done?

Chapter 23

Stacey Smith was reading the pleadings from Sullivan's suit against his old law firm. Whitcomb was making notes across the reception area. Macuzak was buried in the sports section. They sat in another law office in Philadelphia. This one was a plaintiffs' firm on Walnut Street.

"This is getting to be a regular deal with us, huh?" Stacey Smith said.

"Not too bad for you, I hope," Whitcomb said.

"George has me showering like every other day now that we know you might be along," Macuzak said.

Smith brushed at Macuzak's tie. "He doesn't have you being very careful with your ice cream."

"That's tzatziki. One of the vendors had some souvlaki that smelled too good to pass up."

"Where's Roger keeping himself?" Whitcomb said.

"Said he didn't feel well, went back to D.C. right after he dropped Matty at the airport. Offered to take the interview for us another time."

"Really?"

"I mentioned it to Matty when he called," Smith said. "He said not to worry about Roger and get the job done while we were in the neighborhood. 'Keep moving,' he said."

"Huh." Macuzak went back to the newspaper.

A slim woman wearing loud shoes thundered in to fetch them from the reception area. She led them back to an office where Bali Silverstein got up from her desk to greet them. Ms. Silverstein was of medium height, with an attractive face and voluptuous figure. Her choice in clothing and makeup worked to her best advantage and Stacey felt underdressed. She thought Macuzak's eyes would pop out.

Whitcomb took the lead. "Ms. Silverstein, I have to thank you for meeting with us on such short notice."

"Not a problem," Silverstein said. "I gather Mr. Sorenson is not here."

"He's sick," Smith said.

Silverstein laughed. "Sure he is."

Whitcomb peered at his pad through his reading glasses. "Now, we understand that you represented Mr. Sullivan in his claim against his old firm as well as against the restaurant where his wife was killed and I want to make crystal clear that we do not want to put you in a position in which you are violating any privilege. While we were in the area, we thought we might explore your impressions of Mr. Sullivan outside the confines of your attorney-client contacts."

"Mr. Whitcomb?"

"Yes."

"You're the lawyer, right?"

"Correct."

Silverstein continued. "I've done this lawyering thing for a while myself and am comfortable with this interview which you have requested under the parameters of this document."

Silverstein pulled a single page from a folder and slid it across the desk. Macuzak pinned it with a pencil eraser and read aloud.

> *Bali:*
>
> *I hope this letter finds you in good health and high spirits.*
>
> *I anticipate the authorities will be pursuing you for questioning in the near future. If or when such an attempt to contact you is made, I hereby waive any privilege which has ever existed between us and urge you to cooperate with whatever legitimate legal authority presents itself. You are expressly authorized to produce any documents pertaining to our dealings*

which you may still possess at the time the authorities approach you to the extent they do not conflict with some other privilege you conclude to be in play.

This waiver does not encompass and expressly forbids any contact with Roger Sorenson, Special Agent, Federal Bureau of Investigation.

This document is self-proving, and a copy shall be considered as effective as the original to which I have hereunto set my hand this 26th day of December, 2000.

Have a good life.

James Sullivan.

"It's signed."

"When did you get this?" Smith asked.

"I don't recall. Sometime early this year."

"So, months ago?"

"Correct."

"Still have the envelope?" Macuzak said.

"No."

"Any of the documents?"

"No."

"When did you destroy those?"

"When I saw fit."

"But after you got the letter?"

"You're Macuzak right? The psychologist?"

"Just a Master's, not a Ph.D."

Smith wondered if her meds were out of whack again and remembered that she wasn't on them anymore. She stole a glance at Whitcomb. He waved her off with his eyes.

A psychologist? The guy bowls like a consistent 280.

Whitcomb's a lawyer. Feldman's a lawyer. Sorenson's a lawyer. Macuzak's a psychologist.

I'm like intellectual chopped liver sitting here.

"I don't have to answer that question, Mr. Macuzak," Silverstein said.

"Of course," Whitcomb said. "Are there any documents which you know of that fall within the purview of this privilege waiver?"

"No."

"May we take custody of this?"

"Yes."

"Would you like us to arrange for you to receive a copy?"

"I have a copy."

"So, other than opening it and handling it you've also made a copy."

"I also destroyed it. That's a copy."

"When did you destroy it?"

"When I saw fit."

"Any proof of when that might have been?" Smith said.

"You're Smith, the girl on the baseball cards?"

Bitch.

"Are you always this passive-aggressive?" Macuzak said.

"No, not always. To address your question, Lieutenant Smith, I have no documentation of when I destroyed the original letter, but note for your edification that it occurred long before the authorities contacted me. I must also add that you are far more attractive in person than in photos."

Smith felt her face getting hot.

"Ms. Silverstein, we can do this another time," Macuzak said. "Like after you've wolfed down your daily bucket of medication."

Whitcomb picked up the letter and stood. "We'll be back with a subpoena."

"Sit down. I'll play nice."

"I'm getting old and my patience is short. You'll need to impress us."

"All I can tell you is what I know."

"We can start with how long you've known Sullivan," Macuzak said.

"I met him on the first day of law school. They grouped us together alphabetically, Silverstein and Sullivan."

"Sorenson," Stacey said.

"Correct. Bet Roger didn't mention that did he?"

"Yeah, he did."

"Did he mention that we were all in the same study group?"

"Didn't come up," Macuzak said.

"Well, it didn't last all that long. We dumped him after the first semester."

"How'd that work?" Stacey said.

"Study group? We broke up the material among four or five people so that we could divide up the work. You focus on different pieces and depend on the others to digest their segments and give you just the kernels you need. You do the same for them."

Whitcomb was back in his seat. "So, Sullivan and Sorenson have a history of not getting along."

"Jim didn't want to dump Roger. Thought the guy needed all the help he could get and gave him the benefit of the doubt, but it was majority rule and the rest of us ditched him. Roger didn't seem to mind. Had a job all lined up with the FBI before he even showed up for school. He didn't need to worry about money since his family has it."

"We're talking about Roger now?" Stacey said.

"You didn't know that?" Silverstein said. "I'm not surprised. Roger's always been a duplicitous asshole. His grandfather made a lot of money in commodities. His son, who I think is named Roger, too, took a job with the FBI. He came and spoke during a recruiting day and acted like he was doing the world a favor. Patrician jackass. I'm sure that your comrade Roger has the same attitude. He showed up at law school just to punch his ticket. He didn't care if he did well, only that he passed and had a good time."

Whitcomb cleared his throat. "In any event, there was some falling out with Sullivan and Sorenson. You and Sullivan remained friends?"

"There was never any falling out between those two. I mean, Jim was ambivalent about Roger. It was the rest of us who were annoyed that he was around, but to answer your question, Jim and I remained friends."

"Is that all you were?" Macuzak said.

"Yes."

"I don't believe you."

"Too bad."

"You should be a better liar than you are in this line of work."

"Excuse me?"

"Now you're defensive. That's proof that you're feeling vulnerable because you're clicking through your head whether we can catch you in the lie."

"Fine. I made the play, but he didn't go for it."

"He was married, wasn't he?" Smith asked.

Bali Silverstein smirked. "Oh, please. He was there. I was there. He was a good man, a catch. He loved his wife. I tried halfheartedly. It wasn't like I was determined to break his home, just hit it with a hammer to see if it fell down."

"But he held out," Macuzak said.

"Who can blame him? His wife was beautiful. I wanted to think she was this stupid little housewife type, but she had brains, too, the whole package. I got over it. We stayed friends."

"How often would you see each other?"

"In school we saw one another every day. After that it was a lunch once in a while."

"But you were tight enough that he came to you to represent him."

"Correct. But I'm a pretty good plaintiffs' lawyer. It wasn't like he was hiring a shoemaker."

"When did he contact you about suing the firm?"

"He didn't. I went to see him in the hospital. He was almost catatonic. He couldn't care less at that point. After a few weeks, I eventually talked him into going after the firm."

"You solicited him in his hospital bed?" Whitcomb asked.

"I helped out a friend. At that point, I thought he was going to wind up pushing a shopping cart around. I was looking out for him. This was a good man, a strong man. He did everything right, everything he was supposed to do, and this O'Brien creature cost him his whole world. They got off cheap."

"What brought him around?"

"A dog. His wife's dog. The neighbor who was feeding it found it after the house fire and that took him out of the twilight zone. You know, when his house burned down, I had to tell him because there was no one else to do it. I earned my fee just for that."

"What happened to the dog?" Smith asked.

"What do you mean?"

"Did it live, die?"

"Oh, it was fine. I had my assistant minding it until he got out of the hospital. It was a moppy looking little thing, like a bedroom slipper. I'm allergic, so I never got too close."

"Did he get any kind of mental health treatment?" Macuzak said.

"I tried to hook him up, but it was a no go. If we went to trial, that was going to be needed, but O'Brien folded pretty quick once he got to call me a whore and a bitch a few times. He was getting a bargain and knew it since the carrier was footing the whole bill."

"How about in the hospital?"

"There was a therapist who came in, but Jim ignored him."

"Did he make any notes?"

"There were some notes on the chart that he showed up and the patient ignored him."

"I gather you don't think too much of Mr. O'Brien," Whitcomb said.

"He's in my constellation of top five creeps."

"Who else is in there?" Macuzak said.

"One ex-boss, one ex-husband, one soon-to-be-ex-husband, and Roger Sorenson."

"You don't pull many punches."

"Neither did Jim. That's why we liked each other."

"You want to elaborate?"

"Well, in this business, you learn that a lot of stuff is not really all that important. It's smoke and mirrors. You start out thinking you can make this big difference in the world and then it turns out you can't. You're just more aware that you're buried in the bullshit than the schmuck next to you. You have to take your pleasures in small victories. Jim was more of a big-picture kind of guy."

"How's that?" Smith asked.

"He worried about why things were a certain way rather than just being absorbed with what they were. He had this whole engineering part of his brain that protested against things that didn't make any sense. His instinct was to do what made sense instead of what was required by others. That can be counterproductive in the practice of law, or any institution really. I was always amazed that he survived in the army as long as he did."

"So, he wasn't a good lawyer?" Macuzak said.

"Oh, he was a good lawyer. He just was conflicted that big pieces of it don't make any sense. For example, there's this maxim that everyone knows: Ignorance of the law—"

"Is no excuse."

"Right. We talked about this once and he was hung up on the point that if you think about it in light of the criminal requirement for *mens rea*, a guilty mind, it's the only excuse. This is the kind of thing that would stick in his head and annoy him. This isn't to say that he wasn't technically proficient. He was good at his job and able to do it, but he once told me that he felt like the magician at a kid's birthday party, amazing a bunch of people who didn't know any better."

"What did he do for fun?"

"He worked. He had his wife, of course. They used to go on dates once in a while. He told me her favorite date was to go to the supermarket."

"Fun guy," Smith said.

"I was intensely jealous when he told me that. They had one another. They had a whole life. They were happy. I envied that. Wouldn't you?"

"It's not like your life is over," Macuzak said.

"Yeah, I know. I'm going through my second divorce in four years and it's depressing. It's hard to get it right and they seemed to do it right out of the starting gate."

"What else did he do? Any places he liked to visit?"

"He schlepped around the world with the army, but nothing in particular sticks in my mind. You have to understand that he worked all the time. Dennis O'Brien is a notorious slave driver."

"Is that why he was going to leave?"

"What?"

"He had plans to leave the firm," Smith said.

"Really?"

"That's what we've been led to believe."

"Huh. He never told me."

"We were talking about travel," Whitcomb said. "I don't suppose you know where he is now."

"No idea."

"And you got rid of the envelope for that letter."

"Correct."

"Don't remember the return address."

"Sure I do. I even looked it up."

"And?"

"It's Roger Sorenson's apartment in Washington."

"Guess we won't find him there."

"You'd have to ask Roger."

The intercom beeped on Bali Silverstein's desk. She picked up the phone handset and had a discussion with someone. She hung up.

"I have a judge who wants to see me in half an hour," Silverstein said.

"We can resume at another time," Whitcomb said.

"There isn't much else I have to offer."

"We'll review what we have and let you know."

Loud-shoe woman escorted them back to reception. Smith collared Macuzak.

"Dr. Macuzak?" she said.

"Just a master's. It's not like it's helped catch me any crooks."

"I'm impressed."

"Like most of life, more than half the battle is showing up. George and my wife got together and conspired to knock me off my barstool at the VFW so many times that I had it before I knew it. Grants and the department kept paying for it."

"We told him he would never get his degree," Whitcomb said.

"So, of course, I had to show them up. I think it's in the garage somewhere."

"His wife has it framed in the study."

"My study looks like a garage."

"I have to pee before we get out of here," Smith said.

"Sounds like a plan," Macuzak said.

When she was washing her hands, Smith saw Bali Silverstein emerge from a stall with red eyes.

The Dragonlady cries.

"You all right?" Stacey asked.

"Sure. I'll be fine."

Silverstein started working on her makeup. "Look, I didn't mean to be too much of a bitch."

"It's okay. You're just doing your job."

"Yeah, that's kind of the hell of it, right?"

Smith made eye contact in the mirror.

"Can't say that I'm too eager for you to catch him, if he's even still alive," Silverstein said.

"Yeah, we get that a lot."

"So, you work much with Sorenson?"

"He's my partner."

"I guess you know by now to watch your ass."

Smith did not say anything.

"You want to file a harassment claim, or anything else against him, I'm your girl."

"I can handle it."

Silverstein laughed. "I've heard that before."

"Come again?"

"Come on. You haven't checked on your partner?"

"No. Should I?"

"I'll save you the trouble. In addition to being a rich, scheming, back-biting, pompous little son of a bitch, Roger is Mr. Date Rape."

"I'll forget I heard that."

"Why do you think he's not here? Why do you suppose he never even tried to contact me about this whole cavalcade of shit? Why do you suppose that Jim excluded him from questioning me? I've got the goods on him."

"Why didn't you press charges?"

"Me? It wasn't me, sugar. I'm not his type."

"Then what are you talking about?"

"There was a friend of mine first year. Cute girl from California. Japanese. Well, she wasn't. She was born in L.A., but her parents or grandparents came over. Bookworm. Anyway she breaks character and shows up at this mixer. Roger acts like a spider with a moth in its web: pays attention to her, brings her a beer—as in one beer before she goes home and studies some more. The next thing she knows, she wakes up at his place the next afternoon with no idea of how she got there or what happened."

"Did she ever pursue it?"

"No. She transferred out after the first year."

"Sounds pretty thin."

"He even left her with a little souvenir."

"Did she keep it?"

"Not a kid. A tattoo. Tiny. She didn't even know it was there for a week."

"Forensics could have done something with that."

"She thought it was a bruise at first, a tiny little number four on her ass. I found two other girls with the same experience, numbers five and seven."

"He's innocent until proven guilty, but if you want to put me in touch with them, I'll see it gets checked."

Silverstein laughed. "Statute's gone and so are the complainants, honey. I'm telling you for your own benefit. You don't have to worry too much. You're not his type."

"How's that?"

Silverstein straightened her hair and blouse. She reached for the door. "Roger goes for Asian girls. Besides, he won't come after you. You could shoot him."

Smith was left to look at herself in the mirror.

Fabulous.

Chapter 24

The crosshairs moved across the diploma. He could almost read it at this magnification. He reduced the scope's power and looked at the back of Gavigan's head.

These guys fight for the jobs with the office windows and views so they can spend all their time hunched over their paperwork, or looking at some stupid diploma or maybe a print.

Don't be too judgmental; you used to do the same thing. You used to be a suit just like they are.

He may even be working some of your old files at the rate cases move in this town.

Sullivan shuddered at the thought of being there in the office, any office, or any courtroom, or anywhere practicing law.

I'd rather get shot than go back to that bullshit.

Maybe I should shoot him. I'd be doing him a favor.

"Nah."

The HVAC unit below him roared back to life. The machine was deafening. He reinstalled his earplugs.

Sullivan maneuvered the scope's view away from his old office to the one next door.

"Dennis, you're working. And on a Friday at that."

O'Brien sat in his office at the northeast corner of the building. He appeared to be reading, a useless exercise in Sullivan's estimation since

Dennis considered himself a speed reader. His reading comprehension was so bad that O'Brien signed a brief in which Sullivan had sprinkled the word "phlegm" no fewer than forty times over five pages. Sullivan calculated the distance to the back of Dennis O'Brien's head at under 150 yards. At the moment, there was little wind here on the rooftop. A sniper's rifle was not his tool of choice, but this would be an easy shot.

Sullivan parked the crosshairs on the base of O'Brien's skull. He cycled the rifle's bolt to chamber a round.

"Time for a visit from Mr. Boat Tail."

He touched the trigger with his index finger.

"Easy shot from here."

A cloud moved and the sun's glare obscured his view. Sweat ran into Sullivan's eye.

Relax. You'll get another view.

Another cloud blocked the sun. Sullivan went back to controlling his breathing.

Who are you kidding?

"No one."

Sullivan opened the bolt and unloaded the rifle.

He'd kill you in a minute.

"Yeah, but I'm not worth the sweat off his balls."

He laughed and started to break down the rifle, but stopped after removing the bolt.

Leave it pointed at his window. Maybe he'll get the message. Have an epiphany.

"Fat chance."

Sullivan pointed the disarmed rifle at O'Brien's office and rolled a few fingertips on it to ensure usable prints. He adjusted the Swarovski spotting scope he bought the night before for a last look.

"I'm not leaving you behind."

O'Brien was packing two trial bags in his office. Sullivan guessed he was packing only the most crucial papers, which would sit unexamined, if not lost, in his car's trunk for the duration of the weekend or longer. O'Brien waved his arms about and had two secretaries in the room with him who looked frantic. One of them covered her face and ran from the room.

"Don't worry, darlin', nothing's forever."

Sullivan saw Gavigan get up from his desk and reappear in O'Brien's office. The remaining secretary disappeared and O'Brien shut the door. He stood less than a foot from Gavigan and wagged a finger up at him. Gavigan wrote something on a pad and looked at his watch.

"Go ahead, Gavigan, kill him. You know you want to. You can get the charges pleaded down and you'll be out in five to seven. Then you can go get a real job in a real business. Isn't that what the little prick is telling you?"

Maybe I should kill him.

O'Brien made a brief telephone call while he donned his jacket. Gavigan was back in his office packing a bag.

Enough of this shit.

"Show's over folks. Time to get the hell out of Dodge."

Sullivan dropped to the roof and returned to the stairwell, where he discarded his coveralls.

You really need to get a life.

At least I got this nice spotting scope.

"Maybe I should take up serious bird-watching."

He walked down the steps to the elevators, which went all the way down to the parking garage. Once in the garage, he walked toward the stolen Porsche. Dennis O'Brien strode toward him with his two bags.

Shit.

O'Brien stopped and opened the trunk of a black Lexus into which he heaved the bags.

Sullivan took his seat in the Porsche. He could see O'Brien. Sullivan started the Porsche in anticipation of an immediate departure, but O'Brien did not move. He sat in the Lexus and stared back in the direction from which he came. Sullivan would have to drive by him to exit. He loaded a silenced MP-5 submachine gun, and placed it on the seat next to him.

Come on, Denny, what are you waiting for? You don't let me get out of here and I might kill you after all.

O'Brien dialed his telephone and ducked down in the Lexus as though to hide. Gavigan lumbered into view with a single bag. He threw it into the trunk of a red Volvo. Without delay he flopped behind the wheel and pulled out to exit. O'Brien's head popped up and then down with the telephone to his ear. He sat upright after the Volvo passed.

Something stinks.

Sullivan put the Porsche in gear and followed the Volvo, being careful to divert his face as he passed O'Brien. Sullivan caught up to the Volvo in time to cut off an Alfa Romeo, which resulted in the shrieking of the Alfa's obnoxious horn. Its driver made an obscene gesture at Sullivan, but he was able to stay behind the Volvo. Sullivan looked over at the MP-5 and covered it with a newspaper.

Maybe I should go back downstairs and empty a magazine into Dennis.

A Mercedes in front of Gavigan dealt with the attendant in her booth as Sullivan pulled out some cash and watched his mirror to see the Alfa driver exit his car right behind him.

Now what?

The Alfa driver was big with a substantial gut. The cuffs of his shiny suit pants dragged on the ground. His hair glistened and was combed straight back. His hands flickered with gold rings and a bracelet.

Plaintiffs' lawyer. Probably has a nickel-plated .38 strapped to a leg just above his Italian loafers and is all pissed-off because he had to work past lunch on a Friday.

Alfa guy tapped on the Porsche's window. Sullivan lowered it.

"Hey, asshole, you almost hit me."

"Sorry. Why don't you let me cover your parking for your trouble?"

Alfa guy hiked his trousers. "Why don't you roll back and I'll take your spot."

Why don't I put a burst in your chest?

"Relax," Sullivan said. "You look like the top of your head is gonna blow off."

Sullivan noticed the Volvo roll forward. The attendant was an older black woman with enormous glasses. His mirrors revealed no cars behind the Alfa. O'Brien must still be downstairs.

"I'm serious. Move the fuckin' car."

"What, did you run out of Xanax or something?"

Sullivan rolled forward to shorten the gap behind the Volvo. The Alfa guy walked with him. Gavigan awaited his change.

"Hey, pussy, I'm talkin' to you. Stop movin' up. Back up, or I can come inside and kick your ass."

Sullivan whispered with no word intelligible except "mother."

Alfa guy moved closer. "What did you say?"

Sullivan's left hand fired out to grasp the man's testicles, which he jerked down until his grip failed at what seemed to be the man's shins, but it was hard to tell since he folded and collapsed around Sullivan's forearm. Sullivan rolled forward as Gavigan departed.

He gave the attendant a fifty-dollar bill. "Keep the change, but could you call a cab for that guy on the ground? I think he's drunk."

The man from the Alfa rose to his hands and knees so he could vomit. The gate rose.

"Have a nice weekend," Sullivan said.

He stayed close behind the Volvo in the thick center-city traffic. Gavigan worked his way north to extract himself from the worst of it. They were northbound on Broad Street above Vine before Sullivan let the distance expand. No sign of O'Brien's Lexus interrupted the trip into North Philadelphia, but Sullivan had to swerve to avoid a van that popped from a tiny side street right in front of him.

At the next traffic light, Sullivan looked at the van stopped in the lane to his left and experienced a sense of foreboding. The black man in the van's front passenger's seat was in his twenties and wore a stylish leather jacket. Sullivan guessed the colors proclaimed its wearer's allegiance to the Chicago Bulls. A hand emerged from the back of the van and pointed in the direction of the Volvo, now two cars ahead of the Porsche. Sullivan looked again at the van and saw that it advertised Iaccavone Plumbing and Heating Services.

Iaccavone my ass.

The light changed and the van pulled ahead to lurch into the lane right behind the Volvo, causing the driver of a decrepit Plymouth Volare in front of Sullivan to brake and shake her head. Sullivan's view was blocked, so he pulled out to the left in time to see the Volvo make a right turn. He was out of position to follow, but the van did.

Sullivan rocketed the Porsche to the next street and made the next two right turns. His speed down the narrow streets caused some men stripping a Toyota to jump onto the sidewalk. The streets were narrow, filthy strips cut between abandoned row houses, identical to so many he had stalked in pursuit of targets. He came to an intersection where he watched the Volvo proceed east from Sullivan's right to left. He could see that Gavigan read some scrap of paper as he drove. The van had fallen back enough to allow Sullivan to turn left and insert the Porsche behind the Volvo and ahead of the van. The Volvo paused at the next couple of streets while Gavigan appeared to get his bearings, but the van fell way behind Sullivan.

Come on! You're in Indian Country here. You can't possibly be serious about doing business in this neighborhood alone when it's gonna get dark.

Deep inside, Sullivan knew he was wrong. He had done the same thing countless times upon O'Brien's orders. He lost track of his treks into murderous regions to secure a statement, interview witnesses, take photographs, or visit accident scenes. Gavigan thought he was here to do some part of his job and here were these men following him. At that point, Sullivan recalled the context from which he knew the man in the van.

Oh, Denny, you are a bastard.

Sullivan saw that the van had pulled over almost two blocks behind him. He made a U-turn and pulled over to watch it. Sullivan guessed that Gavigan was lost and the guys in the van were not. He watched his rearview mirror to see the Volvo make its own U-turn and head back toward the van. Sullivan took his post behind the Volvo, which paused and turned left into a side street before it reached the van.

The street was a long southbound one with one travel lane and a parking lane to the right, which sat empty except for the hulks of a few stripped cars. There were vacant row houses on the west side and some type of light industrial facility or warehouse on the left. The Volvo parked halfway down the block. Sullivan passed the Volvo. He saw the van turn into the street behind him as Gavigan exited the Volvo and walked back to his car's trunk.

Why is this my problem?

———◆◆◆◆———

Gavigan closed the trunk and hit the remote for the alarm. An African-American man called to him from a van that was coming to a stop in the street.

"Excuse me," he said.

The side door of the van started to slide backward.

Shit. I'm about to be carjacked. Goddamnit.

Gavigan held up his hands.

"What the fuck?" the van's driver said.

The van flew backward more than a car length with a thunderous crash and shattering of glass. Gavigan shielded his face as glass flew, but he could see that a Porsche had backed up into the front of the van at what must have been thirty miles an hour. A man bolted from the Porsche and had something flashing in bursts in his hand as he ran toward and behind the far side of the van. For some reason, the van still seemed to be shedding glass. The Volvo's horn honked as the tremor from the crash triggered its alarm.

Gavigan again noticed the sliding door start to open, but the Porsche driver came from behind the van and walked forward along its passenger side. The man had a gun in his grasp. He pointed it into the side opening of the van and three distinct flashes accompanied by short cracks erupted from the weapon. The man looked back and forth inside the van and turned to face him.

Oh, shit.

"Are you all right?" he asked.

"Yes. I think so," Gavigan said. "Are you all right?"

The man smiled and his whole face crinkled. "Why, yes. Thank you. Do you suppose you could turn that off?"

Gavigan hit the alarm's remote to stop the noise. He saw there was a shotgun inside the van.

"They were going to carjack me weren't they?"

The man looked in the van's passenger window. "Not exactly."

"Are they dead?"

The man reached into the Porsche for something. "Oh, yeah. They're dead."

Gavigan extracted his wireless telephone. "I'll call the police."

The man pulled some bags from the Porsche. "No. Don't do that. Are you armed?"

"No. Of course not."

"Can I put this in your vehicle?"

"Oh, sure."

Gavigan unlocked the Volvo and the man placed the items on the backseat, but still held the submachine gun. A thought surprised Gavigan and the question erupted from his lips.

"Are you going to kill me?"

"Not likely. I just totaled a perfectly good Porsche to make sure that didn't happen. Let's go."

The man sat in the passenger's seat of the Volvo.

Gavigan stuck his head in the driver's door. "What about the police?"

"What about them?"

Gavigan sat behind the wheel with the telephone poised. "We have to call them."

The man fastened his seat belt. "No. That would just involve a lot of irrelevant papers, forms, and tedious interviews. Nice car. Does this have dual airbags?"

"Yes. Look, we can't just leave a bunch of bodies littering the street."

"Sure we can, John. I do it all the time. Let's go."

"What do you mean? How do you know my name?"

"Oh, I'm sorry,"

The man extended his hand, which Gavigan instinctively grasped in a firm shake.

"Jim Sullivan."

"John Ga—Did—did you say Jim Sullivan?"

"Yes. In the flesh. It even sounds funny when I say it. I can't remember the last time I actually introduced myself to someone. How'd I do? Did I make a good impression?"

Gavigan's head sagged onto the wheel. "Oh, Christ."

"Relax. I won't hurt you unless you do something really stupid."

"Look. There are people in that building who are expecting me. Why don't you just leave me here and take the car and, and, and go."

"There's no one there, John. Now, drive."

"This isn't happening. This is a dream. You're not here and neither am I. I finally collapsed from exhaustion and will wake up in some nice emergency room with a pretty nurse who will show genuine concern for my well-being, and—"

Sullivan took the telephone from Gavigan. "Let's go, John."

Gavigan turned his head and looked at Sullivan, who smiled again.

"Still here," he said.

"What do you want me to do?"

"Drive," Sullivan said.

Gavigan dropped the keys in Sullivan's lap where the submachine gun lay. "I'll tell you what. Seriously, you take the car and leave me here."

Sullivan inserted the key into the ignition and started the car. "Drive, John."

Gavigan sighed and reached for his seat belt.

"Leave your belt off. I don't want you tempted to plant the nose of this thing into a bridge abutment."

Gavigan put the car into drive and pulled from the curb to clear the wreckage. "Okay, I'm driving. Where are we going?"

"Go back toward Broad Street and we'll head south toward center city."

Gavigan complied.

"Now where?"

"Keep going."

Gavigan's telephone rang in Sullivan's lap. Gavigan glanced over while Sullivan picked it up. He pressed a button on the keypad and held it to his ear while his right hand shifted the submachine gun.

"Hello?"

"John?"

"I'm sorry. John is indisposed at the moment. May I help you?"

"This is his wife, Christine. Who is this?"

"Hello, Christine. My name is Jim. I'm a client of John's. We're in his car at the moment and he's driving in heavy traffic. I'll be happy to relay any message."

Gavigan reached for the phone. "Let me talk to her."

He felt the muzzle of the weapon in his side. Sullivan shook his head.

"Could you tell him I caught an early flight and I'll see him at home later?"

Sullivan glanced at the clock in the dashboard. "Christine, where are you now?"

"I'm on the plane now, somewhere near Harrisburg."

"I'll tell you what. Why don't we meet you at the airport?"

"No, don't bother. I can catch a train home."

"Nonsense. We're already headed that way. John's going to drop me at the airport."

"If it's no trouble."

"None. What's the flight number?"

Christine supplied it together with the designated arrival gate. Gavigan started to talk, but stopped when the gun moved up to his cheek.

"Well, thanks very much. I'll see you soon."

"Actually, you'll probably only see me in passing. I'll be the one frantically running for my flight."

"You'll fit right in then. Maybe we'll meet another time."

"I hope so."

"Bye-bye."

"Bye-bye."

Sullivan ended the call. "John, that part about letting you talk on the telephone would qualify as something really stupid. I won't hurt her or you if you cooperate."

"You should know that neither one of us has anything to do with drugs. We don't sell and we don't use."

"That's terrific. What does it have to do with anything?"

"Well, you have this hatred of drugs and I want you to know that's not what we're about."

"I don't hate drugs. I think drugs should be legalized so that the drug pushers are forced out of business."

"Sorry. Maybe I'm confused."

"No doubt."

"Look, tell me what you want and we can get this over with."

"Why does Dennis O'Brien want you dead?"

"What?"

"Denny O'Brien, the obnoxious little prick you work for, wants you dead. I want to know why."

"How do you know this?"

"He sent you up here this evening with no notice, right? Probably on some type of rush assignment."

Gavigan's eyes flashed from the street to his passenger. "Do you have our offices bugged?"

"No. I know him as well or maybe better than you do."

"Well, I can't tell you anything. You know that if you're who you say you are."

"John, I'll make this easy for you. I'm not going to let you hide behind any of that Rules of Professional Conduct or client-confidence garbage. You will tell me what I want to know or I will start to shoot off your body parts. You just saw me kill three men in cold blood, whatever that means, so you know I am capable of violence. Therefore, you will have a defense of duress in the unlikely event of any disciplinary proceeding arising as a consequence of you telling me what I want to know. Do you understand?"

"Yes."

"Why does Denny want you dead?"

"I don't know that he does."

Answer only the question asked.

"Why were you parked on that street where I just saved your sorry ass?"

"I was there to meet with someone."

"Who?"

"I don't recall."

"John, quit this answering-only-the-question-asked bullshit. The Rules of Civil Procedure do not apply to the circumstances in which you find yourself. Tell me why you were out in the middle of Indian Country all by yourself with a hit squad on your tail."

"I don't remember who I was to meet. It's written on a piece of paper with the address of the factory where I parked. I was supposed to investigate some accident with a machine press inside."

"Is this an established case?"

"No. There's not even a file number on it yet. The accident happened this afternoon and was called into Dennis right before he left for the weekend."

Sullivan looked out the window. "Who told you to go do this investigation?"

"Dennis."

"Was anyone else present?"

"No."

"Who called it in?"

"A new client, I'm not sure of the name, something Dutch or German, and potentially an important source of new business. O'Brien was kind of vague."

"Gee, I wonder why."

Sullivan pulled the muzzle from Gavigan's side. "Let me ask you this, John: Why didn't he go himself if it was a new and potentially important client?"

"I can't answer that."

"Sure you can. You just don't want to. How do you think I came to be on that street just as you were about to get killed?"

"I have no idea."

"I followed you from the parking garage where I also watched Dennis O'Brien hide in his Lexus and make a telephone call as you pulled away. Guess what I noticed in the van when I peeked inside."

"A cell phone?"

"Very good, John. You're catching on. Turn left and get on the

Vine Expressway. We'll cut over to I-Ninety-five and shoot down to the airport."

Sullivan held a Nokia phone in front of Gavigan's face.

"That's the call log," he said. "Recognize the number?"

"Dennis's cell."

Sullivan hit a button. "Here's the number right before that one. Even I recognize that number."

"Dennis's office."

"Now, why does he want you dead?"

"I still don't know."

"Come on! What have you been working on? What has he been pissed-off about?"

The MP-5 poked Gavigan's side.

"The shark tank," Gavigan said.

"What about it?"

"I was doing some checking on it after I finally got the forensic reports."

"And?"

"He settled the case speedy quick before we had a lot of data, but I didn't know it and he got all worked up about me checking on things."

"Like what?"

"Well, like the forensic reports. I hired this expert from California to review some tissue slides, and he generated these reports that caused Denny to flip out."

"What about the reports?"

"A lot of things, but I thought the most important was that they had no water in them when they died."

"What do you mean?"

"They weren't in the water when they died. They were torn up and there was water in their lungs at a gross level, which was enough for the coroner, but this guy in California did some type of more detailed analysis I had heard about from some diving-board case. I sent him some slides. His tests showed they were already dead when they went into the water, so the sharks could not have been the instrumentality that killed them."

"Sounds like a pretty good defense for the aquarium."

"I thought so, but Denny told me to forget about it and destroy the reports."

"Good defenses don't sell a lot of aquarium tickets, at least not as many as man-eating sharks."

"Yeah, that's what I kind of figured, too."

Sullivan unloaded the MP-5 and started to disassemble it as he spoke. "Is that all you figured?"

"What do you mean?"

"I think Denny staged the whole thing."

"You think he was doing more than just trying to make the best of it after the fact?"

"One of the guys in the van was Reggie Washington. He was one of O'Brien's wayward youth back when he was involved in the Big Brothers organization. Reggie always had the wrong attitude and was tied up in gangs. My guess is that he furnished the two Puerto Rican kids that got fed to the sharks just like he was going to clean up the mess you would create with your forensic reports."

"Jesus Christ."

Both men lapsed into silence during the trip east on Vine Street and then south onto I-95. Sullivan gathered his things until everything seemed packed. He broke the silence near the defunct Philadelphia Naval Shipyard as the Volvo climbed the bridge to cross the Schuylkill River.

"Okay, John, here's the deal. Dennis is going to have you killed. You need to get yourself and your wife out of town. It doesn't matter where, but go. Do—"

"Denny is going to jail for the two kids at the aquarium," Gavigan said. "I saw them, you know."

"No. I didn't know that."

"Sick fuck had me hustle out there with a photographer in the middle of the night."

"Yeah, well, I guess he couldn't set that up ahead of time without drawing too much suspicion.

"So, John, it's imperative that you get Christine and yourself away from here," Sullivan said. "Do you need money?"

Gavigan was surprised at the offer. "No, money's fine right now. Besides, I need to make Dennis pay for this."

"Okay, John, you're not thinking straight. Dennis is not going to jail for any of this. Things are not what they are in a court of law. They are what you can prove them to be, and at this point there is no evidence that will convict him. Your most important task at the moment is to run. Do you understand?"

"Right."

"Don't 'right' me. Let's review. Some men sent by your boss came to kill you tonight. You watched me kill them. While they may have been murderous scum, they were real people with real moms, real dads, and maybe real kids. This isn't some Hollywood bullshit where they're going to get up and be okay. I've brought you here at gunpoint and convinced you that your boss is trying to kill you. Therefore, your career, your life as you've known it, is over. Can you hold yourself together long enough to get your family to safety?"

Gavigan realized that he had disassociated himself from the experiences of the evening somewhere back in North Philadelphia. However, that sense of detachment was not new. He seemed to live with it all the time of late. The sense of reality Sullivan forced upon him was novel only in his admission of it. Gavigan was emerging from a long sleep, a nightmare he did not even realize existed.

"Yeah," he said. "I'll be okay."

Sullivan pointed Gavigan toward the arrival side of the airport. They drove to Christine's terminal.

"Park at the curb," Sullivan said.

"We'll get towed."

"No, we won't. I do it all the time. Nobody gives a rat's ass."

Sullivan took the car keys after turning on the parking lights. They left the Volvo sitting all alone in a tow zone. In the terminal, they climbed to a corridor linked to the departure area and actual gates. Sullivan spoke and handed things to Gavigan as they walked.

"Here's the play, John. Your phone is on the floor of your car. Don't bother with nine-one-one; it's a waste of time. I suggest you call the number on my card here. It will connect you to someone named Feldman. He's bright and efficient. If he's not there, talk to Macuzak or Whitcomb."

Gavigan sorted through the Captain Crack Attack Cards Sullivan proffered. The lecture continued.

"Don't bother talking to Roger Sorenson. He's an idiot and mean-spirited to boot. The others might be able to do something about Dennis or at least help you get away. You can tell them whatever you want about our encounter. However, you should tell them I'm out of play. Tonight only happened because I felt compelled to save your ass. They will never hear from me again. All I ask is that you give me a head start. Otherwise,

I'll have to tape you into the men's room. Agreed?"

"Agreed."

Sullivan turned to descend the departure side of the terminal short of the security checkpoint and gates. He threw the Volvo keys to Gavigan.

"Have a nice life," he said.

As soon as Sullivan fell from view, Gavigan sprinted back toward the arrival side of the airport. The few public telephones along the route were occupied or broken. Down the steps near the baggage claim and doors, he found a functional payphone he used to dial 9-1-1. Somewhere after the twelfth ring, he looked out the window to notice the Volvo had been joined by a dozen other parked cars all with their parking lights glowing. Gavigan shook his head.

Sullivan was right about at least one thing.

No one seemed to give a rat's ass.

Chapter 25

Matty Feldman awoke with heartburn. He blamed no one but himself for eating far too much Chinese food late the night before at a place he had not visited in years. Matty loved Chinese food and savored that which he found in San Francisco far more than anywhere. A double latte did little to assuage his discomfort, but did accelerate the walk to his counsel's office. He checked in with the receptionist, who showed him the coat closet where he hung his suit bag. He sat down just long enough to wonder whether anyone ever purchased *People* magazine or if they simply read it in the offices of doctors, dentists, and lawyers.

The receptionist brought him another cup of coffee as Cornelia Andrews came to retrieve him. As always, she looked fabulous despite the fact that she was not a stunning woman. She dressed well and spent time in salons being processed in manners Feldman could not imagine. Feldman thought he enjoyed seeing Cornelia so much because she served to protect him in what had become an unpleasant divorce proceeding instituted by his wife, Lorraine. They chatted about his flight and hotel as they burrowed into the warren of offices to reach the one belonging to Cornelia. Once inside, she shut the door and they sat on a couch along an interior wall.

"Okay," Cornelia said. "I have good news and bad news."

"Bad news."

"You flew out here for nothing."

"What?"

"The depositions are cancelled, or rather, they will be in a few minutes."

"What's the good news?"

"That was it. You get to go home."

"I don't get it. These have been scheduled for weeks."

"I tried to call you yesterday to cancel your trip, but you had already left."

Feldman had no time or money for gratuitous trips to California. "Why are they cancelled?"

Cornelia pulled a letter from her file and handed it to Feldman. "This. It came over the fax last night."

He scanned it. The author was the attorney representing Lorraine. It stated that Lorraine intended to bring to the depositions her "moral and spiritual adviser, Larissa Frontenac." Feldman read the letter twice and gave it back to Cornelia.

"I don't get it. She's bringing someone to the deposition. So, what?"

"She's bringing Larissa Frontenac to the deposition. You know who that is, don't you?"

"Sure. She's the trailer-trash talk-show princess. She can sit there and hold Lorraine's hand and we can get this over with. I don't have time to be jetting all across the country on personal business."

"She has no right to have this woman present at the deposition. It gives her an unfair advantage that I don't want to concede. Further, it connotes some implication of abuse in the course of the marriage."

"That's bullshit. I never laid a hand on her."

"You know that and I know that, but the crowd who listens to this woman won't make that type of fine distinction. Why let reality get in the way of a juicy story?"

Feldman considered the ramifications of this news. Larissa Frontenac seemed to be everywhere since the casino shoot-out. She had her own talk show, which he gathered did well in some markets. She also colluded with the Captain Crack Attack publishers and posed for some of their product. If she decided to get involved in his divorce, she would not find anything scandalous. She would disseminate whatever information she wanted whether she sat in on a deposition or was somehow barred.

"What are the chances of keeping her out?" Feldman said.

"Hard to say. There's some precedent for the proposition that a deponent gets to have moral support, but they usually are required to make some type of showing first. That hasn't occurred here because they're trying to ambush us. Do you think it was an accident this came over the fax on a weekend?

"On the other hand, the judge assigned to the case is a flake. You met him. He would be one of the more likely people on the bench to actually buy into this crap. Under any circumstances, we should be able to keep her cameras out, although the notice of deposition we got from your wife awhile back was for a videotaped deposition."

"I think we should just push ahead and get this over with," Feldman said.

"Out of the question."

"Cornelia, I don't have time for this. The deps have been set and reset. I've got a million friggin' things to do back east. I spent the weekend prepping some U.S. attorney in Chicago on a monster case that's going to trial soon. That's why I blew off our prep meeting for yesterday. The net result of that lost weekend in Chicago is that they need me more than they thought and I've got to go back next weekend. That's the kind of thing I have to squeeze in and around this manhunt fiasco. I haven't slept in my own bed in over three weeks. I can't be flying to California all the time just because I had the bad judgment to get married here a long time ago."

"Well, as I've told you before, I think you have a good chance of counterfiling in Virginia to get a forum closer to home. You have not lived in California since you were first married. You've lived in Virginia for the last ten years."

"I don't have the money to pay you, let alone another lawyer in Virginia. Besides, I haven't been in Virginia in weeks. Let's stop the hemorrhage and get this over with."

"Not a chance."

"Look, this Frontenac woman's cameras can be kept out, right?"

"If the judge goes along with it, but we need to get a motion filed and that means response time. So, we would be off for today anyway."

"Can't we just get the putz on the phone?"

"I can try, but that might just piss him off. Even if we do, we have to wait to see if she tries to rumble in here with her crew so that we have the problem defined for the court."

"Let's try it."

"I advise against it."

"Cornelia, if you've bought any Captain Crack Attack Trading Cards lately, you'll realize I'm busy tracking someone who has killed—no, no, no,— 'eradicated' is the word they use. He has eradicated scores of people. I do not have time for some talk-show host putting this nonsense in my way."

"Fine, but you're doing this against my advice and that'll be noted in the file."

"Stop worrying about covering your ass. I'm not going to sue you."

Feldman's pager sounded.

"Sure," Cornelia said. "That's what they all say."

Feldman recognized the display on his pager as Sorenson's wireless telephone number. "Oh. And I want to go first. Can I use your phone? I'll put it on my calling card."

Cornelia pointed at a telephone next to her couch. "Look. I've angled to have her go first because she's the plaintiff. It's up to her to make her case. Don't sabotage your own defense."

"She can have the divorce. Why are we even fighting about this? She can't get blood from a stone. What do I do, dial a nine?"

Feldman put his reading glasses on as he studied the telephone's multitudinous features.

"No. Just dial it straight. That thing will automatically put the call through and put it on your bill. She won't agree to an amicable proceeding. Maybe she thinks there's a book in it."

Feldman could hear ringing through the handset. "A book?"

"There's a book in everything these days. You're high profile with this vigilante fellow you're after. It's very Elliott Ness."

"A book. Who's got time to read anyway?"

"Well, whatever—a screenplay then."

Feldman held up a hand as he heard the ringing stop. "Roger, Matty returning your page. Can you hold on just a second?"

"So, what's the bullet?" he asked Cornelia.

"My advice is as follows," Cornelia said.

"One. We cancel the depositions for today so that I can file a motion to get this Frontenac bitch excluded. In the process, I'll ask for costs on the motion and the costs on you appearing today.

"Two. If you won't go along with my first piece of advice, then let me depose Lorraine first so that we're fully informed of the allegations she's making before you testify.

"That's where we are right now."

Feldman leaned forward on the sofa with his hand over the telephone's mouthpiece.

"The judge is an asshole, so option one is a waste of time. How long will it take to depose Lorraine?"

"Depends on what she has to say. Could spill into tomorrow easy."

"That eliminates option two. This is Monday right? I've got a briefing tomorrow in Washington. My flight out leaves around seven and I want to bump it up if I can."

"I told you to block open at least three days for this."

"I did. Events kind of overtook things. So I'm a day late and I have to leave a day early. It's not like I can tell people to wait when they tell me I've got to respond to a situation. I work more than one case you know, despite what Captain Crack Attack, Incorporated, says."

"Look. It's bad enough that we lost yesterday as prep time. If we stall on your testimony, then we have tonight to get you ready for tomorrow."

"No. In and out. I have nothing to hide."

"You're killin' me here, Matty. You know that, don't you?"

Feldman smiled at Cornelia and returned to the telephone.

"Sorry, Roger. What's up?" he said into the telephone.

"We have a situation here," Sorenson said.

Feldman pulled a pen and index cards from his jacket. "How's that?"

"He's made contact."

"When did he call?"

"He didn't. He kidnapped one of O'Brien's people."

Feldman snapped his fingers at Cornelia to draw her attention from her self-appointed task to get more coffee. "Say again, Roger."

"Sullivan abducted one of O'Brien's people."

"Fatal?"

"No. Released already."

"Unharmed?"

"Yes, sir."

"When?"

"Friday."

"Why am I just finding out about this?"

"I just found out about it myself. Apparently the report went to the Philly cops who sat with it for a while before kicking it over to the field office, which then left voice mail in D.C., but they were working on the system and lost all the messages. Your basic cluster fuck, sir."

"Okay, Roger, where are you?"

"In the car."

"You're on a cell phone?"

"Correct."

"All right. Get yourself to a secure land line and call me back at—" Feldman looked to his attorney for the number, which she supplied and he passed along. "Make sure that you get everyone in the room and we'll do a conference call. Understood?"

"Yes, sir." Sorenson sounded irritated.

"I'll wait to hear from you," Feldman hung up and added, "asshole."

Cornelia arched her eyebrows. "Something happening?"

"Yeah. Are your telephones secure?"

"As far as I know. I mean we're not the CIA, or anything like that."

"Okay. Remember everything I said about the depositions happening today? Forget it."

"Excellent. I love it when I get my way."

"Yeah," Feldman felt his heartburn surge. "Excellent."

———■◆■———

"All right? First, who is on the phone?"

Matty Feldman was curled into the fetal position on a windowsill in his stocking feet with his cheek pressed against the glass in an attempt to view a patch of San Francisco Bay.

"This is George Whitcomb in Washington. With me are Detectives Smith and Macuzak. We also have present, for the moment, John Gavigan, who had contact with Mr. Sullivan last Friday evening in Philadelphia. A stenographer is standing by as I am advised that is standard procedure. We can proceed with a synopsis, and Mr. Gavigan has been kind enough to make himself voluntarily available for questioning. Is that how you would like to proceed, Matty?"

"Yeah, let's get the brief rundown and I'd love to ask questions of Mr. Gavigan, if he's okay with that? But before we start, where is Special Agent Sorenson?"

"Here. I'm on a secure line at Quantico. I can access any resources we might need rapidly from here and I have already requested additional tactical people be sent to Philadelphia. They should be there within the hour. The investigative support unit is standing by to render assistance as requested, and I have Dr. Funtz on his way."

"I see," Feldman said.

Sorenson must have been all the way down in Myrtle Beach if the best he could do was get back to Quantico. Feldman wondered how many rounds of golf Roger had played before he had to hurry north. Of course, he probably started back before his initial call to Feldman.

"Okay. Give me the rundown now and we'll see what else we need."

Feldman eased off the windowsill to sit at a conference table where he could write notes. He smiled when he heard Smith start to give the details. Whitcomb and Macuzak were giving her room to run and show off in front of the boss, something Sorenson would never allow.

"John Gavigan is an attorney who works directly with Dennis O'Brien at Sullivan's old firm. He never worked directly with Sullivan and never met him before Friday night. Sometime between seven-thirty and eight o'clock that evening—"

"Sorry, Stacey," Sorenson said. "With all due respect to Mr. Gavigan, are we sure this was Sullivan?"

"We matched a left thumbprint from a cell phone, Roger. We've got two cars and a van still to process, but we should get moving and wait for forensics to catch up," Smith said.

Feldman smiled. "Please continue, Stacey."

Smith continued uninterrupted for twenty minutes. She related the substance of what had happened to John Gavigan. Feldman scrawled indecipherable notes. He visualized Sorenson staring at the acoustic ceiling tiles in one of countless fluorescent-washed concrete rooms at the FBI's training facility, occasionally playing solitaire on his computer. Smith finished the tale, including the delay in routing the issue to the FBI under those circumstances where Gavigan first called the local police.

"Good briefing, Stacey," Feldman said.

"Yeah, really good," Gavigan said. "You covered everything. Even the part where we found out the FBI takes weekends off."

"Mr. Gavigan?" Feldman said.

"Yeah?"

"First, I need to know if you've been offered any type of psychological counseling since these events. If not, you may want that option right away; although I will admit I'd like to ask you a few questions if you're up to it."

"Well, yeah, they asked," Gavigan said. "I'm okay, I think. It was —and is—all kind of surreal. Sullivan said to me at one point, 'I just killed three men—are you okay with that,' like he was saying to me 'I just stomped three cockroaches, any problem?' I mean, what am I supposed to say? I didn't really even see him do it. He just kind of buzzed the car and bang, he's done. I mean I'm glad they didn't kill me, but I didn't ask for Captain Crack Attack to swoop in and save my butt. Know what I mean?"

"Yeah," Smith said.

"Okay, then, if I may—" Feldman said.

"Well, one other thing that I would like to emphasize," Gavigan said. "And I've rationalized the way I can talk about this attorney-client situation because I'm convinced Dennis, my client in his guise as the aquarium, is trying to commit another crime, specifically kill me. In fact, Sullivan's the one who convinced me of that fact. So, I'm kind of through the looking glass here and would like to know what is happening as far as picking up Dennis and any cohorts he may have in this."

"Just so you're aware, boss," Macuzak said. "O'Brien seems to have disappeared. No one at his office knows where he is and his counsel denies any knowledge of his whereabouts. We've told him we want to talk to him and he will be picked up unless he surrenders. As Stacey noted, we've linked him to at least one of the dead shooters in the van."

"You don't have enough for a warrant," Sorenson said.

"Doesn't mean we can't roust him," Smith said.

"But you don't want to taint—"

"Enough," Feldman said. "Mr. Gavigan, we're going to enter a phase in our discussions which I would prefer we insulate you from."

"So you'd like me to step outside?" Gavigan said.

"Yes, but I don't want you in and out of the room like a yo-yo. So, before you go, is there anything else you would like to add or amplify in the summary Detective Smith furnished?"

"No. She was really thorough. I just want to make sure I'm not going to get gunned down crossing the street."

"Sullivan's come and gone. He won't bother you again. It's part of his Robin Hood delusion," Sorenson said.

"You're not hearing me," Gavigan said. "I'm worried about Dennis, not Sullivan."

"I understand completely," Feldman said. "Do we have protection established for Mr. Gavigan?"

"Four agents for right now, in a safe house," Whitcomb said. "Mrs. Gavigan is out of town at her husband's request."

"Good. We'll develop that more when I get back."

"Okay, Mr. Gavigan, let's put you in possession of those agents right away. If there's anything you need, ask. We'll meet when I get there tonight. Does he have beeper numbers?"

"Yes, sir," Smith said.

"Okay, he's gone," Macuzak said.

Feldman looked back out the window as he pondered developments. "All right, people, we're going proactive. We'll bait Sullivan out using Gavigan."

"Don't you think O'Brien might be a more effective person to use?" Sorenson said.

"Negative. Sullivan approached Gavigan and specifically told him to run and hide from O'Brien. Besides, Sullivan could have popped O'Brien a million times in the last few years. The thing that drew him out was this shark-tank thing. We're going to want to check on the publicity that got, since Sullivan must have seen it, but I would guess a story that gruesome got spread around."

"I remember seeing it on the news," Macuzak said.

"Put the squeeze on O'Brien's partners," Feldman said. "I want to flush him out. He might be involved in another attempt on Gavigan for all we know. Have the firm vote to suspend his draw, or however he gets paid. Hook Gavigan up with a good lawyer to sue the balls off the firm. Maybe he can impound O'Brien's money. Suggest that he use the same one Sullivan did when he took them to the cleaners, that Bali woman. If that doesn't gain him any actual ground, then at least it should force O'Brien to the surface.

"This Gavigan is our key. We have to get him on board and happy with the arrangement. That probably means money and lots of protection. We'll protect him, but maybe we can get O'Brien to finance the rest. These are things I want you to think about. We'll flesh this out more later. I'll be on a plane back this afternoon. Roger, you pick me up at the airport in Philadelphia.

"Questions?"

Feldman ended the call with a sense of direction that he felt the pursuit had lacked from the start. They now had some area where they might predict Sullivan's behavior. Feldman started to write a note to himself to call a friend in agent recruiting about Stacey Smith, but stopped himself by making the call immediately.

＊＊＊

Matty accepted Cornelia's offer of a ride to the airport. He had nothing to check and headed straight for his gate. When he was partway down the concourse he saw a light come on, a bright, shining portable sun affixed to the front of a television camera. He had to get past it to board his aircraft, but knew that he had been seen. The inevitable came like a wave he watched forming off the beach.

"Mr. Feldman, Larissa Frontenac," the woman said.

Feldman shook the extended right hand and ignored the microphone in the left.

"May I have a word, sir?"

Feldman did not break stride. "No. No comment."

He'd had more than his share of practice brushing off the press, if not talk-show hosts who considered themselves part of the press corps. Frontenac pivoted and kept pace, no mean feat in her short, tight skirt and spiked heels.

"Can you comment on the status of your pursuit of Captain Crack Attack?"

"No. Other than to say that we don't use that term which, if I understand correctly, is a registered trademark."

Feldman was out in front, stretching his legs, but the cameraman was tall and kept pace walking backwards. Frontenac struggled to keep up. Waves of fellow travelers parted to allow the spectacle to pass.

"You have nothing to tell the American people on this subject?"

"Not at present. Besides, last time I checked, you weren't the American people."

"How much is being spent on the investigation?"

"No comment."

"We've uncovered the figure of two million dollars per week. Do you dispute that?"

"No comment."

Feldman stuffed his anger. He felt his heartburn return with a vengeance.

"Then you don't dispute it?"

"No comment."

Feldman turned into the gate with his boarding pass in hand. The aircraft was loading and the line was short. Frontenac was almost out of time.

"Do you dispute your wife's allegations of abuse during the course of your stormy marriage?"

"No comment."

"Then you admit that you are a woman beater?"

There was just enough of a questioning intonation to beat a libel suit. Feldman knew that Frontenac and her producer's lawyers were always careful with this accusation, which was posed during almost every show.

"No comment."

Feldman gave his pass to the gate agent and stepped through the door onto the jet way.

"Isn't it true you're having an affair with your subordinate Stacey Smith?" Frontenac yelled into the tunnel of the jet way.

Matty Feldman was too busy biting his tongue and fighting heartburn to answer.

Chapter 26

James Sullivan opened his eyes and put his sunglasses back on the bridge of his nose. He sat in a wooden chair on a luxuriant lawn not far from an inviting swimming pool. He spied the delivery of his lemonade and the newspaper he'd requested. He thanked the young Hispanic man and wondered whether he had relatives to the south who went thirsty while places like the Arizona Biltmore diverted water to grow grass in the desert. He would leave a large tip for the man, who pretended not to notice the scars on Sullivan's torso where the surgeon had gone hunting Walter Cole's bullets.

I wonder how old Walt is doing.

He studied the brilliant sky for a cloud, but none was there to be seen. The stark mountains stood in flinty contrast to the blue backdrop. It felt good to be in the sunshine, but Sullivan concluded after a few hours that recreation in the greater Phoenix area focused on golf or experiencing the desert. He loathed golf and had had more than his fill of the desert while in the army.

He sat up and the coughing started. He was improving, but whatever he had inhaled in lower Manhattan took its toll.

Everything. You inhaled everything.

He shifted and pain shot down the back of his leg.

Another region heard from.

Like so many other firefighters, Joe Murphy became a volunteer at the site of the World Trade Center collapse. He dug, hauled buckets of debris, breathed who knows what, and shed tears. He even caught a glimpse of Sorenson at the command post.

No doubt making a nuisance of himself.

Sullivan pushed past the first few pages of the news.

Bastards.

You should have been killing those sons of bitches.

Sullivan heard a wireless telephone chirping for the seventh time since he took his place on the manicured grass. He did not look up to examine the recipient of the call. It was the corpulent tanned man sitting about fifty feet away on an identical chair, who had taken six calls and originated twice as many. He was somewhere between fifty and eighty, although it was hard to tell under the hairpiece, cosmetic surgery, and the massive terry-cloth robe the hotel furnished. In a minute the man would start to stride with the telephone and discuss "the project." As he paced about on the grass, he would puff on a cigar the size of a Buick and drop matches in the grass, which would need to be recovered by the hotel workers. Sullivan took an instant dislike to the man, which was shared by at least a few of the callers based on the tones of the conversations. Sullivan got a whiff of the distant cigar.

At least it overrides the electrical-fire smell.

He peered over his newspaper at the telephone pacer on the brilliant green lawn under the cloudless blue sky.

They must have invented blue and green here.

At that moment Sullivan decided he would kill the phone man if he walked ten steps toward where he sat. Sullivan counted the man's steps. He turned back at seven steps. Sullivan went back to his paper.

Now, now. Try to control those impulses. You don't kill people anymore. If you're going to try to be normal you have to tolerate people even if they annoy you.

A few weeks earlier, he had sat outside a Krispy Kreme shop in Pensacola. The man in the pickup next to him smoked like a chimney. Sullivan listened to the man's young daughter wheeze from the smoke. He screwed the silencer onto a .45, ready to kill the man on principle.

"It's got to stop," he said. "This is the place where it stops."

He left the man to smoke, the daughter to suffocate.

Sullivan flipped through a few pages of advertising to find something else of interest. "Leave it alone."

He noticed the phone man pivot at the far end of his saunter across the lawn. He could not help but count his approaching steps. He turned away on the ninth step.

Leave it alone. It's none of your business.

Sullivan continued his journey through the newspaper looking for anything other than terrorism news. He found the article about John Gavigan on page twenty-four. He read it three times.

I should have left the MP-5 in the car. It had my prints all over it. Still, they should have lifted them from somewhere in the car. I even gave him a card. Couldn't they find any of my DNA?

A rasp rattled Sullivan's paper. "Excuse me."

He lowered the paper to see the phone pacer standing two feet away, the telephone tilted away from his mouth, but still rooted in his ear. He must have taken thirty steps to arrive at where he stood.

"Helluva thing, huh?" he said.

Sullivan could see the pores in the man's large nose and knew that he could break it and drive it back into his brain, or deliver a kick to his neck that would crush his windpipe. Sullivan visualized a crew of Hispanic men trying to remove bodily fluids from the grass and raking furiously at the tire tracks left by the ambulance that would transport his victim in a frantic but futile trip to the hospital.

"Sorry?" Sullivan said.

"Terrorists," the man said. "We need to kill all the cocksuckers."

"Oh, right."

"At least there's some upside."

"How's that?"

"We practically have this place to ourselves."

Sullivan looked around at the empty lawn.

No witnesses.

"I was here last year at this time and it was packed," the man said.

"Yeah, well people may be saving their vacation for Thanksgiving."

"Have you got a light?"

"No," Sullivan said. "Sorry."

"Lost my damn lighter on the golf course," the man said. "Been using matches, but ran out."

"That's too bad."

Sullivan thought of three other ways to kill the wretch in front of him, but knew he would not use any of them.

The man withdrew another massive cigar from his robe pocket. "Want one?"

"No, thank you."

The man waved it about like a magic wand. "They're Cuuuuu-baaaahhnnnn."

"I don't smoke, but thanks anyway."

The man turned with a wave. "Suit yourself."

Sullivan's command voice shot after the man. "Hey."

The man turned to see what was about to hit him.

"Hope you find your lighter," Sullivan said.

The phone pacer put the telephone back to his ear from where it had dropped. "Yeah, thanks."

That went well. You almost had a real conversation with a loathsome stranger who—you didn't kill.

Now, if you can fix this mess you created for Gavigan, you'll be all set. Maybe you can even learn to play golf.

⎯⎯⎯⎯⎯◆⎯⎯⎯⎯⎯

The telephone did not break Feldman's concentration on the computer screen.

"Feldman."

"Hey, baby, what are you wearing?" Cornelia Andrews said.

"A suit, the same suit for three days now, but underneath I have on a camisole and garter belt."

"Oooooowwwww. You're making me too hot too soon."

"Well, Cornelia, that's what I would be wearing if all of what little money I have weren't going to a high-priced lawyer in San Francisco. By the way, are you billing me for the first thirty seconds of this call?"

"Of course. It's just like if we talked about the weather instead of sexual role-playing. But, if you want to continue with that, you need to give me a major credit card number together with the expiration date and the name as it appears on the card."

"As I said, I'm all tapped out. Besides, no one wants to get involved with a wife beater."

"Well, you know that is all just too much bullshit to be believed. That Frontenac woman is a one-trick pony and, quite frankly, she's history since nine eleven. How you doing?"

"How do you think?" Feldman said.

"Busy, huh?"

"Like the proverbial one-armed paper hanger."

"Are you eating?"

Feldman looked at the pizza box on the corner of his desk. "Sort of."

"Sleeping?"

"Yesterday."

"I'm worried about you."

"Me, too. So, what's up?"

"Your favorite judge decided your deposition has to happen."

"No can do. All tied up."

"Have to or you'll find your ass in contempt."

"Nope. Chasing public enemy number one and still after my buddy Captain Crack Attack who's fallen to number, like, ninety-eight at this point. I'm like the Manhattan Project. He can't touch me."

"Not to make you feel insignificant, Matty dearest, but yeah, he can."

"How about if I get an order from a federal judge that says I'm too important to be bothered right now? I can probably get one of the U. S. attorneys to fetch that for me."

"That's only going to piss our judge off. Further, it would not be binding on him."

"What about your awesome powers of persuasion? I'll give you my credit card number and you can talk dirty to him instead."

"That is just too revolting to contemplate. Besides, I'm not sure he's straight. We're left with you coming out and getting this finished."

"Can't do it."

"Matty, lookit, I've stalled this thing for weeks, but the judge ain't buying it at this point."

"When?"

"He's pushing to close the file by the end of the year, so we've got to get it in before Thanksgiving. I don't suppose you can give me any prep time."

"No way."

"How about this: You fly out this Friday, we prep on Saturday, and do the dep on Sunday."

"Can you make them work on a Sunday?"

"The judge can."

Feldman looked at the folded newspaper on his desk. The story had burned out days ago. He needed things to cool down before Gavigan would get more coverage. He could fly the trip as an air marshal.

"Come on out Friday," Cornelia said. "We'll have dinner."

"Fine. I'll probably be on a late flight and no place too expensive. I can't afford it."

"Dinner's on me. Least I can do for one of our terror hunters. We'll eat real Chinese. That way no one else in the place will know what we're talking about."

"Sounds like a plan. Let me know if you can sell it."

"Consider it sold. Make your reservation and get yourself out here. Call or e-mail with your flight info and I'll have you picked up."

"Yes ma'am."

"Ciao."

"Bye."

Matty sometimes wanted to be like Cornelia, but he knew he could never be someone who used Italian to sign off the telephone or wore anything other than a white shirt and tie to work. He looked back at the newspaper and then out the window. The pieces were in place. He could run things from afar and rush back if needed. Whitcomb and Macuzak could handle things that might happen while he was in transit. He decided to take care of business in San Francisco.

John Gavigan stared at his raincoat and realized that the feature was an odd distraction since his office door was almost always open. He rotated his chair so he could stare out at the city's lights for a while. It was past eight and he thought about eating, going to the gym, or going home. His eyes wandered to the sky to track an airliner and he wondered whether anyone planned to crash it into a building. He reached for the telephone to call Christine for the twelfth time that day, but stopped himself. His telephone was bugged by the government to the point that a technician warned him about the radiation hazard if he kept the handset to his ear for too long. Besides, the call would be for his benefit rather than hers.

Gavigan longed for some work to do, but all his files had been redistributed. Matty Feldman sold his proposal to the partners. They pulled all his cases in turn for a healthy sum and his cooperation in waiting for Sullivan to make contact. The partners seemed eager to help the government since it helped to free them from Dennis O'Brien. They were all happy with Dennis's prolonged disappearance with the exception of Walter Cole, who made himself scarce but had not disappeared.

Gavigan was bored. He had few diversions apart from his practice. Earlier in the afternoon, he found himself envying the people who went to the movies on Chestnut Street in the middle of the day. He pondered booking a trip to Colorado for the weekend and wondered whether the FBI agent sitting down the hall would have to go along. After all, Feldman was flying to San Francisco for the weekend. Maybe he could take enough time to drive the Volvo out for Christine's use. Either the firm or the feds would provide him with a vehicle. With the priority on the antiterror front, nothing would happen for weeks or months in exposing Sullivan.

Gavigan was not even sure what he was doing in his office. He was scheduled for another briefing the following week on how to manipulate the contact to the pursuers' best advantage. He rotated his chair to look back out the window. A few moments later, his dozing evaporated in the face of a faint chirping sound. Gavigan searched the raincoat's pockets for his wireless telephone. He drew it out in the hope of speaking with Christine, but could not help himself from uttering his normal telephone response.

"John Gavigan."

"Do you recognize my voice?"

Gavigan searched his memories of male voices and went cold inside within one second. "Oh, shit."

"I'll take that as an affirmation."

"How the hell did you get this number?"

Gavigan visualized Sullivan using the telephone in the Volvo and knew the answer before he finished the question.

"Listen carefully," Sullivan said. "I will deliver to you a package that will exonerate you under the condition that you get yourself and your wife out of there before Dennis has you killed. Do you understand?"

Gavigan's mind raced through the things he supposed the FBI would want him to say. "No. Say this again."

"Dennis will kill you. You are implicated in the homicides of the men in the van. I can help you with these issues. Have you been drinking?"

Gavigan wondered how he could get the attention of the agent down the hall. He took his desk telephone off the hook.

"I may have had one or two," he said.

"Drinking is probably not a constructive activity at the moment."

"You're the one who called after hours."

"Pay attention. You will receive a package that will absolve you of the homicides provided that you flee Philadelphia and Dennis O'Brien."

"Okay. I'm on track. Where do we meet?"

"We don't. I'll send it to you. Give me an address."

"I don't have that option. I've been frozen out by the cops. They say my place is a crime scene."

"Then I'll send it to you at the firm."

"Forget that, too. I cleared out my desk and don't trust them to give me my mail."

"Where's your wife?"

"Don't you go near her, or I'll find you and kill you myself."

"Fair enough. I gather that you have at least moved her to somewhere safe."

"You stay the hell away from her!"

"Not a problem. I'm trying to help you here. Do you agree to my terms?"

"What terms? The firm fired my ass. There's nothing to keep me here. I just need whatever the package is unless it's going to blow up or something. What's in it?"

"The weapon I used. Who's your lawyer?"

"You're talking to him."

"You're kidding."

"Do I sound like I'm kidding? Do you know what criminal defense attorneys cost? Drug dealers have priced most of the rest of us criminals right out of the market. I shot my wad hiding my wife and making bail."

"No friends from school you trust?"

"My abrasive personality didn't help me there too much, and the few I still have aren't answering the phone since I made the papers."

Gavigan felt like he was walking a tightrope; the only safety net was the fact that at least some of his words were truthful.

"Be in the lobby of the Bellevue tomorrow evening at this time," Sullivan said. "Make sure your telephone is switched on."

"What time?"

"Don't set a trap. If you do, I'll kill Christine. I'll let you live with that fact for weeks, or months, then, I'll kill you. Good night, John."

"How's the murder weapon supposed to help me?" Gavigan said.

There was no answer.

"Hello? Hello? Hello?" he repeated. "Shit."

Chapter 27

Stacey Smith lost track of the quantity of coffee and cigarettes she had consumed since Macuzak and Whitcomb had picked her up late last night. She knew she looked a mess with her pulled-up hair and stretchy knit dress in all its unwashed glory, but no one else looked dapper this morning, either, after spending the night mobilizing assets to capture Sullivan. She did not even care to consider the wreckage of her eleventh attempt to stop smoking since the beginning of the New Year. Whitcomb and Macuzak returned with bags of danish.

"It took you long enough," Sorenson said.

"Where's Gavigan?" Macuzak asked.

"I sent him home for a shower and some rest," Sorenson said.

"Who is with him?" Whitcomb said.

Sorenson leered in Smith's direction. "In the shower? I assume he's alone since his wife is out of town, but you never know."

"Are there agents with him?" Macuzak asked.

"He's got two agents watching him from a discreet distance."

"Are the jump-out squads ready?"

"We have a tactical team in place," Sorenson said. "It will go on alert this evening. A backup team is also on its way, but won't be on site when we take him."

"Just one team?" Whitcomb said.

"One should be more than adequate," Sorenson said. "In fact, you folks don't even need to be there if you're too tired."

"How big is the squad?" Macuzak said.

"Seven," Sorenson said.

"So, twelve with all of us."

"That enough?" Smith said.

"More than enough," Sorenson said.

"We should be okay," Whitcomb said.

"He's not gonna shoot at us anyway," Macuzak said.

"I hope he tries," Sorenson said.

Smith decided she had to lay off the coffee. Her hands were shaking too much.

———◆◆◆———

Word of Sullivan's surfacing did not reach Matty Feldman in time to catch a late-night flight, but he was racing to make an early morning direct flight from San Francisco to Philadelphia that should put him on site for the capture, or more likely shooting, of James Sullivan. He associated the numbness and tingling in his arm with the pressure he had put on a nerve passing through the cubital space at his elbow while leaning on the car door with his telephone glued to his left ear for the last thirty minutes. He also had some pain in his jaw and neck but attributed that to a poor night's rest followed by endless telephone calls. The shortest call he had made this morning was from a pay telephone outside a convenience store, and that was only because there were some things he did not want to disseminate over radio waves. Further, he did not want to share all his thoughts with O'Malley and Richards, the two field agents driving him.

Feldman looked at his watch as the FBI sedan parked at the departure curb. His plane was scheduled to leave six minutes earlier, but Feldman wielded enough influence at the moment to hold it at the gate. The three men met with a waiting airport policeman who walked them through the terminal to the gate. Feldman shook hands with O'Malley, Richards, and the policeman while the gate agent snatched his boarding papers. Once Feldman was on the aircraft, the jet way began retracting before the cabin door closed. Feldman found an aisle seat well back in coach after running a gauntlet of irritated looks from his fellow passengers.

———◆◆◆———

O'Malley started and ended the conversation on his pocket telephone just after Matty Feldman's aircraft left the gate. "Package's on the way."

Richards looked out the window with an air of disinterest.

"You gonna tell me who that was?" He asked.

"Old friend from the academy," O'Malley said.

"Must be a good friend to have you standing around in the airport acting like you're on *X-Files*."

"Come on. I'll buy breakfast."

"Naw, naw, naw. This is so important that you're making secret phone calls; we better wait for the plane to go. So, who is she?"

"Who?"

"The chick on the phone."

"If Special Agent Legs-That-Go-on-Forever hears you use the word 'chick' your ass'll be up on charges of sex discrimination," O'Malley said.

"Just answer the question."

"There is no chick."

"So, you are gay. Excellent. I just won the pool."

O'Malley's cool broke for the first time that morning. "What pool?"

"Nothing."

O'Malley turned back to the glass. "You're just busting my balls."

"So, who was it on the phone?"

"Guy named Sorenson. He works for Feldman on this bullshit task force they have going."

"Roger Sorenson?"

"You know him?"

"The father or the son?"

"The son."

"Yeah. I know him."

"And?"

"And what?"

"You want to tell me something about him."

"I didn't say anything." Richards said.

"You didn't have to."

"My mother told me more than once that if you can't say anything nice, say nothing at all."

"And you're gonna suddenly start taking this advice?"

"I'll just tell you to watch your back."

"Why?"

"The guy's a weasel."

"And you know this how?"

"We were both in New York at the same time. I worked a white-collar case with him for almost two years. Just as we were about to roll it up, I got transfer orders to Vegas. Sorenson took it over at the finish line and I got dick for credit."

"You never made any noise about it?" O'Malley said.

"Naw, I started digging out from under in my new slot and let it slide."

"Huh."

"I did hear that Sorenson became Mr. New York. Loved the place. Moved into Chinatown. Even kept evidence in the Towers after he went to Washington."

"Well, you can bet that stuff is gone."

"You know his old man?"

"I know he's connected."

"Oh. Well, there you go," Richards said.

Feldman's seatmate was Dennis Wilson, age nine. Dennis was the only offspring of a four-year marriage between a dentist and an attorney. Dennis's parents' divorce had been so acrimonious that all adults involved in the process believed it a positive development when they moved to different coasts. As a consequence of his parents' career choices, Dennis had fallen victim to daycare or some other form of parenting for hire since he was seven weeks old. Due to his unfortunate name selection, a fading fund of accurate knowledge about television characters from earlier decades, and his demeanor, the child came to be referred to as "Dennis the Menace" by anyone out of his parents' earshot. Nevertheless, a bitter custody battle over him resulted in a visitation order that caused Dennis to fly across the country twelve to fifteen times each year despite the fact that neither of his parents spent substantial time with him after arrival. Indeed, Dennis's mother could not tolerate his "behavioral problems" absent his Ritalin. Dennis's father, who put him on the flight back to his ex-wife, had neglected to administer this medication to his son for the last three weeks but did provide him with four large Ghirardelli chocolate bars for the trip.

Dennis struggled against his seat belt as Feldman stuffed his briefcase under the seat. "I know you! I know you! I know you!"

"That's nice," Feldman said.

He surveyed the cabin for another seat he could occupy once they were airborne. The plane seemed warm and he could feel his pulse pounding in his ears from the rushed trip through the terminal.

Dennis was on one knee despite his fastened seat belt. "I have you! I have you!"

"Terrific."

Feldman knew from similar encounters that the boy was referring to one of the infamous Captain Crack Attack trading cards. He had autographed a dozen or more of the things over the past few months. Sweat poured down his face and neck. He reached overhead to open the air vent.

Dennis dove under the seat in front of him to rummage through his carry-on luggage. A safety video blared to life on the cabin's central line of television screens. Matty slouched to look out the window across the aisle. He felt sad to leave San Francisco and realized that he always felt this way when he left the city. He tried to remember how many places he had lived during his career, but his musings were interrupted by an announcement from the flight deck apologizing for the late departure but noting that the plane was next to depart although it had just started to taxi. The flight attendants hustled around the cabin checking seat belts.

Dennis exploded from under the seat and shoved one of the Captain Crack Attack cards into Matty's hand. "Lookit!"

"Great."

Matty examined it and recognized the image as one that must have been lifted from footage shot by Larissa Frontenac's video crew when he last passed through this airport.

Dennis stood upright on his seat and bumped his head on the overhead compartment. "Can you sign it? Pleeeeeeeease?"

Matty was reaching for his pen before the question came. "Sure."

A flight attendant leaned into Matty's row. "Excuse me, sir. Dennis, we talked before about how you had to stay in your seat."

"Yes, sir," Dennis seized the autographed card from Feldman.

As Dennis fidgeted with his seat belt clasp under the gaze of the flight attendant, Matty Feldman felt a momentary, enormous pressure behind his sternum. He dropped his pen as his hands flew to his chest. A loud croak erupted from his throat.

The flight attendant looked down in time to see Matty's eyes roll back in their sockets. He grabbed Feldman's neck and each wrist in search of a pulse.

"Oh, shit," he said.

O'Malley and Richards stood at the end of the concourse sipping lattes. Their position allowed a view across the ramp and taxiways to where Feldman's plane moved down the runway. It turned off onto a taxiway.

"What have we here?" Richards said.

"That is his plane, isn't it?" O'Malley said.

"One and the same."

"Probably some mechanical problem. Mr. Feldman might be buying us breakfast."

A red flashing light appeared on the concourse where they had parted company with Feldman. It was atop a golf cart that served as an ambulance within the airport. An ambulance and a fire truck sped along the tarmac.

"You might want to give your little weasel friend a call," Richards said.

O'Malley had already hit the redial button on his cell phone.

"Okay. Keep me posted."

Sorenson hung up. Hot Stacey and the Jersey Clowns were in the conference room with him. Sorenson regretted having shared with them that he was keeping tabs on Feldman's progress through the airport. A glance from Macuzak demanded an explanation.

"Feldman's plane appears to be delayed," Sorenson said.

"How long?" Smith asked.

"Not sure. Anyway, we have enough time to actually get some rest before the big show, which will go on whether Feldman is here or not. I suggest that we head for our respective rooms and catch some of the sleep that escaped last night."

No one argued.

———————◆◆◆———————

Richards and O'Malley stood around in a curtained area of the emergency room. They had watched Feldman being removed from the aircraft and had hurtled after the ambulance. They detected the change in demeanor of the EMT who continued chest compressions right into the hospital despite the fact that his attention seemed to be elsewhere. They knew what they would hear as soon as the doctors and nurses finished their efforts. They watched a physician emerge from the treatment area through the same automatic doors that had opened to accept the stretcher a half hour earlier.

"Are you the FBI guys?" he asked.

"Yeah," O'Malley answered.

The doctor looked down at a form on a clipboard to make sure he got the name right. "Mr. Feldman did not survive, I'm sorry to say."

O'Malley already had the telephone to his ear.

Chapter 28

Sorenson drummed his fingers on the conference room table. The assistant U.S. attorney next to him reached over and touched his hand to stop the movement. Sorenson looked at her. She was quite attractive, but for a change he was detached from her femininity as he considered the day's events and looked at his watch. It was just after four in the afternoon. When he had learned of Matty Feldman's death, Sorenson knew that opportunity had not only knocked, it had kicked in his door, grabbed him by the lapels and demanded that he act.

Act he did.

Within thirty minutes of Feldman's death, Sorenson convinced two of three assistant directors to give him temporary control of the task force under those circumstances where an arrest was possible within hours. The ad hoc committee on the telephone told him that a meeting would convene over the weekend to sort out the future structure of the task force. Sorenson was to be in Washington the next day at noon. In the meantime, they placed Sorenson in command while neglecting to tell him not to do anything drastic.

Sorenson had not looked back since that telephone conference. He spent every minute tracking down Dennis O'Brien, meeting with lawyers, and working the telephones. He had not consulted anyone inside the Bureau, not even his father. Then, he moved himself into the conference room where he now sat.

Across the table, Dennis O'Brien and Sean O'Donnell reviewed the third and final immunity agreement of the day. They were taking too much time since the district court approved the document. The agreement was simple. It provided blanket immunity from federal prosecution for anything O'Brien might have done up to the time of its execution. It mirrored the agreements that Sorenson pushed prosecutors in Pennsylvania and New Jersey to ram through their court systems in record time. Now, O'Brien and O'Donnell had all three agreements arrayed on the table for comparison purposes.

"Is there some problem?"

The question came from the assistant attorney general from New Jersey. He sat next to the assistant U.S. attorney. Beyond him was an assistant district attorney from Philadelphia, who made notes on a trial transcript. All three prosecutors had been pulled from other matters to deal with an immunity agreement for someone they did not know represented by a criminal defense attorney more experienced than all three of them combined.

Sean O'Donnell pulled himself upright in his chair and out of the huddle with Dennis O'Brien. He turned to the court reporter waiting behind her equipment at the end of the table and flashed his dazzling smile.

"I think we can proceed," he said. "Let's go on the record. Please swear the witness."

The court reporter asked Dennis O'Brien if he swore to tell the truth. He did.

O'Donnell fanned the immunity agreements across the table. "I would like to have these marked and made a part of the record."

The court reporter leaned away from her machine to hunt for exhibit labels. "Any particular order?"

"Any of you have a preference?" O'Donnell said.

"What's the procedure you're following here?" the Philadelphia ADA asked.

"I want to establish the existence and terms of the agreements through a colloquy before Dennis starts to answer questions," O'Donnell said.

The New Jersey AAG looked at his watch. "Is that really necessary? I've got a night box filing in Trenton that really needs my attention. I don't want to spend the next three hours going through these agreements, the terms of which we already know since we've worked on them all afternoon, under those circumstances where your client is going to say that he cheated on his tax returns. I mean, it's not like he killed anybody, right?"

The lines in Sean O'Donnell's forehead deepened. "I have to represent my client as I see fit. The terms precedent to his agreeing to answer questions are encompassed within those agreements. I need to establish for the record that they exist and what they mean. Now, the reality is they mean what they say, so I don't think that part of this exercise is going to take three hours. If you're pressed for time, maybe we can deal with the New Jersey agreement first if your colleagues agree."

"No problem," the assistant U.S. attorney said. "Besides, this is my office, so I'm here for the duration."

"I'd like to go second if I could," the Philadelphia ADA said. "I've got some stuff to attend to back at the office."

"Sure. We should mark the Jersey deal one, Pennsylvania two, and mine three," the assistant U.S. attorney said.

"Back on the record," O'Donnell said.

He turned to his client. "Please state your name for the record."

"Dennis O'Brien."

The polished senior partner was haggard. Sorenson guessed he had not shaved in days. His attire was casual with a rumpled blue blazer donned as a token to mark the significance of the occasion. O'Brien's red-rimmed eyes betrayed lack of sleep.

"What is your date of birth?" O'Donnell asked.

O'Brien answered that question followed by a host of others, including his Social Security number, driver's license number, attorney identification number, businesses in which he was or ever had been a principal, places of residence for his entire life, and so on. As O'Brien answered, Sorenson saw a broken man and thought about what a fool Feldman had been to conclude that O'Brien could not be trusted to help capture Sullivan. The man Sorenson saw would do anything to help the FBI. Instead, they had wasted so much effort with this Gavigan idiot. Feldman even got the firm to float a raft of money to gain his cooperation. It bordered on extortion. Jew boy had even thought that Sullivan would be stupid enough to show for a meeting tonight.

And don't forget about the rifle. It was pointed right at O'Brien's office with Sullivan's prints all over it! Fucking Feldman tried to explain it away as some kind of message.

"Now, Mr. O'Brien, we have an agreement marked as exhibit one," O'Donnell said.

He handed the marked copy to his client. "Can you identify that for me?"

"Yes, I can. It's an immunity agreement between me and the State of New Jersey together with its political subdivisions."

"Is it your understanding that the agreement is in effect at this time?"

"Yes."

"Now, I know the document speaks for itself, but what is your summary understanding of the agreement?"

"Well, the exhibit does speak for itself, but generally, it provides blanket immunity from prosecution for any crimes or offenses I may have committed in the State of New Jersey from the date of my birth to the present time provided that I disclose the existence of such offenses during the course of this interrogation. It provides me with absolute immunity in that jurisdiction superior to mere transactional or use immunity in turn for my cooperation in assisting the efforts to capture James Sullivan by submitting to this interview. In contractual terms, the consideration supporting the agreement comprises immunity in exchange for cooperation"

"And is it your understanding that the blanket immunity agreement was approved by a New Jersey court this afternoon?"

"It is," O'Brien said. "I would not be here otherwise."

O'Donnell turned to the New Jersey assistant attorney general. "Is that your understanding of the agreement as well?"

"Are you talking to me?" the AAG said.

"Yes. I asked if your understanding of the agreement conforms to that of my client. You executed it together with him prior to its presentation to the court," O'Donnell said.

The prosecutor leaned forward as he dropped his transcript in apparent disgust. "One, I'm not here to answer questions.

"Two, no one cares what I think the agreement means because I am not a judge and neither is your client.

"Three, the agreement means what it says within its four corners. I'm only here because the FBI is doing a full-court press to secure your client's cooperation. To my knowledge, your client hasn't done anything wrong in New Jersey. I would wager that this vast waste of time comes about so that your client can reveal some insignificant violation of the state's tax code, while the rapist whose appeal I'm combating is getting a chance at a new trial because I'm sitting here in this goddamned room. So, with that said, let me ask your client what he has done in New Jersey that gives rise to the necessity for this immunity agreement."

O'Donnell held his hand across O'Brien's chest in a gesture of control. "Don't say anything. My client will not answer any questions until we have established the terms of the agreements in all jurisdictions represented here today. To my satisfaction, that has occurred with regard to New Jersey."

The assistant attorney general stuffed the transcript he had been reading into his bag and started for the door. "Fine. I need to get moving. Let me know if anything major comes from this."

As the New Jersey prosecutor shook hands and made for the door, Sorenson's telephone vibrated in his pocket. He answered it.

"Sorenson."

Smith's voice shot through the connection. "Roger, where are you and what the hell is going on? Some of the locals are telling us that Matty is dead. Is that true?"

Christ. Like I have time to deal with this bimbo.

"Stacey, I'm in a meeting. Let me break away and call you back within a minute or two."

Sorenson closed the connection. He excused himself from the conference room with the understanding that the lawyers would continue with the colloquy. After he went to the men's room, he called Smith from the hall outside the conference room.

He started to pace the hall with the opening of the conversation. "Stacey, it's Sorenson."

"Roger, we're getting word that Matty had a heart attack this morning in San Francisco. Do you know about this?"

"Yes. I found out about it after you went to get some sleep."

"Why the hell didn't you tell us?"

You'd shit your silky panties if I told you half the things I know.

"I've been busy trying to pick up the pieces. Besides, there's nothing for you to do about it."

"Our information is that it was fatal. Is that your understanding?"

Smith's voice had a steely quality, as though she were playing the part of someone capable of posing coherent inquiries under stress. Sorenson assumed that Whitcomb must be feeding her questions. He turned in his pacing to see the Philadelphia assistant district attorney leaving the conference room. They would be discussing the federal immunity agreement while he wasted his time talking to Smith and company.

"Yes," Sorenson said.

"Where does that leave us?"

Smith's question came after a long pause. Sorenson was convinced that Whitcomb or Macuzak was steering the conversation.

"Proceed as scheduled," he said. "I'll get there when I can, but I expect that it will be after everyone is already in position."

"The tactical people have already sent themselves over from what we understand. Who exactly is in charge? Have they told you?"

"I am," Sorenson said. He wanted Hot Stacey and the Jersey boys to savor that for a while before he made them choke on it.

"No one from Washington?"

Sorenson felt an urge to fire Smith right now, over the telephone.

"Stacey," he said. "I *am* from Washington. Now, you and the others can get yourselves into position. I've already spoken with the tactical people. They know what to do. Just stay out of their way in case anything happens."

"Do you know anything about the arrangements?"

"I just told you about those," Sorenson said.

Dumb bitch.

"Get to the scene and stay—"

"Not the arrest plan," Smith said. "Matty's funeral arrangements."

Sorenson hesitated. He had not considered the fact that Feldman would have a funeral. There would be many important Bureau people there: assistant directors; deputy directors; the director himself maybe; the attorney general. He would be expected to attend, perhaps even say a few words.

"I haven't heard anything about it," Sorenson said.

"He was Jewish."

Duh.

"I suppose."

"Jews are usually buried pretty quickly, aren't they?"

He needed to focus on what was happening in the conference room. "I'm not sure of all the details. I'll make a few calls after I'm done here and then let you know."

Sorenson ended the call. He might have to wait until after the funeral to fire his colleagues. They had to go, but he did not want an awkward public confrontation at Feldman's funeral. For the moment, his fatigue and time constraints frustrated his favored game of office intrigue. He checked to ensure that his fly was closed before opening the door to the conference room. As he did so, he was almost run down by the assistant U.S. attorney who was emerging to look for him.

Sorenson and the attorney turned back into the room. Sorenson flipped open his laptop computer and searched for the file with his questions for Dennis O'Brien. There were not all that many. He wanted to outline some details of what he expected as far as cooperation in capturing Sullivan. He assumed command of the floor.

"Now, Mr. O'Brien, I want to ask you a few questions be—"

O'Donnell held up his hand. "My client will not answer any questions until he is afforded an opportunity to articulate facts underlying any possible offenses subject to the approved immunity agreements previously marked and incorporated into the record as exhibits one through three, inclusive."

"Mr. O'Donnell, I am under some time constraints this afternoon, now, evening," Sorenson said. "I just want to go over what is expected of your client before midnight."

"My client is acutely aware that you have bargained for his cooperation in capturing one of the most dangerous men in America. We will not go any further unless he is allowed to enumerate his offenses and/or possible offenses in accord with the agreements."

Sorenson slumped into his chair and opened the games file on his laptop. "Fine. Enumerate away."

Dennis O'Brien started to speak in a monotone while consulting his digital assistant. He read a prepared statement from the tiny device. As the New Jersey assistant attorney general had guessed, he spoke about tax evasion in the Garden State as well as in Pennsylvania. He also confessed to eluding federal income taxes as an individual, corporation, and partner. Every tax return he ever filed had been fraudulent. He spirited income offshore. He commingled funds of clients. He kited checks. He engaged in a host of fraudulent enterprises which Sorenson ignored. Indeed, after fifteen minutes of O'Brien's droning about his transgressions Sorenson felt fatigue start to overcome him. The droning continued.

Wonder what Stacey's gonna wear tonight.

"I utilized my law firm, aquarium, restaurants, and their associated subsidiaries as criminal enterprises, including but not limited to laundering of illicit funds acquired from illegal drug distribution and vending organizations in which I also conspired and worked as a stakeholder."

I wonder if that scar on her thigh messes up her ass.

"I conspired in and participated in the attempted murder of my associate, John Gavigan, and the felony murders of any and all individuals killed on...," O'Brien consulted a ragged piece of paper pulled from his pocket and supplied a date and location together with some names corresponding to Sullivan's meeting with Gavigan. "This includes, but is not limited to, the demise of one of my criminal associates, Reggie Washington."

"Oh, shit," the assistant U.S. attorney said.

She leaned forward to break Sorenson's reverie. "Hold it right now."

"No," O'Donnell said. "Keep going."

Sorenson looked up at O'Brien and noticed that his color had returned, together with a coat of perspiration. O'Brien picked up the pace.

"I conspired in, and participated in the abduction, torture, and homicides of...," O'Brien peered through reading glasses as he stumbled through the Hispanic names noted on the crumpled piece of paper, "who died at the shark tank in my aquarium."

O'Donnell slipped a piece of paper to the court reporter with the names already typed out to avoid an interruption in his client's diatribe. Sorenson started to speak, but O'Donnell silenced him by holding up his hand. The court reporter, who Sorenson now recalled had been engaged through O'Donnell's office, ignored the attempted interruption and kept recording O'Brien's rapid-fire speech.

"I conspired in and participated in the attempted homicide of James Sullivan on...," O'Brien supplied the date from his crib sheet.

"I conspired in and participated in a number of homicides and felony murders which occurred in Philadelphia on...," again, he secured the date from his sheet, "including that of Ginger Sullivan, deceased wife of James Sullivan.

"Finally, and in furtherance of my ongoing criminal enterprises and conspiracies as well as to conceal those illicit activities, I killed my law partner Mr. Bard in conspiracy with others who made his death appear accidental and/or natural because said Bard engaged Ginger Sullivan as an independent auditor in an attempt to discover and disclose the previously referenced criminal activities. Each and all of these offenses occurred in furtherance of ongoing criminal enterprises and involved inter- and intrastate use of mail, telephone, wire, and computer connections in and among the jurisdictions referenced in exhibits one through three, inclusive."

With the completion of his monologue, the hunted, haggard look of Dennis O'Brien was replaced with the countenance of a winner. He took a long drink of water. The knot that had formed somewhere near Sorenson's scrotum a minute earlier felt like it would choke him on its way to blowing through the top of his head. The assistant U.S. attorney let her face drop into her left hand while she reviewed the notes on her legal pad, as if searching for the precise moment when her prosecutorial career had ended.

Sean O'Donnell leaned back in his chair and clasped his hands behind his head. The lines that had etched his forehead were gone. He showed his dazzling capped teeth as he broke the silence and articulated a note for the record.

"My client, who enjoys full immunity for any offenses arising from the articulated facts, will now entertain questions.

"Mr. Sorenson?"

Chapter 29

Sullivan drove the Porsche north on Broad Street in South Philadelphia. He traveled in the left lane to avoid the double-parked cars, trucks, and casino buses common in this part of the city. It had taken him over three hours to make the trip from Maryland. His back ached. Only his pain medicine made the ride tolerable. During the trip he counted no fewer than six Porsches similar to the one he drove. As he crossed Passyunk Avenue he saw a seventh Porsche. He was enjoying the ride. For a moment he considered turning away from the city and Gavigan.

Stop screwing around and get your head in the game.

He tried to focus as the meeting place drew near. He crossed Locust Street and surveyed the scene to his left in front of the hotel. He was surprised by what he saw. There were no fewer than three unmarked police cars on Broad Street, including one parked in front of the doors to the Bellevue where he had planned to buy Gavigan dinner. He assumed the two shiny black Suburbans with the darkened windows belonged to a tactical team. Sullivan continued with the flow of traffic past the hotel and north toward City Hall.

"Gee. I guess this is a trap."

Didn't they think I would do my reconnaissance before I showed? Hell, I'm not even an hour early and these clowns are still setting the trap. At least they could have parked in a less obvious spot.

"Oh, well. So much for dinner at the Palm. I guess Roger's gonna be blackballed from there."

Sullivan turned east onto Market Street from City Hall. He drove past the federal courthouse at Sixth and Market Streets and went north on Fifth to Arch, where he doubled back to look at the federal office building in which the FBI maintained its local office together with other organs of the federal bureaucracy. He doubled back again and drove into the garage most of the federal people used.

He found Gavigan's Volvo parked on the first level.

"Well. I guess my little buddy turned me in."

———◆◆◆———

Gavigan paced the lobby of what had once been the Bellevue Stratford Hotel. Following the outbreak of Legionnaires' disease at the hotel back in 1977, it had closed and been resurrected as an office building with some upscale shopping and a much smaller hotel on its upper floors. Gavigan looked at the interior display window of the Ralph Lauren store for what seemed the four hundredth time since his arrival.

The display window confined an antique bed festooned with dark sheets, comforters, and more pillows than he could count. On the floor next to the bed stood a pair of ancient leather riding boots with a riding crop balanced across their tops where someone's calves would be if they were worn. The boots seemed made for a man, but the feet seemed small, maybe a size six or seven.

In the rear corner of the display stood another antique, a desk. It was accompanied by a small chair. Some masculine accessories were strewn across its top and a picture frame held a photograph of a stunning blond woman atop a horse. He doubted whether anyone lived in a place like that which the window portrayed. It must be a fiction contrived by some flamboyant window dresser.

No. It was too perfect—too contrived for somebody as creative as a window dresser.

This was created by some computer program that consumed demographics about purchasers and decided what merchandise should be put where. The display was a huge kit that came from a warehouse in some place like Hoboken or Cleveland. The window dresser had to assemble it according to minute directions formulated to foster that

Jane Austin-meets-Bill Gates feel that they were trying to capture. It was more like assembling a child's toy on Christmas Eve than a creative process. It probably prescribed the angle for the riding crop perched atop the boots.

Gavigan looked at his watch. Sullivan was ninety minutes late. Smith, the pretty agent, and the two older detectives met with him before setting him out to decoy Sullivan. He had not seen Sorenson, who was in some type of meeting because Feldman had dropped dead that morning, but Gavigan was assured that he would be on scene listening through the microphone taped to his chest by the appointed time of the meeting with Sullivan.

Gavigan felt unstable sitting in this trap, but the host of SWAT guys lurking nearby comforted him. He again pulled his wireless telephone from his pocket. Its little display continued to indicate its willingness to ring and the strength of its battery. Gavigan left the phone in his hand, but let it drop to his side.

Having already read all the fronts of the book jackets, reviewed the expensive truffles, and glanced at the cosmetics and the evening gowns in the other windows, he returned his attention to the bedroom in the window with its old leather, high-count cotton, and photograph. He spoke into the glass.

"That must be the jockey's girlfriend."

These were the first words he had spoken aloud in fifteen minutes. The last ones had been, "He's not coming." Ten minutes before that he said aloud, "He's a no-show." Neither comment drew a response from Sorenson or his minions.

"I wonder if she's a lesbian," Gavigan said.

His cellular phone rang within fifteen seconds. He let it ring four times.

"Hello?"

"Listen. Are you talking about lesbians and jockeys, or are we having some type of communications snafu?"

"Sorenson, nice of you to show up. Look, he's not—"

"Don't use my name. Follow the protocol and act like you're talking to your wife or girlfriend!"

"Okay, bitch. He's not gonna show. Now get your sweet ass down here and pick me up!"

Gavigan flipped the phone closed to end the call. For a split second he pondered the consequences of talking to his wife in such a fashion. It made him shudder.

Within fifteen seconds, Sorenson charged through the lobby doors opening from Walnut Street. He started screaming at Gavigan before he came within fifty feet of him.

Sorenson pointed his index finger. "I don't need this shit from you!"

"No," Gavigan said. "What you need is a course in Cop one-oh-one! You think this guy is gonna waltz in here to meet me when you've got cop cars parked all over the place!"

Gavigan noticed a pair of black-clad figures emerging from behind a column on the mezzanine. Their submachine guns pointed toward the ceiling. He saw the two detectives follow the pretty agent through the same doors Sorenson had used. Gavigan loosened his tie and unbuttoned his shirt to pull at the microphone taped there.

"Okay, folks! Show's over. Miller time. Goin' to Disney World and all that."

Sorenson rested his hands on his hips and cocked his head up at the larger man. "You know, I don't need this shit from you anymore. I don't think you can deliver the goods and I now have someone who can."

Smith pushed herself between the two men and rearranged Gavigan's shirt so that the wire was covered. "Hi, Roger, what's going on?"

"No, no, no, let him pull it apart. We don't need this guy anymore," Sorenson said.

"Why don't we do this somewhere more private," Whitcomb said.

Sorenson spoke into his radio. "We're blown. Let's pack up and get out."

A half dozen black-clad figures emerged as if from the woodwork of the building. They gestured the receipt of the command and walked toward a small meeting room where they could shed their weapons and tactical clothing before walking onto the street.

"Roger," Smith said, "John here may have a point about the cars. I know they're unmarked, but they're sort of conspicuous. We asked the guys to move them, but they said you specifically told them to park them out front."

"That's a misunderstanding," Sorenson said. "Let's drop the load here back at the office and go pick up O'Brien. He's my new bait."

"You made a deal with Dennis O'Brien?" Macuzak said.

Gavigan laughed.

"That must have cost you something pretty hefty. At least one count of attempted murder on me."

"Matty expressly refused to deal with O'Brien," Whitcomb said. "He believed the man could not be trusted."

Sorenson stepped close to Gavigan. "Cost me? Your boss got immunity to lure out Sullivan and it cost me plenty, but it will be worth it."

"What the hell are you talking about?" Gavigan said.

Sorenson pointed a trembling index finger at Gavigan. "Just this: If your friend Sullivan ever shows up, or calls you, or contacts you in any way, which I surely doubt, make sure that the first thing you say to him is that Dennis O'Brien put a contract out on his wife and had her killed."

"Have you been drinking?"

"Say that with me won't you? 'Dennis O'Brien killed your wife.' Come on, it's easy."

"Are you out of your mind?" Gavigan said. "You really did get him immunity, didn't you?"

Sorenson turned and walked away.

"Oh, my God," Whitcomb said.

———◆———

Two hours later, Gavigan walked like a zombie through the parking garage. For the first time since Sullivan had left him at the airport, he was alone. Sorenson cashiered him as bait for Sullivan, an act for which Gavigan demanded a document executed in Sorenson's own hand. He reached for the telephone in his pocket and upon failing to locate it remembered that it was in his briefcase. He needed to speak with Christine and replay with her some of the evening's events.

Gavigan could not believe what he had heard from a law-school classmate of his who worked for the U.S. attorney's office. She had sat in on Roger Sorenson's dealings with Dennis O'Brien that day and was frantic because she now assumed she would lose her job. She even asked Gavigan if he knew of any openings at firms in town. She wanted to move before word of the immunity fiasco became associated with her. Sullivan had been correct when he said that Dennis was smart. The deal he worked on Sorenson was extraordinary not only for the protection it afforded an admitted killer, but the fact that Sorenson seemed oblivious to the fact that he had gotten nothing in return.

Gavigan pointed the keyless remote at the Volvo and pushed the button. The car flashed its lights in acknowledgment and unlocked itself. He opened the driver's side rear door and rummaged in his briefcase for his phone.

"Hi, John."

The voice was so close that Gavigan jumped a bit and bumped his head on the roof of the car. He turned to see James Sullivan standing not four feet from him. Sullivan threw a valise at Gavigan's chest, which the larger man fumbled to the ground.

"I brought you something," Sullivan said. "Open it."

Gavigan's hand quivered a bit as he bent over and unzipped the case while watching the killer. He allowed a quick glance into the bag to see a submachine gun.

"Delivered as promised," Sullivan said. "Although I am a bit disappointed that we couldn't enjoy a nice meal. What with the FBI lurking behind the nearest potted palm, I suspect that we wouldn't even have gotten through the appet—"

"Dennis O'Brien killed your wife," Gavigan said.

Of course, he had. Dennis had killed this man's wife with his drug-dealing pawns. Dennis had brought on the rage that had cost so many lives. Gavigan stayed down on the ground with the bag so that he did not see Sullivan looking down at him. A long time passed before Sullivan spoke.

"How do you know?"

The question sounded to Gavigan like that of a teacher asking a pupil to prove a theorem. There was not a hint of doubt, just a need to hear the whole reason for the right answer that had been blurted from the back of the room.

"He found out that Bard had your wife doing some independent auditing on the sly. He knew that she would find out that he was laundering drug money through the firm, so he had her killed. He took care of Bard later. You must have just gotten lucky."

"Get in the trunk, John."

The bigger man paused, but then rose with the bag in hand. For a moment he thought about jerking the weapon from the bag. That thought triggered a chain of questions. Would this be his last chance at survival? Was the gun loaded? How did it work? Would Sullivan shoot him down before he even got it out of the bag? Was he even in danger?

"You knew it didn't you?" Gavigan said.

"No."

"But you suspected?"

"Get in the trunk, John."

Determination reigned in Sullivan's voice. His eyes were cold and clear. Some wild piece of Sullivan was in command and Gavigan knew that someone would die because of what he had said to him.

"No." Gavigan stood a bit taller with the utterance that he couldn't believe had slipped from him.

"You won't be harmed if you cooperate. All I ask is that you get in the trunk."

Gavigan's eyes scanned the garage for help. "No. You're just gonna kill me. Take your best shot!"

Gavigan threw the valise and charged Sullivan as the smaller man reached under his jacket. The distance was short, but Gavigan managed enough acceleration to put his mass to use. He felt his right shoulder bury itself into Sullivan's abdomen and rode him onto the pavement. But Gavigan's speed was not great enough to entrap Sullivan's right hand. The last thing Gavigan saw was a white flash near his left ear.

Chapter 30

S tacey Smith stood next to the hulking driver of the bomb disposal truck so she could inhale his secondary cigarette smoke, although the ostensible reason was so that she could watch the small monitor that depicted the progress of the robot approaching the Porsche in the garage. The breeze swirled on Sixth Street and she looked south to keep dust from blowing in her eyes. She could see the crawling traffic on Walnut Street in the distance, the closest street flowing west. Several blocks around the scene were empty with the exception of a swarm of news vans and helicopters that had somehow secured exemptions from the restrictions.

Sorenson paced ten yards away with his telephone glued to his ear. He was accompanied by a handful of officers from the police and fire departments. They enjoyed a van equipped as a mobile command post complete with a revolving green light to indicate its presence, but they were either too anxious to spend much time inside or had been crowded out by the bomb squad. Macuzak and Whitcomb leaned on the hood of their sedan. Smith strolled over to them and took a sip of Whitcomb's coffee.

"Are we there yet?" Macuzak asked.

"Not quite, bomb guys are always pretty slow."

"Understandable."

"I should have taken the keys," Whitcomb said.

"There might be a trip wire," Smith said. "You did the right thing. Besides, Roger already called the bomb squad."

Macuzak nodded at the monitor. "There."

Smith sauntered back to her post near the truck driver. On the television, she saw the front of the Porsche, which was backed into a parking place. The driver adjusted the brightness on the screen and she could make out the word BOMB scrawled across the car's windshield.

She turned to Macuzak who now stood close behind her. "That's written in lipstick?"

"That's what it looked like. Can you pan down on the bumper?"

"I'm not running it," the driver said. "They're doin' it from downstairs. This is just a repeater of what they're seeing."

Smith had watched the bomb-disposal team go into the garage almost an hour earlier. They emerged later a few members short and without the mass of equipment they had set up. Her understanding was that two team members encased in blast-proof suits were running the robot from a safe distance. They were linked to the rest of the world through an umbilical of cables and fire hoses. Macuzak and Whitcomb had walked right up to the Porsche before anyone arrived and scoffed a bit about the need for such precautions. When the telephone tip about the bomb reached Sorenson, they went to investigate over his objections.

"Here we go," Macuzak said. "There. See the 'T'?"

Smith squinted at the screen and after adjusting the brightness she could make out a "T" as well as a "G" and the second "R."

"TRIGGER is written right across the hood with an arrow pointing down to the remote key chain," Whitcomb said.

"What I would like to know is why he did this, assuming it's our guy, that is?" Smith said.

The roar of one of the fire trucks intensified and caused Smith to survey the scene. She could see six pieces of fire apparatus, fifteen police vehicles, seven or eight cars belonging to various federal agencies, and five television vans. Her gaze met Macuzak's and the two stared at one another for what seemed like a long time.

Shit!

"Where did Gavigan park?" Whitcomb said.

Smith put her telephone to her ear. Gavigan's number rang until she reached his voice mail. She left an urgent message. After she hung up she followed the two detectives to an audience with Sorenson.

"It's just a ploy," Whitcomb was saying as she arrived. Sorenson shook him off and slipped an orange vest over his head. It featured yellow reflective tape and strings of lights that pulsated above the four-inch stenciled letters IC above five more lines in smaller type declaring INCI/DENT/COM/MAN/DER.

Smith inserted herself into the tightening circle around Sorenson. "I couldn't reach him."

"It's a diversion," Macuzak said. "He's snapped up Gavigan."

"You don't know that," Sorenson said.

"Why else would Sullivan be in the garage?" Whitcomb said. "You just said that you provided Gavigan with a pass for this garage earlier in the week. We're standing here with half the police department because he wants us to. We should be running wants on Gavigan's Volvo while we still have a chance."

"I have a situation here. I don't have time for speculation," Sorenson said.

"Come on, Roger," Macuzak said. "You must have recognized his voice from the call."

"I told you the connection was bad. It was wireless and came off that array." Sorenson pointed with a radio aerial at the top of a building across Independence Mall.

Whitcomb ran his hand over his face. "Look, the car is a Porsche. We know he has a predilection for them. You wouldn't be 'Incident Commander' if you weren't sure it was Sullivan. Knowing that—"

"Negative. I'm in charge by virtue of the fact that the tip came to the FBI and constitutes a viable terrorist threat to the national security of the United States and its installations, wholly apart from the pursuit of Mr. Sullivan." Sorenson's arms swept the Mall, part of Independence National Historic Park, and the two federal buildings behind him.

"Assuming it could be Sullivan," Whitcomb said, "we should try to find John Gavigan, since he is the most likely reason Sullivan would have been in the garage in the first place."

A member of the bomb squad called through the open door of the command post. "The disrupter's ready."

"Okay," Sorenson said. "Get the firemen in position."

Smith watched eight firemen lumber into the garage in response to a radio call from one of the fire officers. They made a definite show of turning off their radios and inserting ear plugs before they entered.

"You're gonna try to detonate it?" Macuzak asked.

"It's the safest way," Sorenson said.

"Just go get the keys. There's probably a note on disarming in the car."

"We don't know that."

Macuzak used his hands as if he could shape the words so that they would penetrate Sorenson's skull. "He's not out to hurt cops, Roger. That's not his style. Setting up a big diversion is his style."

"Nonetheless, I won't order anyone to go get the keys."

"I'll do it," Smith said.

The bomb squad members rotated their heads to see if it was the good-looking fed they had scoped out earlier who was willing to blow herself up.

"I'll go with her," Whitcomb said, just before Macuzak could.

"No. We'll detonate in place."

"Aren't you worried about secondary devices?" Smith asked.

"He hasn—"

"You can't have it both ways, Roger," Whitcomb said.

Sorenson grinned in Whitcomb's face. "Sure I can, old man. Watch me."

Sorenson pushed his way into the command van. Smith was back on the telephone to Gavigan. Macuzak was calling dispatchers in southern New Jersey where he said they would broadcast a search directive for Gavigan's car.

Whitcomb walked back toward the bomb-disposal truck's monitor with the others. "Might as well watch the fire while Nero fiddles."

———————————⋄———————————

There was the ringing again. It coordinated itself with the pulsating pain in his head.

After the ringing stopped, he let his eyes blink open a few times. This did not seem to aggravate the pain, but he doubted his eyes worked because he could see nothing other than black. He tried to rise, but his face hit something after moving just a few inches. His legs were bent so that he could not extend them without hitting something. An object rested close to his torso. He felt it leaning against him and recovered his identity in the scratchy Cordura fabric and grassy smell.

John Gavigan felt the upper end of the oblong item and found the head of his driver jutting from the top of his golf bag. This meant he was in the trunk of his car. A conclusion that seemed odd since the last thing he remembered was walking out of the federal building in Philadelphia. He had some kind of meeting with an old friend, something about getting her a job.

The ringing started again. He recognized the insistent call of his telephone coming from beyond the golf clubs. He tried to recall the last time he'd played golf. It had been in the autumn. He remembered the leaves were falling. He had played with a couple of adjusters and one of the partners in some tournament. Gavigan played badly. One of the adjusters told him he needed to play more. He remembered that he felt like telling the client he never had time to play but bit his tongue. That night Christine was really upset when he showed up well past dinnertime with a few drinks in him.

"Oh, shit."

He remembered things now. He felt his head. It did not feel wet. Sullivan must have hit him with something. He was stuffed into his trunk. He was alive. The ringing started again.

Gavigan knew his telephone was in his briefcase on the backseat. He recalled that this car had a little hatch that went from the trunk through the middle of the backseat. The idea behind it was that you could carry long objects, like skis, inside the car. He never used the feature except to lug an easel Dennis used at a trial in Newark. Gavigan laughed out loud when he thought of the idea that he would ever go skiing.

He strained to reach past the golf bag. He located the hatch and opened it without a problem. The center armrest pushed down, but he could not reach his briefcase. The ringing had stopped, but he continued to stretch his arm. He managed to heave himself over the golf bag for better access. With effort that seemed to dislocate his shoulder he grabbed the edge of the briefcase and dragged it toward the hatch. There was no way it would pass through the hole, but he found the telephone inside by feel. As he pulled the telephone through the gap, it started to ring again.

———◆———

Stacey Smith strained to hear against the background noise. "Hello? John?"

She was almost sure she heard someone answer. "John Gavigan? It's Stacey Smith."

"Yeah, I'm here."

The voice sounded like it was dislocated from its owner.

Smith waved to get Whitcomb's attention. "John, are you all right?"

"Head hurts pretty bad."

"John, where are you?"

"In the trunk of my car."

One of the bomb-squad guys yelled out the door of the command post. "Fire in the hole!"

Smith saw the disrupter whack the place on the Porsche where the remote sat. The device punched a dent into the hood while the key ring fell out of the picture. The car did not explode. She focused on her call through the din.

"Do you know where you are?"

"No."

"Is the car moving?"

Smith mouthed the word "trace" to Macuzak who started the process with his own phone.

"No. I'm parked somewhere."

"Are you hurt?"

"My head is killing me. Sullivan clocked me with something."

Smith hesitated for just a minute. "John, is Sullivan still with you?"

"I don't think so. He was waiting for me in the garage."

"John, what garage?"

"Near the federal building."

"Can you hold on for just a minute, John?"

Smith turned her head from the telephone without waiting for an answer. She yelled to Sorenson. "Roger, stop!"

The bomb-squad technicians in the command post turned in response to the commotion. The robot's arm was about to grasp the key ring complete with alarm transmitter. One of them covered the microphone on his headset and leaned back to Sorenson.

"You want us to tell them to stop?" he asked.

"No, no, no. She's probably hysterical about something stupid," Sorenson said. "Go ahead."

Smith poked her head into the command post. "Gavigan may be in the garage. We better check and see."

"We don't have time for this," Sorenson said.

The bomb technician still had his hand over his microphone. "What do you want to do? I need to tell them pretty quick if you want to stop."

The television screen in the command post turned to snow shortly before the muffled thud rattled everything in the van.

"Too late," the bomb-squad technician said.

Another screen showed bomb disposal men in the garage still at their post behind lots of concrete. The men in the trailer tried to reestablish communications. The firemen pushed into the television picture within a few seconds. They knocked down the fire within ninety seconds. Nineteen automobiles were demolished; forty-six others were damaged. Smith's connection to Gavigan was gone. She looked Sorenson in the eye.

"If Gavigan was in there, I'll have your fucking badge."

———•◆•———

Willy Jefferson put his microphone back in the retainer on the dashboard. He sighed and reached into his briefcase for a telephone as his backup pulled in next to him so that its headlights shone on the back of the parked car in front of him. Willy got out of the patrol car and nodded for Pete Resch to cover his advance. He walked to the rear of the car and felt for the trunk release. To his surprise, it depressed and he raised the lid. Inside, he saw a big white guy crammed around a golf bag.

Willy beamed. He had never worked on a kidnapping. "Mr. Gavigan, I presume."

Gavigan waved his telephone at the policeman. "Yeah, I was talking to someone a while ago, but my batteries went dead."

"We have an ambulance on the way, sir."

"Never mind that, I need to call someone. Have you got a phone?"

"Yes, sir, but my understanding is there's a federal agent named Smith who wants to know if we really found you. They've been applying major heat to find your car."

"Fine. I'll talk to her. Have you got the number?"

Jefferson dialed the number he had gotten from the dispatcher just a moment before and presented his telephone to Gavigan as it started to ring.

"Smith."

"John Gavigan here."

"John, are you all right?"

"I think so. My head still hurts, but I'll live."

"Where are you?"

Gavigan looked at Jefferson with a gesture of his shoulders. Jefferson supplied the answer, which Gavigan relayed.

"I'm in a big empty parking lot in Haddonfield, New Jersey."

"Is there any sign that Sullivan is still around?"

"No, but listen, I remember telling him what Sorenson told me to say."

Gavigan was conscious of Jefferson's presence. "Do you remember? In the hotel lobby?"

"You mean about killing his wife?"

"Exactly. I told him and it was like the lights went out. I thought I was dead for sure."

"How long ago was that?"

"No idea."

Gavigan turned to Jefferson and asked him the time. After getting the answer, he said to Smith, "I have no idea how long I've been here."

Jefferson interrupted as an ambulance's whine came within earshot. "Sir, I can tell you that this car was not here forty-five minutes ago when I passed through."

Gavigan relayed the information.

"So, it's possible that Sullivan may take a whack at O'Brien. Macuzak's been trying to find O'Brien, but he's not answering his phones. Do you know where he might be?"

"It's the weekend, right?" Gavigan said. "He's probably in his office with half a load on calling people at home and asking them why they aren't at work."

"Is that his pattern?"

"It was before he started the disappearing act."

"Did you mention that to Sullivan?"

"No, but if he worked for O'Brien for any length of time, he was probably subject to it. The prick calls you up at one A.M. on Sunday morning and starts to ask you about depositions you took three weeks earlier. Wants to know why you're not there to immediately answer his inane questions. Listen, they're about to shove me into an ambulance and I need to call my wife. What else do you need?"

"Sorry, John, you take care. You sure that you're generally okay?"

"Yeah, I think so, but the cops are gonna make me go."

"Who's the cop who found you?"

Gavigan read it off the officer's chest. "Jefferson. Yeah, Jefferson."

"You tell Officer Jefferson excellent work. Someone will be over to secure the scene. We'll check with him so that we can catch up to you."

Willy Jefferson would receive a commendation for rescuing a kidnap victim. Gavigan climbed aboard the ambulance under his own power. The next day he would start his drive to Colorado and a new life. On Sixth Street, Stacey Smith rummaged through the files in the trunk of her car looking for some telephone numbers. When she thought no one was looking, she stuffed two extra magazines for her sidearm into her jacket pockets.

Chapter 31

Macuzak ended the call just as the battery on his telephone died. He studied the display under the dome light of the sedan to confirm its demise.

"I'm out," he said as though he were throwing in a poker hand.

"What did she have to say?" Whitcomb said.

"Mrs. O'Brien relates that she has not seen her husband since early this afternoon. They had lunch together in Stone Harbor. He borrowed her car, a Chevrolet Tahoe, your basic urban assault vehicle, and went to the city, something about a meeting with the FBI. He's not answering his cell phone because it's mounted in his Lexus, which she's driving. Her guess is that he might be in his office. Of course, all this information comes filtered through the fifth of Absolut she seems to have sucked down since lunch."

"I say we go to the office," Smith said. "We've got nowhere else to look. His lawyer doesn't know where he is and Gavigan says he gets off on going in late at night."

"Let's go see what there is to see," Macuzak said.

Smith opened the car's door. "I'll tell Roger. He'll probably want the National Guard activated."

Sorenson had doffed his orange vest and was walking toward the sedan where the other team members were changing seats.

"Roger," Smith said. "Gavigan's been found locked in the trunk of his car. He—"

"Is he dead?" Sorenson said.

"No. Let me finish," Smith said.

Macuzak and Whitcomb joined the circle outside the car.

She pointed to where smoke still curled from the garage entrance. "Gavigan was abducted from that parking garage."

"What time?" Sorenson said.

"He's not sure, but we know his car hasn't been parked where they found it for more than about fifty minutes."

"How do we know that?"

Macuzak sighed and looked at the sky.

Sorenson turned his attention to the detective. "What's your problem?"

"He has difficulty controlling his anger in the face of unbridled stupidity," Whitcomb said. "Why don't you let Stacey finish briefing you before you interrupt with a lot of questions that are irrelevant at this point?"

"Why don't you go fuck yourself?" Sorenson said.

"Good, Roger," Smith said. "Let's revert to the schoolyard while Sullivan gets away. Your ego is wasting our time."

"I am in charge here. I will no longer tolerate this Keystone Cops bullshit. You people are all out.

"Fired.

"Terminated.

"Finished."

Sorenson pointed at Macuzak and Whitcomb. "You fossils can bounce back to Jersey. And Dorothy here can go back to Kansas, or Hooterville, or wherever the hell it is she comes from."

Smith felt a sudden stillness in the midst of all the commotion on the Mall. She saw that Whitcomb and Macuzak were both looking around. Sorenson turned to march off. In the five seconds that followed, Whitcomb fired his foot into Sorenson's groin; Macuzak caught the crumbling agent; and the two of them bundled him into Smith's car. There followed a lull in the conversation while Sorenson tried to retain his stomach's contents and everyone scurried into the sedan.

"You assholes are dead," Sorenson said.

"So," Macuzak said, "Stacey here was briefing us on current events in the investigation before she was rudely interrupted."

Smith looked back and forth between the two older detectives. Their expressions were nonchalant, as though they beat up FBI agents everyday.

"You guys are dead," Sorenson repeated. "Assaulting a federal agent. In front of a witness no less. I knew you were stupid, but not that stupid."

"Do you know what he's talking about, George?" Macuzak said.

"Must have been having a senior moment."

"Stacey?" Macuzak said.

Sorenson started to laugh. "She saw the whole thing. You guys are dead."

"I didn't see anything," Smith said.

The laugh was silenced. She looked right into Sorenson's face. "You know, Roger, you don't look so good. That flu you were complaining about earlier might be getting the best of you."

"This is bullshit," Sorenson said.

"As I was saying, Roger," Smith said. "Sullivan left Gavigan locked in his trunk maybe an hour ago. He knows that O'Brien killed his wife because Gavigan told him. He also knows that O'Brien might be in his office right now. Where does that overeducated brain of yours tell you Sullivan might be right now?"

"At his office?" Sorenson said.

"Now you're talking," Macuzak said.

"He wouldn't dare," Sorenson said. "He knows we're all over the place. He wouldn't hit right under my nose."

"We're not all over the place," Whitcomb said. "We're here. Concentrated away from the place where we should be. As far as hitting right under your nose, I recall him doing precisely that in Washington."

"What we propose," Smith said, "is that we take a ride over to O'Brien's place just to check things out. Why don't you come with us?"

"I don't think so."

Smith gestured for the two detectives to leave the backseat where they all but enveloped Sorenson. "Why don't you guys go on ahead while Roger and I reach an understanding?"

Macuzak and Whitcomb exited from either side of the sedan. Sorenson started to follow.

"Sit down, Roger," Smith said.

"These guys are going down for this," Sorenson said.

Smith poked him in the chest. "No they aren't. You give them a hard time and I'll find some assistant director who wants to hear about your sexual advances and innuendo."

"I never touched you," Sorenson said.

"You don't have to. Besides, I might not remember it that way."

"No one will believe you."

"Sure they will. Look at me."

Smith tossed her hair.

"I'm a babe. You're a pig. Besides, I already went to Matty about it. So, there's a history that predates your wild accusations about my colleagues who at worst may have tried to set you straight about your improper advances. Of course, that's the fall-back position assuming that you want to have your bruised balls put into evidence. I bet some of these techies floating around have a telephoto lens if you want to document the present condition of your private parts."

"Fine," Sorenson said. "We'll check the office."

———◆◆◆———

Sullivan stopped in the alley behind the building, really a small one-way street that ran for a few blocks parallel to Market Street. The walk from the PATCO train had been short, but he was glad to stop since Gavigan had re-broken some of his ribs with his heroics before Sullivan had clubbed him unconscious with a sap. He swallowed two more Percocet for the ribs as well as for his nagging back pain.

Sullivan noticed a Chevrolet Tahoe double-parked on the sidewalk behind the building. It bore a personalized New Jersey license plate he recognized as belonging to Dennis O'Brien's wife. Sullivan recalled that she kept her legal residence in New Jersey after losing her driver's license in Pennsylvania due to her drunken driving habit.

Great. She's got a tank now. She'll probably crush some struggling graduate student in a Toyota moments before he's destined to win a Nobel Prize.

Sullivan walked around to the front of the building where the lobby opened onto Market Street. He strode to the glass lobby doors and made a show of crashing into it with a lot of noise despite the sign that hung in the doorway indicating the entrance was locked. The noise drew the attention of the lobby guard who lounged behind a desk some fifty feet from the door. The guard leaned on the intercom switch to speak with the moron who had just walked into the door.

"Can I hep you?" Sullivan heard through the intercom next to the door adjacent to the locked revolving door. He looked over to where the intercom rested in the door frame and ignored the call from inside, but instead started to rattle the revolving door.

"That door locked. May I hep you?"

Sullivan looked around in wonder for the voice, adjusted the thick-framed spectacles he had donned for the occasion, and peered into the intercom as though he heard a voice from another planet. He approached the intercom but said nothing.

The guard enunciated with extra effort. "Good evening. May I help you?"

"Bon, er ah, good eveneeng," Sullivan said. "Pleeezze, I am to conference Monsieur Cole, thunk you so uver very much."

He resumed rattling the revolving door.

"Who are you here to see, sir?"

Sullivan ignored the latest call on the intercom and waved a business card through the glass at the guard visible within while he rattled the door ever louder. He pushed and held the button next to the intercom that served as a doorbell and uttered "Pleezze" followed by "thunk you so uver very much." The guard groaned from his chair and let Sullivan inside.

Sullivan knocked the guard down behind the desk and shoved his Beretta into the back of his neck. After recovering a Glock from under the desk, he trussed and gagged the guard with duct tape in a maintenance closet. He returned to the lobby desk to view a bank of video monitors and tape machines situated under the desk. He saw Dennis O'Brien pass across one screen and then another before he used the silenced submachine gun to destroy the equipment. As Sullivan rode the elevator upward he confirmed the guard's Glock was loaded and put it in his back pocket. He checked the MP-5 which, to his surprise, was empty. In all his shooting he had never emptied a magazine except on a firing range.

Poor fire discipline. What's that about?

He put the reloaded MP-5 into the valise and selected some items for his jacket pockets before the elevator reached the floor where he knew O'Brien waited.

———————•◦•———————

Whitcomb studied the stream of creeping tail lights on the Vine Street Expressway as they inched forward and then stopped yet again. Even at this late hour, westbound traffic stood still. Macuzak fiddled with the car's radio in an effort to learn the nature of the delay. He found an all-news station that advised of an accident.

Macuzak's fingers drummed the steering wheel. "We should've taken Sansom Street. Do you have your cell phone? We should call and tell them we're hung up."

"The battery on mine went dead earlier tonight. I can never remember to charge the damn thing. They are probably mired in the same traffic. We can try to raise them on the radio, but I would prefer not to speak with Sorenson at the moment."

"Can't say that I'm that anxious to call them up."

Whitcomb looked over at Macuzak in the darkness. "Striking Sorenson might not have been the shrewdest course of action."

"As you would say, Georgie, 'I am acutely aware of that fact.' But the asshole had it comin' from a mile away. Besides, we're fired. We knew that as soon as Matty died. We only have tonight to get a shot at this guy."

Whitcomb shook his head in the darkness. "It did feel good to wail on his white ass."

"Why, yes, George. I suppose that it did."

Whitcomb's radio squawked to life. He acknowledged the call. "This is Whitcomb. Please repeat. Over."

"This is Sorenson. Where are you? Over."

"Stuck in traffic about one quarter mile from the Twenty-third Street exit off Vine. Where are you? Over."

"We're in front of the building. Over."

"I guess they're not stuck in traffic," Macuzak said.

Whitcomb spoke into the radio. "We'll be there in a matter of a few minutes once we clear traffic. Over."

"We'll go in to see what the status is with O'Brien. When you arrive wait behind the building for further instructions. Sorenson out."

"Acknowledged," Whitcomb spoke into the radio and released the transmission button before adding, "asshole."

Chapter 32

S ullivan broke the door with the pry bar from his valise. This technique produced more noise than he desired, but he felt a sense of urgency rooted in the mess he had left in the lobby. Once in the firm's reception area, he heard loud voices and moved through the semidarkness toward them. He had not moved more than twenty feet before the chill down his back confirmed that one of the voices belonged to Dennis O'Brien. In another ten feet he identified the other voice as Walter Cole's. He froze in his tracks and recalled the evening years before when Walter shot him.

Although they never spoke after the event, Sullivan guessed that Cole only had done what he thought necessary in order to stop his boss from being killed. He had heard from one of the nurses that Cole had come to see him in the hospital, but his nerve had failed somewhere between the nurses' station and the room where Sullivan recuperated. Sullivan concluded years before that the shooting was nothing personal. It was just Walt doing his job. Sullivan stood in shadow and hoped he would not encounter Cole. He did not fear Walter and his trusty six-shooter, if he still had it. Rather, Sullivan did not want to deal with the embarrassment that old friends feel when they meet and know that it has been too long since they last spoke.

He eased down the hallway. Cole's voice assumed an unrecognizable tone. It radiated fury, something Sullivan had never heard from Cole during their years of shared frustration. Sullivan was always the hothead of the two, while Cole had been the rational force that accepted injustice whether from a court or the caprice of O'Brien. Sullivan strained to hear the men speak.

"There was no need to fire her!" Cole screamed.

"Fuck her! She's dead weight and has been dead weight since fucking day one, Wally! She only fucking lasted this long because you fucking wanted her to!"

"She said you enjoyed firing her! You just called her up and told her she was fired! She thought it was a joke until you insisted you were serious!"

"I did enjoy firing the cunt! She was fucking useless—no, no, no, she was worse than useless! She was a fucking disaster area! She was so fucking stupid, I don't know how she managed to pass the bar! You probably helped her with that, too!"

Cole said something that Sullivan could not hear. He moved closer to the corner office and took a position crouched behind a secretarial desk about thirty feet from the office where he could see through the doorway. A pile of folders stood in the hall outside the door leading to O'Brien's office. Someone launched another case file onto the growing pile.

"Besides, it doesn't matter anyway!" O'Brien said. "The whole fucking place is shutting down! We're all fucked!"

"What do you mean?" Cole said.

"That's it! It's all she wrote! Fucking *hasta la vista,* motherfucker! I'm closing up shop. We're all out of a job.

"Oh, and by the way, Wally, I fingered you for shooting Jimmy."

"What?"

"I believe my exact words were, 'I conspired with Walter Cole and participated with him in the shooting of James Sullivan,' or some such bullshit. Anyway, I've got immunity and enough free publicity coming that I won't be able to sell enough aquarium tickets. The feds handed me this and they don't even know what to fucking ask for in return. Talk about dumb motherfuckers."

Cole walked from the office and down the hall to the next door. Sullivan leaned back under the desk where he hid, but he could not go too far since the area was cluttered with women's shoes and shopping bags belonging to some secretary who would learn on Monday that she had no job.

Well, I didn't come here to hide under a desk.

Sullivan looked down at the MP-5, but did not move.

I'll have to hit Walter with some pepper foam.

Stop stalling.

Gunfire erupted behind him. Sullivan tumbled behind another secretarial station and felt around for blood or some evidence of a wound, but none existed. He looked back toward the direction from where the shots came.

Shit! What happened?

"Fuck!" O'Brien screamed in a tone audible despite the ringing in Sullivan's ears.

Sullivan scrambled to where the corner office door stood open. Dennis O'Brien lay flat on his back with his green sweater soaked an almost brown color. Only a small red fountain pulsating in the middle of the stain indicated it was blood. Sullivan noticed holes in some of the windows and more blood, lots more blood, sprayed across the glass. Walter Cole stood over O'Brien with his father's old service revolver.

"Fuck you, Wally, you cocksucking motherfucker," O'Brien said.

The pulsing fountain slowed to an oozing well. O'Brien's eyes fixed on the ceiling, but looked well beyond it and everything else.

Sullivan stood in the door. "Walt, are you okay?"

Cole turned his head to face Sullivan with the revolver in his hand. He made no effort to point it at Sullivan.

"I killed the bastard," Cole said.

He looked back down at the body of Dennis O'Brien. "I should have let you do it years ago."

Sullivan set his MP-5 on the floor. "Walt, why don't you put down the weapon?"

"Don't you think those were really appropriate last words coming from Dennis?"

"Yeah, well, he never could construct a sentence without 'fuck' in it."

Cole laughed with wet eyes. "Well, anyway…"

"Walt, this is not a problem. Give me the piece and you can say that I did it. You can walk away from this clean. There's no way they'll think you did it with me around."

Cole gestured at a small camera mounted over the door. "Actually, it's all on film."

"Forget that. I shot up all the monitors before I came up. I'm telling you, you can walk away from this. Do you still have that old leather chair? Come on, I'll tape you to it before I leave. I've got a whole roll of duct tape in my bag."

Cole did not budge. "You know, he fired Melinda."

"Yeah, I heard."

"She called me in tears. She told me if I couldn't do anything, then we were through. What else could I do?"

"Well, there's time for all that later."

"No. I'm tired of all the bullshit. I'm just… just really tired. Do you know what I mean?"

"Yeah, Walt, I know. You can take a rest now. We can talk about all this later."

Cole's hand flexed its grip on the revolver.

Sullivan was conscious of time passing. The police would be along soon enough.

"Walt, how are the kids?"

"My wife bolted and took them a couple years ago."

"Oh, I'm sorry, Walt. I didn't know."

Moron. Nice topic to pick at a time like this. What was the old rule of cross-examination? Never ask a question to which you don't already know the answer.

"Well, how could you? Anyway, I hate to admit it, but I don't even miss them anymore."

"We're getting way off the subject, Walt. I was telling you how to get away with this. Let's go in your office and—"

Cole smiled. "Jim, it was really good to see you."

He then raised his revolver and put the muzzle in his mouth.

———◆———

Smith shivered against the wind outside the building's lobby. "I don't like this, Roger. We should call for backup."

"Nonsense. We'll break the door. Besides, I don't really care what you think."

"You need a warrant to do that."

He fumbled through the trunk for a jack handle. "I don't have time for a warrant. Besides, there are exigent circumstances present which obviate the need for a warrant."

"Like?"

Sorenson strode toward the lobby door while he tested the weight of the jack handle. "That's O'Brien's vehicle we saw out back, and he's a flight risk based on events of the last few hours since I haven't been able to get hold of him. Therefore, I am justified in breaking into this building in the immediate interests of detaining and protecting a material witness. Besides, you're the one who wanted to come over here."

"He's not a flight risk," Smith said. "There is no way this can be right."

Sorenson applied the jack handle. He turned around with a grin after clearing the remaining glass from the door frame. "You were saying?"

Sorenson stepped through the door frame and walked toward the lobby desk. Smith followed him.

"I'm serious, Roger. You are out of control."

Sorenson looked at the computerized directory on the lobby desk. "Now, let's see."

Smith drew her weapon. Sorenson drew his sidearm and looked around the lobby.

"What is it? What do you see?" he said.

"He's here," she said.

"Where?"

"In the building. I can feel it."

Sorenson put his weapon away. "The firm is on the twentieth floor. I doubt that you can sense his presence that far away. You need to relax. Put that away."

"I'm serious, Roger. He's here."

Smith spoke into her radio. "Smith to Whitcomb."

"Whitcomb here. Go ahead."

"Sullivan's in the building. Call for the tactical squad. Make sure they know there are plainclothes officers on the scene. Over."

"Acknowledged."

Sorenson ran behind her and spoke into his radio. "Sorenson to Whitcomb."

"Whitcomb."

"Cancel that tactical squad. We haven't confirmed Sullivan's here."

Sorenson placed his hand on Smith's shoulder to keep her from getting too far away. Their eyes locked for a long time before he looked away to yell into his radio. "Whitcomb, acknowledge!"

"Whitcomb. Go," crackled from the speaker after a pause.

"Cancel the SWAT team. We'll check the building first."

"Acknowledged. No TAC team yet. Do you still want us to cover the rear?"

"Yeah. Cover the back and we'll call you as needed. Sorenson out."

"Whitcomb out."

Smith looked behind the lobby desk to see the shattered video monitors and empty 9 mm shell casings deposited by the MP-5. She said nothing to Sorenson but walked to the elevator to press the button for the twentieth floor. Sorenson followed and blocked open the door when the car arrived.

"Stacey, you have to snap out of this episode you're having. Do you hear me?"

She fingered an extra magazine for her Smith & Wesson in her jacket pocket. "Roger, I have to go upstairs."

"We should find the lobby guard."

"He's probably tied up in a closet."

"He's probably taking a dump or looking at a porno magazine somewhere."

"Roger, all the surveillance stuff behind the counter is shot to shit. Sullivan's either still here, or just left. I've gotta go. You can either let go of the door and wait here, or strap it on and come with me. Either way, call for some backup."

On their way to the twentieth floor, Sorenson tried in vain to summon assistance with his radio. The signal never left the dense concrete walls of the elevator shaft. They heard the sound of muffled gunshots from above the elevator. Sorenson looked over at her, but Smith just looked at the floor and shook her head.

———◆◆◆———

"Shots fired. Call for backup. Plainclothes officers on the scene. Acknowledge."

"Acknowledged. Backup summoned," Whitcomb said into the radio.

"Make sure they're my people, not the locals," Sorenson blared through the little speaker.

Macuzak ran for the pay telephone on the corner next to the bar.

Whitcomb looked up the side of the building as he exited the car now parked on the tiny street behind the office tower. He walked back to the trunk and realized that Macuzak had run off with the keys. He looked to see Macuzak returning from the telephone.

Macuzak was a bit winded from the short run. "Okay, feebs are on the way, but locals would be faster."

"Open the trunk."

Macuzak opened the trunk and reached for the valise containing their body armor. Whitcomb looked back up the side of the office tower as if he might see a clue to the events unfolding inside.

"Whitcomb to Smith. Over."

"Smith."

"Joe and I are in position. We'll be with you in a minute. Please advise as to your location. Over."

"Negative. Watch the fire stairs in case he gets by me. Out."

"Whitcomb out."

Whitcomb thought about Stacey Smith. Her tone betrayed that she had no illusions of assistance from Sorenson and knew that she was confronting a practiced killer. She still had her composure. Feldman had been right when he said that Smith had balls of brass. He looked at Macuzak who fumbled with Velcro closures on the dark Kevlar and ceramic vest emblazoned with the yellow letters: "FBI."

"We should have had her ride with us," Whitcomb said.

Macuzak reached for the gun case buried even further in the trunk. "Spilled milk. Shouldn't there be periods after these letters?"

"They make up for that error by correctly emphasizing these are bullet-resistant vests, rather than bulletproof."

Macuzak held two Remington shotguns pointed skyward with their butts resting on the trunk's sill.

"Are those loaded?"

"All except for the chambers."

Whitcomb extracted two shells from his coat pocket. "Here you go."

Macuzak loaded as Whitcomb again looked up the side of the building for guidance. His eyes passed down to the ground floor where two metal doors stood on either side of the glass door to the elevator lobby. The main lobby on the front of the building was visible through the elevator lobby. He looked at his watch. Macuzak handed him a shotgun and the two men walked toward the glass door.

"How long before Roger's ninjas arrive?"

"I'd guess no more than fifteen minutes, but that comes from someone who thought he could get somewhere on the Vine Street Expressway."

The two men stood some distance from the glass door.

"What do you think?" Whitcomb said.

"This looks pretty good. If he uses the elevators we can shoot him through the glass and we can hit either fire door from here."

"I'll tell Stacey."

"Whitcomb to Smith. Over."

Smith cringed as she heard the transmission blare to her right. The sound came not from her radio, but Sorenson's. He had not only failed to turn down the volume but had increased it at some point since they tumbled out of the elevator and advanced through the broken door. She held her finger to her lips in the semidarkness, but continued to train her pistol down the hallway. The last shot seemed to have come from the direction they now followed toward a corner of the building. She recalled that O'Brien's office lay in that direction.

She motioned for Sorenson to advance. As he had on two other occasions, he hesitated and then moved no more than ten feet forward. She took her turn and moved twice as far just as she had each time she had moved ahead of Sorenson.

Light streamed from O'Brien's doorway. Sorenson was well behind her in the hallway. She scrambled into a secretary's area near the office and peered into the room. She saw O'Brien down and the feet of another body. She crossed the hall to hug the wall next to the door. She looked down the hall to see Sorenson behind a desk fifty feet away training his weapon in her general direction.

She rolled around the threshold with her firearm and only enough of her eye exposed to allow her to aim. The feet belonged to someone whose head was now split open. Seeing no one else in the room, she eased herself in to confirm that both occupants were dead and that the second one was Walter Cole. A silenced submachine gun lay on the floor. A revolver rested near Cole.

She heard a cry from the hallway and switched off the room's lights.

She heard things falling to the floor and rolled into the hallway back to the secretary's desk. A figure well down the hallway ran for the front door. Smith ran after the shape.

Shooting erupted out of the dark to her right and ahead of her. Smith dove under a desk while she listened to Roger Sorenson scream and shoot at random around the office until he exhausted the .40-caliber rounds in his magazine. After Sorenson depleted his ammunition, Smith found him staggering around like a blind man. She punched him in the face to keep him from reloading and regretted it as her hand started to burn with some gummy substance deposited on Sorenson's face.

"He maced me! The fucker maced me!" Sorenson screamed.

Smith kicked Sorenson's weapon away so he would not find it. "Roger! Shut up and stay down! I gotta go after him. You'll be fine."

Smith ran down the hallway behind her pistol. She heard the elevator bell signal its arrival as she reached the front doors and hauled the broken one open. With the door halfway open she saw him fully for the first time. He saw her, too, she knew.

In fact, he was way ahead of her. The Texan stood there rock solid. He had had a haircut and a shave, but she recognized him. She would have been able to pick him out on the street if the chance had come, but now here he stood fifteen feet away with a Beretta pointed right at her head. There was no mistaking that he had her cold.

She froze in position in the doorway with her burning hand grasping her Smith & Wesson which, despite her best efforts, came through the doorway pointed at the floor.

The elevator doors opened across the lobby from where he stood, but he did not flinch. His face moved and she watched his mouth form the last words she thought she would hear.

"Congratulations," he said.

"What?" She answered after a pause.

"The ring. It's an engagement ring isn't it?"

She smiled for an instant. "Yeah. It is. Thank you."

The elevator stood there, but he didn't move toward it.

"How's the leg?"

He remembered her.

"Good as new."

"That's great. Well, I've got to be going. Good night."

He took a step toward the elevator and blocked the doorjamb with his foot.

She raised her pistol. "Freeze!"

I might get a cardiac hit on him.

He'll still hit you between the eyes.

"Stacey, we both know I've got you here. So, just let me board the car and no one gets hurt."

"I can't do that. Besides you're not gonna shoot me."

"Now, why do you say that?"

"You didn't kill Roger. Besides, if you shoot me then all that work you did on me in the casino would be wasted."

He rolled his eyes to the ceiling and after a moment pointed the gun up at it.

"Okay. You've got me. I'm putting down my weapon."

He crouched and put the Beretta on the floor. Smith saw a ring on the floor next to the gun before she noticed the object rolling from Sullivan's left hand as he stood. It exploded with a flash and a thundering bang.

Smith fired twice into the place she last saw Sullivan, but fell back from the flash, which filled the elevator lobby. She advanced toward the elevator car, but found the doors shut. She stepped on the Beretta, which still rested on the carpet. She looked back up to see blood on the elevator doors' casement along with some tissue. She checked the hall, but did not see Sullivan. She drew the radio from the pocket where she put it so long ago.

"Smith to Whitcomb or Macuzak. Over."

"Macuzak. Go."

"Suspect Sullivan escaped the twentieth floor. He's wearing a dark suit. I think I winged him. He took one of the elevators to the east side of the building but might bail out before the ground floor. Over."

"Are you all right?"

"Roger that. We're fine. There are two stiffs here, but I'm not sure they're his. He's got some of those flash/bang grenades, so watch out. Over."

"Are you sure you're okay?"

"Yeah. We're fine."

"Okay. Hold your position and we'll hit him on the way out or send in the ninjas if he's hiding. Macuzak out."

She looked down at the Beretta on the floor and the blood on the frame of the elevator door. After a moment, she spoke into her radio.

"Listen. I'm not sure that Sullivan's still armed. Over."

She listened for an answer from the tiny speaker, but none came. She spoke again into the radio.

"Did you copy my last transmission? Over."

No response came. She let the radio drop to her side. She leaned down near the elevator to retrieve a watch. It was a Rolex with a broken band. She turned it around and read the inscription on the back: DON'T YOU LOVE ME MADLY?

She wiped her eyes with her sleeve on the walk back to where Sorenson wailed and told herself that the grenade's smoke must have contained tear gas.

Sullivan ripped a piece of duct tape from the roll to secure the combat dressing to his shoulder. He had feeling in his right arm, but he had little doubt that his shoulder was shattered. Sergeant Smith managed to place at least one if not two rounds just above the protection provided by his ballistic vest.

This'll probably take a few operations to get fixed, if I ever get out of here.

From the third floor, he could see that the street behind the building held fewer than three cars with only one of them qualifying as a potential police car. He was still too high to see if anyone stood near the building.

Well, I can't wait forever. Percocet's gonna start to wear off.

Time to go.

Sullivan looked at his wrist and noticed that his Rolex was gone. To his surprise, the sense of loss was not all that great.

I guess she's really gone for good.

Sullivan shoved the guard's Glock into his left coat pocket and palmed a thunder/flash grenade in his left hand. He was able to hold O'Brien's car keys in his right hand. Leaving behind everything else, including his blood-soaked bullet-resistant vest, he entered a stairwell and ran down the remaining flights to the fire door where he stopped. There was no window. He listened but heard nothing through the door. He eased the pin from the grenade with his left thumb and opened the heavy door just enough to slip out.

The lobby lights sharpened the outlines of the two men standing near the building to his left. They raised their weapons in his direction. Sullivan needed to cover twenty yards to where O'Brien left his sport utility vehicle.

He heard "Freeze!" and "Police!"

That's not very original. Haven't they thought this out? Don't I even rate a derisive epithet? Not even a "Scumbag"?

Sullivan did not freeze as he knew he never would when confronted with this situation. He kept walking to the right like an associate on his way to lunch after working at his desk all morning, but still the men screamed at him, as if they were trying to convince themselves of their identities and the importance of their commands.

Better than halfway there. Keep moving. They're not supposed to shoot someone just walking away.

The grenade dropped from his hand and still he did not stop, or even slow. Only with the explosion behind him did he begin to run. The noise from the grenade was deafening as usual, so he never heard the shotgun blasts that knocked him down just fifteen feet from the Tahoe. One moment he ran and the next he had the concrete pressing into his face.

Chapter 33

S tacey Smith sat behind the wheel of the Crown Victoria in a cloud of cigarette smoke. She had taken a Marlboro offered by one of the tactical operators. At the time, she thought she would just take a puff to calm her nerves. Less than ten hours later, she was almost finished with her second pack.

The crime scene had been a mess. Some EMTs arrived within a few minutes of the tactical agents. Sorenson screamed at the tactical people to search the building and ordered the EMTs to commence resuscitation efforts on O'Brien. The EMTs assessed both bodies and advised Sorenson that they could do nothing, which only seemed to aggravate Sorenson, who muttered something about needing O'Brien for bait.

Smith inhaled and watched George Whitcomb emerge from the surgical supply store across the street. He put his parcel in the backseat of the sedan. She noted the full-size tire fitted to the rear passenger side of the vehicle. She had not seen Macuzak at all, but spoke with him over the telephone for just a moment. The discussion was cursory. Macuzak wanted to slip back into a hot tub to alleviate the pain he felt from an old aggravated back injury.

She had cornered Whitcomb earlier that morning to ask what happened. He repeated the story that Sullivan had slipped past them in the alley when they went to the lobby. He shot out a tire on their sedan and stole the O'Brien sport utility vehicle. He was driving away as they returned to the alley. They fired their shotguns and gave chase on foot for the length of the block, but made no headway. During this process, Macuzak injured his back and returned to his hotel room while Whitcomb came back to the crime scene about a half hour after the shooting. Their radios, Whitcomb explained, had been damaged and they could not call for help.

Sorenson loved the story. It fit his profile of Macuzak and Whitcomb as two oafs wandering the landscape of modern law enforcement. He told Whitcomb to pack his bags and take Macuzak back to New Jersey since their services were no longer required. Smith was finished as well. She had done her job. They were fired. They were all fired for the second time in as many hours.

She followed far behind Whitcomb's car to a neighborhood just a few blocks south of where the O'Brien firm maintained its offices. He turned down a side street, which she recognized as Delancey Place, when she got to the end of the block. Smith continued straight and almost hit a woman crossing the street at the next corner. Smith thought she looked familiar. She circled the block twice before parking on the sidewalk in front of Whitcomb's Ford. Smith looked up and down the block before lifting and then dropping the elaborate knocker on the massive door of the brownstone.

Esther Berman opened the door and after slight hesitation smiled at Stacey Smith. She always smiled as far as Smith could tell.

"Hello, dear. What can I do for you?"

"Hello, Mrs. Berman. Is he here?"

"Why no, dear. Dr. Berman just stepped out to go to the College of Physicians' library. Maybe you can catch him there."

"That's not who I'm talking about, Ma'am. Is James Sullivan here?"

Macuzak appeared in the doorway beyond Mrs. Berman. He turned to yell over his shoulder into the deeper recesses of the house. "It's Stacey."

"Come in, dear," Esther said. "Can I take your things?"

Smith went into the room that once had been a parlor in the old brownstone and now served as Dr. Berman's reception area. Whitcomb emerged from somewhere deeper in the large house.

"Stacey, what a surprise," Whitcomb said. "We were just here checking with the doctor regarding Joseph's recurrent back—"

"Forget it, George," Macuzak said. "She knows."

"How about tea?" Esther said.

Whitcomb beamed like a proud parent. "Really? She knows?"

"That means you owe me twenty." Macuzak backed away from a window. "And she's alone. That makes it a hundred."

"You didn't think I'd fall for that cock-and-bull story about him getting by you, did you?" Smith said.

"Roger seems to have eaten it up," Macuzak said.

"Roger's an idiot. Is he here?"

Footsteps from a hall announced the approach of Dr. Berman. "Is that the shikse I hear?"

"Good morning, Doctor."

Berman kissed her on the cheek. "Good morning, dear. Shoot anybody yet today?"

"No. Not yet."

"Well, it's still early."

Berman turned to Whitcomb and Macuzak. "Well, he can be moved. What's the plan?"

"Actually, Lieutenant Smith's arrival presents something of a problem. You see, she's not actually in league with us," Whitcomb said.

"Let me see him," Smith said.

The conspirators exchanged glances.

"Follow me," Berman said.

Smith followed Dr. Berman down a hall and through a maze of doors in the massive brownstone. They entered a small room where James Sullivan sat on an examining table.

Smith studied her quarry. Scrapes covered the end of his nose and chin and it looked as though he might have lost a tooth or two. He was fit as she could see with his shirt removed. She inventoried the identifying scars from where Walter Cole's bullets had been removed. There was no tattoo on his shoulder as Sorenson had led them to believe for so long. A dressing and air cast enveloped his right shoulder and held his arm against his torso. He looked at her and lines formed around his eyes as they had the night before, the same lines she noticed in the casino even as she almost bled to death.

"Sergeant Smith, long time, no see," Sullivan said. "Come to finish me off have you?"

"Lieutenant Smith."

Macuzak and Whitcomb crowded into the room.

Sullivan looked to Berman. "Hey, Doc, can you leave us alone for a minute?"

Berman whispered into Sullivan's ear loud enough for all to hear. "I don't want to leave you with these Philistines."

"Well, they all shot me at least once and I'm still here. Besides, everything you've done here to this point has been under duress from these two fellows. I don't want you to become an accessory after the fact."

Smith looked over at Macuzak while Sullivan spoke. Macuzak reached into his pocket and held out two oblong plastic objects maybe an inch in diameter. Smith took one and studied it. It was a plastic bullet fired from a shotgun. Macuzak and Whitcomb must have knocked him down and moved in like lightning.

"Bullshit. I've got better lawyers than they do," Berman said. "Say nothing and we can call one right now. If the prosecutor or jury is like most, you might be able to beat any charges."

"My guess is that if things go all right here I might not need one," Sullivan said. "Besides, you know how much I hate lawyers."

"You always were a stupid goddamned Irishman. Holler if you want me."

Berman left, but pivoted back into the room. "Listen, dear, how many times did you shoot him? I found what look like two in-and-out wounds."

"I fired twice."

"What was it? Nine millimeter?"

"Forty caliber."

"Well, it made a mess of his shoulder, I'll tell you that. They ought to make one more gun and then throw them all in the ocean."

"Doc, we need a minute," Sullivan said.

"Right, but if you're going I want to change that packing once more."

"I won't go without saying good-bye. You folks won't stop me from doing that will you?"

Smith was in control. It was up to her to do the talking.

"No," she said.

As Berman left, Whitcomb sniffed the air. "Stacey, have you been smoking again?"

"George, let it go."

The three police officers clustered into a semicircle around Sullivan.

"What's the program?" Sullivan said.

"You tell me," Smith said.

"Perhaps I should do that," Whitcomb said. "Our plan is to set Mr. Sullivan free with several conditions. First, he stops his crime spree."

"He already did that," Macuzak said. "That's why we didn't have any recent assaults."

"Additionally, he must disappear and never be heard from again, something at which he has demonstrated his proficiency," Whitcomb said. "Further, if he is ever captured, he will deny we ever assisted him if questioned on the point."

"Anything else?" Smith said.

"There's the matter of Mr. Sullivan furnishing his services in the war on terror. We've put him in contact with another branch of the government that has expressed an interest in his skills."

"You're dealing him as a hired gun."

"Apparently, his talents are in demand."

"That's the woman I saw in the street," Smith said. "She's CIA."

"We're not exactly sure what letters are on her ID," Macuzak said.

"Anything else?" Smith said.

"No," Whitcomb said.

"No cash, or merchandise, or a draft choice to be named later?"

"That's not what this is about," Macuzak said.

"It is what it's about," Smith said. "We can't let him go. Why should we let him go? We caught him. And what do you mean he stopped his crime spree? What the hell was last night?"

As soon as she uttered the words, Smith remembered that she was only alive because he had not killed her the night before, just as he had kept her from bleeding to death.

"She's right," Sullivan said. "I'm a menace to what passes for society."

Smith turned on Sullivan. "Shut up!"

She wanted to pace, but the room was too crowded.

"How well did you cover your tracks?" Smith asked.

"We recovered the rounds used to stop him," Whitcomb said. "No one saw us remove him from the scene. He destroyed the video equipment covering the lobby and outdoors before he went upstairs."

"What about O'Brien's car?"

"Burned on some railroad tracks early this morning," Macuzak said.

"You could have thought to shoot the tire on your car," Smith said.

"We were a bit pressed for time," Whitcomb said.

Smith looked out a window that faced a small garden hidden behind the house. "I could've helped you out, you know."

"The decision was made not to involve you if this opportunity arose."

She turned to face her partners. "Matty knew about this."

Whitcomb and Macuzak exchanged glances.

"It was his idea," Macuzak said. "He gave us the plastic bullets and the shotguns."

"I should say that Matty arrived at this possible solution in more recent times," Whitcomb said. "He concluded that Sullivan had become dormant some time ago although his continued myth discouraged at least some dealers. He also realized that Mr. Sullivan here is far more rational than Roger has asserted. Further, Matty expressed a pragmatic concern that we might not secure a conviction in light of some of the groundwork laid by Roger as well as the potential that a jury might be reluctant to convict due to the character of the victims. It seems that Roger, well…"

"Roger what?" Smith said.

"Well, Roger was very anal-retentive about keeping control over the case materials and storing everything in his laptop. It seems that he picked up some computer virus somewhere, which damaged all his files whenever he tried to save them. There was also the matter of him storing key physical evidence in New York. It seems that it was destroyed in the Trade Towers collapse. Matty had some nightmares about Roger being kept on the witness stand for weeks."

"When did this happen?" Smith said. "I must have missed a few meetings."

"Over time. It sort of evolved. Matty actually called us on his way to the airport to confirm his feelings on the matter."

Smith turned to Sullivan. "Did you do this thing with the computer?"

"You can't really fault me for remembering my old classmate's fondness for tattooed Asian lesbians who urinate on one another," Sullivan said. "Once someone confides that sort of thing to you, no matter how many beers you've had, you won't forget it."

"So that's it?" Smith said. "You're going to let him go?"

"Not without your agreement," Whitcomb said.

"Roger's gonna figure this out. Hell, I did."

"Don't sell yourself short. Unlike Roger, you're a good cop," Macuzak said.

"A good cop wouldn't let him go." Smith turned back to the window. "Give me a minute here."

Macuzak and Whitcomb turned to leave. Sullivan eased off the table to follow.

Smith reached for her weapon. "You, sit down."

She did not draw, but Sullivan resumed his perch on the table. Smith lit a cigarette.

After a few minutes, Sullivan broke the silence. "Nice shooting."

"Excuse me?" Smith said.

"Gun shoulder," Sullivan said. "Right over the vest? I wouldn't have tried that."

Smith reached for another smoke. "I was aiming for your head."

"Well, I've found that's kind of a tough target," Sullivan said. "So, when's the big day?"

"What?"

"The wedding date."

Smith had not thought of her fiancé for a long time. "None of your damn business."

"Of course."

"June. We're getting married in June."

"That's kind of a cliché, don't you think?"

"Man, you don't know when to shut up, do you?"

"No. It's not one of my strong suits. Lawyer training, I guess. So, what does he do?"

"He's a doctor."

"Really? That's terrific. Someone who does something useful."

"Yeah, well, I met him in the hospital when I was in for the leg. So, I guess I have you to thank for that whole thing, too."

"So, do you love him?"

"What?"

"This doctor you're marrying—do you love him?"

"What kind of question is that? Do I love him? Of course I do."

"Just asking. A lot of people don't really love the person they marry."

"Well, I—we love each other."

"Well, congratulations, or I should say best wishes since you're the bride-to-be. I think you're supposed to congratulate the groom instead of the bride."

"Well, yeah, thanks."

"So, you'll be settling in back home and starting a family I would hope."

"We'll probably have a couple kids soon, but we may be moving around after he finishes his fellowship."

"What type of doctor is he?"

"Plastic surgeon. Reconstructive plastics."

"That's terrific. I hope you have a nice, calm, sedate life after all this."

Smith turned to look out the window. "So, you're retiring?"

"That's the deal, unless some people with trench coats drop me an e-mail for some reason."

"Why should I believe you?"

"You shouldn't. All you have is my word. Of course, that's the way business used to be conducted before we became civilized. If I walk out of here, you'll have no leverage on me whatsoever. I could even blow the whistle on you folks. It's an illegal and unenforceable contract that you don't have the authority to make. By all current interpretation of the law, I should be put in the criminal justice system. We all know how well that works."

Smith thought about the fiasco trials of recent years. She turned back to Sullivan and the question that had gnawed at her erupted. "Why did you do it?"

"Anger," Sullivan said. "Anger and frustration. The system wasn't working for me, so I made up my own. I wish I could tell you that demons spoke to me, or the neighbors' dog commanded my actions, or there's something wrong with my limbic system, or some other acceptable explanation, but that's not the case. I just had enough and snapped. I won't say that I'm sorry. I only stopped because I wasn't getting results."

"So, what? You just decided to go on a killing spree?"

"Well, I kind of got pushed through the door, but then didn't turn back."

"Something set you off?"

"Yeah. Someone shot my dog. Well, my wife's dog. After all the nonsense I went through, a broken back in the army, Ginger's murder,

Walter shooting me, somebody burning down my house, it turned out that someone shooting a dog just made me blow my stack. I had just become the perpetual victim, a statistic. That was not acceptable."

Smith looked out the window. "What were you doing in the casino that night?"

"I was trying to make a weapons connection with Withers. I had my doubts about whether I would need him, but the opportunity was there. I was trying to walk out but the whole thing went bad when Redfeather started shooting."

Smith lit another cigarette. "You're getting off pretty cheap."

"I tend to agree."

"You know, my old partner Williams—he was killed in the casino—"

"Yes. I know."

"Williams has a kid."

"I didn't know that. Boy or girl?"

"Girl."

"Smart?"

"As a whip. At least as far as I can tell, she's only a couple months old."

"Sounds like Harvard material," Sullivan said. "That can get expensive."

"That's what I hear."

"Think you can spell the name right this time?"

Smith turned from the window. "Let me check."

Smith pulled an electronic organizer from her jacket and read the entry for the girl complete with address, Social Security number, and date of birth. Sullivan scrawled on a bandage wrapping held near his entrapped hand.

"Got all that?"

"Never heard it from you."

"Then we have a deal."

"No."

"What do you mean no?"

"I've already got this deal to walk from Macuzak and Whitcomb. There needs to be consideration to support your additional terms."

"I'm letting you go and you want me to put up something else? Is that what you're saying?"

"You're not going to let me go. You won't be able to live with yourself."

"Excuse me?"

"I propose that I leave this building. I will walk counterclockwise around the block three times. During that period, I guarantee that you will have reconsidered this scenario, at which time you can exit the building and attempt an arrest. It will be a genuine arrest since if I see you or your partners on the street, I will shoot you down."

Smith laughed and shook her head.

"Come on," Sullivan said. "This should appeal to your western sensibilities. It's like a movie where the clock ticks toward high noon. It's up to you whether you come out or not. If you do, it looks like you caught me coming from the doctor. Your partners walk away clean. Everybody's a hero unless I kill you. Hell, my gun hand is even immobilized. Of course, you can just sit here for a while and all the other conditions are still in place. It's a no-lose deal for you."

Smith ran a hand through her hair. "Will the Bermans play ball?"

"The Bermans will do what I tell them on this account."

Smith stubbed out the smoke on the sole of her shoe. "Fine. But don't forget that I'm still letting you go."

"Then we have a deal."

Smith huddled with Macuzak and Whitcomb at the exam room door. Sullivan called for Dr. Berman who with his wife started to change the dressing on Sullivan's shoulder. Smith heard Sullivan tell the Bermans that they were always to remember that they treated him at gunpoint and that the police were not involved.

Instructions on wound care tumbled from the doctor. "You have to see a good trauma or orthopedic surgeon within the next twenty-four hours. Do not wait any longer than that or they might have to chop off your arm up near the neck. The wound is as clean as I can get it, but you need exploration and debridement in a surgical suite; probably followed by a reconstruction or two. Keep it immobile and freshen the ice water every hour."

"What should I tell them if they ask what happened?" Sullivan said.

"Motorcycle accident," Berman said. "They ought to throw those damn things in the ocean, too. Tell them you think a fence post or tree branch pierced your shoulder.

"These are Percocet. Take those one or two every six hours for pain, but you'll be zooming, so try to lay off those as much as you can. This is an antibiotic. Take it every four hours until they're all gone, or some doctor tells you to stop. Try to eat something when you take those."

Smith filled in Whitcomb and Macuzak on her conversation with Sullivan. Smith could tell they did not like the idea of a possible shoot-out, but agreed to the terms.

Mrs. Berman filled the air cast with ice water from a portable water cooler designed for the purpose. She refilled the cooler and put it in Sullivan's free hand. Dr. Berman kissed Sullivan on both cheeks and told him to go. Esther kissed and hugged him and Smith heard her whisper with the smile never leaving her face, "Get out of here before these assholes change their minds."

"You *will* disappear," Macuzak said. "You're not going to be like Charles Bronson and come back to make *Death Wish Two* through *Seven* and all that nonsense."

Sullivan eased off the table. "I'm already gone. I gave your little spook friend that e-mail address. It's as good as a dead drop if you need to reach me for some reason."

In the front vestibule, Macuzak handed Sullivan the Glock taken from the guard the night before. "Make that disappear, too."

Sullivan moved the slide and checked the magazine. "Done."

Smith leaned close. She could smell him. "We're even. If I see you again, I'll shoot you down."

"Understood. You've used all your free passes as well," Sullivan said.

"Take a walk."

"Three times counterclockwise around the block. Shouldn't take more than about fifteen minutes."

"You won't see me out there."

"Sure I will, once you've realized what you've done."

Sullivan said nothing further. He walked from the house alone.

Sullivan had been right. After six minutes, Smith popped out the front door with her pistol in hand. Whitcomb and Macuzak followed her for support. Smith scanned the block for Sullivan, but he was nowhere to be seen. She noticed that Whitcomb's back tire was flat.

Macuzak tapped her arm. "Stacey, where's your car?"

Smith looked at the empty spot on the sidewalk where she parked the Ford. Visions of the car stolen from her in Washington flashed before her eyes together with the hundred recriminations she heard from Sorenson about leaving her keys in the ignition.

"Shit. He stole my car. Goddamnit I know I took the keys."

Esther sidled next to Smith and passed her arm through that of the younger woman. "You know, dear, when you visit in the big city, you should always be careful of what you leave unattended. There could be something valuable that someone might take. Like keys, for example."

Smith looked into the older woman's clear blue eyes.

Esther smiled. "How about some brunch?"

Smith answered after only the slightest hesitation. "I'm famished."

Chapter 34

John Gavigan lit the candles on the table and dimmed the lights enough so that he could watch the snow fall through the darkness outside. Christine entered from the kitchen bearing the main course. John had offered to help cook, but was dismissed from the kitchen hours earlier. Christine told him he could make an attempt next year, or perhaps the one after that, as the demands of clinical rotations consumed more of her time. For now, the first year of medical school, she could manage a Christmas Eve feast. John poured the wine.

They sat and toasted the meal; their lives; and, for a change, their actual happiness.

◆

Macuzak handed Whitcomb a cold Red Stripe as he eased his pale bulk onto the chaise lounge. "This was an excellent idea, Georgie."

Whitcomb took a pull from the icy beer bottle and adjusted his sunglasses to meet the demands of the afternoon. "Since we are recreationally engaged, I will let that pass."

The two men had concluded the first annual Christmas shareholders' meeting of their investigative agency moments earlier. Demand for their services was far outpacing supply. They should have been interviewing potential new associates or at least tending to some of their existing work, rather than sitting on a Jamaican beach. However, it was a holiday and they had to meet on administrative matters at some point.

Macuzak nodded down the beach in the direction from which their wives walked through the edge of the surf. "Here they come."

"How come we've never done this in the past?" Whitcomb said.

"Money."

"No. I don't mean that."

"What?"

"Gone on vacation together."

"For purposes of the Internal Revenue Code, this is not a vacation," Macuzak said.

"And I don't mean to Jamaica. Even to the Jersey shore. We haven't really socialized all that much over the years."

Macuzak sipped from his bottle. "Well, you know how exclusive you African-Americans can be."

"I thought it was the awkwardness of not having a fresh corpse around to serve as a conversation piece."

"I thought about bringing one down with me but figured there might be a hassle at customs. Plus, Liz wanted the window seat and I didn't want the two to argue."

"Still," Whitcomb said, "it might have been worth it for the extra peanuts."

The two men laughed as old friends can when they play a joke on the rest of the world.

On his way to get more ice, Roger Sorenson ripped from his refrigerator door the card with the words "Happy Holidays" emblazoned in gold across the front. He spun it toward the trash can but missed. He would leave the card to sit and decay. After his lease expired, it would be part of the accumulated detritus that he would abandon in this hell hole.

Through some beyond-the-last-minute magic his father had worked, Sorenson avoided outright dismissal from the FBI, but drew a punishment that he believed worse on some days.

Days like this.

Sorenson staggered back to his living room. He took another long sip of Canadian Club and surveyed the darkness outside his apartment window. It never really got to be light this time of year and the snow had been falling with a relentlessness that even the locals thought noteworthy. Roger hated the cold and dark. He emptied his glass with the knowledge that he was drinking more than usual, but reassured himself that it was not all that odd a behavior in Alaska.

Roger returned to the kitchen for a refill and took solace from the fact that his posting was at least keeping someone else from being happy. There was no doubt some special agent in Washington, New York, or Los Angeles who longed to be here in Roger's place, just as he longed to be in theirs. He knew that he would be one day.

He would be back.

He just had to take his medicine for a while. That's what his father had said.

They could not keep him on ice forever. This last notion caused Sorenson to break into hysterical laughter since it struck him at that moment he was putting more ice into a fresh whiskey.

Sorenson raged at the darkness through the window. "They can't keep me on ice forever."

The bottle was in his hand now. The glass lay broken on the kitchen floor amid a smattering of ice.

In the apartment downstairs, a couple huddled under their blanket waiting for the drunk upstairs to pass out like he did most nights.

"Hear that?" the woman asked.

"Yeah. He's talkin' about ice again."

"Won't be long now."

"Bet on it?"

"What's in the pool?"

"Gotta be fifty bucks or better."

"I give him five more minutes."

"Candy from a baby. He's good for more than that. Hell, it's only five after ten on Christmas Eve. Guy's gotta liver the size of an Airstream. But if you insist, you're on."

Tonight the woman won the bet. Roger Sorenson blacked out and fell silent even before the couple finished talking.

Stacey Smith opened her eyes and experienced the momentary disorientation that comes with waking in an unfamiliar place. The ceiling was stark white and sunlight started to make its way across the top of the window. She shuffled into the living room and flopped onto the sofa.

The tree stood crooked in the corner farthest from the sliding glass doors that opened onto what passes for a view in Southern California, a sliver of the Pacific Ocean beyond what seemed like a million rooftops. Christmas morning and she was alone. Jeff had explained to her the importance of working through the holidays. It seemed that many patients elected to schedule plastic surgery during the holidays either in order to camouflage the recovery period as much as possible, or to liposuction themselves into impossibly tight holiday dresses. Even the senior members of the practice were operating. They were all working as much as possible. Money flowed into the practice.

Jeff encouraged her not to work, but Stacey was reluctant to quit after surviving the academy and dealing for an assignment to Los Angeles. In her heart, she knew there was another element that kept her working. She did not quite trust Jeff to take care of her forever, but she resolved this conflict by rote with the rationale that she trusted no one that much.

She spied the presents under the tree. The small one she wrapped late last night drew her attention and she retrieved it. She snipped away the wrapping to reveal the small box. She opened it to look at the polished and repaired Rolex and recalled the memorial service for Matty Feldman. It was there that she told Macuzak and Whitcomb about recovering the watch after shooting Sullivan. She had put it in her pocket and forgotten about it until she was packing to leave Philadelphia. Macuzak and Whitcomb advised her to keep or dispose of the watch rather than turn it in, since the FBI would presume she intended to steal it all along. She hoped that by giving the watch to Jeff, she would dissipate the guilt of having kept it. As she watched it sparkle in the morning light, she decided she could not give it to Jeff. She looked at the inscription on the back.

"Don't I love him madly?"

———◆———

Joe Murphy stepped out of his house into the brilliant Vermont sunshine. The air was cold enough to allow the snow to squeak beneath his tread; not even Bob the cat emerged for more than a sniff of the icy air. He abandoned his suit and tie this Christmas in favor of a flannel shirt and jeans that better accommodated the new Cryo Cuff fitted to his right shoulder, an ingenious device that both immobilized his arm and shoulder while furnishing ice water to control inflammation. Since his motorcycle accident, Joe Murphy had endured three surgeries on his right shoulder with the most recent only days earlier. After the holiday, he was to commence what had been described as his last course of physical therapy. The surgeon was confident that the joint would regain full range of motion and strength.

He set down the large Smith & Wesson revolver on the deck railing to give himself a free hand to adjust his sunglasses. The heavy weapon felt odd in his left hand and his balance was thrown off a bit when he unburdened himself of the gun. Against the dazzling brightness, shade crept across the valley floor like a curtain. Murphy was due at Wanda's house for Christmas dinner in less than half an hour, a stray she allowed into her dysfunctional family on major holidays. He lost track of time watching the shadows move and guessed that he must be late for dinner. He could feel the Cryo Cuff turning to slush from the cold. His telephone was ringing. He blew on his fingers to warm them and picked up the Smith & Wesson.

"Time to go."